Books by Barbara Kyle

The Queen's Exiles
Blood Between Queens
The Queen's Gamble
The Queen's Captive
The King's Daughter
The Queen's Lady

The QUEEN'S EXILES

BARBARA KYLE

KENSINGTON BOOKS
www.kensingtonbooks.com

KENSINGTON BOOKS are published by

Kensington Publishing Corp.
119 West 40th Street
New York, NY 10018

All Kensington titles, imprints, and distributed lines are available at
special quantity discounts for bulk purchases for sales promotion, pre-
miums, fund-raising, and educational or institutional use.

Special book excerpts or customized printings can also be created to fit
specific needs. For details, write or phone the office of the Kensington
Special Sales Manager: Kensington Publishing Corp., 119 West 40th
Street, New York, NY 10018. Attn. Special Sales Department. Phone:
1-800-221-2647.

ISBN-13: 978-0-7582-7324-6
ISBN-10: 0-7582-7324-X
First Kensington Trade Paperback Printing: June 2014

eISBN-13: 978-1-61773-206-5
eISBN-10: 1-61773-206-0
First Kensington Electronic Edition: June 2014

10 9 8 7 6 5 4 3 2 1

Printed in the United States of America

HISTORICAL PREFACE

In 1571, Elizabeth I of England, at the age of thirty-eight, had reigned for thirteen years. She was far from secure on her throne. England was a small, weak country with no standing army and an undersized navy. Elizabeth knew that Philip II of Spain, the most powerful monarch in Europe, was poised to invade.

To strike at her, his army would sail from the Netherlands. There, less than a hundred miles off her shores, his troops had already subjugated the Dutch. Philip was lord of Spain, portions of the Italian peninsula, and the Netherlands, whose cities of Antwerp and Bruges were Europe's richest trading centers. He was also stupendously wealthy thanks to his vast New World possessions. The Spanish Main was a scythe-shaped slice of the globe that ran from Florida through Mexico and Central America to the north coast of South America, gateway to Peru. Twice a year the Spanish treasure fleet crossed the Atlantic to deliver hoards of New World gold, silver, and precious gems to Philip's treasury in Spain. He used this constant river of riches to finance his constant wars. Throughout Europe, Spain's armies were feared and triumphant.

Nowhere were they more feared than in the Netherlands. There, Philip's ruthless general the Duke of Alba had crushed Dutch resistance to Spanish rule. As governor from 1567, Alba had set up a special court called the Council of Troubles. Under its authority he executed thousands, including leading Dutch nobles. The people called it the Council of Blood. Prince William of Orange was one of the ten thousand people summoned before the Council. But Prince William escaped. He gathered a rebel army and marched into Brabant, the Dutch heartland. But his troops were inexperienced and untrained, and with winter approaching and money running out, William turned back. He went into exile in the German lands, awaiting his next chance.

Philip of Spain was known as "the most Catholic prince in Christendom." Catholics considered Elizabeth of England a bastard (they did not acknowledge the marriage of her mother, Anne Boleyn, to her father, Henry VIII) and a heretic, for Elizabeth's first act as queen had been a proclamation to make the realm Protestant. It had also made her the supreme head of the church in England, a concept that Catholics found grotesque: a woman as head of a church. In 1570, Pope Pius V excommunicated Elizabeth in a fiery decree, calling her a heretic and "the servant of crime." He released all her subjects from any allegiance to her and excommunicated any who obeyed her orders. Scores of affluent Catholics left England with their families and settled in the Spanish-occupied Netherlands.

These English exiles considered Elizabeth's cousin Mary, Queen of Scots, to be the legitimate claimant to the English throne. Since 1568 Elizabeth had held Mary under house arrest in England, a comfortable captivity in Sheffield Castle. Elizabeth did not dare set Mary free, fearing she would foment an invasion by a Catholic League of Spain, France, and the pope. In the Netherlands the English exiles were plotting to overthrow Elizabeth with military help from their powerful Spanish friends and install Mary in her place. And there, in the Netherlands, a day's sail from the English coast, Spanish troops under the merciless Duke of Alba stood ready should Philip give the invasion order.

But the Dutch rebels had not given up, only gone to ground. They still considered Prince William of Orange their leader. He was keen for a second chance to win back his country for the Dutch. And Elizabeth of England was eager to secretly support him.

That second chance came in the spring of 1572. This time the rebels would not come marching, as an army. They would come— a desperate, motley fleet—from the sea.

❧ 1 ❧

The Prisoner

The Island of Sark: Spring 1572

Fenella Doorn watched the unfamiliar wreck of a ship ghosting into her bay. Crippled by cannon fire, she thought. What else could do such damage? The foremast was blown away, as well as half the mainmast where a jury rig clung to the jagged stump, and shot holes tattered the sails on the mizzen. And yet to Fenella's experienced eye the vessel had an air of defiance. Demi-cannons hulked in the shadowed gun ports. This ship was a fighter, battered but not beaten. With fight still in her, was she friend or foe?

Or faux friend. Fenella kept her anxious gaze fixed on the vessel as she started down the footpath from the cliff overlooking La Coupée Bay. Old Johan followed her, scuffling to keep up. The English Isle of Sark was the smallest of the four major Channel Islands, just a mile long and scarcely a mile and a half wide, so from the cliff top Fenella could see much of the surrounding sea. The few hundred farmers and fishermen who called the island home were never far from the sound of waves smacking the forty miles of rocky coast. Fenella, born a Scot and bred from generations of fishermen, was as familiar with the pulse of the sea as with her own heartbeat.

"She flies no colors," Johan said, suspicion in his voice. Sheep grazing on the cliff top behind them bleated as though echoing the old Dutchman's unease.

"She likely struck her colors in the skirmish," Fenella said.

"Surrendered? Then why wasn't she taken as a prize?"

"Maybe she was, and the prize crew boarded her." Whoever was in command had done a fine piece of seamanship, Fenella thought. The skirmish must have happened far out in the Channel, since no report of it had reached Sark, yet this captain had brought in his ship with one mast shot away and a single lateen sail on the jury-rigged mainmast. Crew now labored at lowering the sails on main and mizzen, the figures too small at this distance to make out features.

"Or maybe she's Spanish," Johan warned. "Spaniards are cunning. Have a care, Nella."

"That's no Spaniard. Her beak's too long. English, maybe." She had decided the ship was not a danger, at least not to the people of Sark. On the contrary, the crew might need victualing, and Sark's crofters would be glad to sell them mutton and the first spring lambs. Fenella saw silver for herself, too. The monotonous clanging aboard, faint at this distance, told her that crew was working the pumps non-stop, which meant there was at least one hole below the waterline. That promised employment for Fenella's shore crew to careen the hull on the beach to make repairs.

Still, something about the crippled vessel unnerved her, as though it had come hunting her personally. She gave a thought to the flintlock pistol that lay in her petticoat pocket beneath her skirt. A foolish fear, she told herself, especially on such a peaceful, sunny day. Her skirt brushed the flowering gorse, releasing its faint perfume into the warm air. The cliff paths all around were brocaded with primroses, dog violets, and yellow celandines. Springtime always lifted Fenella's heart. Yet she had seen death strike often enough amid sunshine and flowers.

She and Johan were almost at the beach, and the cliff path through the gorse was now wide enough for them to walk abreast. Knowing they could be seen from the ship, Fenella took comfort in having the old man at her side. Absurd, she knew, since he was sixty, twice her age, and had just one arm. The other had been hacked off above the elbow when they'd fled the Spanish troops' onslaught of the Netherlands, troops who had butchered the Doorns' village and made Fenella a widow at twenty-five. Johan, her father-in-law, was as stubborn as her late husband, and she knew he would fight for her to the death. She loved the old man for that, but his devotion was also troubling, disabled and frail as he was. She worried about him, for he was getting frailer every day, the cough that had infected his lungs at Christmas persisting despite the spring warmth. Still, she did not slacken her brisk pace on the path as it wound down to the beach. Johan would not want her to.

"More likely she's Dutch," she said to reassure herself and him, "crawling in from a scrape with a Spanish galleon or two." The Dutch hated the brutal Spanish occupation of their country and many had taken to the sea to attack Spanish shipping in the Channel. They had organized themselves into a ragged fleet of a few dozen vessels and with rebel pride called themselves the Sea Beggars. Fenella had refitted several of their vessels that had been shot up by Spanish guns. "The fools never learn," she muttered. She belittled the rebels to mask her admiration for them. But realism outweighed her admiration. Imperial Spain, the most powerful nation on earth, was invincible. The Sea Beggars were minnows attacking sharks.

"That's not Dutch rigging," Johan said. They were crossing the beach, heading for their rowboat, and he raised a hand to shade his rheumy eyes as he studied the ship. "Now that I see her abeam, I think your first guess was right, Nella. She's English."

Nothing unusual about English shipping around Sark. The island lay eighty miles off England's south coast, closer to France, and English trade with France, the Netherlands, Spain, and Portugal was constant. But this ship had been maimed in a battle and England wasn't at war. "An English privateer?" Fenella wondered aloud.

She heard a clank at the bow and saw a dull metallic gleam as the vessel's anchor plunged with a splash. Cable roared through the hawsehole. Fenella knew the anchor would hold well on La Coupée's sandy bottom. This ship was here to stay.

She and Johan reached the rowboat and lifted it to the water's edge, wavelets sloshing at their feet. They climbed aboard and she took the oars. He sat in the stern, squinting at the ship. "God's blood," he said with sudden eagerness, "could it be the baron?"

She scoffed as she rowed. "That fable again, Johan?" He had spoken before about an English privateer, a nobleman who was hitting the Spaniards hard. It was common knowledge that privateers and pirates of many nations prowled the Channel looting their prey—if they weren't sunk first. But a baron? To Fenella it made no sense. Why would an English lord put himself at such risk?

"It's him; I can feel it." Johan's milky eyes shone with excitement. Then, indignation. "And look what the Spanish devils have done to him. Shot him to pieces, damn their hides! I've got to get home, Nella. I've got to go and do my part!"

"You'll do no such thing." He had been harping at her for months to take him back to the Netherlands so he could join the resistance movement. What nonsense. As if a one-armed old man with weak lungs could be of any use. "Might as well spit at a hurricane."

"I beg you, take me back so I can do what I can. Before I breathe my last."

"Enough," she snapped. "I've told you, we'll go nowhere near that madness." Exasperation made her row with such vigor she felt sweat trickle down her back. "You need to look in a mirror, Johan. Fighting's for the young."

"If you won't take me, just give me a boat that I can helm and one brawny crewman. That's all I ask."

"A boat is something I cannot spare. And with one arm you'll find the swim to Amsterdam a long one." Over her shoulder she glimpsed a scatter of men at the ship's rail watching them approach. "Now, keep your nonsense to yourself in front of these visitors and let's earn some coin. Go on, hail them."

Johan shot her a look that said, *You and I are not done yet.* But he squared his shoulders to do business. Cupping his hand to his mouth, he called up to the men at the rail, "Are you English?"

"English, aye!" a voice called down. "We're the *Elizabeth*. Come aboard, if you will!"

Rowing closer, Fenella felt the breeze die in the lee of the tall hull, like a wooden wall, and its shadow engulfed her. Again, she sensed the ship's latent power, like a harpooned whale, weak but still able to crush a boat with a thrash of its tail. But harpooned the ship was. Fenella saw three jagged shot holes in the hull's planking, two forward and one aft, all plugged with oakum-stiffened canvas that dripped water. The gun port sills were stained black with gunpowder, and the acrid smell of it clung to the planks. Fenella sculled the rowboat around and came alongside, and Johan made fast the bowline to the ship's chain plate. The crew tumbled a rope ladder over the side.

Fenella let Johan climb up first, a slow process with his single hand and fluttering empty sleeve. She followed. It was their usual device with strangers. Visitors assumed that the man was in charge and Fenella a mere shore woman. It allowed her a few moments to observe them unwatched before introducing herself as the owner of a salvage enterprise, to their inevitable surprise.

Today, as it turned out, she was mistaken.

"Mistress Doorn?" a man asked, striding toward her. So, they knew of her. He was stocky, bullnecked, and black bearded, his thick lips chapped by the sun. Gun grease streaked his plain gray breeches and doublet, and a grimy bandage wrapped his head, its bloodstain dried to a nut brown.

"Aye, sir," she answered.

"I must say, I expected—" He stopped, looking flustered.

"A hag instead of a beauty?" Johan slyly suggested.

The Englishman collected himself. "Someone older."

Fenella noted the dozen or so crewmen nearby, dirty, barefoot, bleary-eyed. They carried on at their labor, some coiling lines, some snubbing the anchor cable even as they stole glances at her. They had the look of exhausted men relieved to have made safe harbor. No wonder—she had never seen a deck so damaged. The stump of the lost foremast looked like an amputated limb. In the base of the mainmast a thirty-three-pounder cannonball was embedded in the oak. Shot holes peppered the roughly furled sails on the mizzenmast. The bowsprit was blown away, as was the taffrail, and shot had plowed splintered channels in the deck planks. Dried blood stained the deck in red-brown splotches. The scene belowdecks must be as bad or worse, since the clang of the pumps never ceased. The sweating men at the pumps would be sloshing in knee-high bilgewater. The deck itself vibrated underfoot with every clang. She could hear men moaning below, too. The wounded, no doubt.

"I'm Curry," the bearded man said. "James Curry. My gunner's mate was on a Portsmouth carrack you refitted last year, Mistress Doorn, and says you're the best. As you see, we've suffered severe hits. Can you effect repairs?"

"I can, sir." This captain seemed common enough, she thought. *Not Johan's baron privateer.* It brought out the playful devil in her and she asked Curry, with a taunting glance at Johan, "Just one question, sir. Do I address you as *your lordship?*"

Curry looked baffled. Johan winced. Fenella had to smile. But she tempered her mockery as she considered the fine seamanship that had brought the *Elizabeth* into her bay. "Forgive my manners, Master Curry, you are most welcome. And never fear, my shore crew will soon have you refitted to fight another day."

"Was it Spaniards?" Johan asked Curry with grim eagerness.

"Aye, a monster three-decker. But they got the worst of it."

Fenella didn't see how. This ship was a hulk.

Curry grinned. "We sank her."

"Curry, get below." The gruff voice behind Fenella made her turn. A man, tall and lean, was coming up the companionway from belowdecks. His clean-shaven face was smudged with grime like the other men's and his voice was hoarse with fatigue, but his movements were brisk, charged with anger. "Waites is dead. Bring up the damned prisoners. They'll pay for this."

"Aye, aye, sir." Curry knuckled his forehead in salute and hastened down the companionway.

"You there, boatswain," the tall man went on, "go with Curry and tell the—" Seeing the visitors, he came to a sudden halt.

Fenella's heart seemed to stop. Those dark eyes staring at her.

That face sun burnished beneath the dirt. Sir Adam Thornleigh! She had never thought she would see him again, not in this life. And not in the next one, either, for smiling angels would surely welcome him into heaven while she'd likely be kicking at flames in the devil's place.

"Fenella?" he said in amazement. "I'm right, aren't I? Fenella"— he struggled to remember her last name—"Craig?" A faint smile broke over his face. "I'm sorry, perhaps you don't remember me, it's been so long. Edinburgh?" he prompted to jog her memory. "Your fishing boat?"

As if she would ever forget! Their desperate flight to Amsterdam. His kindness to her on the voyage. She had been struck with love for him like a bolt from the blue, and every day since then she'd secretly held him in her heart. "Of course," she managed. "Sir Adam."

"How many years has it been, I wonder?"

"Eleven," she blurted. Then laughed, too thrilled to feel foolish. "You are well met, sir," she said with all the warmth she felt.

He grinned. "So, you're the Siren who lured us poor sailors to your shore. Well met indeed, Fenella."

He looked so pleased it brought joy bubbling up in her, making her laugh again. To think that she had fancied his ship might bring evil! But her happy bubble shattered as she thought of her appearance, disheveled as a fishwife. The damp clumps of auburn hair that had escaped her mobcap. The sweat darkening the underarms of her coarse linen sleeves. Her cheek . . .

He saw it, of course. His eyes locked on the scar. She turned her face away, pretending a consulting look at Johan. *Beauty, ha.* Men admiring her body were content to ignore her ravaged cheek, but she always caught them stealing looks at the scar left by a smashed bottle, compliments of the bastard she had lived with, the Edinburgh garrison commander. The scar had hardened into a white ridge that branched across her cheekbone. After eleven years she rarely gave it a thought, her days too busy for mirrors. But Sir Adam's eyes on it made her cheek burn as if the flesh were gashed anew.

Johan piped up, "One question, sir, if I may. Do we address you as *your lordship?*"

Thornleigh blinked at him. "What?"

"By the fine sound of you you're an English lord, and it seems you've sunk a Spanish man-of-war." With a smug glance at Fenella he went on, "Are you the hell-bent English baron we've heard tell of?"

The brazen interrogation seemed to amuse Thornleigh. "I can't speak to what you've heard, but yes, I'm Baron Thornleigh." He looked at Fenella, jerking his thumb at the old man. "Who's this?"

She could hardly find her voice, appalled at Johan's impertinence and in awe of Thornleigh's exalted new status. New to her, at least. "He's Johan Doorn . . . my lord," she managed. "My master shipwright."

"Good. I'll need you, Doorn." Thornleigh was suddenly all business. "Would you confer with my carpenter? You'll find him in the fo'castle." A nod of agreement from Fenella sent Johan shuffling toward the forecastle. Thornleigh turned to her. "I have wounded men. Is there a doctor ashore?"

"Tomorrow, from Guernsey." She explained, "He comes the last Wednesday of every month." She was glad to turn to business to quell her somersaulting emotions. "How many?"

"Fourteen."

"There's room in the church of St. Magloire. And crofters' wives to nurse them."

"Good." He turned to his watching crew. "Rayner, tell Bates to ready the wounded and get them up on deck." The scrawny crewman dashed to the companionway and clambered down it.

"By the sound of your pumps," Fenella said, "you'll be wanting to careen right soon, my lord. We'll tow you round the headland to the boatyard bay. Good beach, and I can supply all you need there. Stout oak masts, cured planking, plenty of pine pitch. I have carpenters, too, if you lack them, and a sailmaker if you're needing canvas."

He nodded but was clearly distracted, his eyes fixed on the companionway that led below. The scowl she had seen when he first came on deck darkened his face again. Curry was leading up several men, and a crewman below bellowed at them to keep moving. Five emerged, stumbling one by one out onto the deck, squinting at the sudden bright sunshine. From the look of them—filthy, barefoot, in ragged homespun shirts and patched breeches—they were common seamen. Spanish prisoners. She smelled their sweat and fear. The gashed forehead of one oozed blood, and all were bruised and scraped. She imagined them plunging into the sea as their ship sank, flailing in the water in terror, since few seamen could swim, and then, when the *Elizabeth* picked them up, scrambling up the chain plates for dear life, the heaving sea bashing them against the hull, cutting heads, arms, shins.

Another prisoner followed, far better dressed, though his clothes were unkempt: a black satin doublet frothed with gold lace, and black satin breeches embroidered with silver and gold. He wore a jeweled hat of green velvet. A Spanish noble. A don. He stalked a few paces away from the seamen and arrogantly turned his back, proclaiming his status. Fenella felt a shiver. She hated Spaniards.

"Bring ropes," Thornleigh told Curry. "We'll hang them in pairs from the mizzen."

The crew sprang to life with savage eagerness, swarming the prisoners. Fenella's breath caught in her throat. Had she heard aright? *Hang them?*

"Sawyer, lower the longboat," Thornleigh ordered a crewman. "Prepare to ferry the wounded."

The two crew parties set to their tasks. Curry and his men marched the prisoners to the mizzenmast while Sawyer's party set to swinging out the longboat from its boom.

"Move to the mizzen," Curry barked, "or you'll taste Kate Cudgel again." The seamen didn't know the English words, but they understood Curry's raised club. So did Fenella. Their bloody wounds had not come from scrambling aboard in a heaving sea. Thornleigh's men had beaten them. She watched in horrified amazement as Curry's gang hurled two ropes aloft along the mizzen spars. A hangman's noose dangled from the end of each rope.

She spun around to Thornleigh. He was striding across to the port side crew party. She hurried after him. "Sir Adam . . . I mean, my lord—"

"Plain Adam to you, always," he said with a gentle smile. "You saved my life."

It sank the words she'd been about to say. Yes, she had saved him all those years ago, springing him from the garrison jail, but he had been so weak from captivity she thought he'd scarcely noticed her on their flight across to Amsterdam. Now, his look at her said he knew he was in her debt, and it thrilled her.

The terrified jabbering of the Spanish seamen brought her back to the here and now. They were huddled together, quaking in fear, surrounded by the leering crew. She could not see the don past the crowd of crew shouting their bloodlust, but she imagined that even the nobleman now was quaking. "Surely you won't hang them?" she asked Thornleigh.

"Why not?" he snapped.

Her words stalled at his glare. She found her voice. "Send them to the galleys; that's punishment enough. And you can ransom the don."

"I don't need silver."

"But, hang them in cold blood? It's . . . plain murder."

"*They're* the murderers. Attacked my men guarding them. Slit their throats, four good mariners. And a boy, Tim Waites, ten years old. He died in my arms five minutes ago." He turned to Sawyer's men and shouted, "Belay those lines!" They hastened to obey and the longboat splashed into the water, ready to take the wounded. They heaved over the rope ladder.

A wail came from one of the Spanish seamen. He was frantically crossing himself, praying, as a crewman tugged the noose close. Laughing, the crew mimicked the prisoner's action like monkeys.

"Don't, my lord," Fenella said. "This is raw vengeance."

" 'Which is mine, sayeth the Lord.' " The look in his eyes was cruel, bitter. This was not the Adam Thornleigh she remembered. What had happened to harden him so?

"My lord, they're set to swing," Curry called to him.

"Get on with it then," Thornleigh growled.

"No!" Fenella said. "Stop right there, Master Curry!"

They all looked at her in surprise. Thornleigh scowled. "What the devil—"

"The devil's behind what's afoot here, sure enough. I will not have it. This is my bay. You are my guests. Hang those men, and I promise you there will be no respite for your wounded, no refitting of your ship, no victualing. You will not set foot on Sark."

He glowered at her. "Who do you think you are, woman?"

His fury unnerved her. She hardly knew how the steel had come into her to cross him. But she had not escaped war in Scotland and slaughter in the Netherlands, all those mangled bodies that haunted her, to tolerate gross brutality now. Not here. She had come to Sark for peace.

"The Seigneur of Sark gives me authority over this bay," she said, "and I have twenty-three armed men ashore who'll do as I order them. Let these poor wretches loose, I say, or mayhap in the night you'll find your anchor cable cut. You'll drift out to sea and your men at the pumps will finally drop, and your ship will sink."

They stared at each other. Fenella didn't blink, but her mouth was dry as canvas. She said quietly, her heart in her throat, "Stay, my lord. Set them loose. Stay, and make your ship whole."

A faint light came into his eyes. Shame? Amusement? Tedium? Whatever it was, he turned and gave a brusque new order: "Curry, pull down those ropes. No one hangs today."

There was a groan of disappointment from the crew. They didn't immediately obey, anger in their faces. The way they glowered at Fenella sent a spike of fear through her. She thought of the pistol that lay in her petticoat pocket. Idiotic, of course. Her against all of them.

She had to act quickly. She called to the Spanish seamen who were watching, stupefied, "Come on, you poor silly dagos, take the longboat!" She beckoned them over to the waiting boat that nudged the hull. "Come!"

They gaped at her. At Curry. At the English lord who was captain. Thornleigh's eyes stayed fixed on Fenella. Then he bellowed to the prisoners, "You heard her! Move, you damned sea slugs! You're free!"

One more stunned moment and then the prisoners rushed across the deck. Thornleigh stood stony faced, giving no order to halt them as they raced to the boat. Curry and his men watched in amazed silence.

The seamen were clambering over the rail when a man crashed against Fenella's back. She staggered to keep her footing. It was the don, racing after the seamen for the boat. He grappled a prisoner in his way and threw him aside, sending him sprawling. The action knocked off the don's velvet hat. Another prisoner was in his way, starting to climb down the rope ladder. The don spun around, looking for a weapon. Fenella saw his craggy face. Green eyes. Gray-blond hair like bristles. A shock went through her. Five years ago that hair had been bright blond.

The don snatched a belaying pin and turned to the prisoner climbing down and bashed his skull. Blood drops flew and the victim pitched overboard with a scream.

The coldness of a grave settled over Fenella. She was not aware of the time it took to raise her skirt and draw out the pistol, load the finger-sized powder charge, then the ball. She was swift from practice, and a calm corner of her brain knew it took less than a minute. The don had tossed his weapon, the belaying pin, clattering on the deck. He had thrown one leg over the rail.

Fenella cocked the trigger. "Don Alfonso!" she called.

He looked up astride the rail.

She aimed straight at the green eyes and fired.

❧ 2 ❧

The Spanish Threat

Adam Thornleigh stood knee-deep in the water, overseeing the effort to careen the *Elizabeth* onto her starboard beam. The beach rang with the shouts of his crew and the Sark shore crew as they hauled on five taut lines, like whalers struggling to pacify a leviathan. Even lightened of all her stores and water casks the ship resisted. The forward half of her keel was up on the sandy bottom, but her stern slewed stubbornly in deeper water. Adam felt a twinge for her; she seemed to know she'd be defenseless on her side.

He splashed through the shallows to the men with the bowlines, calling, "Haul her in, men! Now! *Haul!*"

With a mighty heave they dragged the ship forward. Her full keel finally plowed along the bottom. The starboard gang seized the moment and hauled her over, and as the larboard side rose Adam saw the two jagged holes from cannonballs that had crashed through the main deck and out the hull, imperiling his vessel and men. The oakum-stiff canvas he'd ordered packed in had only reduced the deadly leaks, not stopped them. High and dry now, the *Elizabeth* shivered for a moment, her timbers creaking. Then, giving up the fight, she surrendered and slumped down on her side like the weary veteran she was. The sweating men shouted victory and danced in the waves she made.

Adam let out a pent-up breath of relief. His ship was out of danger.

He walked out of the water onto the beach. Ahead, the cliff face rose around him in a semi-circle, and crowning it the sunset sky flamed red and orange. Razorbills wheeled in arcs, black and white against the glory of red. Murres swooped in to land on rock ledges on the cliff face. Adam felt a kinship with these birds who spent most of their lives at sea. As he tramped the sand in his sodden boots he suddenly felt sore in every joint. It had taken hours getting his wounded men ashore and getting the *Elizabeth* lightened, towed, and careened. He was hot and sticky and welcomed the cool shore breeze that whispered past his ears. He'd like a wash. His skin was still gritty with gunpowder grains from the morning's action. An action he might regret. Sinking the *Esperanza* hadn't been his intention. He'd only meant to cripple her, but she had blasted the *Elizabeth* with all her murderous firepower, so Adam had blasted back. England and Spain had been on the brink of war for four years. *Have I pushed us over the edge?* If so, he wasn't sorry. He'd long been urging the Queen to take a stand against the tyrant.

Beside him someone coughed. The Sark shipwright, the one-armed old man, Doorn. He stood waiting. While the crew had got in position, he and Adam had been talking about Fenella Craig shooting the Spanish don. She had rowed ashore immediately after, white-faced, too shaken to answer Adam's questions, leaving him with Doorn. Then the urgent careening operation had taken all Adam's attention. Now, his concern flooded back. "Go on, Master Doorn. About the lady. You seem to know her well. Why did she do it?"

"She hates the dagos, my lord."

"Don't we all. But that individual drew her special ire." Adam couldn't help being grimly amused. She had been telling *him* to be merciful.

"Do you hate them indeed, my lord?" Doorn seemed fiercely eager about it.

Adam's amusement drained away as he remembered the terrified Spanish seamen. Had he really been about to hang them? He'd been enraged by their attack on the men he'd posted to guard them. Four of his crew killed, and the boy, Waites. It felt terrible to Adam that the lad's final resting place was this remote island, far from family. But his rage was spent. So much had happened since. Fenella. And the Spanish don.

"I *told* her it was your lordship sailing in," Doorn went on eagerly. "Your men say it was the *Esperanza* you did battle with, a twenty-gun galleon. And you sank her! By Christ, I'd like to have seen it. Were any Sea Beggar ships with you in the fight?"

"No." He was about to add, *Not this time*, but thought better of it. His work with the Dutch rebels was unofficial. For months he'd been harrying Spanish shipping, carrying out the secret wishes of his queen, the *Elizabeth*'s namesake. Sometimes he acted in conjunction with the Sea Beggars, sometimes alone, but always as if on his own initiative with no connection to Elizabeth. She was wary about pushing Spain too far.

"You did it yourself?" Doorn cackled with glee. "By Christ, my lord, you are the terror of the Narrow Sea."

Adam said wryly, "Mistress Craig might better claim that title. Can you shed no light on why she shot the don?"

The old man looked away, quiet now. "You asked before about planking, my lord." He pointed toward a long, low shed with a thatched roof, sheltered in the lee of the cliff, and beckoned Adam to walk with him. "We have stout oak planks from Normandy, well cured. Sturdy Baltic pine, too, for your masts. And plenty of pitch and cordage. We'll soon have you back in fighting shape. Come, I'll show you."

Why deflect my question? Adam thought. *Is he trying to protect Fenella?* But it was no use pretending it hadn't happened. "No, not now," Adam said. The light was fading, and so was he. He still had to visit the wounded to check that they were settled in the church. Tomorrow, too, billets must be found for his men; tonight they would camp on the beach, no hardship in this fine weather. A whiff of roasting meat reached him. His men not involved in the careening were eating around a campfire where they'd rigged a spit. Rabbits? Adam hadn't had a bite since the morning's action, and the smell of the roast meat set his belly to gurgling. He realized he was famished. Some of the men were sharing bottles of sack. A few lolled, drunk already; others were asleep, sprawled by the fire. Adam felt exhausted. The seigneur's chamberlain had sent word offering him a bed in the manor house, the Seigneurie. But the issue of the dead Spaniard could not be ignored. "Fenella—that is, Mistress Craig—she may face rough consequences."

Doorn's eyes snapped to him. "From you, my lord?"

"Me? Never." The Spaniard would rot at the bottom of the bay and good riddance. Adam had watched plenty of his own men plunge into the Channel. And he would never forget Spain's vicious attack four years ago on him and the other ships of Hawkins's expedition to the New World, when scores of English seamen had died, their throats slashed by Spanish swords, limbs ripped off by Spanish cannonballs. Corpses now, fish white in the sunless depths of the Gulf of Mexico. "But she'll have to answer for what she did."

Doorn shrugged. "Seigneur Helier is the Queen's man here and he's over in Jersey, at his manor of Saint-Ouen. Never fear about him, sir; he has lordship of all Sark and he is well pleased with the trade Fenella brings in. The only other authority is the church elders, and they'll shed no tear for a God-cursed dago papist. As for the poxy sailors Nella sent on their way, they won't reach their home soil for weeks, and even when they do, why would they blab against her when she saved their skins?" He added with a growl, "Me, I would've let them swing. But Nella, she's different."

Indeed she is, Adam thought. *Extraordinary woman*. How bold she had been, demanding that he free the Spanish seamen. How paradoxical, killing Don Alfonso. And now, all around him, was the evidence of her small fiefdom. The long shed was the center of her boatyard, and the cottages hugging the low, irregular terraces no doubt housed her shore crew and their families. Out in the bay a smart-looking caravel, Swedish by the look of her rigging, rocked at a mooring, her shrouds pinging musically in the breeze, while four other vessels bobbed alongside the jetty: an expertly refitted Dutch cog, a Highland galley, a serviceable fishing smack that was perhaps French, and a wherry. All belonged to Fenella. Adam thought of that desperate voyage he had made with her from Edinburgh eleven years ago. He had been weak and fevered after months in the Leith garrison, jailed for running arms to the Scottish rebels. All he knew then of Fenella was that she was the mistress of the garrison commander, a brute she'd wanted to escape from, so she sprang Adam from his cell and supplied a fishing boat for them to flee in. Adam owed her his life—the commander would have hanged him. When she proved to be a capable sailor he'd been even more grateful, for he had helmed the boat in a fog of fever.

Not too fevered, though, to notice how fine looking she was. Even with that scar across her cheekbone. Like a white branch, broken. It tugged a string of sadness in him that something so lovely had been marred. A rose with one cankered petal. Oddly, the flaw heightened the beauty of the whole lush bloom. He remembered, when they were at sea, her gouged, bleeding cheek. What kind of brute would do that to a woman? Adam had killed men, but he could not imagine deliberately maiming a woman.

Then he thought of his wife, and knew he was lying to himself. If he had Frances in his grasp he would strike her senseless. *My wife, the traitor.* How close her plot had come to killing the Queen. And how enraged he had been to find Frances had escaped. In the three years since then his agents had scoured Europe for her. Now, one had found her. In Brussels. Reading his agent's letter, Adam had felt the hot excitement of vengeance. When he caught up with Frances he would drag her home to hang.

Except what about Katherine and Robert? She would be twelve now, the boy nine. Every day Adam cursed his wife for taking them. Stealing them. His spry, clever Kate. Robert, his son and heir. Adam so missed their shining faces. They must have been so frightened, torn away from their home and everything they knew. Were they frightened still? And how were they living? What had Frances been *doing* all this time? He looked east across the water, toward the darkness where Europe lay. Weary though he was, he itched to track down the wretched woman. Not to exact vengeance, not anymore—that was a cankerous obsession, and he knew he had to let it go. All he wanted was to get his children back.

It came to him over the echo of a razorbill's cry: *Now is the time to do it.* His ship would be out of commission for weeks, and he couldn't bear to loaf on this island backwater. He'd been on his way home to report to Elizabeth on his mission, first to the Dutch Prince William of Orange in exile on his German estates, then to the French Huguenots in La Rochelle. All these dissidents wanted Elizabeth's support, but first she had to know how strong they were, what real chance they had of disrupting her adversaries, the Catholic kings of France and Spain, so eager for her downfall. She was waiting for Adam's report, but his return to England would now have to wait until his ship was refitted. That didn't mean he had to wait here doing nothing. He could go quietly, privately, to Brussels. If he didn't, Frances might slip through his fingers again. She could slip away to hell for all he cared, but if she left the capital she would take Kate and Robert with her and he'd lose them again, this time perhaps forever. Looking out at the dark horizon, he made his decision. He would go to Brussels, get his children, and take them home.

"Her name's not Craig," Doorn said suddenly.

The words cut into Adam's thoughts. "What?"

"Fenella. After she left Scotland she married."

He felt a prick of disappointment, almost as though he'd lost something. Absurd. He barely knew the woman. But he could not deny his intense curiosity about her. "So her name now is what?"

"Doorn."

Adam blinked at him. She'd married this crippled old man?

"She settled in my village. Polder. It's in Brabant, north of Bergen op Zoom, on the River Scheldt. Her brother left her a little money when he died and she opened a chandlery. Nothing much, just a counter and a shed, but Nella knows boats, and word of her Swedish blocks and quality cordage got round. That's where she met my son, Claes. He was a shipwright like me. I lived with them, my wife and I, and when she died I went on living with them." Doorn was watching the seabirds wheeling around the cliff top. "Glad I am that she died when she did, quiet-like."

The old man's solemn tone gave Adam a twinge of unease. A foreboding.

"Three years Claes and Nella had been married," Doorn went on, "three years to the day. That's when the Spanish soldiers came riding in. Like a squall they hit us. Some folk in the village had been printing pamphlets against the Spanish occupation, tracts against the Duke of Alba, the new governor come to subdue the whole Dutch people." He spat in the sand. "Curse him to hell."

Adam knew all about the pitiless Duke of Alba. The Dutch had paid a bitter price for daring to oppose him.

"He hanged so many in Antwerp, they say the price of rope shot up," Doorn said with grim humor. His look turned grave. "It was a quiet morning in Polder when the soldiers thundered in with sword and axe and pistol. And with fire. We heard screaming and shooting. It was slaughter. Soldiers threw a torch into our house. I took a stick to one of them and cracked his head, but another raised his sword and hacked off my arm." He nodded to his empty sleeve. "I lay there in my blood. Fenella dragged me out. Our house went up in flames." He plucked at the sleeve, picking off a speck of dirt. "They rounded up the village men on the quay. Fenella and I made our way there, me fainting, staggering. We did not dare cross the line of soldiers, but we saw past them, past the screeching women. They tied the men together, two by two, face-to-face. To save the time it would take to hang them. They pushed them into the river. They tied Claes to Vos the bookbinder. I saw them go under. . . ." His voice cracked.

Adam stood silent, picturing it.

"Polder was in flames. . . . Fenella and I, we spent weeks in the forest. She foraged . . . kept me alive." Doorn rasped a cough. It became a spasm of coughing that made his narrow chest crumple and his shoulders shudder. When it passed, he spat, then swallowed, and got control of himself. "The commander that day was a fair-haired Spanish lord, name of Don Alfonso."

Good God, Adam thought. His prisoner. He saw the nobleman again, scrambling for the *Elizabeth*'s longboat. Tumbling overboard, his face blown away, a red pulp of blood and bone.

"Now you know, my lord. Why she hates the dagos."

The sky glittered with stars over Fenella's cottage. The night breeze stole through the open window, jerking the flame of the candle on the table where she stood. The table was spread with boat gear—blocks, sheaves, shackles—crowding the crockery pot of thyme that Fenella grew. She bit off a mouthful of bread slathered with goat cheese and topped with a spring of thyme and chewed it slowly, trying to savor the tang of the cheese and the sweetness of the bread. Trying not to think about the dead Spaniard. *I've done murder.* For one stunning moment when Don Alfonso had pitched overboard she had felt a thrill of satisfaction. If only she could have shot him five years ago! Killed him as he strolled the wharf while his soldiers drowned the men in pairs. She could still see Claes's wild eyes as he hit the river with Vos, arms bound, thrashing like a speared fish.

She closed her eyes to shut out the awful memory. What was the use of remembering? She had long ago forced herself to let the past die.

But what she had done today could not be forgotten. Of all the stupid, impetuous things she had done in her life, killing Don Alfonso was the stupidest. The thrill was gone, swamped now by a fear that made her feel almost sick to her stomach. Was she going to prison? Seigneur Helier was the Queen's authority here, the lord of Sark, but he was Fenella's friend, so could she hope he might turn a blind eye? Lord Thornleigh outranked him, though. Would Thornleigh clap her in irons? Her hand holding the bread trembled. He hadn't detained her—that was a good sign. Besides, he was fighting Spaniards himself, killing them. He'd almost hanged the don.

But even if both the seigneur and Thornleigh turned a blind eye, what about the Spaniards? What would they do when they heard she had killed one of their own? For they would surely hear. The Spanish seamen whose necks she had saved would make landfall in France as soon as they could, at Saint-Malo or Ushant, and there one or more of them would blab. Probably not to inform on her, not with malice, but just because when they reached a tavern the tale was too good not to tell. The "Sea Queen of Sark" who blew off the face of a Spanish grandee. What sailor could resist telling that? Then word would reach Spain. Don Alfonso might well have a powerful family; they might be royal courtiers. They would demand vengeance from King Philip. Panic nipped at her.

She took another bite of bread and cheese to quash it. Manchet bread was her special treat. The fine wheat flour, doubly milled, was expensive. She had it brought from England and baked it herself using her own recipe with rose water and nutmeg. Those items were as dear as diamonds, but a few drops and a few grains scenting the manchet loaf made her feel she was feasting like a duchess. Not tonight. This bite was hard to swallow, her throat had gone so dry.

She forced it down with a mouthful of wine. A Baltic trader had given it to her, three barrels of the renowned wine from Madeira as part payment for what he'd owed her for repairs to his carrack. She had gifted one barrel to the Seigneur of Sark as a mark of their friendship and one barrel to the church elders to keep them out of her hair. The last she savored in the evenings with Johan, or with Madeleine Benoit, the rigger's wife, who liked a laugh as much as Fenella did. She drained the Madeira from her goblet. Johan always scoffed at how she stood to eat when she was by herself. She didn't like sitting at a table alone. Made her feel unready. Though for what, she couldn't say. She set down the empty goblet, her mind on the Spaniards who might soon be coming for her. Her trembling hand made the glass rattle on the wood.

A rasping sound. She glanced at Johan's closed door. A snore? Annoying, but at least it was a healthy sound, not like his awful coughing fits. Johan was getting sicker. It gave her a pang. Was she going to lose him? How bullheaded he was about wanting to go home to fight the occupation. Idiotic. He'd deserved the tongue-lashing she'd given him. The Spaniards would crush him like a bug. And yet something in his fierce wish to go home gave her a twinge of shame. Who was she to say how any man should live his life? Or sacrifice it. The rasp sounded again. Not a snore, she realized, just his window shutter grating on its hinge, nudged by the breeze. A west wind had risen.

Her gaze rose to the loft above his room. That's where she slept. Her big feather bed shared the platform with bolts of canvas and heaps of cordage. She liked the snugness of the loft, like a ship's berth, and loved its window view overlooking the bay and her shipyard. She had taken refuge up there after leaving Thornleigh's ship, her hand still smarting from the kick of the pistol. She had sat stiffly on her bed and watched through the window as the men careened the *Elizabeth*, her crew and Thornleigh's working together.

Adam Thornleigh. The way he'd looked at her as she held the smoking pistol. A look of shock, but something more, too, something mysterious. Admiration? It sent a spark through her. For eleven years Thornleigh had smiled at her in her dreams. Claes Doorn had been a good man, quiet and calm, and he had cherished her. No woman could have asked for a better husband. But he had not fired her blood the way Adam Thornleigh had done with a single glance.

She straightened up in self-disgust. *He looked at me as a murderer.* What else could he see? He, a great lord, a baron, honored at the court of Her Majesty Queen Elizabeth. *Me, as common as barley bread.* Besides, he had a wife. When he and Fenella had left Scotland, in his fever he'd spoken of his wife being with child, their first. *His bairn*, she thought, envying his wife. It tugged an ache inside her. She would be thirty-one at Michaelmas. No man. No bairn.

Foolish, lack-brain thoughts. She had a far bigger problem. The noose. She clapped the crockery lid back on the cheese pot to clear her head and swept bread crumbs off the table. Her noisy bustling brought a whimper from Jenny, the young maid asleep on the straw pallet in the corner by the hearth. Fenella stopped with a sigh. *Let the girl sleep. I should do the same. God knows what tomorrow will bring.*

She took the candle and climbed the stairs to the loft. Sleep didn't seem likely. She set down the candle on her nightstand, a priceless ebony prie-dieu she had salvaged from a Portuguese wreck. She freed her bunched hair from her mobcap and shook it loose. Unlacing her bodice, she undressed down to her shift, then turned to the night-dark window, so black it reflected her image as clearly as a mirror. She kept no mirrors, had no time for them, but now she stood still, hands on her hips, and gazed at herself. The flickering candlelight probed the scar on her cheek. She had long ago come to terms with it. A badge of her independence. In a way, it had saved her. Her life had once depended on her looks. The

Leith garrison commander had wanted her, so she had traded her body for security and bread. But even then, at eighteen, she'd vaguely known that in the future, once beauty was gone, she would have nothing to trade. Her ravaged cheek had forced her to stand on her own early. Hard at first, with some bitter weeping into her pillow, but she had persevered and grown her business. Here on Sark she had prospered.

But now? She felt cold and fearful. Would she wake one morning to see a Spanish pinnace sailing in to hunt her down?

A rap at the door startled her. Who, at this hour? Benoit reporting trouble with the visiting seamen? She had seen them drinking. Brawling sailors were common as sand flies. She didn't need that kind of nuisance now. She whirled on a robe and went down. Jenny was sleepily opening the door, yawning and rubbing her eyes.

Fenella's breath caught. Adam Thornleigh stood in the doorway.

His eyes swept over her loosely tied gown, her tumbled hair. Then back at her face. "Forgive the intrusion at this late hour, Mistress Doorn. But we need to talk."

Had he come to arrest her? But he could have done that hours ago. She found her voice. "Of course, my lord. Come in." He stepped inside, ducking his head under the low doorway. How fine he looked! He had washed, shaved, put on a clean shirt and a doublet of garnet wool. His dark hair, pushed off his forehead, was still damp and glistening. His sheathed sword gleamed in the firelight. She glanced at the dumbstruck maid, whose eyes were big with awe. "To bed with you, Jenny." The girl curtsied, then crept away. Fenella said, "Come through to the parlor, my lord."

He followed her. She closed the door, took a deep breath, then turned to him. "I hope you are comfortable at the Seigneurie?"

"It's fine." He frowned, as though unsure of how to go on. "Couldn't sleep, though."

She waited, her pulse racing. This visit could only be about Don Alfonso. In the silence the wind whispered at the window. A hawthorn bush scratched at the pane. She asked, struggling to sound calm, "Will you take a glass of Madeira?"

"Fenella, you need to leave."

"Leave?"

"It's not safe for you here. The Spaniards. They'll want revenge."

A shiver ran through her. "I know." Yet the shiver was part thrill. He was on her side!

"Do you?" he asked gravely. "I mean that they'll come for you. To hang you."

The word made her flinch. She had seen Spanish torture, executions.

"You need to get yourself to some place safe," he said. "You have family in Scotland, don't you?"

"Family"—that was a word only for a lord. The sunken-eyed kinfolk she'd grown up with had long ago been felled by plague and war. The few who were left were too penniless to feed themselves, let alone another. "My home is here. On Sark." Home, livelihood, everything she had worked to build! Fury boiled up in her at the thought of losing it. At the unfairness of it. At herself for her own brainless act. She lifted her chin, pretending defiance. "Seigneur Helier will stand by me."

"Not against a diplomatic storm raised by Spain in London. If they insist you stand trial, Her Majesty might have to grant their request."

A tremor went through Fenella. Would the great queen order her to swing?

"But that's not likely the route they'll choose, not with relations between the countries so tense. They'll take the quick, quiet way with you instead. They'll come for you themselves."

Her fear swarmed back. "I have guns. From a French carrack that went down in a gale. I salvaged four demi-cannons, fifteen pounders. I'd planned to sell them, but instead I could—"

"Don't even think it. Helier would have to arrest you if you fired on a Spanish ship."

"You *sank* a Spanish ship."

"And will face Her Majesty about that."

His meaning was clear. He was a great lord, a friend of the Queen, who would stand up for him. She was a powerless commoner.

"As for the Spaniards," he went on, "if they want me they'll have to catch me first. But you, you mustn't stay here, an easy target. Even if you could use those guns you can't beat them. They'll come with a hundred men, and if you sink them they'll come back with two hundred."

She couldn't believe such a thing. "They'd send all that manpower, just for me?"

He was looking at her with an odd intensity, as if he'd just realized something astonishing. "My God. You don't know *whom* you killed, do you?"

Of course she did. "Don Alfonso. The devil I watched butcher my village."

"He was Don Alfonso Santillo de Albarado de Cavazos. The nephew of the Duke of Alba."

Alba! In the Netherlands Alba had the power of a king. Her legs felt suddenly weak as reeds. She reached for Thornleigh to keep her knees from buckling.

He gripped her arm. "Don't despair," he said gently. "I won't let them take you. Here's what you have to do. Go to England. You'll be safe there. I'll advise Her Majesty to ensure it."

"She would do that?"

"She's already giving the Sea Beggars safe harbor."

Fury surged in Fenella again. "I'm no beggar!"

He gave her a look of pity, one that said: *Face it, you are now.*

She pulled back. Pulled herself together. "So . . . to England. For how long?"

No answer, just more pity.

"You mean . . . never come back?"

"As long as you're here you're easy to find."

She struggled to take it in. *Go to England . . . maybe forever.* But there was no use arguing. He was right. Stay here and she would swing. "Johan . . . I can't leave Johan Doorn."

"Bring him, too."

"And . . . I'll have to sell everything. Vessels. Buildings. My stock of gear—"

"No, there's no time for that. You have to get away before word reaches Alba."

"Leave behind everything I own?"

"You can build a new business in England."

"That's daft! Pardon, my lord, but the cost—"

"I'll cover it. In fact, I'll buy your vessels and have some of my crew sail them to England." He seemed to read her astonishment and added as though to explain, "Look, I brought this trouble on you. If I hadn't sailed into your bay none of this would have happened. So let me resettle you in England. Anywhere you choose. A southern port might be best. Perhaps the Isle of Wight. Non-stop shipping there. Wherever you decide, I'll supply you with whatever you need. And, of course, my protection."

She could only stare. The enormity of what he was offering! Tears sprang to her eyes, her emotions a storm of confusion and gratitude, anger and relief. She was afraid to lose control and openly weep. To prevent that she forced a laugh. "Partners, you mean?" The baron and the commoner.

His smile was wry. "Why not?" He added quietly, "Fenella, I owe you my life. I won't abandon you now when yours is in jeopardy."

The concern in his voice, in his eyes, warmed her to the core. A vision shone through her misery, a vision of being in England with him, his partner in business, being near him. She swallowed her anger at the coming upheaval. She'd been through worse. Besides, if she wanted to stay alive she had no choice. She clung to the vision. "You are kind, my lord."

"So, you'll go?" he urged. "Immediately?"

She nodded. "Yes. I don't know how to thank you."

"No thanks needed." A change came over his face, and in his voice was a new urgency. "The fact is, now I need *your* help. I need to take one of your boats."

Why? she thought. "The *Elizabeth* will be ready in—"

"I can't wait for that. There's a . . . private matter I must see to."

She longed to ask what the private matter was, but clearly he didn't wish to elaborate. "Of course," she said. "Take the Swedish caravel." The vessel was Fenella's best—and the least she could do for him.

He shook his head. "Too fine a vessel. And too big. I'd need

twenty crew, fifteen at the least. Dangerous. The Spanish port authorities know me."

She didn't understand. "Spanish port?"

"Spanish-occupied. I'm bound for the Netherlands. I'll leave
my crew here and Curry will oversee the work on the *Elizabeth*. I
need to get to Brussels. So I'll buy that little fishing smack of
yours, if I may."

"Brussels?" She was astonished. "But surely that's too dangerous for you." The Spaniards were already offering a bounty for
him, Johan had said, decreed by the Duke of Alba himself. The
danger was even greater now that Adam had sunk a Spanish ship.
"Alba wants your head."

"That's why I need to slip in unnoticed. A modest craft and a
couple of seamen, that's all. I'll be a fisherman bringing a catch
into Antwerp."

What personal business was so crucial that he would take such a
risk? It baffled Fenella. But the mention of Antwerp ignited a stirring thought. Perhaps she would not have to abandon everything
after all. "My lord, I'd like to get to Antwerp, too. I've been sending my profits to a banker there. I want to get my money."

"Leave it. I'll give you the money. Just get yourself to England."

"No, damn it, it's mine." The steel in her voice clearly took him
aback. She regretted speaking so harshly, but she had worked and
sweated for that profit and was not about to let the bloody
Spaniards confiscate it and leave her penniless. She would take to
England what was hers. To soften her outburst she said, "You're already doing enough for me, my lord." She added with pretended
bravado, "And what kind of partner would I be if I didn't bring investment?" He didn't smile, and she saw that he was still concerned. Before he could speak again, she pressed on. "When do
you plan to take the *Odette*?"

"The what?"

"My fishing boat."

"Ah. Soon as she's provisioned."

"I'll have that done for you at first light."

"Good. Then I'll sail with the morning tide."

"And I'll sail with you." She held up her hands to forestall his protest. "Never fear; I'll collect my gold, slip out of Antwerp, and cross to England before the Spaniards get word of Don Alfonso. Besides, my lord, you could use my help to sail in under the nose of the customs. You, the fisherman. Me, the fisherman's wife."

"And me," said a voice at the door.

Fenella whirled around. Johan stood in his nightshirt. When had he opened the door?

"God's hand is in this, Nella—the *Odette*, His Lordship, and you, bound for the Netherlands. Take me, too, and leave me there. I'm not going to England. I'm going home."

∂ 3 ∂

Alba's Commander

Carlos Valverde, commander of cavalry, judged the assembled crowd of Brussels townspeople to be over a thousand. He swept a sharp glance of appraisal over his mounted troop posted along the west edge of the Grote Markt, the town square. It was a sweltering day, freakish for spring, and sweat slicked the brows of his men beneath their helmets. Carlos's own back prickled with sweat under his leather jerkin, and his palms were slippery inside his gauntlets. Even his destrier, a fiery-tempered Andalusian stallion, twitched in the heat. The horse was a gift from the governor, the Duke of Alba, and Carlos wished he were cantering down a shady country lane to give the fine animal his head rather than standing on parade for the unveiling of a statue of the duke. But duty was duty, and Carlos noted with satisfaction that his troop sat their horses with disciplined stillness alongside the sweating infantrymen, four hundred of them posted to keep the peace, including fifty musketeers.

With any luck, he thought, *keeping the peace won't be my concern much longer.* The duke had sent Carlos a note this morning telling him to see him after the unveiling ceremony. *There is news*, Alba had written, terse as always in his communications. Carlos so hoped it was the news he'd been waiting for. The reward he'd been promised. He was eager to tell Isabel and end the tension that for months had been building between them. She was English and had made no secret to him of how she hated Alba's policies of subjugating the Dutch. Almost a thousand had been hanged and the property of over ten thousand confiscated—"Because I cannot execute them all," Alba had dryly told Carlos. Isabel never complained for herself, but after sixteen years of marriage he could read the silent signs of her unhappiness at the year they'd spent here, Carlos enforcing Spanish martial law. Tonight, God willing, that would change. He would take her in his arms and tell her they were going home.

Trumpets bleated from the center of the town square where musicians stood beside the canvas-shrouded statue. Elevated high on a marble pedestal, the statue formed a triangle with the square's two other focal points, the raised pulpit and the gallows. Sermons and hangings were regular occurrences here. Workmen with ropes stood ready to pull away the statue's canvas covering, and the flock of priests around it shuffled in anticipation, along with city councillors, leading guildsmen, and magistrates.

Carlos watched the townspeople. Trouble from this placid lot didn't look likely. They stood waiting in patient, orderly blocks, perspiring under the noonday sun. Wealthy burghers, beneficiaries of the Spanish occupation, sat on tiers of benches where the ladies, suffering in their finery, fanned themselves in the heat. Visiting grandees from the court of Philip of Spain sat on a separate, higher bank of tiers under a shady canopy alongside the duke's lordly lieutenants and advisers. All eyes were on the shrouded statue, whose sharp peaks beneath the canvas put Carlos in mind of the bony old man himself. Dressed in black satin embroidered with gold like glints of sun on shadow, the duke had settled his long, lean frame on a throne-like chair on a dais among the grandees. Alba had always been thin, even when Carlos had last fought for him in the German campaign over twenty years ago, and a recent illness had left him gaunt. His close-cropped hair and trim beard seemed every day more wiry with gray. Still, Carlos knew the old man was feeling better. Commissioning this statue had helped revive him.

The show was pure Alba. He'd ordered the thing made from

melted brass cannon captured from rebel fighters when he'd marched into the Netherlands four years ago. That was before Carlos had arrived from England, but he'd heard how Alba had crushed his enemy at Jemmingen: twelve thousand green rebels led by the brother of the exiled Prince William of Orange against Alba's fifteen thousand battle-hardened troops of Spanish *tercios*. Over six thousand rebels had died that day; just eighty Spaniards. Impressive, Carlos thought. Another victory to burnish the old man's military record, already legendary. Carlos had been less impressed at hearing how Alba's soldiers had pillaged all the way back to Groningen. People said the sky had turned red with the flames of burning houses.

Carlos glanced at the stands, looking for Isabel. She was with child, their fourth, and he hoped this sweltering heat wasn't making her too uncomfortable. He wanted nothing to upset her in this pregnancy. Two years ago they had buried a newborn baby daughter, and he still felt the shadow on his heart. He knew it was worse for Isabel. A scar of grief.

No sign of her yet. Not surprising, really, since she was coming with the Viscountess Quintanilla, a well-fed matron who moved as slowly as a baggage-train mule. She was kind to Isabel, though, and Carlos was grateful for that; the grand lady didn't slight his wife because of *him*. He glanced at his counterpart, the captain of the infantrymen, Don Felipe, son of the Count de Gortera. Carlos himself was plain Señor Valverde; he had no title and likely would never win one from his queen, Elizabeth. Despite all his years in England and his unwavering loyalty to the English Crown, she had not admitted him to the rank of peers alongside Isabel's brother, Adam, Baron Thornleigh. *Because I'm Spanish.* It galled Carlos. And Philip of Spain would never ennoble him, either, although for a different reason. Spaniards were fanatical about lineage. The lords among Alba's commanders acknowledged Carlos's exceptional military experience and of course they bowed to the duke's judgment, but they would never consider Carlos one of their own. Their ladies, meanwhile, could be ruthless, snubbing the wife of any man as baseborn as Carlos, the son of a camp follower who hadn't been sure which of her customers had fathered him. It rankled him to see even the lowest lordlings' wives outranking Isabel when they were seated at Alba's dinners. She laughed it off, saying the women's arrogance was envy because they wished they had husbands who were half the man Carlos was. When she said things like that, so stirringly loyal, he knew he had something more precious than a noble title. He had Isabel.

What he didn't have, and what he needed for his growing family, was money. Two years of evil luck had all but ruined him, starting with disastrous harvests on the manors he owned in Northumberland and Yorkshire. Then plague had killed a third of the tenants on his Somerset manor; he'd visited the hollow-eyed survivors and doled out what relief he could. Last spring his Cornish tin mine flooded, and then the ship with his last stock of tin bound for France was lost in a storm off the Normandy coast. All these losses had left Carlos deep in debt. So, from Yeavering Hall, their home in Northumberland, he'd written to his old commander, the Duke of Alba, offering him a company of horse: English, Italian, and German mercenaries. Carlos had handpicked them, an elite troop, outfitted at his own expense. The duke had welcomed Carlos to his Brussels palace, eager to put him in command of cavalry patrols to hunt down dissidents. Isabel had joined him, bringing their two younger children, Andrew and Nell, while their eldest, Nicolas, stayed in London as company for his grandmother, the Dowager Lady Thornleigh. But Carlos had never dreamed the Brussels posting would cause such tension in his marriage. *Alba's reign of blood*, Isabel would mutter. Her unease had deepened as soon as she knew about the coming child. *I wish this baby could be born at home*, she had said last week. *Alba can't expect you to stay forever.* He hadn't told her he couldn't afford to disband his troop. He was doing this military service for Alba for one reason only: to win a princely pension from the king of Spain. Alba, as close to the King as a brother, had promised Carlos the pension.

There was a flurry among the ladies in the stand: The viscountess and her entourage had arrived. Carlos glimpsed Isabel taking a seat. She looked straight at him and smiled. He had told her this morning about Alba's note and his hope about what it meant. With a royal pension they could go home. At her smile, Carlos felt all the promise of this boost in his fortunes. The coming child was a happy sign. He hoped it would be a girl, for Isabel's sake.

The trumpets blared again. The workmen hauled on the ropes and the canvas slid off the statue. Sunlight gleamed off the bronze figure, larger than life: Alba with his sword arm raised, the blade pointing to heaven, and his booted foot trampling rebellion in the form of a writhing mass of ferret-faced wretches. The burghers and grandees in the stands applauded. The townspeople looked on in silence, a vacant daze on most faces, like cattle. The duke gave the slightest bow of his head in modest, pleased acknowledgment.

Beside the statue a city official, feminine looking in his flowing robes of office, held up a scroll and read from it, raising his voice so it carried across the crowd on the windless air. " 'This monument is erected to Fernando Alvarez de Toledo, Duke of Alba, governor of the Netherlands, for having extinguished sedition, chastised rebellion, restored religion, secured justice, and established peace.' "

Polite applause. Carlos had his eye on the street beyond the square, gauging how quickly his troop could file out and return to barracks once the ceremony ended. There would be speeches and prayers first, of course. Still, he could probably make it to the governor's palace before supper to meet with him.

An odd sound, a *splat*. A gasp from the crowd. Carlos stiffened in his saddle and his attention snapped to the statue. Something dripped, yellow and viscous, from the bronze arm. A raw egg. His gaze swept the crowd. Who had thrown it? A few titters came from the throng as eggshell slithered off the bronze duke. The city councillors glared at the people. In the hush, every face looked up to the flesh-and-blood duke on his dais. Alba did not move, but Carlos saw a twitch of the thin mouth.

Another *splat*. This time, not an egg. Horse shit fouled the bronze Alba's chin. No twitters from the crowd now. A hum of horror rose as, again, every face looked to the living Alba.

Councillors scurried in the square, shouting orders to the militia and pointing at the crowd to reveal the culprit. But they were all pointing to different spots, no one sure where the dung had been hurled from. At the shouting, Carlos's horse tossed his head in nervous excitement, silver harness jangling. Carlos stood up in his stirrups to get a better look at the crowd. A movement caught his eye across the square: the throng parting. Someone running away? He could see no runner, only the effect, like that of a varmint scurrying through a field of grain.

He kicked his horse's flanks and the stallion bolted forward. Carlos called to his lieutenant, "Martinez!" and pointed to the street behind the crowd. That's where the runner was heading. Carlos crossed the square at a gallop, Martinez falling in behind him, hooves clattering. Councillors and priests lurched out of their way. He and Martinez raced past the statue and reached the far edge of the crowd. Guards stiff-armed the people to hold them back and let the horsemen in. Carlos plunged into the mass of people. They stumbled out of his way, a woman screaming. He still could see no one running; he was just following the ghostly path he'd noted. Under his breath he cursed the people for not moving aside fast enough, slowing him. The path had already closed in. He was losing the culprit.

Then he saw a man burst out of the rear of the throng. Skinny like so many of the poor, in grubby homespun clothes, he was racing to escape, not looking back. Carlos kicked his horse and barreled through the last rank of people, finally clear of them. He galloped after the culprit, past houses and shops and pedestrians, gaining on the man. The culprit swerved and ducked down a side street. Carlos reached the intersection and saw the culprit weaving past carts, people, dogs, a farmer with two pigs. With a glance over his shoulder Carlos motioned to Martinez to follow the man. "After him!"

Carlos turned down a lane that ran parallel to the side street. Galloping, he swerved left and bolted through a garden, and when he reached the street he drew rein, halting his horse. The culprit was running straight toward him, so hell-bent on escape he'd almost reached Carlos before he saw him and lurched to a stop. Carlos drew his sword, ready to strike if the culprit made a move to run. The fellow looked up at him, fear in his sunken eyes. Carlos froze. It was a boy. Tall, but still a boy. No more than twelve. Like Carlos's son Andrew. The boy stood frozen, too, trembling. Carlos, shaken, lowered his sword. In the silence between them his horse heaved bellows breaths.

The boy's eyes went wide in surprise, as he sensed he was safe. He bolted for a gap between houses. But Martinez was now bearing down on him. Martinez's horse's chest hit the boy with a thud, knocking the breath from him and sending him sprawling in the dust. Both horsemen trotted up to him.

"Get up," Carlos said. *Run, boy,* he wanted to say. If he'd been alone he might have. But Martinez was already prodding the boy's back with the flat of his sword as the captive struggled to his feet, and people in the street had stopped to watch, others leaning out of windows.

Carlos and Martinez brought the boy back to the market square, swords drawn as they rode behind him. The crowd let out a roar of anticipation when they saw the two horsemen lead in their prisoner. Some of the burghers were on their feet in the stands, applauding. The councillors at the statue glared at the boy, indignant at the disruption that had marred their ceremony.

Guards took hold of the boy. He looked up at Carlos, his face white with dust and fear. "Please, sir . . . they hanged my father . . . and my brothers. Please . . . I'm the last."

It pressed a weight on Carlos's heart that made him angry. *Then why poke the hornet's nest, fool?* Guards dragged the boy before the city officials. The officials looked up at Alba on his shaded dais. They sent a messenger running up the stands to him. Alba exchanged a few words with the messenger, then gave a nod.

The crowd hummed, anxious, excited. Everyone knew the governor's nod was his command.

The boy was hauled to the gallows. He resisted wildly, kicking and squirming and weeping. Carlos watched in pity and disgust. The boy had a chance to die bravely, but he wasn't going to. Carlos trotted back to his position at the head of his troop, wishing the whole God-cursed business were over. *Hang the poor fool, give me my pension, and let me take my family home.*

But the business turned into something worse than a hanging. The noose was dropped over the head of the boy, who squealed in terror, his face red and contorted with crying, and they strung him up. But they'd kept the rope short so it wouldn't break his neck as a normal hanging would. He kicked at the air, strangling, his eyes bulging, his face turning a ghastly gray-blue. The people watched in a hush of horror and fascination. Then the hangman cut the boy down still alive, choking, gasping. Guards stripped off his ragged clothes. He was dragged, naked and half-dead, along the gallows platform so that everyone could see and then laid out on a bench where they tied him down. The executioner stepped forward, his butcher's knife glinting in the sunlight. He slit the boy's abdomen. The boy shrieked. Blood spurted. The knife dug in and its tip tugged out the coil of intestines. The boy's body twitched in spasms. His eyes rolled in their sockets.

A flurry of women's voices sounded from the stands. Carlos looked toward the ladies clustered around the Viscountess Quintanilla. A knot of women were on their feet, agitated, bending over someone. Between them he glimpsed a slumped form. Isabel! She'd fainted. He dug his spurs into his horse and charged over to the stand, calling, "Isabel!"

She was being helped to her feet by two ladies, and at his shout she looked at him, misery in her eyes. He reached the stands and drew rein. Isabel turned away from him, led off by her companions. Carlos watched her go, wanting to leap from the saddle and rush to her. He saw Alba's eyes on him from the shadows of the dais, the gaunt face frowning.

The brothel was beneath a city magistrate's home on the River Scheldt. Faint voices from the nighttime river traffic drifted down the marble staircase from the street-level foyer.

Carlos found the underground room blessedly cool. The walls and columns were tiled with mosaics, and golden light from hanging candelabras gleamed off the mosaics' jewel-like colors. Music lilted from a lute, and perfume scented the cool air. Alba had insisted that Carlos come with him tonight, and as he drank the fine wine Carlos grudgingly admitted that the place was restful, though the wall-sized mosaic of a recumbent man being serviced by a trio of naked women, one with the fellow's cock in her mouth, was hard to ignore. Carlos would have much preferred to have this meeting in Alba's palace.

Alba dealt another hand of cards to Carlos and their two companions. One was Alba's thirty-year-old son, Fadrique, who lolled in his chair watching a girl sway in a languorous dance to the lute music played by a boy. The other was the Count of Monterra, the noble guest Alba was entertaining, although the plump, bare-breasted girl sitting on the count's lap and nibbling his earlobe seemed to have that task firmly under control.

"Valverde led the vanguard," Alba was saying. Dealing cards, he was recounting the battle of Mühlberg over twenty years ago, his first victory as a general under Charles, king of Spain and Holy Roman Emperor, who had sent an army to rout the German forces. Carlos, just twenty-one then, had captained a company of the Emperor's cavalry. Alba was praising him to the count, and Carlos wasn't sorry he had come tonight if the climax of the praise was going to be news of a pension from King Philip. "It was April, mud up to our horses' hocks," Alba went on. Carlos remembered how Alba had ridden a white horse and worn white armor and long white plumes in his helmet. Supposedly, it was so that his men could identify him, but Alba never missed a chance to put on a show. "By the time we reached the bank of the Elbe the enemy's forces had crossed and destroyed the only bridge. That must have satisfied them that we were no threat." He glanced at Carlos with a look of fatherly pride. "And what did Valverde do? Instantly had his horsemen hack down trees and raise a makeshift bridge. We got all our troops across within an hour, and soon after nightfall we came upon the enemy, unprepared, asleep in the woods." He laughed. "We made so many German corpses that night we piled them in heaps."

The count raised his goblet in a toast to Carlos, who gave a polite smile in return, but his thoughts slid back to the grisly execution of the boy in the market square. And to Isabel. When he saw that she'd fainted he feared a miscarriage. He'd sent his squire, Gomez, to the viscontess's house and he brought back the message that Isabel was fine, had suffered nothing worse than a bruised hip. Carlos was relieved, but the scare left him itching to find out when he could take his family home to England. "You honor me, Your Grace," he said now to Alba. "Which makes me bold to ask about the news you mentioned this morning."

But Alba's attention had shifted to his son, who was getting to his feet at the arrival of a courtesan coming to greet him, a slim girl dressed as finely as a duchess except for her hair, which was colored a fantastic blue. Fadrique and the girl ambled off, chatting, toward one of the private baths.

Carlos prompted Alba, "In your note, my lord?"

The duke's steely gray eyes shifted back to him. "Ah yes, good news for you, Valverde." He smiled. "Very good."

Carlos could have whooped for joy. He forced himself not to ask, *How much is the pension? When can I start collecting it?* He kept his question neutral. "From His Majesty?"

"From His Majesty indeed. I am delighted to inform you that His Royal Highness has named you a Companion of the Order of San Baltazar." Alba raised his goblet. "Congratulations."

Carlos wasn't sure he understood. The Order of San Baltazar was a catchall group the King used to reward minor petitioners such as youngest sons of the least of the nobility, or adventurers who'd brought pirate gold to the royal treasury. A lackluster honor at best. Perhaps it was just a formality that went along with any royal pension? But the Count of Monterra's disinterested look seemed proof of the lowly honor, and Alba, picking a candied almond out of a dish of sweets, said nothing more. Carlos wanted to grab him by the sleeve and demand an answer. *Where's my reward for a year of chasing down your damned rebels?* But he held his frustration in check. He could say nothing in front of the count. He would have to get Alba alone. "Thank you, my lord." Carlos managed a courteous bow of the head. "I am surely in your debt."

"Not at all," Alba said breezily. "God knows you've earned it." He added to the count, making the point, "My jails are full to bursting, in large part thanks to Valverde." He looked up as a willowy courtesan joined them, a blonde in see-through gauze. "Ah, Sophie." He rose and beckoned the count, whose own girl hopped off his lap. The two men and their women retired to the private rooms.

The rest of the night was a trial. Carlos sat dealing cards to himself in games of solitaire, his frustration growing as he waited for the three lords to return. He knocked back several more goblets of wine and pretended to enjoy the lute music, and did, in fact, enjoy the attentions of a tired-looking girl who came to massage his shoulders. She'd brought a little monkey on a leash, her pet. She shrugged when Carlos declined to visit her room, then sat with him and drank with him to keep him company, and he almost felt sorry for her in her efforts to cheer him up by having the monkey do tricks for sugared almonds. But he could not muster a smile, and his mood became blacker the longer he waited for his companions.

Dawn smudged the sky by the time the four men climbed into a boat, Fadrique swaying on drunken legs, the count continually burping, Alba wincing at an attack of his gout, Carlos weary and on edge. They were rowed back to the governor's palace, where, under a torch-lit arch of the inner courtyard, Fadrique's wolfhound bounded to him. He clapped a hand on the dog's head to steady himself and stumbled to the staircase that led to his rooms. The count's sleepy entourage of servants and gentlemen hangers-on crossed the courtyard and enveloped him and bore him away to his suite. Alba's white-haired body servant, a veteran soldier, came stumping down the stairs toward him. Carlos gripped the duke's arm. "A word, my lord."

"A word is insufficient," Alba said, suddenly grave now that they were alone. "There is much to say." He held up his hand to the servant, a silent order to leave them. The old fellow turned and went back up the stairs.

Carlos's spirits surged despite his fatigue. "Then His Majesty has granted your request on my behalf?"

"I couldn't tell you this, not with Monterra nearby. His Majesty has declined your pension. And expressed some displeasure at me for championing you."

The statement was crushing. Alba's tone more so, his anger unmistakable. Carlos struggled to find words. *Declined? Why?* Why was he being treated with such disdain, such scorn? He wanted to grab fistfuls of Alba's collar and demand a civil answer. But he could not argue with a duke, let alone a king. He asked as calmly as he could, "For what reason, my lord?"

"Because he does not trust you."

Carlos flinched. Scorn was bad enough, but this was worse. The outright mistrust of the King? Heads rolled for less. "My lord, I assure you I have done nothing to give His Majesty any cause for—"

"You *married,*" Alba snapped. "Remember?" The sharp sarcasm showed he was barely suppressing his rage.

Carlos could only stare at him. What was the man talking about?

"Married an Englishwoman. A Thornleigh. Sister of the pirate."

Good God. So that was it. Carlos's loyalty was in question because of his marauding brother-in-law. Adam Thornleigh.

"That's right, the pirate baron," Alba growled. "The one who brought us to the brink of war four years ago when he attacked His Majesty's pay ship and gave his queen the gold." Carlos knew the tale. He and Isabel had been at home in England when it had happened. Adam had attacked a ship bound from Spain to the Netherlands carrying gold to pay for Alba's troops, and when he told Queen Elizabeth the money was a banker's loan to Philip of Spain she persuaded the banker to loan it to her instead. People at home cheered her for her sly ruse and called Adam a hero. But Alba, outraged, had slapped a freeze on all English assets in the Netherlands. Elizabeth followed suit, freezing all Spanish assets in England. Adam had started a cold war.

"I have credited you with loyalty to me, Valverde, despite the criminal damage your kinsman continues to wreak upon our shipping. But now Thornleigh has gone too far. He has sunk His Majesty's ship *Esperanza* off the Isle of Sark and taken prisoner the nobleman on board, my nephew, Don Alfonso. We have no report of where Thornleigh has gone. I fear for Don Alfonso's life. So does His Majesty. With such a depraved relative, Valverde, can you wonder at His Majesty's displeasure with you? How *can* he trust you? How can *I?*"

"I have not seen my brother-in-law for over a year."

"Not been in contact with him?"

"No. I've been busy in your service, my lord. Thornleigh does for himself . . . what he does."

"And now he has disappeared in the mists of the Channel." His steely eyes bored into Carlos's. "My question about trust was not rhetorical. If you hope to win back His Majesty's confidence you must show me, must *prove* to me, that you can be trusted. Find out where Thornleigh is. Find out how I can capture him. Then we'll discuss your reward."

It was like smoke clearing on a battlefield, showing the extent of the slaughter and ruin. What Carlos saw was the ruin of his hopes.

Carlos's household was abuzz with a morning liveliness he found hard to take. His mind fogged with worry as he walked past the maidservants bustling at setting out breakfast, he didn't acknowledge their curtsies. The smells of ham and vinegary mustard turned his stomach. His daughter rushed to greet him.

"Papa!" she cried, bobbing a distracted curtsy to him. "Nico fell!" Nine years old, Nell was tall for her age, almost up to Andrew's chin, though Andrew, sauntering in behind her, was three years older. Nell was waving a paper. "The doctor has tied sticks to his leg!"

Carlos tried to focus on what she was saying. Nicolas was hurt? "What's this?" He took the paper from her. "A letter?"

"From my lady grandmother. Nico broke his leg!"

"They've probably cut it off by now," Andrew muttered, a dark jest.

"Don't *say* that," she shot back.

Andrew bowed to greet his father. Carlos knew the boy's jest had sprung from jealousy of his elder brother. Carlos himself had no siblings. His children's rivalries baffled him. "I hope it's a clean break," he said, scanning the Dowager Lady Thornleigh's letter. He'd seen shattered shinbones in battle. The thought of his son as a lifelong cripple was terrible.

"He's fine," Isabel said as she joined them, still pinning up her dark hair. "My mother says he's resting and quite comfortable, and complaining that her library has no *Holinshed's Chronicles*."

"What happened?"

"He crashed out of a tree," Nell said, indignant at their lack of horror for the suffering of her favorite brother.

Isabel said, "He was pruning an apple tree for Mother. Fell off the ladder." She took the letter from Carlos. "She wrote this two weeks ago, so he's probably up and walking by now." She was carefully folding the letter, so carefully that Carlos wondered if she was more anxious about Nicolas than she let on. She looked up into his face. "At the palace all night?" She smoothed a smudge from his cheek with a motherly gesture. "Alba really does take liberties. You look terrible." Her lips brushed his, and there was nothing motherly in their invitation. "But I'll forgive him this once," she whispered, "now that we can leave. I can't wait to hear."

He took her hand and squeezed it. How could he tell her? "You're all right?" he asked. Yesterday's execution in the market square seemed ages ago.

She squeezed his hand in return. "Right as rain, my love." She tucked the letter into her pocket. "Come, let's breakfast. You can read all about Nico after."

He looked at his children. They stood waiting for him to sit so they could eat. He had no appetite, couldn't face breakfasting with them as though nothing had happened. "Andrew, did you exercise the gelding?"

The boy looked startled. "This morning? No, sir, not yet."

"Do it."

"Now?"

"Now. He needs it, and you need to master him."

Andrew looked hurt at the rebuke. He marched out to the stables. Carlos turned to his wife and daughter, Nell wide-eyed at his sharp tone, Isabel frowning in concern. Carlos silently cursed Alba. "Go ahead, eat," he told Isabel. "I want to wash."

Upstairs in their bedchamber he pulled off his doublet and shirt and poured water into the basin and whetted his razor.

Isabel came in with a trencher of bread and ham for him. "Why does he keep you so late? You're exhausted."

He soaped his chin. "Plans for the new patrols." He couldn't tell her he'd spent the night at a whorehouse. Playing solitaire, but what wife would believe that? He added, as he set about shaving, "Joint exercises with Don Felipe."

He caught her shudder. " 'Exercises,' " she muttered. "What a word for it." It irked him. He was doing what he'd come to this country to do, damn it. Alba was the lawful authority and Carlos would not apologize for upholding that authority. He and Isabel had been through this before. She knew enough to keep her objections to herself, but those shudders of hers—he felt them like nicks of a blade.

She set down the food for him on the bedside table and picked up his shirt from the bed. Shaving, he saw her in the looking glass as she folded the shirt. "The viscountess invited me to spend June at her country estate once the baby has come. I was so glad to tell her we had other plans." Carlos wiped off the last of the soap, dreading telling her the truth. He splashed water on his face and toweled it dry. She put down the shirt and came to him and rested her hands on his back and pressed her cheek against his shoulder blades. "Home, Carlos. Now that you have the pension, how soon can we go?"

He turned on her so suddenly she lurched back a step.

"Where's your brother?" he demanded.

She blinked at him. "What?"

"Adam. Where is he?"

"I have no idea. Why?"

"Don't pretend you don't know what havoc he's causing in the Channel. He and the cursed Sea Beggars."

She raised her head high. "Of course I know. And I hope they keep at it. The sooner they break Spain's iron grip on this poor country the sooner Alba's reign of blood will end."

"Don't talk nonsense. This country is Spain's forever. When did you last hear from Adam?"

"Goodness. What an inquisition!"

He snatched her wrist. "Isabel, this is no jest. Have you heard from him?"

She tried to tug her arm free, angry, but Carlos held it tight. A look of confusion, close to fear, flitted across her face. "No. I've had no word of him since we came to this godforsaken place."

"Has your mother? Has she written to you about him?"

"No. Why? Carlos, what's this about?"

He dropped her wrist, sick of the fight. All that was left was the truth. "He's lost me my pension."

She gaped at him. "What? But . . . Alba's promise. He said there was news—"

"Oh yes, he gave me the news. The King has made me a member of the illustrious Order of San Baltazar. His dumping ground for slackers. Might as well have been a slap in the face." He saw her shock and longed to soften the blow. But there was no way he could. The only consolation he had to give her was his regret. "Isabel, I'm sorry." He put his arms around her and pulled her close. "We're here to stay."

She stiffened in his embrace. "No." She said it quietly, but there was no mistaking the firmness. She pulled away. "It's time for you to leave."

"I know you've been unhappy here, but—"

"I'm not talking about that. It's you. You've done your service to Alba honorably. But his brutal command has made so many enemies. The people hate him. You need to leave before they rise up."

"These people will not rise up."

"You saw that crowd in the square react to what Alba did to that boy. They were seething."

"They did nothing."

"They already have. Bakers are refusing to bake, brewers to brew."

"Others will bake and brew."

"And if the people take up arms?"

"Against thirteen thousand Spanish troops? They'll be slaughtered."

She was about to speak but stopped. She knew he was right. Her face had gone pale. "Carlos, if you stay *you'll* be doing the slaughter. I'm asking you, please . . . for the sake of our children. Leave this man's service. Come home."

He shook his head. "I can't."

Anger leapt in her eyes. "You mean you won't."

"I mean I can't afford to. My debts." He looked away. "It's worse than I told you."

He felt her eyes on him, felt her absorb this new shock. "How much worse?"

He turned back in scorn. Was *worse* not bad enough?

She rallied. "Mother will help us. Adam will help us."

"Adam?" The name burst from Carlos in fury. Adam, who had already gifted him two manors for his sister's sake, loaned him hundreds of pounds. How much humiliation could a man take? "Enough. The Duke of Alba keeps food on our table and clothes on our children's backs. I am staying and doing my duty to him."

"It's not *my* duty. There's the coming child to think of. I don't want this baby born in Alba's bloody realm. I'm going home, Carlos. Home to Nicolas, who needs me. And I'm taking Andrew and Nell with me."

It stunned him. Never had he expected betrayal from her.

She took a breath, then said steadily, "I hope you'll come with us."

❧ 4 ❧

Fenella's Gold

Two days in Antwerp had made Fenella wonder if she'd been a lunatic to come back. The place frightened her. It had once been an exuberant city, the trading capital of Europe, renowned for tolerance thanks to its multinational merchant and banking population. But she hadn't been here for five years, and in that time nearly eight thousand Dutchmen had been executed, many more had had their property confiscated, and tens of thousands had fled, mostly into the German lands, rather than suffer under the merciless martial rule of the Duke of Alba. Now, Antwerp felt like a city under siege. People kept their eyes down, anxious, wary. Fenella knew she had more to fear than most. It was Alba's kinsman she had killed. She often found herself looking over her shoulder.

For what? she chided herself as she and Johan made their way past the stalls of the Grote Markt. She doubted that news of her crime could have reached Antwerp in the six days since she'd sailed from Sark. She took solace, too, at how well she blended into the crowd. Her clothes, though fine enough in quality, were out-of-date, making her look like so many others among the city's shopkeepers and craftspeople now down-at-heel from lost business. Johan, shuffling beside her, passed as her tired old servant. *As long as I'm careful and quiet,* she told herself, *I'm as good as invisible.*

And yet, as she and Johan passed the cordon of Spanish soldiers and musketeers guarding the municipal buildings that were the center of Spanish authority in the city, a captain's eyes seemed to bore right into her, knowing, accusing. She looked up at the flags emblazoned with Alba's crest fluttering above their heads.

"Alba," Johan growled. He spat in the dirt. "Satan."

"Shush!" Fenella could have pinched him. The soldiers were watching everyone. "Do you want to get us locked up?"

He grunted his contempt. "Smell that? The sulphur of hell."

"It's burnt sugar, you daft man. The refineries." Ships laden with sugarcane and molasses from Spanish plantations in the New World crowded the riverside wharfs, for Antwerp was the sugar capital of Europe, and the nearby refineries belched a bittersweet-smelling smoke. Johan looked ready to spit again but coughed instead, that awful cough that plagued him. He'd started using a handkerchief to cough into, and this morning Fenella had glimpsed alarming spots of blood on it. Now, he balled it secretively in his gnarled fist, which only deepened her worry. "Here," she said. "Turn here."

She hustled him into Zilvermidstraat, relieved to get him away from the eyes of the soldiers. His hatred of the Spanish, her fear that he would do something stupid, had kept her on edge for the two days they'd been at Mevrouw Smit's lodging house on a lane in the shadow of the cathedral. It had taken Fenella that long to find the home address of Joseph Oliveira, the banker who held her bullion. She did not dare call on him at the Bourse, the international money market where merchants and bankers traded under its vast roof. Notice might be taken of her in such a prominent public place. She would keep to Antwerp's byways. Zilvermidstraat, where ordinary people were going about their business in the shops, would lead her to Oliveira's house. She spotted a gallows at the mouth of a side street. It was barren, no "gallows fruit" left hanging to rot and stink as a warning to the people as she'd seen elsewhere in the city. But a black bird sitting atop the scaffold made her shiver, recalling what the landlady had said at breakfast.

"Magpies. They're everywhere." Mevrouw Smit had been talking fretfully about her loose-tongued neighbor, a so-called magpie because his gossip about one of her lodgers being absent at mass had led to the lodger's arrest on suspicion of heresy. Smit was a widow who looked careworn at the burden she'd been left to shoulder. "Anyway, it freed up the chamber for you."

"We won't be staying long," Fenella had said, eager to change the subject. "So many shops are closed." Her story was that she had come from a northern town with her manservant to buy a wedding gift.

"It's the new taxes," Mevrouw Smit had said gloomily. "To pay the Spanish troops. People feel if they have to pay more tax for their goods they'd rather close shop." She shook her head. "I have to go clear down to the wharf these days to find a baker selling bread."

Fenella lurched to a stop in the middle of Zilvermidstraat. A man's corpse was tied to a stake, slumped, mouth agape. A skinny dog had one of the man's ankles in its mouth, tugging the gray flesh, making the corpse jerk as though alive. Fenella stiffened at the stench. The bloody hand of Alba was everywhere.

Johan took her elbow and nudged her forward. "Come on, Nella. Almost there."

She looked at him, glad of his dour resolve, and together they hastened past the corpse. How she hated this place! She couldn't wait to leave it. One more week, then she could sail away. Taste the clean sea air again. Breathe freedom under the open skies. With Adam Thornleigh. How wonderful the voyage from Sark with him had been. The happiest four days of her life. Sunshine and fair winds had smiled on the *Odette*, and the little fishing smack had carved through the Channel as though she, too, yearned for freedom. There were just the three of them aboard, Fenella and Thornleigh and one-armed Johan, and she had loved working alongside Thornleigh at trimming the sails and handling the tacks. In the freshening breeze they had made the *Odette* fairly fly, her bow wave singing under her foredeck, a rainbow sparkling in its mist. On land, the difference in rank between her and Thornleigh was as wide as an ocean, but on the boat they were equals.

Sailing up-Channel they had bisected the shipping roads and

passed ships flying the flags of Spain, France, England, Scotland, Norway, Sweden. Big galleons, carracks, caravels, and bilanders, smaller cogs and yawls and pinnaces—none paid attention to the little fishing smack, unaware that the notorious English "pirate baron" was at her helm. Still, when the *Odette* passed astern of a big twenty-gun Spanish carrack Fenella kept an anxious eye on the carrack until her flags dropped below the horizon.

Fenella and Thornleigh took turns at the night watches, Johan asleep in the cabin, and their final night was one that she would never forget. She had come up from the cabin, rubbing sleep from her eyes, ready to relieve Thornleigh at the helm. The night was clear, with a fresh breeze, the sea sheened with moonlight, the air unusually warm for spring in the North Sea, almost sultry. Thornleigh greeted her with a faint smile. "We'll make landfall before sunrise."

"At Vlissingen," she said, returning the smile, though she wished the voyage with him would never end. From Vlissingen at the mouth of the Scheldt estuary it was only a short sail into Antwerp.

She sat down beside him in the peaceful hush, taking in the conditions of sea and sail to be ready to helm the boat, her senses alive to the murmur of the bow wave and the salt-tanged air. That's when it happened. Thornleigh had spoken his heart to her. Maybe it was because of the hours he'd spent alone in the soul-soothing darkness, or maybe it was the bond they had forged after three days of working together, being at one with their vessel. Whatever was prompting him to confide in her, she drank in his words, sitting next to him under the vault of stars and scarcely moving a muscle lest it break the spell. His manner was as calm as the night, his voice low, his gaze ranging over the sails with an unconscious expertise that matched his relaxed hand on the helm. But an edge in his voice belied his outward calm.

"My children, that's what I'm going for. I know you've wondered." He glanced at her, then back up at the sail. "My wife left England with them three years ago, our son and daughter. Took them away in secret."

Fenella's breath caught. His wife had stolen his children? How cold his voice was when he spoke of her. And no wonder. It sent a thrill through Fenella: *He does not love his wife.* But how had such a breach in his marriage come to pass? How could any woman leave such a fine man? She longed to ask, but something told her to be still. He would say only what he wanted to say. She murmured, "How awful. You must sorely miss them."

"I tracked her first to Ireland, then lost the scent. I've had agents scouring Europe ever since." He eased the helm to starboard in a gust. "Two months ago one reported seeing her. Seems she was in Spain for a time, then moved north."

Fenella guessed the rest. "To Brussels." The capital, a day's ride from Antwerp. He nodded grimly. It gave Fenella a chill. Brussels was the Duke of Alba's seat—Alba, who had set a price on Thornleigh's head. How did Thornleigh dare enter a city so perilous for him? But he knew the dangers. In the silence, the waves murmured past the hull. "Are they safe?" she asked. "Your children?"

"I pray God they are." His eyes were on the luff of the sail. "Frances may have the black heart of a traitor, but she would not harm the children."

"Traitor?" Astounded, Fenella could not squelch her curiosity. "What did she do?"

"Conspired to assassinate the Queen. In our own house. Frances and her cursed brother, may he rot in hell. They undermined the house with gunpowder, blew it up. I got Her Majesty out just in time."

"You saved her?" Fenella was speechless. No wonder the Queen valued him so highly. But what thrilled Fenella again even more was the coldness in how he'd said *Frances.* He seemed to hate his wife's very name.

"I'll find her," he said. "And I'll get my children."

She longed to know more. "What are their names?"

He looked at her and his smile was warm. "Katherine and Robert. Twelve and nine. The boy, he's a quiet one. Kate's not. A born adventurer. Young though she is, she understands ships." He didn't look back at the sails, kept looking at Fenella, his dark eyes aglitter in the moonlight. "Like you. Were you that way at her age?"

She so longed for him she could have wrapped her arms around his neck and kissed him until the sun rose. And for a moment, from the way he was looking at her, she thought surely he felt the same. Then a gust heeled the boat, and to keep her balance she had to pull away from him. "Take the helm?" he said. The freshening wind demanded a trim of the sails.

She set her hand on the tiller, brushing his hand, alive to its warmth, and then he left her side and went forward to harden the sheets. The boat settled and rode smoothly. Fenella found no such harmony in herself, her every sense stirred by that moment with him. He looked back at her, and in the moonlight she saw the tired look in his eyes, and it struck her with a pang that she had been wrong, had misread the moment. He'd been relieved to have her take the helm, that's all. He was just tired. She felt a fool.

"Go, get some sleep," she said, pretending composure. "Don't worry, I'll wake you if I see the lights of Vlissingen."

He gave her a grateful smile, then ducked under the boom and brushed past her. She savored the last sight of his back as he went down into the cabin.

The next morning they passed through customs at Vlissingen without incident, posing as a fisherman and his wife coming in to repair their boat, Johan posing as her garrulous father, whose nattering soon had the overworked official waving them on. Johan winked at Fenella. She had to smile, relieved that it had been so easy.

They sailed up the estuary, and the closer they got to Antwerp the more nervous Fenella felt, for herself and for Thornleigh, both of them outlaws in this land. Ten miles from Antwerp they entered the scatter of low islands that were wooded humps almost barren of people. Thornleigh tacked back and forth, scanning the mainland shore.

"What are you looking for?" Fenella asked, trimming the sail after a tack.

"A cove I remember. An ideal hiding hole. I anchored in it once to wait out a blow." He glanced at her. "I lived in Antwerp years ago. My father had a wool trade business."

"Ah, so that's why your Dutch is so good."

"There." He nodded at the shore as he steered the tiller and sailed toward it. "That's the entrance."

An ideal hiding hole it was indeed, she realized as they followed the passage's scythe-shaped curve—*like a nautilus*, she thought. At its end lay a cove, a snug indent of the sea hidden by the crescent of alder trees crowding the shore. The alders were tall enough to hide the boat's mast from the sea and from inland. Waterweeds nodded in the shallows.

They lowered the sails and dropped anchor. The quiet was so peaceful, with just the spring chirping of birds in the trees. Johan set to work on the foredeck, coiling lines in his surprisingly efficient one-armed way. Fenella and Thornleigh secured the sails. As they worked together to wrap cord around the bunched canvas, his hand brushed hers. They stopped and looked at each other. Neither moved their hands resting on the canvas, fingers touching.

"When you get to Brussels, my lord—"

"Adam," he said, his face earnest. "You really must call me Adam. We're partners now."

She wanted to stay like this forever, his eyes on her, his fingers kissing hers, his body so near she could feel its warmth. "Adam. It will be dangerous for you in Brussels. If you need a . . . a hiding hole . . . I have a friend. He has a barge. Do you know Sint-Gorikseiland?"

He nodded. "The island in the Zenne."

"That's where he lives. His name is Berck Verhulst. If you should need someplace."

"I'll be fine. Promise me you'll keep *your* head down."

"I will. One brainless act was enough."

He smiled. "Ten days, Fenella. We'll meet back here. Yes?"

"Yes." They'd discussed this already. A rendezvous in ten days, he bringing his children, they hoped. They would sail back to Sark, get his ship, and sail to England. To safety.

That night, as Johan snored in the cabin, Fenella lay awake in the cramped stern berth, her thoughts stealing up to the man asleep on deck under the stars. Thornleigh . . . Adam.

Fenella and Johan turned onto Braderijstraat, where Spanish soldiers sauntered under more of Alba's banners fluttering from a church. Fenella was beginning to wonder about her gold. She had not seen Joseph Oliveira in five years. She had sent him her profits twice yearly for safekeeping, because Sark was a frequent stopover for pirates and privateers, not the most law-abiding men. She had a soft spot in her heart for Oliveira, who had helped her after she'd first arrived in the Netherlands when she'd had nothing but the clothes on her back and a handful of her late brother's coins. Oliveira was the first banker she had ever spoken to, nervously approaching him at the Antwerp Bourse about a small loan to start her chandlery in Polder, and she'd been grateful when he'd granted it. His investment had paid off, especially in the last few years as her business on Sark had flourished. She liked the man and trusted him. And now, seeing how much Antwerp had suffered under the Spanish occupation, she wondered how Oliveira had survived it. He came from a Portuguese family of Marranos, Jews forced to convert to Christianity, and all Jews, converts or not, were closely watched with loathing by the authorities of every Catholic country. The Duke of Alba was notoriously bent on making Antwerp spotlessly Catholic. A new thought struck Fenella. "Johan, what if Oliveira has gone?"

"Gone?"

"Fled. Like we did."

He looked puzzled. "At the Bourse they gave me the address of his house."

"The house of his business. But what if it's passed into other hands? Spanish hands."

"He would have sent you word."

"Not if he was running for his life. Or hanged."

They reached the place, a well-kept house neither old nor new that stood inconspicuously on a quiet, narrow side street. Fenella noted its three stories, thinking they likely served the same functions of the homes of well-to-do shopkeepers that she'd seen from Edinburgh to Amsterdam: The street-level floor was the business, the family lived on the second floor, and the third floor attic housed apprentices and servants.

She knocked. A stooped old clerk opened the door, his face deeply furrowed like walnut bark. He bowed to Fenella with a deference she assumed he granted to all potential customers. The dark foyer opened onto a hallway on one side, on the other a staircase that presumably led to the family's quarters. Fenella inquired about Oliveira, showing the clerk a receipt of deposit. As he examined the paper a frown tugged his lined forehead. "Hmm, dated nine months ago." What did that mean? Was Oliveira no longer here? "Kindly come this way," the clerk said, beckoning her.

Fenella followed him along the narrow hallway, and Johan followed her. She could see little of the premises, for the passage was hemmed in by high partitions of dark wood with several closed doors behind which she heard murmurs and clicking sounds, the business of the countinghouse. A young clerk with an armload of papers hustled past her on his way down an intersecting passage. The stooped old clerk knocked on a door, and at the murmured response of "Yes," from within, he opened it. A messenger boy, sitting on a stool just inside the door, jumped up respectfully.

The darkly paneled room was small, with one high window. Shelves covered every wall in a maze of cubbyholes that ran from floor to ceiling, each hole home to a sheaf of papers. At the far side two clerks younger than Fenella stood at tall desks, writing in ledger books. They looked up at her as she walked in, Johan behind her. A counting table covered in green baize held a scale and lead weights, and there a clean-shaven man of about forty sat with his head bent over a scroll, his quill pen scratching across it as he wrote in a swift but meticulous hand. He had the narrow shoulders of someone who haunts a desk, and a paunch curved the belly of his finely tailored doublet of russet velvet. Crisp curls of dark hair sneaked out from under a brown silk cap. He looked up at Fenella and a weight lifted from her heart.

"Joseph Oliveira. You are well met, sir."

He blinked at her, recognition flashing in his eyes. He shot to his feet. "Bless my soul, it's Mevrouw Doorn."

"I was afraid you might not know me, it's been so long."

A blush tinged his cheeks. "The day I forget beauty is the day I leave this world."

She scoffed. Fancy words. "There's beauty in gold, sir, and from the look of you I'd say your stock of it is burgeoning." She grinned. "Mine too, I trust, thanks to your care." She turned to Johan to introduce him. "My father-in-law, Johan Doorn."

Oliveira's bright eyes turned sober. "My condolences, sir, though long overdue. I never met your son, but I know Mevrouw Doorn must have married a good man."

Johan nodded, looking uncomfortable. "He is with God."

Oliveira set down his pen. "Indeed." He tugged the hem of his doublet as though readying to do business and approached Fenella. "Good lady, what brings you to Antwerp? I hope all is well on the Isle of Sark?"

She hesitated. How much should she tell him? The fewer people who knew of her plan to go to England the better. She was taking a chance just in coming here. His clerks now knew she was in the city. "I mean to expand my business, sir. I need capital."

"Excellent. How can I help you? A loan?" He added graciously, "For such a valued client, I am quite satisfied about collateral security."

"No, sir, not a loan. A withdrawal of my funds."

"Ah. To what amount?"

"All of it."

His eyes widened. "Goodness. Your plans must be extensive."

"They are. I'll need all the money I've deposited with you." She handed him a bundle of folded receipts, the top paper giving the sum total. "That's my accounting. I've come to ask you to please ready the bullion for transport."

"In gold or silver?"

"Gold, if you please."

"Of course. Will Tuesday suit you?"

That jarred her. Today was Saturday. She didn't want to hide in Antwerp for three days. "Why not right away?"

If her impatience surprised him, he didn't show it. "Unfortunately, I cannot gather such a sum before today's end of business. Tomorrow we're closed, of course, and Monday is a holiday. The Feast of Saint Venantious." He brightened. "Perhaps you'll join us? My wife is planning a splendid celebration, and we'll have the honor of welcoming an illustrious visiting scholar from Seville, Father Sebastian, as well as Don Antonio de Reina, son-in-law of the Viscount de Zayas."

"Overmighty Spaniards? As your guests?" He looked taken

aback at her tone, and Fenella realized she'd sounded terribly rude. But his casual attitude shocked her. "Forgive me," she said. "It's just that I was hoping to leave Antwerp immediately." She found it hard to compose herself. "In truth, sir, I'm surprised you stay. Are you not worried for your safety? The safety of your family?"

"Safety?" A guarded look. "I'm not sure I know what you mean."

"The executions. The mass arrests. The wholesale tyranny."

"Ah, you're referring to punishment of the enemies of God. Criminals, heretics, fomenters of riots. They were, and are, a terrible threat to the country. We sorely needed stability, and His Highness King Philip, through his exalted governor the Duke of Alba, has delivered stability."

Fenella shuddered. She saw again Polder in flames, Claes drowning, bound and struggling in terror. "Stability," she managed. "At what cost? Slaughter and ruin. Alba is a monster."

Oliveira forced a tolerant smile as though dealing with an obstinate child. "As Alba himself says, 'It is better that a kingdom be laid waste and ruined through war for God and the king, than maintained intact for the devil and his heretical horde.' Wise words, I'm sure you agree."

"Wise?" She could only stare at him, dumbfounded.

"I assure you," he added in an unnaturally loud voice, "I count myself blessed to have the friendship of the distinguished Spanish gentlemen I've just mentioned who honor me with their friendship."

At his odd tone caution prickled her skin. She shot a glance at the two clerks across the room. Their eyes were focused on their open account books, pens poised over the pages, but neither pen moved. *They're listening.* She stiffened. *Magpies.* Dear God, had she said too much? *Curse my rashness! Stupidly condemning Alba . . . like shooting Don Alfonso. Always too rash, too reckless!*

She mumbled an apology to Oliveira, blaming her ill manners on fatigue and a headache, then quickly concluded her business with him, confirming that she would return on Tuesday for her gold. As she turned to the door to go she glanced at the two clerks. Had her rash tongue endangered Oliveira? The clerks were back at work, pens scratching on paper. Once out of the room she followed the old clerk, who led her and Johan back to the door to the street. Coming down the staircase was a pale, pretty woman carrying a baby on her hip. She gave Fenella a fleeting, polite smile before starting the opposite way, down the hall. Oliveira's wife and child?

"That fellow didn't deserve your tongue-lashing," Johan said, coughing, as he and Fenella left the house. "He's just trying to keep his head above water. Like all of us."

Shame surged over her. She could blend into the crowd as a stranger, but Oliveira could not. As a citizen of Jewish descent he would always be suspect in a Christian land.

Johan's cough got worse as they walked to their lodging house. It made him hunch over, hacking into his tightly balled handkerchief as they crossed the Grote Markt. By the time they were in the cathedral's shadows near the house he was weak, the coughing spasms so strong, Fenella had her arm around his shoulders to steady him and keep him upright. It frightened her. His fits had never been this bad before. He looked at her with unfocused eyes, unable to keep his grip on the handkerchief. The linen, red with blood, spread open in his hand like a noxious flower. Fenella bit back her dismay and tried to reassure him. "Just a few more steps, Johan. Then you can lie down."

He dropped the handkerchief and staggered to a halt, swaying. "I don't . . . think I . . ." His legs gave way. He slipped out from under her arm. "Johan!" she cried. He dropped to his knees. But his innate stubbornness, his refusal to submit, kept him from toppling. People passed with furtive glances, careful to give them a wide berth. Fenella managed to get him to his feet and they covered the last steps to the house. By the time she got him up the stairs to his room and let him collapse on the bed she was out of breath and sticky with sweat.

Johan looked barely conscious. His face was gray, his breathing strained, painful sounding. But his terrible spasms of coughing had abated. Feeling shaky, Fenella sat on the edge of the bed and gently laid her hand on his forehead. It was cold, clammy. Blood flecked the linen collar rucked up under his jerkin. His hand was stained with blood. Her heart bled at the thought of losing him. *Don't die, Johan.*

He sank into an exhausted sleep. She got a blanket and settled it over him, then sat beside him, willing him to survive, watching for signs of any strength returning. The afternoon shadows lengthened over his thin body. Several times Fenella was sure he had stopped breathing, but when she placed her palm on his chest she felt his heartbeat, though faint as a bird's. Watching him so intently, her eyes scratchy with fatigue, she had an unnerving memory of lying beside Claes years ago and studying his face as he peacefully slept. How similar they looked, Johan an older, gaunter version of his son. The high cheekbones. The thin lips, wide mouth. The bony eyebrow ridge. But Claes, in death, had found no peace. She rubbed her eyes, rubbing away the memory.

It was near dusk when Johan's eyelids twitched open.

"Not . . . here," he said hoarsely.

She was so relieved to see him return to her. "What's that, Johan?"

"Don't want to die . . . here."

She squeezed his hand. "No one's going to die. You're better already, some color in your cheeks. It's supper you need. We'll get Mevrouw Smit's good sausage and cabbage into you and by tomorrow you'll be dancing a jig."

He feebly shook his head. "I'm done for."

"No, Johan, you just need doctoring and rest. I'll see that you get it in England."

"That's not . . . what I need."

"It is. As soon as we're in England I'll get you the best doctors money can buy. I promise."

He gripped her hand with a desperate strength. "No . . . no England for me. Home, Nella. Take me home."

It was in the village of Halsteren that Fenella first sensed she was being followed. Fleeting glances of a thickset man in a dusty maroon leather jerkin, a drooping, mustard-yellow feather in his cap. She had first noticed him that morning in Ossendrecht, mounting his horse as she and Johan had left the inn's stable on their horses, and then again when they left Bergen op Zoom. Now, passing the church at the market cross in Halsteren, she turned in her saddle to push down the loose flap of her saddlebag and spotted the man disappearing behind the church wall. This time he was on foot.

Perhaps it meant nothing. Farmers and craftsmen traveled back and forth all the time between villages like Halsteren and the big markets of Bergen op Zoom. The man might be one such trader. Might even have come from Antwerp just as she and Johan had. He seemed to be alone, nothing threatening about him. Since he was no longer on horseback, he likely lived here in Halsteren. *So stop imagining things*, she told herself, and nudged her horse on.

She was taking Johan home, just as he had begged. After two days on the road they were close to Polder, and it was unnerving to be back in this countryside where she had lived with Claes. She constantly glimpsed the river to their left, a branch of the Scheldt that led to the North Sea, winding its way past hamlets and farmhouses. In that river Don Alfonso's soldiers had drowned Claes. She didn't like being back here. She wasn't even sure she was doing the right thing in bringing Johan. She'd tried her best to make him agree to come with her to England, but he had been adamant, and she could hardly force him. In truth, his pitiful plea had moved her. He was too weak to go alone, and he insisted that this was what he wanted before he died.

"There," he said now, pointing to the flat fields that lay beyond the last houses of the village. "The farm's not an hour down that road. We'll be able to sup with Wilhelmina. Delicious cheese, she always made."

"That sounds good. I'm hungry." Fenella had met this niece of Johan's wife at her own wedding to Claes but only vaguely remembered her, a stout, big-boned young woman with white-blond hair and pale blue eyes not unlike the Doorns'. Johan had sent her a message from Antwerp and told Fenella he was sure Wilhelmina and her husband would take him in. Fenella found it strange to think of a farm being Johan's new home. He had been a shipwright all his life, always near the sea.

"They kept a fine milk cow, she and Goert." He chuckled. "They're not rich, but we'll eat well."

He was in good spirits. So good, Fenella was beginning to think his sickness was not as threatening as she'd believed. Clearly, he was feeling much better since leaving Antwerp. That cheered her a little. If she could see him contentedly settled with his niece, it would be less painful to leave him. But leave him she must. This country was not safe for her. She was determined to get to England. There was time. She had five days to return to Antwerp and collect her gold from Oliveira, then get back to the sheltered little cove where the *Odette* lay at anchor. Adam would join her there. Would he bring his children? She hoped so. She felt an eager curiosity to see the son and daughter he so obviously loved.

Deep in her heart, though, it was Adam himself she yearned to see and sail away with. She tingled with anticipation, imagining the sea spray, the freedom from fear, and him. She was embarking on a new life. A part of her still chafed at having to leave behind everything she had built on Sark, but she knew it was her own rash fault. Besides, the island had never really been home. *What* is *home?* she wondered. Not the Scotland she had fled eleven years ago. Not Polder; that had been Claes's home. So why not embrace England as the place where she could finally come to rest? She had no doubt that she could rebuild her business, maybe in Portsmouth or Bournemouth, busy centers of shipping. Or maybe on the Isle of Wight; she would have less competition there. It was exciting, really. Because Adam would be her partner in the business.

Only in business? Could she hope for more? He clearly had no love for his wife. Besides, the woman was a traitor, so she could never set foot in England again. He was shackled to her in marriage by the laws of Christendom and nothing but death could change that. But his heart was not shackled. Nor his body. Fenella wanted both. Warm blood fired her cheeks at the thought. True, she was far below him: He was a fine lord, a baron. But on the boat, working together, they had been equals, and why should working together in business not be the same? In England, she felt happily, anything was possible.

A frantic, flapping goose met her and Johan as their horses plodded into his niece's farmyard. The goose honked and flapped aside, and Fenella looked around as she and Johan dismounted. The yard was hemmed in by the two-story house, some ramshackle outbuildings, a pigsty, and a well. She saw no pigs and heard none, but the yard certainly smelled of pig shit. The house was a substantial structure of wattle-and-daub walls and thatched roof, with a cow byre extending from the back. The building, weathered and begrimed, looked forlorn in the shade of a stand of elms. The trees sloped down to a stream, and the smell of decayed vegetation drifted from the overgrown reeds. At the well, a rope creaked in the breeze. No one was in sight. Fenella smelled burning peat, though, so someone must be home. Supper cooking on the hearth? Her mouth watered at the thought of the cheese Johan had promised. She loved the sweet tang of cheese. The goose, waddling toward the stream, disappeared into the reeds.

"Goose for supper, that would be tasty," Johan said as he and Fenella headed for the front door. He grinned at her. She thought the grin looked strained. He was more exhausted than he let on. They passed a chopping block outside the door: a tree stump where an axe stood on its tip buried in the flat top. Flies buzzed around a gleam of blood. Something, goose or otherwise, had just been killed.

Inside, no one greeted them. The house sounded empty. Fenella had expected the noise of children. Johan had said his niece had four little ones when he'd left five years ago. The silence seemed odd. Was the whole family away? "Is it a market day?" Fenella asked.

He was looking around. "What?" He seemed distracted. Fenella noticed the glowing peat fire in the hearth, and the iron pot suspended over it gave off the aroma of an oniony stew. No one home, but supper cooking. Strange. "Where can they be?" she said. Something else was odd, too. She'd seen many farmhouses and this main room looked no different from most, with its wide brick hearth and scuffed wooden table, its cupboards and benches and stools. But it seemed barren of life, with none of the usual family clutter. No hanging herbs. No caked mud on the floor. No basket of linens waiting to be washed, no shirt or breeches left on the table for mending. No tools on the bench. No child's poppet. It was as if no one lived here. Not even a dog.

She heard the low bellow of a cow. "Maybe someone's in the byre," she suggested. Johan seemed engrossed in poking a ladle into the contents of the pot at the hearth, so Fenella decided to check the byre herself. She opened the side door that led outside. A stone path overgrown with nettles took her to the low shed of rough boards. Inside, in the dusty gloom, a solitary cow stood munching. She swung her heavy head toward Fenella, blinked, then turned back to munching. The place was rank with a smell of musty hay. Fenella stood still, taking in the silence. She heard a rustling. She was peering into the gloom beyond a heap of straw when something bolted past her, startling her. A cat. It leapt up to the crossbeam, streaked along it, and disappeared into the shadows.

She turned back toward the door bright with daylight, calling, "Johan, they must have gone to—"

A figure surged at her from the brightness. She gasped. The huge black shape loomed over her, his arms raised above her head, something black stretched between his hands. She saw the outline of a feather in his cap. She lurched back and collided with another man. He grabbed her arms from behind. "Johan!" she yelled. "Run!" The man with the feather jammed the black thing over her head. A sack. She gasped in fear, sucking in dust from the burlap, coughing. Before she could catch her breath the man behind her whipped rough cord around her wrists and yanked them tightly together. "Open it," he ordered. "Then get the other one." Fenella heard the man with the feather scuffle past her. Heard a loud creak.

Blind in the blackness, her hands painfully bound, she twisted around in terror, but the man who'd spoken suddenly lifted her off her feet. He heaved her across his shoulder, his shoulder bone punching the breath from her stomach. Then they were moving. She was jostled so hard she could not catch breath to shout. She heard the heavy thump of his boots, *thud, thud, thud*. She squirmed, coughing, but he held her tight. *Thud, thud, thud*. Then he rocked to a stop. She felt cold air sweep over her. There was a dank, fishy smell. Where was she?

He set her down on her feet. She swayed, struggling to get her balance, blind and bound, out of breath from fear. She heard *thud, thud, thud*. Then, "Put him down." A loud creak like before. The slam of wood on wood. A click.

The sack was wrenched off her head. She stumbled at suddenly being able to see. She jerked her head, taking in what was around her, though the light was dim. A ladder. A trapdoor at the top, dust sifting from the door having been slammed shut. They were beneath the cow byre!

She twisted around. Five strangers, four men. One held a candle, the only light. Beside him, the man with the mustard-colored feather in his cap. And a woman, stout and square jawed. One of the men was pulling the sack off Johan's head. Johan staggered. He blinked at the woman. "Wilhelmina?"

The woman lurched at him with a dagger and held the tip menacingly at his throat. Johan froze. "Never speak that name again," she said. She pressed the tip to his flesh until a bead of blood broke through. "Understand?" He swallowed, his eyes wide. "My name is Sister Martha. Understand?" He nodded.

Fenella watched in amazement. This fearsome woman was Johan's wife's niece?

"How did you know about us?" the woman demanded of Johan. Her red, chapped hand kept the dagger poised at his throat.

"I . . . didn't," he stammered. "I guessed. I . . . hoped."

She studied him for a moment. Then lowered the blade. Johan rubbed his throat. A smile wobbled on his lips. "Thank you . . . Sister Martha."

She marched over to Fenella, asking, "Who's this?"

"Who in hell are *you?*" Fenella demanded. The men certainly weren't Alba's soldiers. They looked like laborers. Homespun clothes, calloused hands, stolid faces.

Sister Martha glared at her for her defiance, and for a moment Fenella was sure she was going to feel the woman's blade.

Johan said, "It's all right, Sister Martha. This is my daughter-in-law."

The woman blinked. "You mean—?"

He nodded. "Yes."

She and the others stared at Fenella in astonishment. She bristled under their scrutiny. What made them so damned interested in her? The man with the feather touched Sister Martha's shoulder as though to rouse her. She flinched, still staring at Fenella. Then she said with a faint rueful smile, "Who in hell, true enough. You might as well know." She leaned around and cut Fenella's bonds, then pointed with her dagger to the men, one after another. "This is Brother Sebastian. Brother Dunstan. Brother Ambrose."

Fenella rubbed her chafed wrists. "Johan, what's happening? Who are these people?"

"Friends," he said, his voice thick with emotion. "Friends of the homeland."

Rebels? She was stunned. And furious. "You said nothing."

"I wasn't sure."

"But you suspected. How could you not *tell* me?"

He spread his hand in a gesture of apology. "You wouldn't have brought me." His eyes gleamed with tears. "Nella, I thank you. I'm home."

"Sister Martha," the yellow-feather man said as the others kept gawping at Fenella, "we need to fetch Brother Domenic. To tell him."

"I know," she snapped.

"No need," the third man said. "He's already here. His boat just landed." He pointed. Fenella looked across the dim room to a dark hallway, narrow and low. A tunnel. It was the source of the dank, fishy smell, she realized.

She'd had enough of this. She could be hanged just for being found with these people. All she wanted was to get out. "Johan, you can stay if you want, but I—"

"Brother Domenic," the woman said, a deferential greeting.

Fenella turned. A thin man emerged from the tunnel, half-crouched from its low ceiling. He carried a lantern, bringing light into the dim space. As he straightened up he raised the lantern high to examine the newcomers.

Fenella's heart gave a painful kick. Then it seemed to stop. Before her, his white-blond hair aglow under the light, stood Claes Doorn. Her husband. A dead man.

❧ 5 ❧

Frances

Footmen swept open the doors to the gallery in the Duke of Alba's palace, bowing to the Duchess of Feria and her companion, and the two ladies strolled into the long, glittering room. Heads turned.

Frances Thornleigh, head high, savored every moment of making this entrance beside her exalted friend Jane, the duchess. The gallery was crowded with the leading men of Brussels and their ladies: magistrates and merchants, churchmen and military men, Dutch lords and visiting Spanish grandees. Some were awaiting an audience with Alba, some milling for gossip and trade talk. Clerks and servants scurried with messages. Sunshine through the floor-to-ceiling windows made everything gleam, from the banner-bright silks and satins on ladies and gentlemen alike to the shell-white marble floor. A sprightly music of lutes and viols lilted above the gabbling throng, and the air was spiced with the perfumes of Spain.

Frances exulted. What a thrill it was to see and be seen in this splendid palace! She was nervous, but only from excited anticipation about her imminent audience with Alba. She and Jane had prepared their appeal with great care. Frances's heart was beating almost painfully fast, but she was ready. After years in exile—three aggrieved, lonely, worry-gnawed years—she was ready to do anything to get back the life in England that had been stolen from her. Winning Alba's support was the key. He had the ear of King Philip, who trusted Alba's judgment and acted on it. And Philip, master of vast armies with which he ruled half of Europe, had the power to knock the heretic Queen Elizabeth off her throne. Then, it would be safe for Frances to return. Restoration of honor. Vindication. She yearned for it. And today, God willing, she would take the first grand step. Success was not guaranteed, of course. She knew there were deep currents and counter-currents in Spain's relations with England, so deep and swirling it was difficult to stay abreast, especially since she lived far from the power centers of either court. But everyone knew that the two countries were on the brink of war. And Frances was in touch with a different source of power. She had brought the proof, a letter, folded in her pocket. A letter so potent it just might turn the tide against England.

She glimpsed a man across the gallery. Wiry, swarthy, almost hidden by the crowd. He stood very still and seemed to be watching her. A hard face, almost scowling, that gave her a prickle of unease. *Should I know him?* she thought.

"They're all looking at you, my dear," Jane whispered. "They're wondering who you are."

Frances turned to her with a rush of delight. It was true: So many people were watching. How delicious, this curiosity she was arousing by her association with her distinguished benefactor. For three years Frances had been careful to stay hidden, bitter years of tedium and resentment, forced to abandon her title as Lady Thornleigh, her status as an English baroness. For her own safety and her children's safety she went by her maiden name, Grenville. But today she had dared to come into this prominent public place, and it was exhilarating to be in society again. She could go on and on basking in people's curiosity if she weren't so keen to see Alba. Then, a pang of apprehension. Might she and her friend be far down the queue of petitioners? After all, Alba had the governance of the whole unruly country; even a duchess might have to wait her turn. "Will we have to wait long?" she asked Jane, who was smiling to acknowledge the bow of a bishop.

Jane shook her head. "As soon as he's finished his dinner. His secretary assured me we are the first of his afternoon appointments."

"Thank heaven. My heart can't take much more of this anxious beating."

"Don't be nervous, my dear. He's not as ferocious as they say. He cultivates the fierce reputation." She added with a sly twinkle in her eye, "It stupefies the ignorant."

Frances smiled. She squeezed Jane's elbow, grateful for her friendship and support. Over twenty years ago, in the bloom of their youth, they had both enjoyed coveted places at the English court as fellow maids of honor to Queen Mary. Jane had been winsome young Jane Dormer then, the daughter of a prosperous Buckinghamshire wool merchant, and had won the heart of the dashing Spanish ambassador to London, Don Gomez Suarez de Figueroa of Cordova, the Duke of Feria. He married her, and Jane had left England as a duchess to live the rest of her life in wealth and splendor in Spain. Now, she was a widow. Frances had been at her side in Spain when Feria died last year and had helped Jane through her grief. Frances felt like a widow herself, cut off as she was from Adam. Forever. His hatred for her was a kind of death. But that pain did not bear dwelling on. It was Jane who was her mainstay now. Frances owed her so much. God knows what she and the children would have done without Jane's help. Though an exile, Frances was living very well as Jane's guest.

"I am nervous, it's true, but eager," she said. "I know the governor will listen to you, his old friend."

"More likely to you, my dear," Jane said, "when I tell him of your bravery in the uprising and how you almost succeeded."

Yet failed, Frances thought grimly. She still felt scarred by that debacle. Worse, she hadn't been brave at all, had only done what her brother had told her to do, making her house in Chelsea available for the attempt on Queen Elizabeth's life. In the end they'd blown up the house but not Elizabeth. Terrified of arrest, Frances had snatched the children and fled. "Anne came nearer success," she said. "I so admire her." Anne, Countess of Northumberland, was another stalwart among their group. Brussels was home to many English Catholic exiles, from nobles and gentlemen and priests to merchants and traders and seminary students. Frances and Jane had come to Brussels expressly to confer with them. "How she has suffered," Frances murmured.

The Northern Uprising, people had called it. Anne's husband, Thomas Percy, Earl of Northumberland, had led it. In Spain Frances had followed the clandestine reports of Northumberland gathering an army of discontented northerners and she had prayed that he would march on London and overthrow the heretic Elizabeth. But that she-devil had more lives than a cat. Her army routed Northumberland's forces before they got farther south than York. Northumberland fled to Scotland, and his wife, Anne, escaped to the Netherlands. Northumberland took refuge with a Scottish border raider. But the vile Scot sold his noble guest to the Earl of Moray. Anne tried to raise enough money to ransom her husband from Moray, persuading King Philip and even the pope to contribute to her cause. All in vain. Elizabeth outbid her! Took charge of Northumberland and executed him. And then, to demonstrate her total power, she executed his chief supporter, the Duke of Norfolk, the foremost peer of the realm. Frances still seethed with indignation. Spain could not move fast enough to bring down Elizabeth.

A hand touched her shoulder, startling her. She turned to see the swarthy man who had been watching her across the room. He wore the well-tailored but sober clothes of a merchant's agent or a gentleman's steward. Crinkly black hair and a chin shadowed with black stubble. The bloodshot whites of his eyes were spidered with red.

He bowed to Jane. "Pardon, Your Grace." Then said to Frances, without bowing, "A word with you, my lady, if you would be so kind."

He spoke English with an Irish accent, and there was a forwardness about him that raised Frances's hackles. The kind of Irish upstart who did not know his place. "What do you want?" she said.

"It's about what *you* will want, my lady. News." He leaned in to speak in her ear, and she grimaced at the sour smell of beer on his breath. He whispered, "About your husband."

A chill touched her scalp. *Adam.*

He gestured toward an alcove where they could speak in some privacy. Frances said, as calmly as she could, "As you wish," and told Jane she would return in a moment.

"Who are you?" she demanded the moment she was alone with the man.

"Leonard Tyrone, at your service, my lady."

"I need no service. How do you know my husband?"

His half smile showed brown teeth. "I work for him."

A jolt of terror. *He's come to drag me back to hang. No*, she thought, willing her frightened heartbeat to settle. If that were Tyrone's mission he would have grabbed her in the dark of night or on a quiet street, not here among this crowd. The crowd, though, made it the ideal place for him to approach her. But for what? She challenged him, suspicious, "What kind of work?"

He shrugged. "I see to His Lordship's interests."

"I don't believe you. My husband has no property in the Netherlands." Nor ever would as long as he was wanted for his criminal pirating against Spain. Frances had heard the stories. Stories told by people who did not know she was Adam's wife. Stories that made her cringe.

"Not that kind of interest," Tyrone said. A sly gleam came into his eyes. "Ireland wasn't to your liking that first year, I imagine, leastways not the tenements of Waterford. I'm sure you found the Duchess of Feria's feather beds in Seville much more pleasant."

Cold fear crept over her. "You've been following me?"

"Not personally. I pieced it together from what I heard here and there." He added with obvious pride, "That's what I'm good at. Tracking."

For Adam. She tried to think past her fear. Why had this Irishman waited until now to approach her? "What do you want?"

"I told you. I've got something *you'll* want. Information."

She relaxed her guard a little. It seemed he hadn't come to harm her. "About him?"

"Now you get my drift."

"What do you know?" She'd had no contact with Adam in three years. "Where is he?"

Tyrone held up his hands to forestall her questions. "Not so fast. We haven't agreed on a price. I've got expenses, my lady, and His Lordship is tardy with his pay." He nodded to her hand. "That ruby will do me fine."

Her other hand darted to cover the ring, protecting it. "You're mad. This gem is worth fifty ducats." Ten times what a maidservant would earn in a year.

His eyes narrowed and his voice was a warning growl. "Is your life not worth a ruby?"

My life? The icy fear surged back. "He's here, isn't he." It wasn't a question. She knew.

Tyrone lifted his head with the satisfaction of a bargainer who knows he's won. "The ruby."

Her hand trembled as she tugged the ring over her knuckle. He held out his hand and she set it on his calloused palm. "Tell me," she said.

He glanced around to make sure no one noticed as he pocketed the ring. "He's in the country, sure enough. Don't know how he managed to slip in, but a week ago he was in the village of Kloster ten miles out from Antwerp. Arrived with a woman and an old man."

Frances stiffened. "A woman?"

"A red-haired beauty. With a scar, here." He slashed his cheek with his fingertip. "Seemed quite fond of her."

Jealousy bit into Frances. She hated the feeling, almost hated herself. After the contempt Adam had shown her! Yet she craved to know. "You saw him with this woman?"

He shook his head. "I wasn't there."

"What? Then how do you know it was him?"

"Like I said, my lady, I'm a good tracker. I pay fellows here and there to keep an ear to the ground. One's in Kloster, and last week he saw these three strangers in the village. The younger man bought three of the ostler's horses and paid in gold. Bought spurs for himself, too, and my fellow heard him mutter to his mare as he mounted, 'Sorry, girl, but we must gallop.' Said it in English."

"What does that signify? English traders come to the Netherlands all the time."

"Not gentlemen sneaking about with gold aplenty. And my fellow in Kloster described him perfect. Tall and sturdy, about forty, dark hair swept straight back off his face. Quick dark eyes."

A pain squeezed her heart, so clear was the picture of Adam.

Tyrone was eyeing the main doors like a man whose business was done. "And now, my lady, I must be going."

"Wait. Where is he now?"

He shrugged. "Don't know. That's all I've heard."

She needed more. "If you've been working for him all this time you must have been in contact with him. Made reports."

"Aye, I have."

"And received orders."

He studied her as though weighing his options. "Give me that silver bracelet and I'll tell you more."

"You'll tell me now, you wretch, or I'll have the governor's marshal search your pockets and you'll be hanged for a thief."

Anger flared in his bloodshot eyes. It died just as quickly, though, and he backed down with a shrug. "Worth a try." He squared his shoulders. "Last report I sent His Lordship in England was at Lent."

"Telling him what?"

"That I'd spotted you here in Brussels." He added grimly, "My advice? Get away, my lady, while you can."

Dread shot through Frances. Adam was coming for her.

"Ready, my dear?"

She twisted around to see Jane smiling at her. "What?" Frances stammered. When she looked back, Tyrone was gone.

"This is Secretary Albornoz," Jane said, indicating the sallow-faced gentleman beside her. "The governor is ready to see us."

Frances struggled with the chaos in her mind. "Just . . . give me a moment." She hastened toward the door, pushing past people, looking for the Irishman. Past the door she caught sight of him starting down the staircase. She hurried after him. "Master Tyrone!"

He turned on the stair. She caught up with him and said, "How do you receive your orders?"

He gave her a scoffing look. "Trade secret."

"Then you have a choice. Keep your secret, and explain to the hangman how you got the ruby. Or tell me, and collect a fee to act in my service from this day forward. Which would you prefer?"

He blinked at her in surprise. Then a grin slowly grew. "*Told* you I could be of service, my lady."

"Good. Now answer me. How does my husband get his orders to you?"

"At the Bourse. The House of Riegert. The banker's head clerk takes his letters."

"So I can reach you there?"

"You can."

"Go. You shall hear from me forthwith."

She rejoined Jane, who gave her a probing look and asked, "Something wrong?"

Frances forced a smile. "Just a pesky bit of business." They followed the Spaniard, Alba's secretary, down the length of the gallery along the wall of windows. Frances was so distraught she felt almost sick. How long did she have until Adam found her? The sun through the windows beat down on her, raising a clammy sweat. She rooted in the sleeve of her gown for a handkerchief and dabbed it to her damp upper lip. Could she move him to mercy for the sake of the children? No, Adam would never, ever forgive her for trying to kill Elizabeth, that witch who held him in thrall. *How can I escape him? Where else can I flee?*

The doors opened. An antechamber, smaller, quieter, but still crowded with petitioners, the air stuffy. They followed Albornoz straight through, all eyes on them, and he opened another door. The private suite of the governor. A high ceiling bright with pink cherubs in a cerulean sky. Gleaming Flemish tapestries on the walls. A long table spread with maps. A heavy oak desk cluttered with papers. Frances knew Alba instantly, for he looked just as Jane had described: the lean cheeks, the cropped gray hair and pointed gray beard, the somber clothing, all black. He sat behind the desk, lifting a spoonful of what looked like custard to his mouth. Albornoz placed a paper in front of him. Alba ignored it, swallowing the custard while looking up at the visitors. Frances curtsied, her legs shaky.

"Ah, good ladies," he said, setting the spoon down on a silver tray with a clatter, "you've caught me out. I snatch my meals as I can. Bad manners learned on the battlefield, I'm afraid." He beckoned them. "Come in, come in."

Jane and Frances approached his desk, Jane smiling as she said, "Here, as there, sir, you are mightily engaged in His Majesty's business. I am only sorry to interrupt you in it."

"Nonsense," he said amiably, beckoning a footman to take the tray away. "Nothing could please me more, madam, than welcoming you to Brussels." They spoke in Spanish and Frances knew enough of the language to follow, but her nervous state had her straining to catch the diplomatic subtleties. Alba lifted an ebony cane hooked on the table edge and with it he pried himself halfway to his feet. Wincing, he fell back as though defeated. "Forgive me, I beg you. I am a prisoner to the gout." He threw up his hands in surrender. "More bad manners."

"Not at all, sir, please do not trouble yourself to stand. You are kindness itself in giving me and my friend this audience." Jane indicated Frances. "May I present Lady Grenville?"

Frances felt Alba's gray eyes slide over her with flat indifference. "Charmed," he said, then looked back at Jane. "I trust our friends in Seville are well? My wife writes that the Countess of Romero's son has made the countess a grandmother."

"Indeed, and they are all very well, sir, I thank you for asking. But now you must forgive *my* bad manners in forestalling any further talk of trifles. Your time is too precious. Lady Grenville has brought important news. About England."

Alba looked at Frances with some curiosity. "Indeed?" He glanced at Albornoz, who stood patiently beside the desk. Alba took up a pen, dipped it in a silver inkwell, and signed the paper. His secretary took it, gave a perfunctory bow of the head to his master and then to the ladies, and left the room. They were alone with the governor.

Jane wasted no time. She explained that the English Catholic exiles had been busy, raising funds and sending the money to the pro-Spanish faction in England in preparation for a strike against Elizabeth. She assured him that thousands of Catholics in England would follow a leader into battle against the heretic queen, a leader committed to returning England to the one true Church.

Alba stroked his beard. "All this, dear lady, is known to His Majesty. He graciously maintains the pension he awarded the Countess of Northumberland, and welcomes all other refugees from England who are staunch in the defense of God's will. But he has always held that the initiative for action must come from within England. You mention a leader. That element remains lacking."

Jane smiled, triumphant. When she spoke again it was in English. "That is why Lady Grenville is here."

He looked at Frances, intrigued now. He switched to English. "Is this the news the duchess referred to?"

Frances's mouth was so dry she had to swallow. "It is, Your Grace. I have—"

"I should have mentioned," Jane put in eagerly, "that Lady Grenville has proved her own loyalty to the Church with courageous action." She explained the attempt on Elizabeth's life at Frances's house three years ago. "Though it ended in failure, it brought an unexpected happy result in a different quarter." She looked to Frances to carry on.

"I have received this letter, Your Grace," Frances said, drawing the folded paper from her pocket. "It is written in the hand of Her Majesty Mary, Queen of the Scots."

He looked astonished. Then frowned, skeptical. Frances understood why. All of Europe knew that Mary, Queen of Scots, deposed in her own realm, was a virtual prisoner in England, kept under house arrest by order of Elizabeth. The Earl of Shrewsbury was Mary's keeper at Tutbury Castle, where she was treated liberally, with her own household, but kept under close guard. "How did you come by such a letter?" Alba asked.

"She addressed it to me."

He practically scoffed. Frances was quick to go on. "I assure Your Grace it is true. After I fled England and reached the safety of His Majesty's realm I took the liberty of writing to Queen Mary. She was close to my brother Christopher, God rest his soul, when first she came into England. My letter was delivered by a young footman, one of ours, in the Earl of Shrewsbury's household. This letter is her reply to me, smuggled out in the shoe of a loyal maid. Your Grace, you know that Mary once led her armies on the battlefield in Scotland. And you know that scores of valiant English noblemen call her *our* rightful queen, a good and pure Catholic. They are ready to follow her with an army that will smash Elizabeth. Mary is the leader we English crave." She handed Alba the letter. "Read, sir. See how Mary says, in her own hand, that she is ready and willing to be that leader."

He took the paper, still looking skeptical. "If she could be freed."

"We are in touch with men who will hazard everything to do so."

He read the letter. Frances waited, trying not to show the hunger that roiled inside her. With Mary on the throne Frances could return to England, where talk of her past treason would be cut off as surely as Elizabeth's head. Mary would reward her, elevate her at court, perhaps even ennoble her as a countess in her own right. Adam could not touch her!

Alba set down the letter on the desk. Something in his face, a hardening, sent a shiver through Frances. "Spain, of course, wants to see England turn back from heresy," he said, "and therefore would be glad to see a Catholic ruler on the throne. But His Majesty does not feel the Scottish queen is the right replacement. She is more French than English. Her overmighty de Guise family practically rules France. That is not an alignment to make His Majesty content."

Frances opened her mouth to speak, but Alba held up a hand to stop her and sternly carried on. "Furthermore, another failed strike against Elizabeth could injure Spain. We have no wish to antagonize England and jeopardize trade. Even if a strike were His Majesty's wish, he could not easily bear the cost. You may have noticed, madam, that His Majesty has the expense of maintaining almost twenty thousand troops here in the Netherlands alone. No, I cannot allow war with England to stretch our resources further." He turned back to Jane. "And now, dear lady, great though my pleasure is at seeing an old friend, the business of this fractious country awaits me."

Fear lurched in Frances. He was dismissing them.

"Do allow Señor Albornoz to help you to some refreshment before you leave the palace," he said. Almost immediately, as if his voice had carried to the anteroom, his secretary reappeared carrying in a sheaf of papers. Jane urged Alba to at least send Mary's letter to His Majesty, but Alba pushed the paper back across the desk to Frances. Frances did not move. She knew she was expected to take the letter, but something in Alba's rebuff told her there might yet be a chance to turn him to their cause. It was nothing he had said; his words had been plain. But she had caught an undertone, a slight reticence, and surely that was unusual in a man renowned for his iron will, his unfettered authority. Could it be that he did not share his king's reluctance to antagonize England? She listened as Jane went staunchly on requesting that he at least keep the letter so he could consider the merit of their case, but Alba was smilingly firm. He tapped the letter. "It is yours, Lady Grenville. Please take it."

She did not move. "That is not my name, sir."

He frowned at her. "Pardon?"

She saw his irritation, as though she were a trifling annoyance he wished to be rid of. Anger stiffened her courage. She would be heard! "I have used the name Grenville, my maiden name, to protect myself and my children from . . . reprisals from England."

He was barely listening. He nodded to Albornoz, who set the sheaf of papers before him. "More death warrants," Alba said with a glance at Jane, an apologetic statement of the burden of his office, and muttered, "How these Dutch vermin breed."

"I am Lady Thornleigh," Frances declared. "Baroness Thornleigh. You know my husband by reputation. He is Adam, Baron Thornleigh."

Alba looked up at her as though struck. Frances saw his intense, naked interest and she exulted. *Ah, you'll listen now.*

He said to Jane, suddenly cautious, "Is this true?" Jane nodded. Alba asked Frances, still wary, "But you live apart from your husband?"

"Yes. I had to flee. His allegiance is to the heretic queen. Mine is to God."

"Where is he?"

Alba's eagerness almost made her smile. Now it was he who wanted something from her. "I do not know. But I may be able to find out."

A shadow passed over his face and she guessed why. He mistrusted a woman who would betray her husband. It raised her bile. What did he know of hiding like a ferret for three years? What did he know of the dread of being found by a husband who could take her home to hang? She stifled her outrage. *Diplomacy,* she told herself. That was the way to deal with this man whose power she needed on her side.

"We all must do God's work, Your Grace," she said with a meek bow of her head. "As you do. My husband is doing the devil's work. He sails alongside the so-called Sea Beggars, heretics all, attacking Spain's shipping. England itself is ruled by a heretic queen who gives the Sea Beggars safe harbor. Your Grace, I know that in your heart you want Elizabeth swept from the throne and a pious Catholic raised in her place. How could you not, since His Holiness the Pope excommunicated Elizabeth and called on all good Catholics to fight her?" She thumped her finger on the letter on the desk. "Here is our chance. Here is the willing agreement of Mary herself. I beg you, sir, reconsider our cause. Recommend it to His Highness."

Alba's shrewd eyes held her for several moments, and she could almost hear the gears of his mind calibrating.

"The plan may have some merit," he said, picking up the letter. He placed it carefully with his other papers. "However, before I could consider embarking on such a grave course, I would need a show of good faith from you, Lady Thornleigh. Bring me information of your husband's whereabouts. Then, we can talk."

❧ 6 ❧

The Mission

"No, wrong box," Sister Martha ordered Fenella. "This one's for weapons. Food goes in that one."

"Sorry," Fenella mumbled, taking out the burlap sack of sausages and cheese.

It was hard to think straight. She'd had no sleep. Yesterday, joy had almost knocked her down at that first sight of Claes . . . alive. She still felt disoriented, off-balance. People around her were busy packing supplies for an undertaking she didn't understand. They were in a hurry. She'd been put to work by Sister Martha and was following orders in a daze. She didn't think it was much past dawn, but it was hard to be sure in this dank underground chamber. She repacked the burlap sack in the box Sister Martha indicated.

She looked around for Claes. Where . . . ? He'd been here a moment ago, giving instructions to the others. It gave her a prick of panic . . . to have him back but now suddenly gone again. A hanging lantern creaked in the draft from the tunnel to the river. Men tramped past her taking boxes and packs of supplies down the tunnel to boats. She glimpsed Johan hustling down the passage with a leather pack slung over his shoulder. Yesterday Johan had been as stunned as she was to see Claes, but then he'd quickly, eagerly become one of the group—while she was still reeling over how she was to fit in with them . . . with Claes. They were going on some kind of mission, but no one had told her the details. Had Claes left? Her head swam with bizarre images: Claes drowning . . . swimming, but dead. "Has he gone already?" she said almost to herself. She wished she knew what was happening.

"Gone? Who?"

"Claes."

Sister Martha snatched her elbow in a grip that almost shook her. "Brother Domenic."

"Sorry . . . yes. Brother Domenic."

Sister Martha studied her, eyes narrowed, hands on hips. "Are you all right?" She didn't trust Fenella; that much was clear. It's all that *was* clear. Fenella had lain awake all night on the narrow mattress she'd shared with Claes in this underground warren of chambers dug into the riverbank. People had been stretched out around them asleep, snoring. Eleven men, two women, a young lad. The Brethren. *Am I all right?* How was she to answer?

Yesterday, stunned at seeing Claes, she had blurted to him, "*How?* I saw you drown."

"You and Vos," said Johan, gazing at his son in wonder. "Roped together."

"I had a knife in my boot." Claes was struggling with his own shock at seeing them. "Poor Vos was already dead. Drowned. I cut the cord. He sank. I made it to the surface. Gasped air."

"The Spaniards didn't see you?" Johan marveled.

Claes shook his head. "There was such chaos. Bodies thrashing in the water. Screaming. They didn't see me drift downriver." His voice went flat. "The hardest part was Vos's deadweight as I cut."

It had made Fenella shudder. She saw he didn't want to speak of it. How he had changed! So thin! An intense new light in his eyes. Johan rushed to him and threw his arm around him. Claes, shaken by his father's disability, embraced him with feeling, and Fenella saw tears well up in the old man's eyes. Then Claes let Johan go and embraced her, and she held on to him tightly, feeling rocked with joy and wonder. All these years she had imagined his agony, his terror, his lungs bursting, water flooding him with death. It didn't happen! She held him, and her own tears spilled.

The others in the group stood watching, joined by a few more men who came in from the tunnel, and they all waited, anxiously curious about the newcomers. Claes awkwardly, proudly presented them: "My father. My wife. Sweet Jesu, I never thought to see either of them again."

There were sympathetic nods from the group, and Fenella sensed they knew the story of how Claes had been separated from her and Johan. Some of the men offered gruff statements of welcome. A scrawny woman offered a jug of ale. Johan took it and gulped the brew, looking around, excited, his eyes constantly lighting back on his son. Claes, with his gaze still on Fenella, called for food. The group surrounded Fenella and she felt herself led away.

They all sat down on benches at a long, scarred table where one of the men, burly like a blacksmith, Brother Dunstan they called him, thumped down jugs of ale and the scrawny woman passed out bowls of oily fish stew. Claes sat at the head of the table, Fenella and Johan on either side of him. She scarcely saw the others or heard their noisy talk as they ate. She saw only Claes. Though she was flushed with gladness at seeing him alive, guilt nipped at her. She felt she had to make him understand. "I was sure you were dead. I saw you die. Or I would never have left." She heard the plea in her voice: *I didn't abandon you.*

"I know," he said gently. "What else could you do but leave? I hid in the woods and met others who'd done the same, and several told me they'd seen you and Father flee. I was just glad you'd survived. But I had nothing . . . no way to find out where you'd gone. I could only pray that your good sense and Father's help would see you through."

"I was no help, Son," Johan said, quaffing ale. "The dagos hacked off my arm. It was Nella who saved *me.*"

Claes looked at her, surprised, pleased.

She was still trying to piece it all together. "Did you go back to Polder?"

He shook his head. "There was nothing for me there. I lived in the woods. Banded with a few men who'd lost everything, like me. We talked of nothing except how we might fight back."

"Ah!" Johan said, a grunt of admiration.

Claes gave him a look both affectionate and sober. "We were vagabonds, living like dogs. But we had conviction, to hit the Spaniards and one day force them out. That sustained us and drew others to our cause."

His words brought a brusque chorus of approval from the others. "Death to the dagos," said Johan's niece Wilhelmina—Sister Martha—her baleful eyes on Fenella as though in a challenge. Johan asked about her family. Her husband had died of fever four winters ago, she said, chewing her stew. She kept the farmhouse but lived with her late husband's parents at their nearby farm with her children. "My eldest is here." She jerked her chin to the strapping lad who ate beside her. "He's with us."

The Brethren didn't take long to finish their meal. Johan shoveled down stew as if he'd been starved. Claes ate a full bowl. Fenella could not touch a bite.

Later, she and Claes sat facing each other on the narrow mattress while the others slept, stretched out around them, a single candle burning. He took her hand and squeezed it. His grip was strong, his hand bony, the skin dry as flour. She gazed at him, still marveling at the sight of him. He'd been growing a belly when they'd lived in Polder; he'd jested that it was her fault, her tasty baking. Now, he was so thin his jutting collarbones were like sticks under his homespun shirt and his cheeks were two long furrows. His nose had a new crook in it. She reached out and touched it, shy as a virgin. "Broken?"

He nodded. "Three years ago. A skirmish with collaborators. The DeGroot family. We burned down their warehouse. But not before they got in a few licks."

How strange it was. Her easygoing shipwright husband transformed into a fighter.

"Fenella," he said, his voice low, intense. "You coming back. It's a sign from God."

Something in her stiffened. "A sign of what?"

"For years I've imagined life after victory, after we win back the country. I've dreamed of the day you'd come home. It's what's kept me going, kept me building the Brethren. Just knowing you were all right. Flourishing."

She didn't understand. "But . . . you *didn't* know."

He smiled as though holding a secret. "Two years ago I was in Rotterdam organizing a joint mission with a group there. In a tavern I heard a German seaman speak of a woman on Sark. A fine-looking woman who ran a ship repair business, and with her was an old man named Doorn. I was amazed. It could only be you and Father." He added with emphasis, "Amazed and so happy. You've prospered. Just as you should."

That shocked her. He had known where she was but did nothing? "You could have sent for me."

He shook his head. "I made a choice, Fenella. A hard choice. The life I was living was too rough. More important, my work was too dangerous—for you. It was best to keep you out of it, for your own safety. You see that, don't you?"

It struck her that he felt some of the same guilt she did. Her heart softened, sadness flooding her at the ill luck of their long separation, five lost years. Such different choices they had made! She had fled the Spaniards, wanting only freedom, while he had chosen to stay and fight. Would she have stayed if she'd known he was alive? Of course. He was her husband. But what he had said needled her—that he had learned where *she* was and yet had sent no word.

"But that's all in the past," he said with sudden fervor. "Now . . ." He squeezed her hand again, his eyes aglow. "My dear wife, don't you see? My dream is fulfilled. It's God's sign that victory is nigh."

His talk of God gave her a cold feeling in the bottom of her stomach. Claes hadn't used to be especially pious. They were man and wife, yet she had the sense that she hardly knew him. His work with these people, the Brethren, had become his whole life. He was clearly the leader of this group. They were a dour lot. She had met many rough men on Sark, pirates, privateers, rovers, and rogues, but most of them had been fired with a hungry zest for life. She had not seen one of these Brethren smile.

"But, tell me," he said eagerly, "what made you come home? Why now?"

It shook her out of her callous thoughts. Who was she to pass judgment on others? She, a murderer! Lowering her voice, she told him what had happened on Sark. How an English corsair had come into her bay with Spanish captives, among them the commander who had sent the men of Polder to their death, including Claes.

He gaped at her. "Don Alfonso?"

"The same. I had a pistol. Every thought in my head vanished except the memory of you drowning. I shot him. Dead."

Amazement broke over Claes's face. Then a smile of awe. He pulled her to him and held her. She could not move, he held her so tightly. She felt his body tremble. She realized she was trembling, too. He pulled her away again, his hands still on her shoulders. "Dear wife. You are truly one of us."

It shook her. Was she? She struggled with the storm of her thoughts. *Finish the story,* she told herself. "I knew they would come after me. Don Alfonso is the nephew of the mighty Duke of Alba. So I left. Sailed away on my fishing smack and left everything. Claes, I can't go back. But as for coming here . . . I only came to get the gold I keep with an Antwerp banker, and to bring Johan home. It's what he wanted." *I didn't.* She bit her lip, those words unsaid but churning inside her. *Finish.* "I've left my boat near Antwerp. My plan is . . . was . . . to get far away. To England. Start afresh." She feared she was babbling. "But now . . . here *you* are."

"England?" He was clearly astonished.

What reason could she give for that? She had not mentioned Adam Thornleigh, her promise to rendezvous with him five days from now. Nor *would* she mention it. Struggling for an explanation, she snatched one. "The English queen is a friend of the Dutch. She gives the Sea Beggars safe harbor."

Claes's whole expression changed. Sympathetic interest hardened to a steely keenness. "What do you know about the Sea Beggars?"

"I've met a few. They roam the Channel, dozens of vessels, harassing Spanish shipping. Captain La Marck—they call him the Admiral—he came in last year to repair his shot-up carrack. Captain Abels came in twice over the winter for new masts."

"You know La Marck?" he said eagerly. "I haven't met him, but Fenella, we're in contact with the Sea Beggars. We all support

William, Prince of Orange. One day, when we've finally sent the Spaniards home or to hell, William will be our king." The light leapt in his eyes again and she knew it wasn't for her. "Tell me," he said, taking her hand, "did you ever see an Englishman, a captain, in the company of La Marck's fleet? There's a lord, a Baron Thornleigh, who attacks with his own ship in solidarity with the Sea Beggars, and he's hit the Spaniards hard."

She felt something inside her shrink back from him. She wanted to keep the knowledge of Adam Thornleigh all to herself. She had an urge to slide her hand from Claes's, but she forced herself to be still. Holding back from him was folly. And wrong. There was a struggle building inside her over her future. If she was to have any hope of making a decision, she must not poison this moment with a lie. "Thornleigh. Yes. He's the one who brought in Don Alfonso."

Claes let out a laugh of surprise. Of delight. "God's sign, Fenella, you see? Ah, I'd like to meet that Englishman."

She wanted to speak no more of him. "Claes, what exactly do you do, you and this group of yours? The Brethren. You say you fight. But how?"

He seemed about to speak, charged by that inner light. But then something shifted in his eyes, like a door closing. "This has been an extraordinary day. You must be very weary. And early tomorrow all of us must be about our business. Rest now, Fenella. Tomorrow, we'll talk."

She lay down beside him on that narrow mattress and listened to his breathing, tight at first, keyed up like she was, then becoming regular, slow. He slept. All night, she scarcely closed her eyes.

Now, packing supplies alongside Sister Martha, she heard someone shout, "Stand aside!"

Fenella turned. It was the blacksmith, Brother Dunstan, rumbling an eight-foot cannon toward the tunnel. He and another man came at a jog, hauling the big gun by ropes like oxen. Sister Martha lurched aside. A hand grabbed Fenella's arm and pulled her out of the way and she staggered as the wooden wheels of the gun growled by, brushing her skirt, a sharp metallic smell rising from the scabby barrel. She'd seen enough small cannon to know it was a saker. A six pounder. She turned. It was Claes who had pulled her clear.

"We need a name for you," he said gently. He had a leather satchel with him, its strap slung over his shoulder. "Saint Brendan was the patron saint of sailors. Shall you be Sister Brenda?"

She could only blink at him. His white-blond hair lifting in the dank river draft. Unease spreading through her like icy water.

"Brother Domenic," a man called from the tunnel entrance, wiping his brow with his sleeve. "We've loaded all the shot. Which boat for the saker?"

"Number three," Claes told him. "Don't use clean tarpaulins as cover. Dirty them with fish guts."

The man nodded, and the gun and its crew rolled past him and he fell in behind them. Johan came hustling in, coming the other way. "Sun'll soon burn off the fog," he declared to the room at large, catching his breath. "Time to get moving." Three men were hefting boxes past him toward the tunnel and one grunted, "When Brother Domenic gives the word."

"Provisions almost ready," Sister Martha reported over the packed boxes of food.

Johan beamed when he saw Fenella and Claes standing together. He joined them. "All set, my boy." He winked at Fenella. "I'm pilot of boat four." He chuckled, stifling a cough. "Haven't been told yet where we're going, but once I know I'll get us there. These blacksmiths and farmers and brewers are good men, to be sure, but me, I know these waters' spidery ways."

Fenella smiled in spite of her anxious state. She had never seen Johan so happy.

"Father, here are sealed charts," Claes told him, pulling folded papers from his satchel. "Give them to the other pilots, would you?"

Johan nodded as he took them, his eyes sparkling. "I will, I will." He gave Fenella a long, contented look. "Sun'll soon burn off the fog. Time to go."

She reached for Johan's hand. Her own was unsteady. "Take care."

"Aye, we'll take care of the dagos." Chuckling at his jest, he hustled back down the tunnel.

Fenella felt Claes's eyes on her. "You'll be safe here," he said. "Sister Agatha will be staying with you. There's plenty of food up in the house. We won't be more than a few days."

"Claes, you said we'd talk this morning. What's happening? Where are you going?"

His thumb twitched at the satchel strap on his shoulder. He seemed in a struggle over how to answer. "I wish we had more time." He looked away.

She followed his gaze to Sister Martha, who was watching her, distrust in her eyes. Or was it jealousy? Despite the monkish names that Claes and his people had adopted, Fenella didn't expect he'd lived like a monk for the last five years. She turned away from the woman. "I think I have a right to know. Especially if they do kill you this time."

A faint smile tugged his mouth. "You always did speak your mind." He shot a commanding look at Sister Martha, who stiffly turned, picked up a box in her sturdy arms, and carried it toward the tunnel. They were alone.

"Bergen op Zoom," Claes told Fenella. "We're going to ambush a troop coming to reinforce the garrison."

Her breath caught. "The fortress."

He nodded. "One of their main armories."

She knew the city. The old town was surrounded by marshes and diked fields that could easily be flooded, a distinctly Dutch defense action. "They'll be fearsome," she said. The famous Spanish *tercios* had been masters of European battlefields for generations. Claes's little band could not possibly hope to beat such hardened professionals. But he had mentioned there were other rebel groups, too. Maybe they were not going alone? "Do you have the strength in men to win?"

He shrugged. "Not yet. This time we'll do some damage, then vanish. It's our way. One day, though, we'll take that city. With it we'll be able to get reinforcements and supplies by sea. Use it as a base to take back our country."

He took a step closer to her with a yearning look. She knew he was going to embrace her. Kiss her. She stiffened. "Claes, I . . . I think it's good, what you're doing. Brave. I wish you Godspeed. But I—"

"Fenella, I'd love to have you with me in this fight."

She looked into his shining eyes. She was his wife. Her duty was to be with him. A pain squeezed her heart at the thought of Adam Thornleigh sailing away, sailing out of her life forever. She forced herself to take a deep breath to stifle the pain. Her heart thrummed in her ears. She made her decision. "If that's what you want, Claes, I'll stay."

He took her by the shoulders. "No, you don't understand. I told you, God has sent you as a sign that victory is near. *Near*—but not yet. There's still hard work to be done. Much fighting. Some dying. I'd love to have you with me in this fight, but more than that I want you with me when it's safe. When we've won." He touched her scarred cheek. "You've suffered enough. I don't want this danger for you. Go. Get your money in Antwerp and go to England. Be safe there. Be happy."

She felt frozen. Humbled. Grateful. England . . . exactly what she wanted to hear! But his words, so unexpected, so generous, brought no joy. *Some dying*, he'd said. She had lost him once to death. She could not bear to have him die again. Impulsively, she grabbed his hand. "Come with me. You've fought for five years. Let others carry on. Come with me to England."

His smile was rueful. "There are no Spaniards to vanquish in England. No, dear wife, my work is here. A Dutchman I was born, and a Dutchman I shall die."

She saw that there was no way to persuade him. Nothing more to say. A guilty thrill of relief coursed through her. She could leave! It made her feel ashamed.

"Money," she blurted. "Let me send you money from Antwerp. I have plenty. Let me give you that, at least. For your cause."

He shook his head. "We are provided for. Brother Sebastian's family is wealthy and supports us amply with—" He stopped, a thought cutting off his words. "Do you really have enough to give some away?"

"Yes. Truly. More than enough. And will gladly give you what you need."

"You must keep enough, though, to live in England. Live well."

How kind he was. "Don't worry, Claes, I'll be fine. Now, how much do you need?"

"Not me. There is a branch of the Brethren that desperately needs help. Could you take them some of your gold before you leave?"

She quickly calculated. Could she get to Antwerp for her money, make this delivery to the Brethren, then get back to the boat in time to meet Thornleigh? Yes, if she set out this very moment she could make it. "I'll do it. Where is this branch of your people?"

"Brussels."

❧ 7 ❧

"Mares' Tails and Mackerel Scales"

Never underestimate the enemy. Adam Thornleigh had learned that lesson in fighting Spaniards, but now he realized he had failed to follow it. The enemy here in Brussels was his wife.

He stood in Balienplein Place, a busy square lined with the stone mansions of the wealthy, and studied the one with four gray granite columns. More like a palace. According to Tyrone's last report, this was where Frances was living. It unnerved Adam. For three years he had held a mental picture of his wife on the run, scuttling from one bleak hiding hole to the next with their two children in tow, her money dwindling, no social connections to turn to, barely getting by. He had cursed her for dragging Kate and Robert into such a desolate life, and his fears for them had stoked his resolve to track her down and rescue the children. He'd imagined it as a simple thing once he found her, Frances weeping and wailing, no doubt, but powerless to stop him.

Now, he saw that he'd made a serious miscalculation. His wife had at least one powerful friend in a very high place: This mansion belonged to the Duchess of Feria. He could not just march in, take Robert and Kate, and march out. The duchess would have dozens of servants and armed retainers, and if Frances screamed for help he would be in a very dangerous position. He was a wanted man, and soldiers were everywhere. Across the city, at the Grote Markt, he had passed harquebusiers standing in formation with their long guns guarding City Hall and the King's House. Cavalrymen patrolled the streets on horseback. Off-duty infantrymen lounged in groups outside taverns. Adam had left his sword behind so as to pass as a menial commoner, and now he was keenly aware of how ill-armed he was with only a dagger.

He looked around the Balienplein Place square. Executions took place regularly here. So did festivities. *Swords and sausages,* he thought wryly, *the twin sides of the governance coin.* Today there was a market, drawing scores of people. Farmers were selling cabbages and strawberries; bakers were hawking rye seed loaves. Ribbon sellers and knife sharpeners bawled inducements to passing customers. A knot of gentlemen stood talking under a chestnut tree. There was a smell of burning charcoal in the air. Scanning the rooftops of the duchess's mansion, Adam read the sky, a seaman's habit. Wispy white clouds—mares' tails, sailors called them—led to a sea of rippled clouds that sailors nicknamed mackerel scales. Clear signs that rain was coming within twenty-four hours. Likely a storm. A vivid memory tugged at his heart of Kate, age four, sitting on his shoulders as he strolled through the orchard one autumn day in Chelsea, the two of them looking at clouds. He'd taught her the old proverb and she'd repeated it over and over in her child's singsong voice: *Mares' tails and mackerel scales tell tall ships to lower sails.*

He heard children's laughter and looked to a fountain in the city conduit where two boys and a little girl were floating toy boats. Their excited chatter sounded so like Robert and Kate. It gave him a pang. What if he could not reach them? What if they were lost to him?

No, he would not let his thoughts run in that hopeless direction. A plan was what he needed. And first, facts. After all, Tyrone's last report was old. For four months Adam had been away, working alongside the Sea Beggars harassing Spanish shipping, then in the German lands on his mission for Elizabeth to the prince of Orange.

In that time Frances and the children might have moved on. That was the first thing he had to find out.

He didn't have much time. In four days he had to meet Fenella at the cove outside Antwerp and sail to Sark to get his refitted ship. They needed to leave Sark before the Spaniards came looking for them both. Head home to England. Elizabeth was waiting for his report about the prince. But right now home seemed a long way away. He would not leave Brussels without his children.

"Pig's foot, *meinheer?*"

Adam turned to see a scruffy boy of seven or eight offering him a stick stuck with morsels of charred pork. He realized he was hungry. He paid the boy and munched the gristly meat as he made his way through the crowd toward the duchess's house, thinking: Could he get inside by posing as a servant? He looked convincing enough in this garb: homespun shirt, scuffed leather jerkin, coarse breeches the color of burrs. He'd stabled his horse, a telltale sign of affluence, back at the inn. He recalled what Fenella had said as they'd parted, that he would also have to hide *the air of the lord about you*, as she'd put it.

"Air?" he'd said, doubtful. His lofty rank was a recent thing. He'd spent much of his life at sea.

"Because you know the world is yours."

She was clever, Fenella. Warmhearted, too, for all her independence. He had taken an intense pleasure in the days they'd spent coming from Sark the peace, the fine sailing, the easy camaraderie with her. Thinking of her brought a rush of feeling that surprised him. He remembered a moment one night, a sultry night under a star-spangled sky when she had sat beside him at the helm and he'd told her about his children. She'd listened with a sympathy that had moved him.

Be honest, he told himself. *You want her*. Everything about her tempted him. Her lush body, close enough to him that night that he'd felt her warmth. The scent of her skin, like rose water tanged with sea salt. Her loose sunset-colored hair fingered by the breeze like a lover. Her smooth forearm, the sleeve pushed back, brushing his hand as she took over the helm. He'd had to force his eyes off her and up at the sails, unnerved by the jolt of desire. It had felt like a betrayal of Elizabeth.

Was it? That bond had been forged so many years ago. Elizabeth had been a frightened princess of twenty and had needed him, but he knew now, in a way that saddened him, that the passing years had slackened the bond. Over a decade ago she had taken possession of the kingdom and had become a skillful monarch, and he had long known that his place could never be by her side. He would always defend her as his queen in any way that she still needed him; it was why he was helping the Sea Beggars, to check Spain's power, a threat to Elizabeth and to England. She had told him she would not openly endorse his actions because she feared Spain raging against her, so he had taken the role of pirate. That was the stark fact: They both had roles to play. They were monarch and subject, moving in separate spheres. Their brief time together as mere man and woman was long past.

Fenella was different. As they sailed together, he had sometimes felt her watching him and would turn to find her sea-green eyes on him as warm as summer pools. She was beautiful and warmhearted and thrillingly near, and on the day they anchored in that quiet cove and worked together to secure the sail their hands had touched, fingers lingering, and she had not moved away. In that moment he'd imagined what it would be like to have her in his arms and make love to her.

Fool, he told himself. With a marriage as fouled as his, naturally he hungered for Fenella. The lust of a dissatisfied man. It was pathetic, really, the stuff of gross comedy in a play. She was a brave and spirited soul. She deserved better.

He swallowed the last of the pork and tossed the stick, his eyes on the mansion's grounds. The property was walled, but the massed treetops told him the grounds extended far back from the square, some of the trees frothed with white cherry blossoms. He turned into a lane that led between the houses, narrow and muddy. A dirty lad was tugging a stubborn pig by a rope. The cart of a rag-and-bone man rattled past. A couple of workmen were pushing barrows through the open wooden gate that led into the duchess's property.

Gardeners? Their barrows were piled with pungent-smelling dung. Manure for the flower beds and fruit trees, no doubt.

The gate was closing behind the gardeners. Adam ran for it and caught it with his boot. "The Duchess of Feria lives here?" he asked. They looked him up and down skeptically. One said, "What's your business with Her Ladyship?"

No business of yours, he almost said, but remembered Fenella's advice. *Act subservient.* "My master has sent a message for her steward," he said. *Would a magistrate's name sound convincing?* "From Meinheer Dekker."

The man grunted, flies buzzing around his cartload of dung. "That way." He pointed through the trees toward the house. "Round to the west. Steward's rooms are over the main gatehouse." The other man closed the garden gate.

Adam walked briskly down the path through the orchard. He passed gardeners at work on their knees, housemaids carrying baskets of laundry out of the rear of the house, a footman lugging in a load of firewood. No one stopped him. No one spoke to him. He walked straight through the bustling kitchen, humid with steam and smelling of onions, then along a flagstone passage. A few of the servants he passed glanced at him, but he marched on as if he knew where he was going, then up a dim, narrow flight of stairs where, blessedly, he seemed to be alone. He passed through a heavy door and knew he'd reached the family's quarters: The marble corridor was broad and airy, its walls hung with tapestries. He saw a housemaid with an armload of linens coming toward him, a puzzled look on her face as though she wondered who he was. He ducked into a side corridor and kept walking, looking over his shoulder, thinking he was a fool to have come inside this place. What was he going to do, ask a maid where to find his wife? Insane.

Then he saw her. At the far end of the corridor, coming out of a room. Frances. Her back was to him, but he instantly recognized that ramrod posture. She wore a gown of rich black taffeta, Spanish-style, with a stiff white ruff. She patted the lace coif over her hair as she walked away, and he saw that her hand was heavily jeweled with rings. She reached another door and opened it and disappeared inside.

He felt a lash of fury. The plot she had abetted to assassinate Elizabeth had almost succeeded, yet Frances had not only escaped, she'd also found this luxurious haven. If she had fled alone he might merely have cursed her and considered her dead to him, glad to be rid of her. But she had stolen his children, and for three years he'd lived in an agony of worry, wondering if they were even alive. He reached the door and gripped the handle, burning to march in and shake Frances until her teeth chattered.

He quickly came to his senses. A half-dozen people might be in that room with her, ladies come to play cards, or the duchess herself entertaining visitors. Or might Kate and Robert themselves be in there? It was torture to think that only an inch of wooden door might separate him from them. But if Frances saw him she could raise an alarm, and then armed retainers would come pounding in. His powerless state was a bitter thing, hard to stomach. Frances had everything on her side. Control of the children. Protection. Influence. He dare not confront her. Could not let her see him, or even know that he was in the city. If she did, she might hustle the children into a coach and bolt with them. Then he might never find them.

He let go of the door handle, tense with frustration. He told himself that at least he'd confirmed she was staying in this house. That meant Kate and Robert were, too.

Voices. Adam saw a stairway at the end of the corridor. People were coming down it from the floor above. He turned and quickly went back the way he'd come. Servants eyed him as he went through the kitchen, but he made it outside without being questioned, then back out through the garden gate.

At the Balienplein Place market he slipped into the crowd with the galling sense of being beaten in a skirmish, forced to retreat before he'd even seen his enemy face-to-face.

The Black Boar Tavern lay just inside the Anderlecht Gate in the city wall, set in a row of shops and alehouses crammed together like crooked teeth. The tavern was the address Adam had used to correspond with his agent, Leonard Tyrone.

"The Irishman?" the barkeep said in answer to Adam's question. Stained wooden cups lay in a tub of scummy water behind the bar, dousing any thirst Adam might have had. "He moved out."

"When?"

"Two days ago. Had his bags sent. You want his room?"

No, nor the lice that came with it. "Where did you send his bags?"

It was a short walk to the new address, a leafy cul-de-sac where four houses nestled in the lee of a quaint old church. The house was a fine stone structure with red gables, making Adam wonder if the barkeep had made a mistake. Three years ago when he'd hired Tyrone to search for Frances around Dublin, the Irishman had been scrounging for work. If he did live here he'd certainly moved up in the world.

Adam knocked. A thickset maidservant with a hooked nose frowned at him as though doubting such a common fellow could have business with her master and grudgingly led him through to a parlor. A trunk and boxes lay open, half their contents unpacked. Tyrone was lounging at a small table, eating alone, a half-consumed leg of capon before him and a flagon of wine. His goblet was halfway to his lips when he saw Adam. Startled, he jumped up.

"Your Lordship . . ." he stammered.

Adam caught the maid's wide-eyed look before she curtsied and left, closing the door. "Sorry to barge in on you, Tyrone." They eyed each other. It had been a long time since they'd been face-to-face. "Your last report. About my wife. That's why I'm here."

Tyrone blinked at him. Swallowed hard. He looked rattled, almost panicky. "My lord, please let me explain—"

"No need. You did good work, tracking her. I was just there, at the duchess's house, and I caught a glimpse of my wife. Now I need your help." He nodded to the wine. "Can you spare a glass? I'm parched."

Tyrone relaxed a little, though Adam thought he still looked uneasy. "Of course, your lordship . . . of course." He moved quickly to fetch a goblet from a sideboard. He poured the wine so fast it splashed over the rim.

Adam took a large swallow. An excellent Burgundy. He set

down the goblet and wiped his mouth with the back of his hand, glancing around at the gold brocade curtains, the ornately carved bench by the oriel window. The place must have come furnished if Tyrone had just moved in. "You're doing well," he said. "Other enterprises on the go?"

Tyrone was fussing with setting out another plate and shot him a glance. "A lucky windfall, your lordship. A relative died. Will you join me in a bite to eat?"

"No thank you, no time. I have a job for you. You found my wife and I thank you for that. Now I've come about my children."

"Ah," Tyrone said, as though struggling to catch up. "The young Lord Robert and your daughter?"

"Katherine. Yes. Can you confirm that they're living in the duchess's house with Lady Thornleigh?"

"Grenville, my lord."

"Pardon?"

"That's the name your wife is using. Lady Grenville."

Her maiden name. It gave Adam a sting of disgust. The Grenville family had caused his own family so much misery and grief. But something in him was glad that she no longer used his name.

"You've found out a lot. That's good. I need you to find more. About the layout of the house, and where exactly in it my children stay. And about my wife's routine, and the children's routine. I know you're clever, Tyrone, and you have contacts. I need information about how and where I can reach Robert and Katherine alone."

The Irishman's eyes went wide. "You intend to reclaim your children?"

Not your business, Adam thought. "I'm their father. I intend to talk to them."

Tyrone made a groveling bow as though aware he'd gone too far. "Of course, your lordship."

"The thing is, I need to keep my head down. That means you don't know I'm in this city. Understood?"

"Perfectly, my lord."

"So, can you find out what I need?"

"The fact is, I am in quite a good position to help your lordship. In my investigation about the whereabouts of Lady Gren—I mean Lady Thornleigh, I got to know some people of the duchess's household. I made a friend of one in particular, your children's tutor, Goert Peterszen."

"Does he live in the house?"

"He does."

"Good. Grease his palm if you need to." Adam drew a few ducats from his pocket. "I'll need the information as soon as possible."

Tyrone took the coins, pocketed them, then tugged down his doublet. "I'll go right away. Shouldn't take long." He reached for his cap. "And where shall I report to you, my lord? Where are you staying?"

Adam shook his head. The last thing he wanted was to loaf around at his inn all day, waiting to hear. "I'll come back. Be here at seven this evening."

Adam walked briskly across the city, heading for the Willebroek Canal. Near the Grote Markt he noticed a half-dozen soldiers on horseback trotting toward him. He kept his eyes on the ground, plodding on like a laborer until they trotted past him.

Crossing the Grote Markt, he passed a towering statue of the Duke of Alba with sword drawn, his fierce bronze eyes seeming to look straight at Adam. He looked up at the grand Gothic façade of the King's House, Alba's palatial seat. Inside those rooms five years ago the captive leaders of the Dutch resistance, Count Egmont and Count Hoorn, had spent their last night on earth. The next morning Alba had them beheaded in the Grote Markt. It was the beginning of what the people called Alba's reign of blood.

Adam passed the phalanx of Spanish harquebusiers stationed outside the palace with their long guns. They had the bored, arrogant look of entrenched victors. He thought of his sister Isabel's husband, Carlos. A good man, Adam had always thought. Carlos had once saved his life. But now, Carlos was somewhere in this city, a part and prop of Alba's martial power. *Once a mercenary, always a mercenary*, Adam thought with disgust. How could Isabel stand being here?

He made his way westward toward the canal, past houses and churches and shops, gauging how long it would take to reach the canal from the duchess's house on Balienplein Square. This was the route he would take with Kate and Robert once he had them. A quick dash and the three of them would be on a canal boat heading to Antwerp before Frances could rouse her friend's retainers. He felt buoyed with cautious hope. Would he finally have his children back?

He stood on the busy quay and looked out at the ships and barges and wherries, and took a deep breath of the fresh, waterborne air. What a marvel the canal was. Dug eleven years ago, a length of almost eighteen miles, with four locks that lifted the vessels uphill. It let ships avoid navigating the sandy little Zenne River, and gave direct access to the Scheldt River and thence to the port of Antwerp and the North Sea. Watching the crew of a ship with Swedish flags haul in their anchor cable and prepare to set sail, Adam couldn't help admiring Spanish enterprise in overseeing the construction of this canal. England had nothing to match it.

A barge alongside the wharf was being loaded with bawling sheep. He remembered what Fenella had said when they'd reached the cove, that she had a friend here with a barge. Not on the canal, but on Sint-Gorikseiland near the city center. It touched him that she'd been thinking of his safety. He hoped *she* was safe, hoped she'd got her gold from the banker and was already headed back to the cove. With luck, he'd be on his way there tomorrow with his own gold: Robert and Kate.

Dusk was darkening the city as he made his way back toward Tyrone's house. The streets were full of people heading home. Hawkers around the Anderlecht Gate were packing up their wares, hoisting baskets onto carts and satchels over their shoulders. Church bells clanged from the cathedral. Seven o'clock. Adam's stomach growled; he'd had nothing all day but those morsels of pork at the market and a few swallows of Tyrone's wine. He was hungry for a real meal. But hungrier to hear what the Irishman had found out about the children.

In the quiet cul-de-sac Adam waited in the tree-cast shadows outside the red-gabled house. No need to show his face again to Tyrone's inquisitive maid. Overcautious he might be, but it didn't hurt to assume that a servant who knew he was a foreign lord might blab about that. A bat streaked past his ear. He went a few paces toward the mouth of the cul-de-sac. A horse clopped past. Then, in the silence, he heard footsteps. He stepped out from the shadows and intercepted Tyrone.

"Ah, my lord! You startled me." He glanced over his shoulder as though to check that no one had followed him. Adam was glad the fellow was diligent about that.

"It's all right; we're alone. Did you see the tutor?"

"Aye, that I did."

"And? What did you find out?"

Tyrone's smile was one of satisfaction. "More than we'd even hoped, my lord. Peterszen told me that tomorrow morning Lady Thornleigh will accompany the duchess to visit friends near the Coudenberg Palace. While she is away young Lord Robert and his sister will go to the Church of Saint Nicholas for their regular instruction."

"Instruction?"

"In the catechism. Seems they see the priest every Wednesday morning at ten."

Adam groaned. His children were English, brought up as Protestants, but it was no surprise that Frances had wrenched them back to popish ways. It irked him. But he understood what Tyrone was implying and was glad of the opportunity it gave him. When Robert and Kate were with the priest they'd be far from Frances, and from the duchess's men. "Where is this church?"

"On Boterstraat, my lord. Behind the Bourse. Peterszen says the children meet the priest in the side chapel of the Holy Virgin."

Adam clapped his agent on the shoulder. "Well done, Tyrone. I owe you."

The next morning, thunder rumbled above the leaden skies of Brussels. *Rain's not far off,* Adam thought as he left his inn and made his way toward Boterstraat. It was just after nine. He wanted to get to the church early. The blithe townsfolk took no notice of the impending rough weather. The streets were filled with maids carrying baskets to and from market, and carts clattered by as apprentices, farmers, clerks, and priests went about their business. The hammers of bricklayers and masons clanged on a half-finished house. Adam's eyes were on the steeple of the Church of Saint Nicholas to give him his bearings as he navigated the narrow streets toward the steeple. A wagon piled with ale kegs rolled past, the rear wheel just missing his foot, and he lurched back. He was so keyed up to see Robert and Kate he wasn't being careful where he stepped.

He carried on and turned the corner. There, across the street, beyond the passersby, rose the church, a soot-grimed, centuries-old building, oddly asymmetrical. He stopped. Four people stood outside its doors between the stone pillars. Two burly men and two women, one gray haired and dour faced, dressed in the apron and shawl of a waiting woman, the other slender, shrouded in a pale gray cloak, its hood up, her face turned away. By her posture she was much younger. Could it possibly be Kate? No, his daughter was a child and this was a young woman, quite tall. Then she glanced his way and his heart gave a kick. *Kate!* Good God, how she'd grown! She turned away again, and he almost lurched in disappointment at having seen her face for only that moment. He was very glad he'd come early. It was not yet ten. He studied the two men with her. Retainers of the duchess? Likely, for they were armed with swords.

One opened the church door for Kate and she went in. Alone. Adam held his breath. Where was Robert? Inside already? No, Kate's party had arrived early. Had Robert not come at all? That was a blow. Adam had imagined the children coming together, as Tyrone had said. He took a breath, forcing himself to move past the disappointment. He had found Kate, at least. He would have to find another way to get Robert.

He longed to go in after her, but he held himself back. Impossible to go through that door without passing the pair of armed men. They were chatting with the waiting woman. Clearly, they were letting Kate take her religious instruction in private. Reason told Adam he should turn around and leave. Wait for another opportunity to get both children together. But reason fought with his burning desire to see his daughter.

As the three servants chatted he quickly crossed the street and slipped down the lane beside the church. It curved around, and he gripped the handle of the dagger at his belt, half-expecting to come face-to-face with some of Alba's soldiers. The lane was narrow and he had to squeeze past an old woman leading a donkey laden with firewood. He was looking for a door into the rear of the church.

He saw one ahead, a low, arched door studded with nails. He tried the latch. It opened. A musty passage led into the whitewashed sacristy, a workmanlike room whose single, high window spilled gray light onto the vestment wardrobes, the stone basin, the crucifix on the wall. The room was deserted, no priests. That was lucky, and Adam was grateful. He opened the inner door and immediately found himself behind the apse, another world of rosy light filtered through stained glass and incense-scented air. Gold and silver gleamed on the altar, and beyond it rose the polished wood of the choir stalls and the carved rood screen. Over all was the hushed vault of the high-columned nave.

The side chapel. That's where Tyrone said the priest gave the children instruction. Around to Adam's left he saw it, an alcove where votive candles flickered beside an ornate marble altar. Above the altar stood a statue of the Virgin Mary painted in gold and bright sky blue. Adam saw no priest. Just Kate, kneeling at the altar, her head bowed. She held up a golden crucifix on a chain round her neck, held it with both hands as though offering it up to the statue while keeping her head humbly lowered. Then she raised her face to the Virgin, and Adam's breath caught. How like his sister she looked. The same wide-set dark eyes, small nose, full lips. His daughter, his sweet girl . . . now almost a woman.

"Kate!" The name burst from his mouth as he went to her.

She looked startled. She jumped to her feet with a wide-eyed look of surprise. "Father?" Confusion rushed over her face. Then dismay. *Who can blame her?* he thought, his heart aching. *We've been apart so long.*

He reached her and enfolded her in his arms. "Kate, my chick.

It's so wonderful to see you!" She'd been just nine when he'd last seen her and now she was as tall as his shoulder. A laugh of joy escaped him and he pulled her away to arm's length. "Let me look at you. Good Christ, you're so grown. And a beauty, by heaven." Yet her skin was so pale. Did she never see the sun?

She lurched back, away from him. "Sir, you . . . blaspheme," she stammered. "In a house of God."

That threw him. Frances's work, of course, pounding religion into the girl. But he was too happy to let it bother him. "You're right. Sorry. It's just a shock to see you. A *good* shock, I assure you." He looked around, realizing he'd been a fool not to keep his voice down. Was the priest near? It struck him how quiet the church was, as though deserted. He lowered his voice. "Where's your brother? Still at the duchess's house?"

"No . . . he—" She stopped herself. She looked utterly bewildered.

"Never mind. We'll get him later." He held out his hand for hers. "Come, we haven't got much time."

"Time?"

"I'm taking you home."

"I . . . don't understand. Home with Mother?"

"No, your real home. England. As soon as I can get Robert, too."

"England?" she said. Her voice was thin. She sounded horrified. "No."

No? He laughed, a nervous laugh. It had never occurred to him that she would not want to go. "Kate, look, I know I've startled you, surprising you like this, but—"

"You abandoned us," she blurted.

"I what?"

"It's been years. You haven't come to see us. Haven't written to us. Why would we want to go back to England?" Her misery and confusion cut him. "You don't care a whit about us."

Fury tightened his throat. What tales had Frances told them? What lies? "That's not true," he said as calmly as he could. "I've been trying all this time to find you. I love you, both of you."

A thud sounded down the nave. "Christ, is that the bloody priest?" Kate gasped again at his profanity. "There's no time to talk," he said quietly. "You've got to come with me, right now." He took her by the hand. "Come. Out the back."

She snatched back her hand. "I'm not going anywhere with you." She clutched her crucifix, gripping it to her chest with both hands as though for protection. "Father Hubert will soon be here. I'm taking lessons with him. Studying."

"Lessons?" He was struggling to think of how to get her to come. How to break through her resistance.

"Perfection of our daily duties. Purity of intention. The patience and perseverance of prayer."

He whistled in mock bemusement. "That's a lot of *p*'s." A thin jest, a desperate jest.

She glared at him and went on doggedly, "The ceremony for taking the first habit. The needed virtues of a sister."

"Habit? You don't mean . . . a nunnery?"

"Of course. The Cistercian abbey at Ixelles. Robert's there, too; we're staying at the school." She raised her chin proudly. "In two weeks I'll enter the order as a novice."

He was appalled. *A nun?* It was grotesque. "This is your mother's doing."

"God's doing," Kate said with spirit. "I have a calling, sir."

"You have a scheming mother. She can't marry you off since you have no dowry and no family connections, so this is her solution. But I'll see hell freeze before I let her entomb you in a convent."

She gaped at him, appalled and angry and hurt. Her chin trembled. "My mother loves God. And you, sir . . . you should fear Him for your sins."

"My sins? I'm here because of your damned *mother's* sins. She's a traitor."

She gasped. "How dare you!"

Good Christ. She had no idea what Frances had done. "Why do you think she snatched you and Robert and fled England?"

"She said you . . . abused her."

He could hardly breathe for fury. "She tried to kill the Queen. She fled to escape being hanged!"

Kate's face was pale, her eyes deep pools of confusion. It broke Adam's heart. His rage at Frances drained as love for his daughter flooded in. She was really still a child and he hated to hurt her. The church bell clanged, startling him, a clangor like thunder in a cave. Bells across the city pealed as if in echo, ringing the hour. Ten o'clock. He gently reached for her hand. "Kate, I'll explain everything. How she's lied to you. But not now. Now we have to go, before—"

"No!" She snatched back her hand again. She gripped her cloak tightly to her chest. "I will not stay and hear this." She bolted out of the chapel. Turned down the nave. She was heading for the front doors.

"Don't!" Adam ran after her, hurrying past rows of empty benches. "Kate, stop!"

But she was swift. She had one of the double doors partway open by the time he reached her. He snatched her by the shoulders and yanked her backward. She stumbled against him with a small cry, her back to his chest, and he held her to steady her. He looked across the top of her head through the half-open door and froze at what he saw. Armed men. Six of them in the green livery of the Duchess of Feria, their swords at the ready. The bearing of soldiers. They stood with the two retainers and the serving woman who'd come with Kate. And beside them another woman, her back to him, richly dressed in a cape of blue silk. She turned sharply to look at the street, her face in profile. Adam's stomach lurched. *Frances.*

She hadn't seen him. She and the soldiers had moved a little away from the church doors and were watching the street. *Waiting for me*, he realized. The truth came crashing in on him. He'd been betrayed. But how? Who?

The church bell stopped its clangor. Adam ducked behind the open door. They had not heard Kate open it amid the noise of the bells, but closing it now might draw their attention. "Kate," he whispered, "there are soldiers outside. Do you see them? They must not find me."

She looked at them. At him. "Why not?"

"Just trust me, please. Come with me now, quietly, out the back."

"What have you done?" She shook her head. "No, I told you, I'm not going."

She wasn't budging. He had to shock her to move. "Your mother is out there, too. Do you see her? She brought the soldiers."

Kate looked out again. Then back at him, blinking, struggling to make sense of it. "Maybe she's come to fetch me."

"So she sent you here?"

"Yes, who else?"

"But you said you're staying at the convent. How long have you been there?"

"Since Friday."

The day after he'd landed. How could Frances have known that?

"Or maybe," Kate said innocently, "she's come to speak to Father Hubert."

"Where *is* Father Hubert? Not here, because she told him not to come, to keep the way clear for the soldiers to take me. Why do you think the church is empty? They sent everyone out."

Her eyes darted from him to the group outside and back again, like a hunted doe hiding in bracken. He reached out for her, a silent request that she give him her hand. She did not move.

"Kate, listen to me. Your mother has used you to lure me here. Used you as bait."

She was as still as if caught in a spell, her eyes huge. He felt that if he said one wrong word he would lose her.

"Think," he whispered. "Have I ever lied to you?"

Her mouth trembled. She swallowed. "You're lying now." She pulled open the door with such force it scraped the stone and the handle clanked.

Adam saw Frances whirl around at the sound. She pointed to him and cried, "There he is!"

The soldiers rushed up the steps, raising their swords. Adam grabbed Kate's arm and ran, pulling her. She kept pace with him to avoid stumbling, but she was straining back, resisting. He dragged her on past the empty benches. Heard the soldiers pounding after them. "Halt!" the leader yelled.

Adam and Kate were almost at the crossing, the rood screen and choir stalls just ahead. His only hope was to get out the way he'd come, around the apse, through the sacristy, and out into the lane.

But Kate was balking and squirming, holding him back. She grabbed hold of a bench and anchored herself, wrenching Adam to a halt.

The soldiers pounded closer, their swords gleaming red from the light of the stained glass windows. Every instinct told Adam to protect his daughter from their weapons. He turned to face them, dragging Kate behind him, screening her with his body. He whipped out his dagger.

The benches on either side forced four of the soldiers to bunch up behind the first two, so the rear ones veered sideways, two to the left, two to the right, to attack his flank. Impeded by the benches, they jumped over them but were still slower than the front two who came straight at Adam. One lunged at him. Adam lunged at the same moment with a stab that missed, but it surprised the man enough that his sword sliced the air wide of Adam's shoulder and the man stumbled aside. The next one swung at Adam, and his blade tip gouged the side of Adam's neck. It felt like a punch. Blood wetted his shirt.

"Father!" Kate cried at seeing his blood. She reached out for him.

"Stay back!" he said, pushing her clear of the two men coming from the right.

She whirled off her cloak and threw it at the two men. It fell on the sword of one. He struggled to disentangle it.

Kate cried, "Go, Father! Run!"

He looked at his daughter for one agonizing moment. Then he turned and crashed through the rood screen. A soldier pounded after him to the altar. Adam grabbed the golden cross as long as his arm and hacked at the man's sword. The sword fell with a clatter and the man staggered, off-balance.

"Don't let him escape!" Frances shouted, rushing down the nave. She reached Kate and snatched her.

Two more soldiers charged Adam.

"Run, Father!"

He turned and ran.

✂ 8 ✂

The Bargeman

Her horse plodded through Brussels, head down, under heavy rain. Wet and saddle-sore, Fenella kept her head down, too, though much good it did. One shoulder of her cloak was soaked through, and water dribbled down her hood and found the opening under her chin, letting chilly drops snake down her neck. She shivered and with one sodden leather glove bunched the fabric more tightly at her throat. Plodding on through the half-deserted streets, she thought wryly, *Sensible people are indoors.*

My own fault, she told herself. She'd be dry and comfortable if she had stopped at an inn on the road when the downpour started. But she was impatient to get her business here in the capital done and over with. In Antwerp she had returned to her banker and taken a portion of her gold, which now lay tucked inside her saddlebags, destined for the Brussels group of the Brethren. Claes had insisted that she take a servant as an escort, but the fellow slowed her down, slogging behind her, hunched over in his saddle, looking glum in the rain. So she had left him at an inn outside Antwerp and told him to return to Polder. Good riddance. She was used to taking care of herself. She just wanted to get her task done and get back to Antwerp to rendezvous with Adam Thornleigh on the boat. Then she would be off to England with him. Baron Thornleigh. *Call me Adam.* The thought of him buoyed her spirits. She lifted her shoulder to shrug off the drenched patch of cloak, telling herself, *It's only water.*

Drumbeats sounded, and Fenella's horse shied back a step. She steadied the animal as a small troop of soldiers marched out from a side street. A captain led the way, followed by five foot soldiers, then another horseman leading a prisoner by a rope. The rope ended in a noose around the prisoner's neck, and he staggered along, wrists bound at his back, his filthy clothes drenched. Five more foot soldiers brought up the rear, followed by two drummers. A straggle of people plodded behind, among them a weeping woman with a child clutching her hand. The drummers beat out the flat drumrolls that signaled an execution. The prisoner was on his way to hang.

What had the poor fool done? Fenella wondered. Stolen a rich man's purse? Spoken out against the Duke of Alba's tyranny? Those crimes were nothing compared to hers. She had murdered Alba's kinsman. And she was about to commit another crime, bringing aid to men who were fighting Alba. She shuddered, thinking of that noose around the prisoner's neck. She could see herself on the scaffold . . . the scratchy rope . . . you dropped so violently it snapped your neck.

Stop it, she told herself. *No good will come of frightening myself.* She was about to turn her horse and carry on when her eyes were drawn to the captain on the lead horse. He wore a breastplate and a helmet with a white plume. She'd been in the city long enough to know that the plume marked him as one of Alba's commanders. He looked familiar. Where had she seen him before? A young man on the street lurched forward as though to stop him, and the commander scowled and his fighting hand went to his sword. Then his expression relaxed, for it was clear the young man was no threat, weeping and pulling his hair and swaying on his feet. The commander's hand settled and he looked forward again.

That martial action of his jolted Fenella's memory. *Edinburgh.* The garrison at Leith! She'd been eighteen and so miserably poor she had let the garrison commander, a Frenchman named D'Oysel, make her his mistress. But he'd turned out to be a brute, and when he cut her face she'd been so desperate to escape him she had asked for help from a captain of cavalry—this same commander who was riding toward her now. His name came back to her in a rush. *Carlos Valverde*. She blushed to remember how she had offered him her body in asking for his help. But help her he did, in exchange for *her* help in getting his kinsman out of jail. Adam Thornleigh. That was the first time she had ever seen Adam. She struggled to remember exactly how the two men were related. Cousins? No, brothers-in-law, that was it. Adam's sister was Valverde's wife. Questions reared up. What was he doing in Brussels? How had he come to work for Alba?

Her horse jerked up its head with an anxious whinny. That drew a glance from Valverde, and Fenella quickly turned so he would not see her face. She could not risk him noticing her. She had killed a Spanish don and Valverde had the power to arrest. Her horse danced nervously on the spot, a rear hoof skidding on the wet cobbles. She tightened her grip on the reins and got control of the horse. The execution party carried on, swallowed by the gray rain.

God, get me out of here, she thought. She kicked the horse's flanks and it broke into a trot. Her heart was beating fast, out of time with the drums fading behind her. When she was well past the party she reined in her horse to a steady walk. *Finish what you came for, then get out of this God-cursed country.*

She was determined to see her task through. She'd promised this to Claes, her contribution to his cause. It was the least she could do, she had told him, and now she felt how true those words were. Guilt needled her. Hers was a paltry contribution. In fighting Alba, Claes was risking his very life.

But it's not my cause, she thought irritably. Claes had agreed. *Go to England*, he had said. *Be safe there. Be happy.* And go she certainly would. It was the only sane thing to do. Yet guilt had wormed its way into her heart and settled there. She could not shake the sense that she was abandoning her husband.

He had given her directions to the house of the Brethren. It lay just inside the southern wall, by the Anderlecht Gate. Her route would take her right through the city, and Fenella was aware that she must look unusual, even suspicious, riding alone in a downpour when most people were indoors. She could not afford to attract attention. She would be glad, too, to change into dry clothes before going to see the Brethren. So she decided to go first to her old friend Berck Verhulst. He and his wife might offer her a bed to return to for the night after she'd concluded her business with the Brethren. If they were not home, she would finish her business and then find an inn.

The Grote Markt was behind her now, and the Bourse, too. Water trickled off the slate roof of a house to her right and poured from the eaves of a cobbler's shop to her left, splashing mud up to her stirrups. Between the buildings she saw the bridge ahead, a skeletal shape in the rain. It led to Sint-Gorikseiland, the island in the shallow Zenne River that wound through the city center. Her horse clomped onto the bridge, its hooves sounding hollowly on the wooden planks. The island was home to fishermen and fishmongers, and Fenella smelled its fishy reek and heard the *plash* of a watermill. The Low Countries had been well named. This marshy country, level with the sea, was a world of water.

And of rubbish, by the stench. People seemed to use the river as a sewer. She saw the half carcass of a pig, the nether half, floating toward the bridge. Overhanging branches on the riverbank snagged it, and the leafy tips trailing in the water covered it, only a black hoof protruding. That pig will stink come Sunday, Fenella thought as she reached the other side and turned her horse.

She stopped beside a couple of muddy children on their knees in the grass, harvesting worms wriggling to the surface from the rain. She asked if they knew Meinheer Verhulst. "The *Pelican*," they said, and pointed down the path that ran beside the riverbank.

Fenella carried on down the path, past dripping trees and dripping cottages, until she reached the jetty where Berck Verhulst's barge was tethered, a long, low vessel with two stubby masts. Berck, the gentle giant, she thought with a smile as she tied her horse to the rail under a tree. She hadn't seen him in over five years. In Polder he had been one of her best customers at the chandlery. He owned the *Pelican* and lived aboard it, ferrying cargo between Brussels and Antwerp—grain, sheep, ale, horses, whatever paid—and had often come to buy Fenella's gear. So often, in fact, she remembered Claes once muttering, *Verhulst again?* But Claes had had no reason to be jealous; she thought of Berck like a brother. Not long before the slaughter of Polder he'd married a woman from Brussels and they'd moved here. Fenella had never met his wife. Did they have children now? Bairns brought up on a barge? Well, she thought, they'd see more interesting sights than many a pampered young lord in a moat-bound castle. She crossed the spongy grass and stepped onto the jetty.

When she came alongside the boat and took in its condition she felt a pinch of worry. It hadn't left shore for some time; that was clear from the slime of black mold on the lines that tethered it to the bollard. And the furled sails, dripping with rain, sagged with age and neglect. Did Berck not live aboard anymore? She heard sounds belowdecks, a faint clanging and scraping. Hard to tell what caused them with the rain drumming so loudly on the deck.

She lifted the wet skirt of her cloak to step safely onboard and went amidships to the small cabin and knocked. "Hello?" she called. The clanging and scraping went on. She opened the hatch. The cabin was not much bigger than a closet and empty but for a begrimed stool and a heap of frayed hemp line. She closed the hatch, happy to be out of the rain, and threw off her sodden hood. A companionway led to the lower deck. She went down the steps, blinking as her eyes adjusted to the dim light, and found herself in the galley. A low brick hearth. A scatter of splintered crates. A hanging lantern in which a guttering candle gave off the only light and its tallow a rank smell. And there was Berck, on his knees at the cold hearth, his back to her, laying bricks with a clang and scrape of his trowel. He hadn't heard her with the din of the rain above.

She came to him. "Berck."

He swung around. A beard covered half his face, a ragged bush like black wires, and his black hair, too, was shaggy and unkempt. His eyes lit up. "Fenella Doorn?" He got to his feet, looming over her, his head brushing the deck head. Legs like tree trunks and hands like hams.

"None other," she said with a smile.

He grinned. "Christ on the cross." His voice was a deep rumble. "You're a sight to make a man dance a jig."

She grinned back but thought with a sad twinge that Berck's jig days seemed over. His wrestler's body had gone to fat. He was sweating from his labor, and his dingy linen shirt, big as a sail, clung in damp patches to his paunchy torso. She playfully poked his belly. "Someone's been feeding you well, my friend." She glanced around for his wife.

He winked at her. "And someone needs to fatten you up. Come, sit you down, Fenella, and tell me what brings you here. Christ almighty, you're soaked as a stowaway rat."

She laughed. "God's truth, I'll be glad to get myself dry."

The moment she mentioned the baggage on her horse he was on his way to fetch it. He climbed the companionway with unexpected liveliness for a man so big. She heard his thumping gait across the deck. Waiting, she took in her surroundings. Unwashed wooden cups and trenchers. Mud-matted straw on the floor. A threadbare blanket on a berth that was littered with cracked blocks and broken sheaves. A sour smell like old cheese. The squalor surprised her. Berck used to be a proud seaman and kept his vessel in good order.

When he came back she changed her dress and stockings in the privacy of the stern cabin where his berth was a narrow, lumpy bed. The cabin was as dirty as the galley, but the dry clothes felt very good and she was happy to return to the galley and sit at Berck's scuffed table and accept a mug of ale that he drew from a keg almost half his size. He thudded down on the bench across from her with his own full mug and told her he had heard about the tragedy in Polder five years ago. "Lost your man, I heard. Bad luck, Fenella. A hard blow, I warrant."

She looked down at her ale. No need to tell him that Claes had survived. Claes was safer if everyone thought him dead. She told Berck how she'd gone to Sark and established her business there.

A grin spread under his bush of beard. "Aye, you're a woman bound to get on in the world wherever the devil drops you." He raised his mug in a salute.

She smiled and clinked mugs with him and they drank. He

downed his ale in four huge gulps, then refilled it from the keg. An oversized thirst, Fenella thought wryly. Now she knew where that big belly came from. "Shall I meet your wife?" she asked. "She hasn't been caught out in this downpour, I hope."

He spat into the hearth. "Caught by the devil, for all I care." Fenella listened with growing concern as he told her how his wife had left him three years ago. "Said I was always at the cockfights, always off wagering." He upended his mug to finish the ale and his eyes grew misty with anger. "God knows I only did it to keep her in style. Her with her frippery and gewgaws."

So his gambling had ruptured his marriage. She guessed why. "You fell into debt?"

He nodded. "Deeper than a sea sinkhole. And then, when I hit the bottom, she ran off with a hot-gospeller. A right knave, babbled like a baby about being saved by Jesus. And she fell in with his claptrap. Bah! The devil take 'em both."

A melancholy tale, Fenella thought. She reached across the table and took his hand. "I'm sorry."

He looked at her morosely and then with sudden energy clapped his big hand over hers. There was a new gleam in his eyes. "We're both of us alone now, eh, Fenella?"

Uneasy, she slipped her hand back, not answering, and took a swallow of ale. "And your business, Berck? How does it fare?"

He heaved himself up from the table and shuffled to the keg to refill his mug. "Gone, three years now. I couldn't pay the license to work the boat. That's over."

She was shocked. "How do you live?"

"With my hands. Dug the canal, me and a gang glad of the wage. There's many in this city that grouse about the Spaniards, but I say the Spaniards have put bread on many a workingman's table."

"And now?" she asked. The canal was finished.

"My place is at the lock. I help warp the vessels in and out. When I'm needed. Not today." He raised his mug and winked. "There's luck, eh?"

A dockhand. It was a living, yes, but he was no longer his own master. It made Fenella sadder than she could say. Perhaps he read her face, for he raised his head with a look of wounded pride. "I get by just fine. That ale you're drinking is the personal gift of a Spanish don. Came off an overloaded barge, the don's own supply, three kegs that rolled off and would've sunk if my mates and me hadn't salvaged 'em."

Scrabbling for Spanish charity. This was sadder still. And a chilling reminder that she had to be careful about what she said. Thank God she had not mentioned Claes. Berck worked for the city, so his livelihood, meager though it was, came from the magistrates' collaboration with the Spanish overlords. If he heard of a rebel, Berck might well turn him in.

He slammed his hand on the table like a slab of meat and said with sudden, brash cheerfulness, "To good days ahead, eh, Fenella?" He raised his mug again in a toast.

His bravado touched her. She managed a smile. "To good days for us all, Berck." She toasted him. They both drank.

"Now," he said, wiping his ale-damp beard with his hand, "what brings you to Brussels?"

"Business. And a chance to see old friends, like you."

"Have you somewhere to stay? You're welcome to a berth here."

She hated to tell him that she would rather ride in the rain than sleep on this dirty boat. Besides, she'd expected to find a married couple, not a bachelor.

Perhaps he read her face. "The stern cabin would be all yours," he assured her.

"That's kind," she said, "but I must see to my business before it gets dark. My customer is beyond the Anderlecht Gate. There's bound to be an inn thereabouts." She cocked her head, eyes on the ceiling. The din on deck had stopped. "Listen, the rain's let up."

The truth was, something else was troubling her, Berck's tale of how his wife had run out on him. *A disloyal wife*, she thought. *Is that what I am?* Claes had gone on a mission that was clearly dangerous, and what if he was hurt? Or killed? If he died, God forbid, she could only mourn him . . . for the second time. But if he was hurt? A wife's place was with her husband, to help him and comfort him. That was the marriage vow, and she had taken it with her eyes open. She sensed that Claes's stern-faced comrade, Sister Martha, would like to take her place. *But I'm his lawful wife.*

No, he set me free, the voice inside her pleaded. *Go to England,* he had said. *Be safe there. Be happy.* And she had been so relieved to hear that. She wanted no part of the life Claes had chosen in leading the Brethren, hiding underground like rats, always in fear. His hope of vanquishing the mighty Spaniards seemed daft to her, like the wishful thinking of a child. Yet the question needled her without pity: *Was* she free? What if Claes one day realized how hopeless the fight was and left the Brethren? Shouldn't she then come back and live with him as his wife? And if that was the case, how could she start life in England as Adam Thornleigh's business partner, so near him that she would always be yearning for him? How could she put her heart into rebuilding her business there if one day she would have to go back to Claes?

"You'll come back, though, won't you?" Berck was saying.

"What?"

"After your business is done. We've got lots to catch up on. Old times."

She looked at him, the spidery red threads that webbed his cheeks, the morose yet hopeful look in his eyes. "I'll try," she lied. She fetched her satchel, readying to leave, and took out five gold ducats and pressed them into his beefy hand.

He looked taken aback. "What's this?" He sounded on the verge of taking offense.

"To hell with Spaniards," she said slyly. "Buy your own kegs."

He barked a laugh and closed his fist around the coins. "Ha! So I will." He grinned. "You're a woman in a million, Fenella."

She was already going up the steps, her satchel strap over one shoulder, her damp cloak over the other arm. "Here, I'll help you onto your horse," Berck said, following.

Up on deck she opened the cabin door. The rain had stopped, but heavy gray clouds still massed above, allowing no sun. Evening was drawing near. She stepped onto the jetty and turned to say good-bye to Berck on deck. A dog was yapping onshore. Fenella glanced at it. It was crouched on the riverside path barking frantically at something. Through the screen of trees that lined the path Fenella saw a figure coming toward the dog—a man, looking over his shoulder, his face turned away, his steps erratic. He cleared the trees, and she saw that blood soaked his shirtsleeve and half his jerkin. He looked forward again and she saw his face. Her breath caught. Adam Thornleigh!

She dumped the satchel and cloak and ran. At the foot of the jetty she intercepted him. "Adam!"

He looked stunned to see her. "Fenella . . ." His shirt was drenched with blood and water, his hair and face wet with rain. The shoulder of his sleeve was ripped and she saw the gash in his flesh, the muscle glistening red.

"Dear God, you're wounded."

He managed a tortured smile. "Sorry, this was the nearest place. Your friend. You said, remember?"

"Yes, yes, of course."

"Need a place to lie low. The blood . . . hard to hide." The dog, smelling the blood, growled at him and bared its teeth. Fenella picked up a stone and hurled it at the animal, striking its side. It yipped and bounded off into the trees. Adam was looking at the barge where Berck still stood. "Is this the boat? That's your friend?"

"Yes. What happened? Who did this to you?" He was a wanted man. "Alba's men?"

He said nothing, just winced. The pain must be awful, she realized. His face was so pale! "Come aboard," she said, indicating the boat. "You need help."

He frowned, hesitating. "Didn't expect you here . . . don't want to get you into trouble." He looked so doubtful, she was afraid he would turn and go.

"You won't. Really," she insisted. "Come aboard. Let me see to your wound."

He was looking past her. "Sure your friend won't mind?" She turned to see Berck coming down the jetty toward them, scowling. He held a dagger.

"I'll deal with him," she said, though her heart was racing with alarm as Berck reached them. The two men eyed each other. "This is Berck Verhulst," she told Adam. Then to Berck, "This is . . .

Adams. A friend from Sark." If he was on the run from Alba's men she must not disclose his identity. "You can see he's badly hurt. Help me get him below."

Berck blocked the way. "What happened to you, mate?"

Adam looked him in the eye. "Scurvy fellow thought he'd be happier with my purse."

Berck didn't budge, his face dark, hostile.

Adam gave the barest nod. "Right. I'll be on my way." He turned to go, grimacing in pain.

"No!" Fenella cried, and caught his good arm to stop him. "You can scarcely stand. Berck, you can't turn him away. He's a fellow seaman."

Berck grunted, considering it. He glanced at a cottage across the path. "We can't stand here. Neighbors will be nosing out their window." He sheathed his dagger. "Bring him below."

Thank God! At Fenella's urging Adam wrapped his good arm around her shoulder and she guided him aboard and down the companionway. The way he leaned on her both thrilled and alarmed her. He would not do so unless awfully weak. How long had he been walking the streets in this condition? Berck followed her down, bringing her satchel, and she asked, "Where can we rest him?" Berck pointed to the berth littered with gear. She swept the blocks and sheaves to the foot of the berth and Adam sat down on it, his eyes on her. He said very quietly, "I won't stay long, Fenella. Not good for you."

"Hush. Lie back."

He looked reluctant to relax his guard by lying down. Instead, he swung his boots up onto the berth and eased his back against the bulkhead, like a soldier still on watch. Fenella leaned over him and carefully lifted the bloodied, torn edge on his sleeve to look at his gashed shoulder. Even in the dim light the wound gleamed wetly.

"Bandages," she said, turning to Berck. He stood with arms folded, watching Adam, curious or suspicious or both. *No bloody help*, she thought. "Berck, do you have anything clean we can use? A freshly laundered sheet?" He looked at her as if she'd ordered a roast pheasant. "Never mind," she said, and unsheathed the dirk at her belt. She always carried this knife. Lifting the hem of her dress, she used the dirk to cut two long strips off the bottom of her underskirt. "Can you fetch some rainwater?" Berck nodded and clomped up the steps. She resheathed the knife and turned to Adam with the makeshift bandages but hesitated. With a wound so painful could he take off his jerkin and shirt? But he saw what she was doing and didn't need to be asked. He unbuckled the jerkin and shrugged out of it. Then, wincing at the pain, he pulled the shirt off over his head. Fenella felt a clutch at her heart. Half-naked, blood streaking his chest, he looked both more virile and more vulnerable.

Berck brought a mug of water and Fenella sat on the edge of the berth and used a balled strip of her underskirt to gently sponge Adam's wound. Sensing his eyes on her, she felt warm blood flush her cheeks. She readied the other, longer strip and without a word Adam raised his arm and she wound the linen around his shoulder and under his armpit, careful to lay it gently but firmly against the tender wound.

"Thank you," he whispered.

Their eyes met, and the warmth in his sent a flutter to her belly. She swallowed. "You must be parched." She looked over her shoulder. "Berck, draw a mug of ale for him, would you?"

She was tying off the ends of the linen strip when Berck shoved a foaming mug at Adam. "Drink up, mate." He said it as if he wished it were poison. She longed to ask Adam how he had really been wounded—she doubted his tale about a thief—but she could not with Berck near. He'd sat down on his bench at the table with his own full mug. Her questions would have to wait.

Adam raised his mug to Berck. "I thank you for your hospitality."

Berck eyed him in silence and took a mouthful of ale. Fenella asked him for a clean shirt for Adam, whose own was foul with blood. Berck brought one, dingy and threadbare, but at least it was dry. As Fenella helped Adam pull it on she tingled at the touch of his skin. He had finished half the ale and already it was having its effect. His eyelids looked heavy. *He needs sleep,* she thought. She took the mug from him and urged him to lie down. He let himself slump, too weary to keep sitting. She looked around for a pillow and wasn't surprised to see none. From her satchel she took a shawl and folded it and snugged it under his head. He smiled at her, a sad smile like an apology. Then his eyes closed.

"He's out." Berck let out a burp. "On the run, is he?" His words were a little slurred by the drink. "What's he done?"

She looked at him. "I don't know yet." It was only half a lie.

"Why'd he come here?"

"I told him you were a friend." She looked at Adam, glad to hear his steady breathing. "He can't be moved until he gets back his strength. All right if we stay the night?"

Berck gave her a knowing look that said, *So now my boat's satisfactory?* "I told you before, the stern cabin's yours." He looked away, muttering, "You paid for it."

Anger flickered in her at his tone, but she doused it when she saw him stumble off to a berth in the abandoned quarters where he'd once had crew.

She left Adam and closed the door of the stern cabin and lay down on Berck's berth in her clothes, ready to jump up if Adam should need her in the night. Worry about him kept her awake. Was he on the run as Berck suspected? Were Alba's men after him? She lay atop the blanket listening to the sounds outside. Above her, rainwater dripping off the rigging onto the deck. Onshore, a barking dog. She tried to think about tomorrow, about delivering the money to the Brethren, but thoughts of Adam kept surging back. His grateful, weary smile. His whispered, *Thank you.* The warmth of his skin on her fingertips. The warmth spread through her, down to her belly, both thrilling and frustrating. When she finally sank into sleep, it was in a dream of sinking into his arms, her hands on his body.

The next morning Berck was bleary-eyed and heavy-footed from drink, his hair a rat's nest. He downed a cup of ale to fortify himself to go to work at the lock. When he went up on deck to leave, Fenella came up after him to say good-bye. The rising sun pinked the sky, promising a fair day. She squeezed his elbow. "Thank you. For the safe haven."

Sullenness darkened his bloodshot eyes. "Any port in a storm, eh?"

His morose tone irked her. Why did he wallow in gloom? "You

need to pull yourself together, Berck. Clean up this dirty boat. Clean *yourself* up."

He flinched as if she'd slapped him.

She wasn't sorry. Whatever his troubles were, they were nothing compared to Adam's. *Or mine.* "Rolling that big ale keg into the river would be a start."

"Who are you to talk to me like that?"

"Your friend. I mean it, Berck. You need to find a way to *live* again."

They stood for a moment eye to eye, glaring at each other, like two wrestlers about to set on each other. The thought made a laugh bubble up in Fenella. She, wrestle this mountain of a man? She chuckled.

"What's funny?" He looked flummoxed.

"Nothing. Go on now, get to work."

He gave her a last bewildered look, then trudged off down the jetty. She watched him tramp down the riverbank path. Her heart was lighter. Now she could talk to Adam.

He was sitting on the edge of the berth when she came below. No blood had wept through the bandage onto the shirt. A good sign. And he looked well rested. "How's the wound?"

"Better," he said with a smile. "Thanks to you."

She needed to do something, to be busy, else she'd gaze at him like some daft girl. "Hungry?"

"Famished."

She found cold porridge in a crock, and a congealed leg of roasted rabbit. At least she hoped it was rabbit. She set about fixing a trencher for each of them, spooning out the porridge. There was no way to heat it with the galley hearth in a shambles. "It's not the fare from the Queen's banquet table that you're used to, but at least we won't starve."

He watched her as she worked. "First Edinburgh, now here, that's twice you've saved my life," he said quietly. "You mend my ship. You mend my body. I think, Fenella, you could mend a man's soul."

It took her breath away. "My lord . . ." she stammered, looking down.

"You really must call me Adam."

She looked up. His smile, slightly crooked, sent a tingle down her backbone. "Adam," she said, her hand with the spoon almost trembling.

"I never thought to find you here," he said. "I thought you were going north."

"I did. I got my money and then took Johan home. He was happy to see his niece. I left him there, at her farm." She said nothing about Claes. And would not. *It's safer for Claes this way*, she told herself, though she knew such caution wasn't necessary with Adam. He was on the side of the rebels and would never betray a fellow fighter in the cause. No, there was a deeper reason that she could not deny—or face. She did not *want* Adam to know her husband was alive.

"And then?" he asked. "What brought you to Brussels?"

"Wanted to see old friends. Berck and . . . other friends. I'll go see them today." She wanted no more questions about herself. "Here," she said, bringing him the trencher. "You need to build your strength." She sat beside him. They ate in silence. Fenella tasted nothing as she chewed and swallowed. Her eyes were on her food, but her mind was locked on every slight movement he made, every breath he took. When they finished, she took the trenchers back to the table, then sat down beside him again. His good arm was next to her. An inch closer and she would feel its warmth. She hated that inch of air.

"Adam . . ." The name, so intimate, still felt new on her tongue. Felt wonderful. "What happened? Who hurt you?"

He ran a hand through his tangled hair. He was clearly troubled. "I told you I was going to get my children. I saw my daughter, Kate. Spoke to her." He shook his head. "Then lost her."

Fenella gasped. "How?"

"Treachery."

He told her how his agent had said the children would be at the Church of Saint Nicholas for instruction with the priest, how he had gone there and seen his daughter outside with an escort of two men. When she went in he slipped in through a back door and found her praying. "She looked at me like I was the devil." His tone was bitter. "It's her mother. She'd poisoned Kate's mind about me. I told Kate the truth, and I think I could have persuaded her to come. But her mother had put her in that church as bait. To capture me. She arrived with half a dozen soldiers."

"They attacked you?"

He nodded. "I had to run."

Fenella's heart ached at the pain in his voice. "How did she know you'd be there?"

"My agent, Tyrone. Had to be him, he's the only person who knew I was in the city." He gritted his teeth. "Frances put the children in a convent. Days ago, Kate said. Somehow, Frances knew I was coming. It can only have been through Tyrone. So she hid them, then brought out Kate to lure me."

He turned to her and she saw the haggard look in his eyes. "Fenella, you know I have to get home to report to the Queen. That's what we planned, you and I, to get my ship and hasten to England. But I can't leave yet. I have to try to get Kate and Robert." He rubbed the back of his neck, thinking. "I can't do it alone. Their mother will have them well guarded."

"I'll help you. Gladly. What can I do?"

He looked at her in surprise. Affection shone in his eyes. "You stand by your friends so loyally. Johan. Me. You have a good heart."

I'm a witch, she thought. *I want to leave Claes and live in England with you. Forever.*

"But I would never involve you in this," he said. "Too dangerous."

"You can't do it alone; you just said so. Look how narrowly you escaped. And they've already hurt you."

"I know someone who may help." He gave her a look so tender it pierced her heart. "I'm so glad you're here. To talk to. It's such a . . . blessing. But it's dangerous for you. There's a price on my head. You mustn't be seen with me." He took her hand and squeezed it. "I'm going to go."

"Where?"

"I left my horse at an inn near the Antwerp Gate. Too far to go last night, covered in blood. Would have attracted suspicion. But now I'll make my way there." He added quietly but firmly, "You shouldn't stay in this city."

He didn't mention her crime. He didn't have to. "A price on both our heads," she said, then jested with a bravado she did not feel, "Valuable folk, aren't we?"

"You are," he said warmly. "Above rubies." He hesitated. Then murmured, "I wish . . ." He didn't finish, but the searching look he gave her made her burn to know what it was he wished.

"I'll see you aboard the *Odette*, though, won't I?" she said. She was suddenly afraid that something would foul their plan. Afraid that this might be the last time she would see him. "We'll rendezvous at the cove?"

"Yes, just as we planned. We said two days from now, but now I'll need longer."

"Four days?"

He nodded. "Four days, good. I'll be there. I hope to God it's with my children."

"I'll be there, too." She would sail with him to England. And never come back. "Adam, if anything should hold you up—"

"It won't. Whatever happens," he added grimly, "with or without Robert and Kate, I must report to the Queen."

"But if you're stopped, or if you need help, send me a message. To that stable in the village by the cove. Remember? The ostler?"

He nodded. "The ostler."

"Promise me."

He smiled. "I promise."

"What were you about to say, before? That you wish . . ."

He looked away. "If wishes were ponies . . ."

She raised her hand to his cheek and drew his face back to her and whispered, "No nursery rhymes."

He gazed at her for a long moment as though struggling over whether to speak what he felt. Then he said quietly, simply, his eyes never leaving hers, "I wish I'd met you years ago. Before I married."

The words sent a thrill through her. She couldn't stop herself. She let her fingertips slide over his lips. He clapped his hand over hers as though to stop her, but instead he pressed her hand tight against his cheek.

"Adam," she breathed.

He bent his head and kissed her. A hesitant kiss, so light it made her yearn for more. He drew back a little and his eyes searched hers with such a naked need she knew he yearned as she did. Then his arm was around her waist, pressing her body to his.

"Your wound—"

He stopped her words with a kiss so hungry it took her breath away.

9

Isabel

Isabel Valverde couldn't bear to stay in the candlelit opulence of the Duchess of Feria's long gallery a moment longer.

It wasn't the stuffy heat, nor the headache-making babble of the well-heeled throng. In coming here with Carlos, Isabel had known full well what the crowd would be: a mix of arrogant Spaniards, toadying Dutch sycophants, and English Catholic exiles, near traitors in Isabel's opinion. She'd been ready for all that, ready to be gracious for her husband's sake. But among the crowd was a face she had never anticipated. Her brother Adam's traitorous wife! There Frances brazenly stood, chatting with the Duchess of Feria and the Duke of Alba, apparently unaware of Isabel's presence. Isabel was finding it hard to absorb the shock.

"Carlos," she whispered with as much control as she could muster, "I won't stay. I can't."

"I swear to you," he said tightly, "I didn't know she'd be here."

Her anger spurted. "Really?" She loathed his closeness to Alba.

"You think I knew the guest list? I've been on horseback for the last fourteen hours, coordinating patrols with the Mechelen garrison. I barely had time to change my clothes."

She bit back further harsh words. He was clearly as astonished to see Frances as she was.

"What am I bid for this exquisite work of art?" called the auctioneer. The crowd murmured in excitement as servants held up a painting, the property of a merchant arrested at Alba's command for speaking out against the Spanish occupation. The gentlemen and ladies here were all keen to snap up such confiscated treasures. The English-born Duchess of Feria was hosting the event to raise money for her exiled countrymen, and Alba's attendance gave luster to the exiles' cause. The whole event disgusted and disturbed Isabel.

She knew she should not blame Carlos . . . yet part of her did. He *knew* how she felt about these people, about the wretched Spanish occupation. After witnessing the boy's awful execution in the market square she had told Carlos she was going home and taking the children with her. She'd immediately regretted that angry outburst, though. After all, she had willingly come to the Netherlands with him. In sixteen years of marriage they had rarely been apart. In Peru, when he'd been captain of the viceroy's guard, she had accompanied him to his postings throughout that country and enjoyed it. Their one separation had been eleven years ago when he'd gone to Scotland, and that strained episode had taught her that she hated being apart from him.

But she also hated the brutality she saw every day in Brussels. If there was anything she could do to stop it she would, but that was impossible, of course. Ludicrous. Like hoping to stop a marching army from squashing an ant. Besides, given the precarious state of their personal finances she knew how much Carlos wanted and needed the Spanish pension that he'd earned but that Alba had yet to deliver. So she and Carlos had forged a compromise. He had promised her that if the pension did not come within six months they would go home. She had hesitated, because she felt that her first duty had to be the welfare of their children. Brussels was a hideous place for them and the new babe was due in less than two months. But she'd seen how much her threat to leave had hurt Carlos, and that broke her heart. So she had agreed. Six months.

Now, though, once she had seen Frances, six *hours* seemed too long.

"Wait until the auction's over," Carlos urged. "We can't leave now; we just got here."

You can't, perhaps. I don't work for Alba. She had her eyes on Alba as he smiled and chatted with Frances. "Look, he's her champion. All these people are, I warrant. To them she's the long-suffering wife of the Englishman they hate. The pirate baron." She fumed at the injustice. "I swear, Carlos, if I have to speak to her I may spit in her face."

"The two of you were friends once," he reminded her.

"The more fool I. Who knew she would try to murder the Queen? And Adam barely escaped with his life."

"She's paid for it, by the look of her." Isabel had to admit that might be true: Frances had become thin. She'd always been angular and now the angles had sharpened, her chin more pointed, her elbows sharp. "Three years on the run," Carlos added.

"With Robert and Katherine in tow, poor things. Adam's had men looking for them all this time." A terrible thought struck her. "Carlos, I've heard talk about these exiles. They're urging Philip of Spain to back an invasion of England and put Mary of Scotland on the throne. Do you think Frances could be part of that cabal?"

He scoffed. "Gossip. The King's not going to invade anyone. He has his hands full fighting the Turks plus keeping these Dutch in line. People spread rumors to sound important."

"But Frances committed treason once. Why not again? And look at the people she's consorting with. There, see, by the window? That's the Countess of Northumberland. Her husband *was* a traitor. He raised the Northern Uprising and took Durham before Her Majesty put it down and executed him. Everyone knows his wife burns to avenge his death."

As though Frances had heard, she suddenly caught sight of Carlos and Isabel. Frances stared, clearly as astonished as Isabel had been. But she held her head high. *No wonder,* Isabel thought grimly. *She's among powerful friends. To these people, I'm the outsider.*

A man hustled past Carlos and Isabel toward the auction activity and knocked her side. Instinctively, she laid a protective hand on the babe in her belly. Carlos shot the man a fierce look, saying, "Watch where you're going."

"Oh no," she whispered, stiffening. Frances was coming this

way. Carlos let out a low groan as they watched Alba stroll along-side Frances to join them.

"Señora Valverde," Alba said. "What a pleasure to see you again."

Isabel dipped a curtsy and murmured as politely as she could, "Your Grace."

"Hello, Isabel," Frances said. Her thin lips formed a tense smile. "Hello, Carlos,"

Carlos jerked a bow of his head. "Lady Thornleigh."

"It has been a long time," she said to Isabel, tentative but friendly, an overture apparently.

What mischief was she brewing? Isabel struggled to set a sociable face over her disgust. "Indeed it has. Your travels kept you away from us in England."

Alba went on, "I have only recently met your charming sister-in-law, a welcome addition to our city." He added smoothly to Carlos, "Tell me, Valverde, are all the ladies of this family blessed with such beauty?"

Isabel bristled, guessing what he was really asking: *Where does your wife's loyalty lie?* Carlos replied steadily, as though he, too, caught the meaning, "Every one, my lord."

The auctioneer's voice rang out announcing the opening of bids for an emerald necklace. "Will you pardon me?" Alba said. "I promised the duchess I would bid on this for my wife at home in Spain." With a courtly bow of the head to the ladies, he turned and left them.

Frances's eyes flicked to the mound of Isabel's belly. "Your fourth, I think?" Her tone turned wistful. "I well remember your help in delivering my Katherine. We were close, then, you and I. I hope we can be friends again. It's been . . . lonely."

Isabel felt thrown, almost moved. "Have my niece and nephew come to Brussels with you?"

Frances stiffened. All she'd heard was the rebuff. "My children are well. I shall tell them you asked after them."

Isabel impulsively took her sister-in-law's hand. "Frances, this is no life for them. Exiled from home, no country to call their own. Send them back to Adam. Don't make them pay for your crime."

Frances withdrew her hand with icy forbearance. "In this land, my dear, it is your brother who is the criminal."

Isabel flinched. Was this a threat?

Frances went on, her voice hard, "I came to give you a kind word, for your sake." She glanced at Carlos. "Both your sakes. A warning for Adam. Tell him, if he values his head, to keep his distance."

"Your kindness is not required," Isabel replied steadily. "I never see my brother."

Frances held her gaze for a moment as though gauging the truth of her words. Then she proudly lifted her chin again. "Excuse me. I, too, will join the bidding. My dear friend the duchess hopes to raise a sizable purse to comfort the poor souls who've fled England for their faith."

"Poor?" Isabel challenged. "The Countess of Northumberland and her wealthy friends? They're all drawing pensions from the pope."

"There are carters and coopers and cloth workers, too. Would you have them starve?"

"I would have them loyal to Her Majesty."

Frances seemed to bite back a reply. "I shall pray," she said evenly, "that God will grant you a safe delivery." She turned on her heel and walked away.

Isabel was trembling with indignation. "I won't stay in the same room with her. Or these people. I'm going home. This moment." She turned to leave.

Carlos took her elbow to stop her. "Isabel, I can't go until—"

"Then don't," she snapped. "I don't need you."

Across the room Alba was watching them. Carlos looked loath to be seen arguing with his wife. "I'll take you," he told her. He guided her by the elbow toward the gallery doors. "I'll tell him you aren't feeling well."

"That's right, lie. This place makes liars of everyone." She shot a hostile glance over her shoulder at Alba. "Everyone toadies to him."

"That's enough," Carlos said, marching her through the open doors. "We need him."

"We need to get home to England."

"And live on what?"

"At least we *would* live. Here he's going to get you killed." They were on their way down the stairs, their eyes on a trio of chatting Spanish grandees coming up, and she said nothing until the Spaniards had passed. Then she went on, "He has forced this country to its knees and they're going to turn on him, and when that happens I'm afraid you'll be fighting for him."

"I am *bound* to fight for him."

"Bound? By what law?"

"By honor. And by our need."

"My need is to get our children out of this madhouse of a country. Get them safe home. If you won't go, I'll take them myself."

"No. I need you to stay."

"Why? When you know how I feel. We just quarrel. Why *shouldn't* I go?"

Because the travel is rough and I'm afraid you'll miscarry. Because I want you by my side. Because you and the children are everything. That's what Carlos had felt when she'd hurled the question at him an hour ago on the duchess's staircase. He hadn't been able to put the feelings into words. All he'd managed was a terse, "Because you're my wife."

"Obedience, is that it?" she had said. He saw that he had hurt her, though he could not fathom how. How he hated this wrangling! At the duchess's front doors he'd called for the litter Isabel had come in and seen her into it, and when his horse was brought he'd swung up into the saddle.

Now, keeping his horse to a walk, he rode beside her litter through the dark streets, both of them silent in the presence of their two servants led by a linkboy with a torch. Carlos could not get over how strange and uncomfortable the meeting with Frances had been. It made him all the more uneasy because he had not told Isabel what Alba had said that night at the brothel, that there was one sure way to prove his loyalty and secure the pension: track down Adam.

The night was windy, sending broken twigs scurrying along the cobbles of the courtyard at the Valverdes' house. Carlos dismounted and his groom took the horse to the stable. Handing Isabel from the litter, Carlos saw her stormy face, so he sent the servants ahead to bed, not wanting them to see the discord between him and his wife. With no torch, there was only candlelight from the windows to light their way to the front door. Isabel stumbled on an uneven stone. He put out his hand to steady her. She pulled back, refusing his help. It hurt him more than all her angry words.

Wind rustled the high bushes that flanked the door, and Carlos caught a glint of something among the branches. A form stepped out, a man, cloaked. Black in the shadows, he stood barring their way. Carlos pulled Isabel behind him to shield her as he drew his sword. "Who's there?"

"A friend."

Friends don't accost friends. "Who are you? What do you want?"

The man held up his hands in surrender to Carlos's blade. "A word. No more." With one hand still raised he used the other to push his hood back from his face.

"Adam!" Isabel cried. She rushed out from behind Carlos.

Carlos froze. *Thornleigh.* His heart thumped. His mind galloped. *Deliver him to Alba. Win the pension. . . .*

Isabel threw her arms around her brother's neck. He flinched as though in pain. "Adam, what—"

"Not here," Carlos warned, sheathing his sword. *Be friends. Get him into the house.* He glanced at the upper windows of the neighbors' houses on either side visible above the courtyard wall. Some windows were dark. In others, candles flickered. "God knows who's watching. Come inside."

"Oh yes," Isabel whispered, sobered. "Adam, they mustn't see you." She pulled his hood up to shadow his face. "Nor our servants, either."

They brought him inside, passing the servants, and led him into the parlor. Carlos closed the door. When he turned back Thornleigh had again pushed back the hood. Their eyes locked.

"Christ, Thornleigh. You're taking a chance."

"I know."

"*Do* you? Do you know my position here?"

"Yes."

"Then you know I cannot—"

"Hush, Carlos," Isabel said. "Of course we can. Adam, you're most welcome." She was removing his cloak. The shirt he wore was loose at the neck and got tugged off his shoulder. She gasped. "You're hurt!"

Carlos saw the bandage and the small bloom of blood that had wept through it. Thornleigh gave his sister a crooked smile. "Blame your enthusiastic greeting."

"Not for that wound," Carlos shot back.

"Who hurt you?" she said, a cry of concern.

Thornleigh didn't answer. His eyes had not left Carlos. "You're one of Alba's commanders. I know that. We hold different . . . positions. But you're also my sister's husband. And my friend."

"I was." He saw that Thornleigh had no weapon. It would take only a moment to subdue him.

Isabel's eyes flicked between them, agonizing. "Carlos, stop this. Of course you're friends. He's *kin*. Adam, you're in trouble, that's clear. What's happened?"

Doubt flickered across Thornleigh's face. "I need . . . your husband's help."

"Of course," she said. "How?"

"It's about Robert and Kate."

That startled Carlos. He shared a glance with Isabel. She looked as surprised as he was. She said, "We just saw Frances at the Duchess of Feria's house. Frances is staying with her. She assured me the children are fine."

"They're not fine," Adam growled. "They belong in England, with me. I mean to take them home. But she has them hidden away, and well guarded." He looked at Carlos. "I can't do it alone."

Carlos couldn't believe what he was hearing. "You want my help to . . . ?" He almost laughed. "You're brainsick." *And as good as dead if you barge into the duchess's house. Her men will have you in chains.*

"No, Carlos, he's not. This is our niece and nephew. We can't abandon them." Isabel came to him. Her voice softened. "You taught Kate how to shoot a bow and arrow, remember? Her seventh birthday, when we visited them, everyone so merry? And you're Robert's godfather. We stood together at his christening. Please. Isn't there some way?"

She looked up into his face, waiting. . . . Thornleigh stood looking, too, waiting. Carlos suddenly knew: *I'm the one who's brainsick.* Turn Thornleigh over to Alba? No, he could never do that. He had let Alba believe that he might track Thornleigh down, but that was only a tactic to get a step closer to a pension from the King. Thornleigh was Spain's enemy; there was no doubt of that. He had hit Alba hard by pirating a pay ship with gold meant for Alba's troops and he was still hitting Spanish shipping. So Thornleigh might still have to fight for his life. *But not at my hands,* Carlos thought. *We are not foes.*

And there was Isabel. He knew that she and her brother were waiting for him to say something, but he wanted to hold on to this moment, savor Isabel's beseeching look. It wasn't about winning their quarrel. It was about what he saw shining in her eyes. Trust. It warmed him. Made him feel strong.

But strong enough to defy Alba? That brought him crashing up against reality. Anyone found aiding the enemy would get a savage response from Alba. *He could throw me in chains. Hang me. Then what would Isabel do, with Nicolas and Andrew and Nell to raise and the new child on the way?*

She squeezed his arm. "Carlos? Please?"

❧10❧

Enemies Unseen

Carlos galloped through the open gates of the Cistercian abbey. Fifteen of his best men rode behind him, thundering in under the gatehouse arch, hooves clanging on the cobbles. A young kitchen maid, the first to see them, screamed.

"Spread out!" he ordered his men. "Shut the gate!" Their swords scraped from scabbards. The maid dropped her basket. Cabbages rolled from it like heads. She ran.

The horsemen fanned out, cloaks rippling. They cantered alongside the two low wings that formed the north and south sides of the quadrangle. Carlos galloped across to the east side formed by the church, sending terrified nuns scurrying out of his path. The raid had to be quick. The daylight was fading. He'd waited all day so he could hit the place at sunset.

He drew rein beside an old woman who cowered, looking up at him, the sunset's rays reddening his steel breastplate and helmet. He hadn't drawn his sword. It might have been years since the older cloistered women had seen a soldier and there was no need to cause terror. Surprise was all he needed, and by the sound of the screams and shouts and the flurry of nuns scattering from his men he'd accomplished that. "Where's your abbess?" he asked the old woman.

Trembling, she pointed to a stone house beside the bell tower of the church. Carlos was about to say, *Fetch her,* when he saw a tall woman stride out the door of the house, passing helmeted horsemen and frightened nuns. Her haste in marching toward Carlos sent the white scapular over her black habit fluttering. Her blunt features were set in stern dismay at the chaos. "What is the meaning of this?" she demanded as she reached him. "Who are you?"

From the saddle, he jerked a respectful bow of the head. "Valverde. Commander of the Brussels Guard in the service of the governor, His Grace the Duke of Alba. You're the abbess?"

"Yes. What—"

A clang and a shout. They both looked to the main entrance under the gatehouse. His lieutenant, Martinez, had closed the gate. Carlos turned back to the abbess. "Reverend Mother, I have information that an enemy of Spain has taken refuge inside your walls. I've come to search the abbey for him."

"Enemy?" She blinked in amazement. Carlos's horse tossed his head with a snort and a jangle of harness. Carlos glanced across the quadrangle. Trotting ahead of Martinez was Adam Thornleigh in helmet and breastplate and armed with a sword. Carlos prayed that Thornleigh looked enough like one of them. *Get this over with fast,* he told himself. He was jittery at the terrible chance he was taking. If even one person suspected Thornleigh it could light a fuse of questions burning a path straight to Carlos. *Enough to throw nooses over both our necks.*

"But . . . we are a community of women," the abbess said, shaken. "If such a man were here—*any* man—I would know of it."

"I believe he's in hiding. Pardon the inconvenience, but my men will search the buildings."

She seemed about to say more but stopped. Though disturbed, she accepted his authority. His horsemen were already posting themselves at doorways along the wings. "Yes, of course, if you must."

"You run a school here, I understand. Where is it?"

She pointed to the corner of the southern wing. "There. Why?"

"My information is that the criminal is hiding in the children's quarters. That wing must be cleared."

Her hand went to her mouth in concern. "The children? Are they in danger?"

He didn't answer. The more confusion he could create, the better Thornleigh's chances. "To carry out a thorough search I must insist that *all* inmates leave their quarters. The sisters, the children, servants. Everyone will congregate here in the courtyard. I ask that you assist us."

She looked appalled. "Everyone? But we have sick patients in the infirmary. And elderly sisters who—"

"The patients can stay. Everyone else, outside. This man is dangerous, Reverend Mother. A killer. He would slit the throat of any nun in his way. Or take a child as hostage." The young ones here were children of the lesser nobility, worth a ransom. "You understand?"

That hit home. "Dear Lord. Yes . . . yes, I'll see to it. I'll order the alarm bell rung."

"Good. And one more thing. We'll question the children separately. Have them grouped over by those trees." He pointed to the far edge of the quadrangle, a sitting area of benches inside a circle of apple trees.

For half an hour it was a noisy, harried business as Carlos's men searched the buildings, the church bell clanging the alarm nonstop. They searched in earnest, for he had told them they were looking for a rebel and ordered them to question every nun. They didn't know the true identity of the foreigner riding with them. Carlos had introduced Thornleigh as the troop was about to ride out from barracks, telling them he was a Scottish lieutenant, an exiled Catholic eager to help Spain. His men had accepted that without question as they rode for Ixelles past the southern boundary of Brussels and into the abbey.

Dusk had fallen by the time all the inmates were herded into the quadrangle. A woman had fainted and nuns were clustered around her. Young novices clutched each other's hands, wide-eyed as they watched the horsemen trot by. Scullery servants from the kitchens huddled together. A lapdog ran in frantic circles, yipping.

Carlos, overseeing from horseback in the middle of the quadrangle, heard a child crying under the apple trees. He had not gone near the children grouped there, afraid that if his niece and nephew recognized him they might call out to him. Had Thornleigh found them yet? Where was he, anyway? The last Carlos had seen of him, Thornleigh was trotting in circles around the children as they were led to the spot by two nuns. Carlos looked around for him, cursing the time this was taking. They'd spent too long here already. Too many people had seen Thornleigh's face. Carlos saw the abbess march toward him. No fugitive criminal had been found, and of course none of the nuns or children questioned had reported spotting any suspicious man. Carlos spurred his horse away from the abbess to avoid her.

He trotted closer to the children under the apple trees. There were about twenty, girls and boys, the smaller ones in nightgowns, all agog at the horsemen. The two nuns had organized them, got them sitting on the grass. A few of the boys, excited, stood on their knees to watch the commotion. Carlos scanned the faces as he trotted by. He hadn't seen Thornleigh's children for years. Would he recognize them?

Then he spotted two and was sure they were Katherine and Robert. They stood hand in hand, she talking earnestly to an angry-faced nun. They hadn't seen him. They had grown so much, Kate looked almost a woman now, yet Carlos knew them right away. The boy was not as tall, nor as robust looking, but seemed full of curiosity. Carlos felt a queer turbulence in his chest, relief to see them safe and pity for Thornleigh, whose wife had taken them away.

Where the devil *was* Thornleigh?

Carlos looked around at his men, who sat their horses awaiting his orders, their search inside completed. Two trotted aimlessly back and forth by the upset, massed inmates. The church bell had fallen silent. Carlos felt the abbess's questioning eyes on him. He could stay no longer. If she raised an objection about his methods to the bishop he would face questions that could get him thrown into one of Alba's prisons. He rode back to her, told her he was satisfied that the abbey was safe, and thanked her for her cooperation. He called his men together and they rode out the gates, Carlos at the head of the troop.

Thornleigh, wherever he was, would have to manage the rest on his own.

The quadrangle lay deserted in the darkness. The abbey's dozens of windows were dark, too, except for a few where candlelight flickered. Night wind rode through the apple trees, rustling the leaves with a sound that seemed to Adam like the sea. *Ears playing tricks on me,* he thought. Maybe because he was so keyed up. He was crouched at the base of an apple tree, his eyes on the south wing, focused on the door to the children's quarters. He'd been watching it for so long he was fighting a cramp in his leg. His bandaged shoulder beneath the breastplate ached.

An owl hooted from the roof above the door. The roof masked the moon, leaving the doorway in darkness, while out in the quadrangle moonlight silvered the grass and the gravel paths and the apple boughs. Adam had pulled his cloak around him to prevent the moonlight glinting off the steel breastplate. The helmet lay beside him in the grass, tucked into the shadows at the base of the tree.

Would Kate and Robert come out? He had snatched a few words with his daughter, that was all. She'd been standing at the edge of the circle of children under these trees, stunned to see him, and had gaped up at him as he'd leaned down from his horse and whispered, "Meet me here after dark. Right here. Bring Robert." Questions had flared in her eyes, but she'd kept silent as one of Carlos's men trotted near. Clever girl! Adam had seen Robert, too, just steps away from Kate, but Robert had not seen him. How the boy had grown! But he looked unhappy. A nun held him roughly by the arm and shook her finger at him. Robert stood tense in her grip, and his head jerked, not just once but several times as the nun went on scolding him. His jerks of the head seemed involuntary. A tic? Pity shot through Adam as the boy hung his head in shame. Then the nun cuffed him, a slap on the ear. Adam's blood boiled. She had no right! But he had to trot away, could not risk his son noticing him. When he glanced back over his shoulder Kate was taking Robert's hand and the nun moved away. Kate's arm went around her brother's shoulders, a protective gesture that touched Adam deeply.

He had pulled away from the pack of children and trotted down a path alongside the church. It led to a vegetable garden with a shed. There was no one in sight. Hoes and baskets lay at the edge of the garden, abandoned when the nuns working there had been herded to the quadrangle with the others. Chickens clucked from an enclosure of low stone walls. Adam tied his horse to a tree behind the shed, out of sight of the quadrangle, and sat down on a bench inside the shed to wait. Soon he heard Carlos and his troop ride out. Heard the nuns calling the children back inside, and tramping feet and chattering voices as the quadrangle emptied. Night fell. No one came to the shed. Adam had walked back to the quadrangle, staying close to the church wall lest a nun at a dormitory window catch sight of him. He'd slipped in among the apple trees.

Hunkered down now at the base of the tree, waiting, he wondered if he was mad to expect his children to come out to him. Their mother had hidden them here to keep them from him. He felt a punch of shock, remembering Frances's face in the Church of Saint Nicholas, her fierce look as she'd shouted to the soldiers, *Don't let him escape!* What an astounding change in her! Frances, once so possessive, so jealous of Elizabeth, so cloying in her love for him that he had relished his days at sea just to be away from her. Of course, *everything* had changed when she had committed treason, and never again would they live as man and wife, even in the uneasy partnership that had been their marriage. But at that church she had actually connived for his capture. Had arranged it by luring him to Kate and bringing soldiers. A capture that could have led to his death. It rocked him.

And Tyrone. He had changed, too, had become the enemy. Had Tyrone gone to Frances, or had Frances sought out Tyrone? Either way, Adam was convinced that the Irishman had betrayed him to her.

The other changed person was Kate, and that was a change that cheered his soul. Frances had surely done her best to poison the children's minds against him—he'd seen that in Kate's horrified look at first seeing him in the church—yet his daughter's true allegiance had burst forth when she saw the soldiers attack him. Pride swelled his heart as he remembered how she had hurled her cape over the oncoming sword. It had let Adam escape. Now, having witnessed her self-control at seeing him ride in with Carlos's troop, he felt buoyed with hope. If there was a way to get out of the dormitory with Robert, his daughter would find it.

If. What if the nuns locked the dormitory at night and the children could not leave? He would wait for hours if he had to, but he must not be here come sunrise. He stared at the door, willing them to come through it.

The owl lifted from the dormitory roof and flapped across to the apple tree and landed on a bough above Adam's head. Glancing up at it, he felt his sword scabbard scrape the damp grass. He was grateful to Carlos for the weapon, grateful for Carlos's plan to get him inside the abbey and flush out the children. Whatever their differences in allegiance—and they were huge—Adam had gambled that family ties would tug Carlos enough to help him reach Robert and Kate. He'd been right. Thanks to Isabel.

He'd noticed she was pregnant. He hadn't known, it was so long since he'd been in touch with her. A fourth child, that was a fine thing. Carlos was a lucky man, happy with his wife. Adam could scarcely imagine what that felt like, his own marriage being so fouled. Frances had failed to murder Elizabeth, but the attempt had murdered their marriage. Had it ever really lived? A stillborn marriage. Even in its early years when they'd each tried to accommodate the other, never once had he felt the true bond of husband and wife, man and woman united in spirit, one flesh.

Spirit and flesh. *Fenella.* The memory of their lovemaking on the barge came over him with a rush so powerful he laid his hand on the tree trunk to steady himself. Fenella's mouth opening under his. Her body pressed against his. Her breath hot and moist on his neck. Her lips on his throat. He had groaned.

She'd stiffened in concern. "Your wound?"

No, it was not pain he felt but a craving for her that throbbed through his body. She had gone still, as though afraid their embrace had hurt his shoulder. It was enough to bring him to his senses. "I'm sorry . . ." he stammered. "I . . . have no right."

"You do," she breathed. "Adam, I am yours."

He'd plowed his hands through her hair and kissed her, and when he tugged down her chemise and her breasts spilled free he felt he could not get enough of her fast enough. Her nipples taut as berries against his palms. Her yielding mouth. He pushed up her skirt and his hand slid up the warm skin of her thigh, and when his fingers reached the warm, wet cleft she gasped. She pushed him gently onto his back. She straddled him. Never had he felt such a ravenous need. Unfastening himself, he gripped her hips and thrust into her, his desire ferocious, his eyes feasting on her mouth, her hair tumbled over her breasts. When they lay together after, spent, catching their breath, he marveled at the pure joy he felt. She amazed him. Her bold confidence. Her lush beauty. Her eager abandon. The glow of her. Sailing from Sark they had bonded in spirit, and now their union was complete, consummated. She was his, all of her. And he was hers. A marriage truer than he had ever known.

"If I were free," he'd said, gazing into her eyes, "to make you my wife—"

"Shhh." She had stopped his words with a kiss. "We'll be together, that's enough. In England. Soon."

He felt the thrill of her still, his hand pressing the tree trunk, and a smile spread through him. England, where peace beckoned. The future glowed for him and Fenella. A partnership in every sense, loving and lasting.

A screech shredded his dream. The owl had pounced near him and lifted from the grass, wings beating, with a captive vole squirming in its talons.

He saw something else. The door to the children's dormitory had opened, just a crack. He jumped to his feet. The faintest light shone through the crack. Adam awaited, his heart in his throat. The door slowly opened. A shape in the shadows. Two shapes. Kate and Robert! Cautiously, Kate put her head out past the doorjamb and looked both ways along the exterior of the wing. Adam's thoughts flew to her, excitement thrumming through him: *You're safe. Come!*

They stepped out, hand in hand. Kate carefully, quietly closed the door, and then they hurried across the quadrangle straight toward Adam. He snatched the helmet from the grass and pulled it on, ready to go, keeping an eye on the door in case someone came after them.

"Father," Kate whispered as they reached him. He read a flurry of emotions on her face: amazement, confusion, relief. "I thought they'd killed you . . . Mother's men . . . in the church. I saw your blood. Then she dragged me out."

"You were so brave. I got away because of you."

Tears gleamed in her eyes. "Why would Mother do that?"

He shook his head, wincing. How could he begin to explain to his daughter the animosity between her parents?

Kate said, her voice shaky, "She's wrong about you. About . . . everything."

His throat was so choked with emotion all he could manage was, "Bless you." He threw an arm around her and hugged her. "Bless you. Both of you." He reached out for Robert, too, but the boy stood frozen, transfixed. Was it the breastplate and helmet, so fearsome looking? "It's me, Robin. It's been so long, I know I may look different. But it's me."

The boy's head jerked, a small spasm. The tic. "Mother said . . . to stay away from you."

Adam said gently, "And yet you came."

The tic again. "Kate said to." It was a statement of complete trust. Adam looked at Kate with a wondering smile. Had she been the boy's only friend in their lonely exile?

There was no time for this. He had to get them both moving. "Listen to me, both of you. I'm taking you home. To England. We're leaving right now."

Kate's eyes went wide. "How?"

"We'll ride to the canal. We'll be a sight, the three of us ahorse, but we'll get there, and we'll get a boat." He was gambling that his military garb from Carlos would be his passport through Brussels and all the way to Antwerp. "All right?"

She nodded, anxious but also excited. How he loved her for that!

Robert just stared. Something inside Adam lurched. What if his son refused? Adam might be able to manhandle him onto the horse, but if the boy protested, cried out, people would come running. He glanced at Kate, hoping for help. She took her brother's hand and said gently, "Don't worry, Robin, they won't hurt you. Not anymore. You'll never have to come back here."

Adam wasn't sure what she meant, but he saw the bond between his son and daughter and it moved him. He recognized it, the same bond that men in his crew shared who'd been through battle together. Kate and Robert were comrades in arms.

He suddenly noticed that it wasn't Robert's hand Kate held but his wrist, as though his hand was hurt. Adam took the boy's hand. Robert flinched. Adam was shocked at what he saw. Red welts crisscrossed the small palm. He took the boy's other hand. More welts. Adam gritted his teeth. "The nuns did this?"

Robert shrank back in his grasp. His head jerked in a spasm. The tic. Kate answered quietly for him, "To beat the devil out of him. The devil that makes him do that."

Revulsion churned Adam's stomach. He could never forgive Frances for what she'd done to their children. Kate, sent to be swallowed by the convent as a nun, sacrificed on the altar of Frances's religion. Robert, beaten by the nuns.

He went down on one knee so that he and the boy were eye to eye, and laid a gentle hand on Robert's shoulder. "Remember your first pony? You loved that pony. Loved riding him. What was his name? Horatio?"

Bright-eyed for the first time, the boy looked at Adam. "Hector."

"That's right. Hector. Tonight, as we ride, you can hold the horse's mane. Would you like that?"

Robert nodded eagerly. His head jerked. The tic.

Adam tousled the boy's hair. Then looked at Kate and smiled. "Let's go."

Taking the path to the garden shed, Adam kept them in the shadows by the church wall. He untied the horse and swung up into the saddle, then pulled Robert up to sit in front of him, then pulled Kate up to ride pillion behind him. They were as crowded as eels in a barrel, but Adam loved having their warm bodies pressed against him. He realized how deeply he'd missed them, apart for so long. He took the reins, his arms on either side of Robert, who gripped the horse's mane. Kate held tight to Adam, her arms around his waist. They rode slowly past the church, Adam keeping the horse at a walk and again keeping to the shadows. They crossed the quadrangle, heading for the main gate, and he scanned the dark windows and doorways of the wings on either side. He knew Kate and Robert were doing the same, perhaps expecting angry nuns to come pouring out with torches. He glowed with pride at how courageously calm his children remained.

They reached the gate. It was closed, but locked only by a bar across two iron brackets. "Kate, I need you to get off and lift the bar, all right?"

"Yes," she said eagerly. She slid off the horse.

"Slow and quiet," Adam said. "No noise."

She did it beautifully. Lifted the bar off with such care it barely scraped, then gingerly propped it against the wall. She opened one side of the double wooden gate, very slowly, so the creak of the hinges was only faint. Then she hastened back to the horse, whispering, "I did it," her eyes aglow.

"Well done," Adam said with a smile, never prouder. He reached down to swing her up onto the horse. She reached up for his outstretched hand.

Crack! Something punched Adam's breastplate with a screech of metal. He lurched in the saddle, hurled back by the punch. A bullet! The reins flew from his hand. Robert tumbled off the horse with a cry. Adam heard him thud on the ground. *Robert! Is he hit?* The horse staggered with a terrified whinny, knocking Kate over. She sprawled on the ground on her back. "Kate!" Adam cried. He groped for the reins, his mind thrashing to understand. Was *she* hit? No, the bullet had screeched off the edge of his breastplate at the collar. The steel was dented. His collarbone throbbed from the force.

But his son lay motionless on his side, a crumpled shape on the black earth. "Robert!" Adam had got hold of the reins, but the horse in its terror wildly tore away from the gate.

Kate was scrambling to get up. "Father!"

Adam got control of the maddened horse and wrenched its head around. *Crack!* He felt the whistle of a bullet whiz past his ear. His eyes raked the roof by the gate for the gunman. He saw only blackness. Black lead roof agleam in the moonlight. Black chimney.

On the ground his son lay still as death. His daughter ran to her brother and dropped to her knees beside him. Adam kicked the horse's flanks and bolted for Robert. "Is he hit?"

"No, he's all right!" Kate cried, her hand on Robert's face. Adam saw the boy move, his pale face dazed. But alive! Adam galloped toward them.

Crack! The bullet singed the horse's rump, grazing its hide. It whinnied in terror and made a tight frenzied circle. Adam saw blood glisten in a streak through the hair of the horse's rump. His eyes again shot up to the roof. A man was crouched by the chimney! He was just a silhouette in the moonlight, but there was no mistaking the pistol in his hand. An assassin.

Sent by Alba? *But how could Alba know I'm here?*

The awful thought struck: *Carlos?*

No time to think. The gunman was loading the pistol to fire again. Adam had only one thought: *Get the children.* The gate stood open. The street lay beyond. He kicked the horse so hard it jumped. He rode for Robert and Kate.

She was running to him. A bullet whizzed between them and rammed the dirt at her feet. She froze, listing back on her heels. Adam drew rein so suddenly the horse staggered. The bullet had plowed a channel in the earth mere inches from his daughter's foot. She looked up at the roof. Adam smelled the gunpowder. *It's me he's after, but a bullet could kill her.*

"Kate, come! We'll get Robert!"

She twisted back to him. Adam reached out for her. She reached out for him. A bullet tore across his sleeve. He and Kate lurched apart.

"Father, go!" she cried. "He'll kill you!"

"No. Robert—"

"I'll take care of him. Go!"

Adam looked up at the black shape on the roof. The pistol was raised, motionless in the moonlight. Aiming.

"Please," Kate begged. "Go!"

Adam threw an agonized look at Robert. The boy lay on his back but had made it up onto one elbow, stunned, watching his father. Fury choked Adam. If he stayed he would die, shot down in front of his children. Tears stung his eyes. "Kate . . . Robert . . . I'll be back!"

He kicked the horse and bolted into the street. The bullet crashed into the wooden gate.

Adam rode for the canal, galloping through the dark streets in rage, in sorrow, in confusion. In hate.

❧ 11 ❧

Silken Ribbons and
Gold Lace

The young street seller offered up a cone to Fenella, a hand-sized confection of spun sugar brimming with ripe strawberries. Their fragrance was intoxicating. Fenella was in a hurry, on her way to deliver her satchel of gold to the Brethren, but she could not resist. She bought the cone and slipped an extra coin to the seller, a barefoot girl of about ten who beamed her thanks. Walking on, Fenella popped strawberries in her mouth and licked the ruby-colored juice from her fingertips, savoring the tangy sweetness, a taste like summer itself. She basked in the sunshine smiling on Brussels from a clear blue sky, a delight after the deluge of rain that had driven her to Berck's barge two days ago. But she blessed that rain, too. It had brought Adam Thornleigh into her arms.

Her heart danced at the memory of their lovemaking, a burst of passion that had overwhelmed them both. She had savored the dizzying memory over and over since they'd parted. Almost as exciting were the daydreams she now indulged of the future with him in England, a life together, building her business. They would often be sharing their days, so why not nights, too, sharing their passion? She felt a sting of guilt about Claes. She was still his wife. And Adam didn't even know about him. But Claes had released her, had virtually ordered her to go to England and leave him to the dangerous work that consumed him. Even before that, he had known she was living on Sark yet had not sent for her. How could he do that if he cared about her? He didn't care, at least not deeply, it seemed to her. He felt a bond with her as his wife, but only the kind he would feel for any close relation. What he really cared about was the work he was doing. In effect, by his words and actions, Claes had left the marriage. Did that mean she was free?

She *felt* free. Maybe that was sinful of her, because she knew the answer to her question: *till death do us part*. But she could not deny how eager and excited she was to start a new life. She wanted Adam and he wanted her, and they would take whatever happiness they could get together. She could never be his wife—he was bound in marriage to a woman who'd cut herself adrift from him—but Fenella reveled in knowing that she had what his wife did not: his love. Adam had made that thrillingly clear, and it still amazed her. In all the years that she had secretly held him in her heart she had never dreamed this could come to pass. Her lowborn world was as far beneath his as a cave was from the clouds. That they had even crossed paths again had been a small miracle. Yet now, he was hers.

Her heart was so brimful of love she felt the joy might burst out of her in song.

Or laughter—which it did as she passed a couple of boys racing toy boats in the pool of a fountain. One lifted his and leapfrogged it over his opponent's, splashing it down at the finish line. Fenella laughed out loud. What a saucy way to win!

It suddenly struck her that those boys might be the age of Adam's son. Or his daughter. Would they be with him when Fenella joined him on the *Odette* in the cove? That had been his vow, to bring them home, and if she knew anything about Adam Thornleigh it was that nothing would stop him when he set his mind to a mission. The thought of being in the company of his children as they sailed to England sent a pleasant flutter to her stomach. Robert and Katherine. Kate, Adam called the girl. A loving father, to be sure. It gave her a rush of happiness. Who in the world could not love such a man?

The strawberries were gone. She nibbled the sugar cone, keeping an eye out for her destination, a shop under the sign of the dolphin. She was very near it, yet the fashionable street was a surprise. When Claes had told her about the Brussels Brethren she had imagined hard-up men living in a rackety tenement or perhaps some underground hiding hole like the one beneath the farmhouse where she'd first encountered him and his fellow rebels. But this neighborhood she had entered was a prosperous one near the Coudenberg Palace, with leafy chestnut trees and stone mansions and window-bright shops, and the gentlemen and ladies she saw coming and going were dressed showily and expensively. *How dull I must appear,* she thought. Her clothes, though not exactly humble, were far from fashionable. *Never mind,* she told herself. *Let them turn up their noses.* The gold in her satchel could buy the finery off a dozen ladies' backs.

The sign of the dolphin hung at the intersection with a jeweler's shop, just where Claes had said. Yet when Fenella opened the door and stepped inside she thought there must be some mistake. No rebel Brethren could live here. The shop was for ladies, and great ladies at that, a place where stylish headdresses were created. She had stepped into a perfumed place of feathers and spangles and lace. Wooden heads lined the counters, all adorned with fanciful creations on wrought-metal frames that rose in crescents dressed with silk ribbons, gauze, sprays of feathers, pearls, silver lace, gold thread, and ornaments such as tiny jeweled birds. Some of the frames rose from full wigs; others were meant to dress the customers' own hair. Some had long, luxurious curls dangling on either side.

"Looking to sell?" a female voice inquired in foreign-accented Dutch.

Fenella turned. A short woman of perhaps forty, plump as a partridge, regarded her with a condescending smile. Her own headdress was a stylish example of the shop's craft. "Pardon?" Fenella said.

"Auburn hair. It is always profitable." The woman reached out to touch a thick red lock that had tumbled from beneath Fenella's cap, examining it like an item at a market stall. *"Charmant."*

Fenella stepped back, startled. *Of course: the wigs and curls.* In Edinburgh she had known young women who'd sold their hair to help their families survive the winter. This shop woman must think she was one such seller. "No," she said quickly, bluntly, "quite the opposite. I'm here as a . . . patron."

The woman's condescension brightened into keen-eyed interest. "Dear lady, please forgive the error of a foolish Frenchwoman. I am Madame Beaumont, and I am at your service. How may I help you?" Without a beat she smoothly went on, "One of our new Turkish arrangements, perhaps?" She gestured to a towering concoction of striped silks and feathers and pearls.

"Heavens, no."

"Ah, I see." Madame Beaumont instantly took the cue. "Something more quiet. Perhaps it is for a christening?" Her tone became sensitive, sympathetic. "Or a funeral? We would be happy to create a mourning arrangement to your exact specifications."

"No. Thank you. I'm looking for someone. I was told I could find him here."

A blink. "Oh? And who might that be?"

Fenella hesitated. She wasn't at all sure she had come to the right place, and the Brethren were dangerous company to be associated with. Loose talk with a shop worker might lead to trouble for the rebels, perhaps for Fenella herself. Yet this was where Claes had sent her. "I'd like to speak to the shop owner. Is he here?"

"Madame, I own the shop."

Fenella heard pride in the woman's voice. So, a fellow businesswoman. Somehow that settled her uneasiness a little. She glanced around. They were alone. Nevertheless, she said very quietly, "I am looking for Brother Ambrose."

"Brother?" Puzzlement flitted across the Frenchwoman's face. "I do not understand. Do you mean *your* brother?"

"No, no. He is no relation to me. Just . . . Brother Ambrose."

Madame Beaumont looked irritated, as though Fenella were a vagrant who had wandered into her shop. "To seek a monk, perhaps you should visit a monastery. I am sorry, madame, I cannot help you." She made a stiff bow of the head, a clear signal of dismissal. "I wish you good day." Turning her back, she moved to the counter, where she busied herself with adjusting a jeweled ornament in a headdress of lace and gold ribbons.

Fenella had obviously come to the wrong address. It frustrated her acutely. Yet Claes had given her no other information. What to do? She could not make inquiries in the neighborhood. That could jeopardize the Brethren. Could even get her arrested by association. Then her murder of the don would be discovered and her next stop would be the scaffold. She shuddered at the thought. But, curse it, she had made a promise to Claes and she was determined to fulfill it. It was the one thing she could do to help him in his cause. Wrestling with these thoughts, she watched the Frenchwoman's nimble fingers adjust the jeweled ornament in the lace: a tiny ship, its masts topped with emeralds, its rigging picked out in sapphires.

Madame Beaumont frowned at her over her shoulder, a look dark with suspicion. "We keep no other gemstones here," she said, a warning that there was no cache of jewels to steal. "Our ladies bring their own."

But it was not the ornament Fenella was staring at. It was the woman's fingernails. Blue-black crescents of grime beneath the nails. It seemed odd, wrong—this fastidiously dressed shop owner primping the immaculate lace with dirty fingers. A shiver ran up Fenella's spine. *It's not dirt.* She had seen fingernails that blue-black color before, in Polder. Her neighbor Vos, the bookbinder. The one the Spaniards had tied to Claes and shoved into the river to drown. Vos's fingernails had been permanently begrimed. Stained with ink.

Her mind leapt at the connection. She said to the Frenchwoman's back, *"Bruinvissen."* Dutch for "porpoises."

Madame Beaumont's fingers stilled on the lace. Silence. She did not turn, did not move an inch. "Pardon, madame?" She sounded wary. "I did not hear what you said. Could you repeat that?"

"Bruinvissen." Fenella stepped closer so she was by the

woman's side and could see her face in profile. "So perhaps you have something to say to me?"

Madame Beaumont looked at her. All artifice had vanished from her face. Her gaze was clear-eyed, keen. *"Zeemeeuw,"* she replied. Dutch for "seagull."

Fenella felt a thrill. She had come to the right place after all. Their eyes locked. "Brother Ambrose is here, isn't he?" It was a statement. They understood each other now. "He'll want to see what I've brought him. From Brother Domenic."

At the second name Madame Beaumont blinked in surprise. She seemed suddenly to decide. "Come," she said simply. She went to the front door and locked it by sliding a bolt, then beckoned Fenella to follow her behind the counter to a door decorated with silver gauze and pink silk rosebuds. Fenella hitched the satchel over her shoulder and the Frenchwoman guided her through the door and closed it behind them. Here there was no trace of the stylish whimsy of the shop, just a plain passage of bare boards. They reached a door on which Madame Beaumont rapped her knuckles lightly in a rhythm of three quick taps and after a pause repeated the trio of raps. The door opened. A balding, sallow-faced man regarded Fenella with a frown. He wore an ink-stained canvas apron over his stocky frame. In the small, stuffy room behind him the single window was boarded up. Fenella smelled the coppery tang of ink. Lamplight glinted off the dark metal of machinery. A printing press.

"It's all right," Madame Beaumont told the man. "She's from Polder."

Ushered in, Fenella felt her head brush sheets of inked pages pegged to dry on twine that crisscrossed the space above them like spiderwebs. On a table beside the press were trays of movable type. Beneath the table, casks of ink. She did not have to read the words that hung above her to guess what these people published: illegal Protestant broadsheets. They were probably Calvinists. Printers of such contraband were regularly arrested and imprisoned. Many stubbornly had held to their heretical beliefs, refusing to recant when given the chance, and been burned at the stake. Martyrs. Such people baffled Fenella. She pitied their suffering but could not help thinking them fools. Why accept tortured death to uphold a mere belief, a cause? What cause could be worth such agony?

The man had taken up a position to block the door, keep Fenella here. She felt that after passing Madame Beaumont's test she was being tested again. "Brother Ambrose?" she asked.

"Not I, mistress," he said guardedly, wiping his hands on his apron. "I'm just a laborer."

"My cousin is too modest," said Madame Beaumont. "He has felt the bite of prison manacles in Paris and has the scars to prove it."

Fenella was beginning to understand. "You're Huguenots?" Her sea-roving customers on Sark had kept her abreast about the French Protestants whose base was the port of La Rochelle. The French king had made annihilation of the Huguenots his priority. Many had fled to Protestant England. Her thoughts jumped to Adam. When his ship had limped into Sark he'd said he was returning from a mission for Queen Elizabeth. Fenella had heard of the Queen's stealthy support of the religious subversive leaders in France, as well as William of Orange, the Dutch prince in exile. Had she sent Adam to meet with such leaders?

"All who follow the true word of God must work together," was Madame Beaumont's sturdy reply. "One day we'll be back in France."

The man was eyeing Fenella, still frowning. "From Polder, eh? Proof?"

Fenella lifted the flap of her satchel and took out the note Claes had written vouching for her and introducing her as Sister Anne. The made-up name made her uncomfortable, but she knew that Claes meant only to protect her.

The man's eyes widened as he read Claes's words, and a new note of awe came into his voice as he said, "Brother Domenic himself." He handed the note to the woman and when she read it Fenella saw that she was equally impressed. Claes obviously meant a great deal to them. To the whole underground movement, perhaps. A leader. She felt an unexpected twinge of pride.

"I can always tell," Madame Beaumont said with a proprietary smile of approval at Fenella. It made Fenella feel like a workhorse being bought. *It's Claes they admire. I'm just his messenger.* The Frenchwoman went on, "You are most welcome, Sister Anne. I am Sister Agatha."

Fenella stifled a shiver at being called something she was not. Caution pricked her again. She was on her own here. She took back the note and tore it up. She wanted no evidence to connect her with these people. Nor should she tarry long among them. Their crimes could stain her as surely as their ink. She asked, "Where can I find Brother Ambrose? I have something to give him."

"Instructions?" the man asked.

Fenella hesitated. Claes had told her to deliver the money only to Brother Ambrose. But how was she to do that unless these people took her to him? She had come too far to turn back. "No," she said, hitching the satchel higher on her shoulder. "Gold."

The woman's expression became eager, her eyes on the satchel. "Brother Domenic has sent us gold? Oh, thank the Lord, we are sorely in need of it."

Fenella bristled. *It's from me. Am I to get no thanks?* But her hurt pride died as quickly as it had flashed. It was childish to want thanks. This was the least she could do for Claes. "Yes. But I will deliver it only to Brother Ambrose. I hope I've come to the right address."

"You have. He is my husband."

Fenella didn't know why that should surprise her, but it did. The plump proprietor of the ladies' shop didn't seem suited to such risky business. Altogether too soft. Yet she was clearly a committed partner. No longer Madame Beaumont but Sister Agatha. "Is he here?"

"Upstairs. Come."

"No," the man told her. "He left."

This was clearly news to the lady. "Where?"

He shrugged. "Young Brother Pieter came running in the back and dashed upstairs. Then Brother Ambrose came hurrying down with him and they left."

Sister Agatha gave him a knowing look. Her voice dropped to a conspiratorial hush. "To Zilvermidstraat?"

Another shrug. "No one tells me." He laid his hand on a lever of the press as though wanting to get back to work and gave Fenella a dark, quirky smile. "And that's the way I like it."

"Come," Sister Agatha told Fenella with fresh energy. "I know where Brother Ambrose has gone. I'll take you to him. Let me just get my shawl."

When she came downstairs she had removed her fanciful headdress and wore a simple lace coif over her neat, brown hair. Leaving the shop, they passed the fountain where Fenella had seen the boys with the boats. The boys were gone. She and Sister Agatha set out across the city. *We look like two housewives on our way to market*, Fenella thought. It made her feel calmer.

"Forgive my caution when you asked in the shop for my husband," her companion said. "We have to be very careful. Two weeks ago there was a raid on the Mechelen Brethren. One of Alba's agents had infiltrated their group to entrap them. They are a small chapter, only seven. All are now in prison."

Fenella was sorry for the poor souls but had no wish to know any more about them. Thankfully, Sister Agatha did not chatter, despite some sidelong glances that spoke of her curiosity to know more about Fenella. She was clearly following the Brethren's guiding principle that the less the members knew about one another the safer they all were. That was fine with Fenella. They walked the rest of the way in silence.

People hurried past them along the street. Fenella did not know Brussels well, but she knew they were getting close to the city's center, where the great buildings of state surrounded the Grote Markt. She and her quiet companion skirted the edge of the Grote Markt, avoiding its wide expanse. More people hustled by them. A burly man knocked Sister Agatha in his haste. "Why is everyone in such a hurry?" she grumbled, rubbing her banged shoulder.

"Is it much farther?" Fenella asked. She longed to have this business done with. She had left her horse on Berck's island a half hour's walk away and was eager to get it and then be on her way to Antwerp. But she couldn't say that was the reason for her impatience. "Carrying so much gold makes me nervous. Thieves."

"We're almost there. Turn here, Zilvermidstraat. It's a house at the corner, there."

Thank goodness. Fenella smiled inside, thinking how free she would feel leaving the city, lightened of her burden, both the gold and her fear of capture. A day's ride would bring her to the cove where the *Odette* lay at anchor. To Adam.

"Hush," Sister Agatha said suddenly, halting in mid-stride.

Fenella stopped. "What is it?"

"Hear that?"

Fenella strained to listen. Two women ran past her, one tugging a child. Fenella heard, past the buildings, a hum like a flock of raucous starlings thronging a tree. She realized it was a throng of people. Excited people. There was another sound, too, a rumbling beneath the hum.

Her skin prickled. The sound was drums. *An execution.*

Sister Agatha turned to her, her face tense. She, too, knew what was happening. "It's big. Look at all these people."

Men and women were flocking along Zilvermidstraat and turning at the corner onto a street that led to the Grote Markt. Sister Agatha tugged Fenella's arm. "Come."

Fenella balked. She had no wish to see poor folk hanged. "No, we need to get to Brother Ambrose."

"Later. Now, we must bear witness." The words were stern. "It's what the Brethren do."

Fenella had no choice. To get to Brother Ambrose she had to stick with his wife. They followed the people hurrying toward the public square. Men and women and children fairly ran in their excitement. Fenella and Sister Agatha grimly marched.

They reached the edge of the Grote Markt and pushed through the gathering throng, and when they broke through to the front they saw the execution party coming toward them. Six soldiers on horseback led it, followed by at least two dozen prisoners in dirty clothing, their hands bound at their backs, shuffling single file. Ropes around their waists tethered them together like packhorses. They were flanked by ten soldiers on foot on either side of the column. Four drummers brought up the rear.

Fenella's eyes were drawn to the commander who rode the lead horse. *Valverde, again.* Instinctively, she turned away so he would not see her, though scores of people separated them.

"Oh, dear God," Sister Agatha moaned. "Our Brethren."

Fenella didn't want to turn around. Had Valverde passed them yet? But the Huguenot woman tugged Fenella's sleeve and said in an agonized whisper, "Bear witness, Sister Anne. These are your people."

Fenella shivered. *Not mine.* She cautiously turned, and saw the back of Valverde as he rode on. Relaxing a little, she watched the prisoners who now shuffled past, ragged men with blood-caked noses and bruised faces. Some walked with their heads down; some looked straight ahead in a daze of terror. A few faces looked familiar. Where had she seen these men? A winter crept over her skin. She'd met them in the underground warren beneath the farmhouse. *Your people.* The Brethren of Polder!

She spotted an old man . . . with one arm. Her heart punched up in her throat.

Johan!

She clutched Sister Agatha's arm for support. Behind Johan a tall prisoner shuffled, his face a blue-black mottle of bruises and scabs. The shock was a bullet to Fenella's chest.

The prisoner was Claes.

❧12❧

The Letter

"Look at him kick!" a man crowed.

"Can't see anything with you in the way," someone grumbled. "Shove aside!"

Fenella thought she might vomit. Five prisoners swung from the gallows across the square. In a stupor of shock she had watched the guards string them up. The floor had dropped out from under them. Their necks snapped. They kicked the air. The crowd roared.

"May God have mercy on their souls," Sister Agatha murmured.

The five corpses hung limp. Guards cut them down and hauled them to the side of the scaffold. The floor was raised again. Below the scaffold the rest of the prisoners stood packed behind a rope barrier like animals in a pen. Fenella thought wildly, *Johan and Claes are among them . . . but where?* Bodies jostled her, hemming her in, blocking her view. She gripped Sister Agatha's arm. She had to, just to stay standing. Her legs felt as spongy as moss. She sucked in sharp breaths to steady herself.

The drums rumbled again. "Now the next ones," Sister Agatha said grimly. The crowd gabbled in excitement. The hangings were about to continue.

Fenella craned to see past the people, past the soldiers patrolling on horseback and the guards on foot. It was a sea of heads and backs and pikes and horses. Then, through a crack between

shoulders she glimpsed guards pushing the next group of condemned up the steps onto the scaffold. Five . . . but she couldn't
see who! *Johan? Claes?* Panic swarmed over her. She had to see!
She bolted forward. The satchel slid off her shoulder and dropped.
She barged on, shoving men and women out of her way. They
grunted in anger, and a fat woman lost her balance and fell. Curses
rained on Fenella. She barged on, her eyes fixed on the prisoners
who were stumbling up the steps, arms bound at their backs. She
had almost reached the front of the crowd. A thin line of steel-
helmeted guards stood facing the people, spread out, one to her
left, one to her right. Could she dash through the break between
them? She squeezed through to the front rank.

A hand snatched the back of her collar. She struggled, off-
balance. The hand was Sister Agatha's. "Let me go!" Fenella
cried. "I have to—"

"You can't get to them," Sister Agatha warned in a fierce whisper. She had picked up Fenella's dropped satchel and slung it over
her shoulder. "Even if you made it across the square they'd stop
you. There's no—"

"Marguerite!" a man called. He was forcing his way toward
them through the crowd, squeezing past people, his arm outstretched.

"Jacques!" Sister Agatha reached out to him. They clasped
hands above the head of a child whose parents stood agog at the
scaffold activity.

"Pieter told me." The man's hushed voice was tight with emotion. "I had to see if it was true." He and Sister Agatha gripped
each other's hands. For reassurance, it seemed to Fenella. For
strength. The unmistakable bond of man and wife. *This has to be
Brother Ambrose.* He added in a louder, forced cheerful tone clearly
meant for the people around them, "Our 'prentices love a free afternoon, my dear." A young man beside him gave a friendly nod of
agreement.

Fenella understood with a jolt: Officials had given the city's apprentices leave to attend the hangings. *To watch Johan and Claes
and their friends die.* She thought she might scream. Sister Agatha
still held her by the collar and the crowd had closed around them.

Fenella craned to see. Which prisoners were being led to the gallows? "Let me go!" she cried.

Brother Ambrose shot her a dark look. "Who's this?"

"The visitor we were expecting," said his wife. "From your cousins in the north, remember?"

A gap opened ahead and Fenella could suddenly see the prisoners on the scaffold. Five. Her heart thumped. *Johan!* She bolted, breaking Sister Agatha's grip. The guard closest to her had turned to watch a commotion in a far section of the crowd. An empty swath of the square stretched between her and the scaffold. She burst out of the front rank.

A horseman trotted past her, his eyes on the scaffold. Fenella froze. The rider was Valverde. In his wake she smelled leather and steel and horse. She gulped a breath. He hadn't noticed her.

She darted past his horse's rump and dashed for the scaffold. More horsemen were not far away, but her raw need to reach Johan kept her running. It was hard to breathe, dust clogging her throat. In her ears the hum of the crowd. The rumble of the drums.

The scaffold was now just a stone's throw away. Beside it, the pack of prisoners stood behind a screen of guards. She was so near she heard their murmurs of despair, smelled their sweat, their fear. She looked up at the five on the scaffold. Johan stood swaying, weak. A rope wrapped around his waist pinned his single arm against his body. The hangman dropped a noose over his head. Fenella opened her mouth to cry out, *No!* but choked as she glimpsed Claes in the pack. His beaten face . . . his haggard eyes locked on Johan. *Claes!*

Two guards marched forward to block her. "Halt there!"

She tried to dash around them. One grabbed her arm and she staggered. They manhandled her backward, used to dealing with people who'd lost their senses. She struggled and squirmed to get free. She had no mind, only a burning need to reach Claes . . . reach Johan. "Let me go!"

At her cry Johan turned his face. His gaunt eyes met hers. Her heart wailed: *Johan! I'm here!* But she saw that he scarcely recognized her. He coughed. That raw cough that she'd so long feared would kill him. The pitiful thought cut her to her soul. Disoriented, dazed, Johan blinked and looked across at the prisoners in the pack. Looking at Claes? A silent good-bye to his son? It tore Fenella's heart. She writhed, trying to break free of the guards, her arm outstretched toward Johan.

Hands gripped her shoulders from behind. "We've got her now, sir," Brother Ambrose said, his voice meek, deferential. "She's with us."

The guard threatened, "If she wants to join the ones on the gallows we can do that."

"My wife's cousin, sir, please forgive her." Brother Ambrose touched his temple. "She's never been quite right in the head."

The guard grunted, relenting. "Take her away."

"Come now, dear," Sister Agatha coaxed her. "Let's get you home."

Fenella shook off their hands.

"Come!" Brother Ambrose ordered.

Fenella swung a fist at him. He caught her arm. She stumbled. The two of them dragged her backward toward the crowd. "No!" she cried, straining to look over her shoulder at Claes. At Johan. "I've got to stop them!"

"Be quiet," Sister Agatha whispered tightly.

"Or I'll *make* you quiet," Sister Agatha's husband warned, his grip like claws on Fenella's arm, dragging her. They reached the front rank of the crowd.

"Please," she begged, her throat raw. "I'll be still. Just let me see!"

The drums stopped. A thud from the scaffold. A roar from the crowd.

Fenella spun around.

The five men hung from the gallows. Johan's body twisted slowly. Head bent. Neck broken.

Horror roared through Fenella's head. *No! . . . No! . . . No!*

A horse cantered past her. A whiff of leather and steel. Valverde. She did not move. *Could* not move. The wailing child inside her said, *If you don't move, this didn't happen! If you don't move, Johan's still alive!*

The Brethren couple were whispering intensely. "What are

they doing?" . . . "Singling him out?" . . . "Oh, dear God, is he next?"

Fenella tore her eyes from Johan's broken body. Valverde had trotted over to the pack of condemned prisoners. He was beckoning one man out. Claes.

Fenella's heart banged in her chest. Looking stunned, Claes stepped forward from the pack of doomed prisoners. He blinked in confusion, gazing up at Valverde on his horse. Valverde motioned to another horseman to join him. The two of them flanked Claes. Horror crawled over Fenella. *He's next.* Valverde motioned Claes to move.

But wait . . . Valverde and the other horseman were guiding Claes in the other direction . . . *away* from the pack.

"What are they doing?" Brother Ambrose whispered in awe to his wife. "He's not going to hang?"

Fenella felt a punch of hope. "Spared?" Her horror drained so fast she felt light-headed. "Yes! Look, he's been spared!"

"But where are they taking him?"

Feet tramped on the scaffold. Fenella looked back. Guards were cutting down the dead men. Five more were being led to the gallows. The drums rolled. A guard dragged Johan's corpse to the edge of the platform. Dropped him with the others.

The horror rushed back and she felt she would retch. *Johan.* He'd come home to fight. To die fighting. *They killed you before you could try.*

Her vision darkened. She swayed. The light died.

A flowery smell. Perfume. Tainted by another smell. Ink?

Fenella opened her eyes. Had she been asleep? The bed she lay on was soft, plump with pillows. The filmy bed-curtains, drawn aside, stirred in a draft from the open door. She started to rise. It was a struggle, her limbs as heavy as though weighted by rocks. She sank back.

"Better?" Sister Agatha sat beside the bed sewing lace onto a beribboned length of gauze.

Fenella tried to speak, but her tongue felt thick as cloth.

"It will wear off." Sister Agatha regarded her over the needle-work. "Ah, I see you don't remember. I thought it best to give you a sleeping draft."

Shards of memory flashed. Lying on the ground, the crowd looking down at her. Brother Ambrose slapping her cheek to rouse her from her faint. Walking back through the city between the couple to their shop, her weakened muscles twitching, her mind thrashing. *Johan dead . . . Claes, taken where?* Stumbling through their door, up the stairs. Someone handing her a goblet of wine. Swallowing. A bitter taste. Then, all fog.

"A bad day," Sister Agatha said. Her nimble fingers plied the needle with relaxed skill and anyone might think she had spoken of nothing worse than unpleasant weather. But her face was pale and her lips pursed with tension. Her eyes flicked up to Fenella. "Mark me, you're going to need a thicker skin for this work."

Work? The horror rolled back. Johan swinging . . . the corpses . . . Valverde . . . the condemned pack . . . *Claes!* She snatched that ray of hope. "Did they let Claes go?"

The woman's eyes snapped in anger. "*Never* say that name."

Fenella struggled to remember the name they used. "I mean . . . Brother Domenic. The commander led him away from the con-demned. You saw that, didn't you?"

"We don't know what all that was about. We're waiting to hear."

She managed to push herself up onto her elbow. She had to know! "But have they set him free?"

"Patience, Sister Anne. Brother Ambrose has gone to find out."

Fenella sank back down, her head still foggy. *Brother . . . Sister.* She remembered the moment when the couple had called to each other in the crowd: *Marguerite! Jacques!* Their public names. Through the open door Fenella glimpsed the staircase that led down to the room with the printing press, the room behind the ladies' shop. The couple must be known locally as Jacques and Marguerite Beaumont, the French emigrants who ran the shop, but Fenella knew they were disciplined Brethren, using "Sister" and "Brother" for their risky work. Yet she had also seen them des-perately clasp hands to comfort each other and give each other strength. Husband and wife. Marguerite and Jacques would be the names they murmured to each other in private. Now, she could think of them no other way.

"When will he be back? Brother Ambrose, I mean."

Marguerite shook her head but did not miss a stitch. "I told you, have patience."

Fenella heard a new edge in the Frenchwoman's voice. Bitterness? Fear? A wave of guilt rushed over her, for she suddenly realized that her reckless action at the hangings might have dangerous repercussions. "Have I . . . put you in danger?" she asked.

A hard look. "We accept danger. And loss. You must learn to do the same."

Fenella swallowed. Never had she felt such a turmoil of grief and remorse.

A new look of kindness softened the Frenchwoman's face. "I'm sorry. Those were good men. We have said a prayer for their souls. When you feel strong enough to get up we'll pray for them together."

Fenella felt a twitch of fury. What good were prayers to a dead man?

Marguerite said, obviously curious, "One was your particular friend, that's clear."

"Friend." The word pierced Fenella's heart. "Yes . . . he was. I wish I could tell you . . . his name." Johan. Her companion after the hellish massacre of Polder. Her comrade through the lonely years on Sark. Her right-hand man in the business, his knowledge of ships and shipbuilding second to none. Argumentative, sharp-tongued, loyal old Johan. Tears stung her eyes. *Claes saw them hang his father!* Her tears spilled.

"There, there." Marguerite patted her hand, all sympathy. "We are fighters, my dear, but we are women, too. So weep for your friend. Pray for him. And never forget him."

Fenella swiped away the tears, angry at herself. Tears were as useless as prayers. "You say you are fighters. But can you *win?*"

Marguerite looked taken aback at her sudden intensity. Fenella hardly knew herself where the harsh passion had come from.

"I can tell you this much. The gold you brought will go a long way to sustaining the fight."

"My satchel!" It had slipped off her shoulder when she'd bolted through the crowd.

"Don't worry, I brought it back. The gold is here, safe."

A sound downstairs. A door closing? They shared a glance. Hope shot through Fenella. "He's back."

"Perhaps." Marguerite stood up. Her control masked the anxiety that Fenella knew gripped her. Was it her husband . . . or Spanish soldiers?

They strained to listen in the silence. The wait was torture. Forcing her heavy limbs to obey, Fenella pushed herself up onto her elbow and swung her legs over the edge of the bed, her feet onto the floor. Faint footsteps sounded downstairs. Her hope surged back. It could not be soldiers; they would make far more noise. It had to be Jacques. Was Claes out of danger? Free? Had Jacques brought Claes with him? She pushed herself off the bed and stood up.

Louder footsteps on the stairs. They both watched the doorway.

"Jacques," Marguerite breathed in relief as he stepped in and closed the door behind him.

Fenella felt a shiver at that closed door. "Where is Brother Domenic?"

Jacques looked at her, his face haggard. "They've taken him to prison. The one beneath the King's House. It seems that Alba has . . . a special plan for him."

"Oh no," Marguerite said in hushed horror. She went to him and they clasped hands. "Just as I feared."

A chill crawled over Fenella's skin. "Special?"

They looked at her, their faces drawn. "Because he's such an effective leader," Marguerite said.

Jacques nodded. "My informant in the palace said—" His voice faltered.

"Tell me," Fenella demanded.

"Alba is going to make an example of him. Brother Domenic alone . . . in the market square. A show execution."

A show. Fenella knew the Spaniards, knew the nightmare possibilities. Torture on the rack to break limbs. Hanged until almost dead and cut down alive. Castrated. Abdomen slit and entrails drawn, the victim still conscious.

The couple bowed their heads, still holding hands. They murmured in unison, "May God have mercy on his soul."

Fenella felt a coldness steal through her bones. There would be no mercy for Claes's body. Her heartbeat, quickening moments ago in hope, then in fear, now slowed and beat with a rhythm as steady as the execution drums. A word rose to her throat. For a moment it stuck there, hard as a stone. She forced it out. "No."

They looked up at her in surprise. "No?"

"I can't let that happen."

The Frenchman said with pity, "It is in God's hands."

No, in mine. An insane thought, maybe. How could she possibly prevent Claes's death? But somehow she had to try. And if she was to have any hope of succeeding she would need the Beaumonts' help.

"There's something you need to know," she said. They were still holding hands. Man and wife. It gave her the courage to go on. "Brother Domenic is my husband."

Adam awoke on the boat from a dream of Fenella, wanting her, his body's need as intense as a schoolboy's. He sat up in the cramped berth and rubbed his face hard to break the longing. The *Odette*, at anchor, rocked beneath him slowly, gently with the motion of the ebbing tide.

He pushed off the berth, got to his feet, pulled on his boots. *Get moving.* The lure of Fenella lingered, warming him. Today he would see her. Today she would come to the boat. He had held on to the sweet anticipation of that since he'd come aboard yesterday. Had filled his mind with Fenella, willing the thought of her to keep at bay his torment about Kate and Robert.

That memory still made him feel sick. Leaving them behind, galloping away from the gunman on the roof, not knowing what had happened to them. He told himself that they would be cared for by the nuns, that they were not in danger. But he had failed to get them out, and the bitterness of that made a fist of his stomach. He would not be bringing his children home.

He grabbed his hat. Food. Get some food for Fenella. Stay busy while waiting for her. Otherwise he'd torture himself about Robert and Kate. There was some biscuit and small beer on the boat, but he wanted something better for Fenella. She liked manchet bread, he remembered, made with fine white flour. Little hope of finding such a thing in the village, but at least it gave him a mission.

He came up on deck, rotating his shoulder to ease the soreness. The wound was no longer painful, but the muscle was still tender. The sun was burning through the morning mist. Shreds of fog hung in the trees that crowded the shore. Ducks bobbed in the reeds, fishing for breakfast. There was a faint smell of wood smoke from the village. He hoped this might be a market day. If not, there would be a cookhouse. If the place was too poor even for that, he'd inquire if some housewife had fresh bread to sell.

He climbed into the little skiff and rowed for shore, and with every pull of the oars he asked himself again: Who had tried to shoot him? The question had plagued him on his overnight ride to Antwerp and the next day all the way to the cove, and it plagued him still. The Duke of Alba wanted him dead, but how could Alba have known he would be at the abbey? One sickening possibility was Isabel's husband. *Did Carlos betray me?* But that made no sense. *Carlos risked himself to help me.* Unless . . . if Alba suspected what Carlos had done he might have forced the information from him. But Adam couldn't imagine Carlos breaking like that. Even if he had, Alba commanded thousands of soldiers, so why not send several to be sure of success? Why a lone, hidden gunman?

No, Alba was not behind this. So who else wanted him dead? His thoughts had wound this tortuous route again and again since he'd galloped out of Brussels, and he always came up hard against the same answer: *Frances.* Four days ago she had lured him to the church using their daughter as bait. She had to be working with Tyrone, who had certainly betrayed him that day, no doubt for a bountiful reward from Frances. But Adam had assumed that Frances had set that trap as a display of her strength, to show him he could not get the children, then she would send him on his way. At the very worst she might have delivered him to Alba. Would she actually go so far as to hire a man to *kill* him?

It seemed astounding, inconceivable. His own wife, who had once been so cloyingly devoted to him. But her act of treason had severed their marriage as surely as an executioner's axe, and she had certainly hidden Robert and Kate in the convent to keep them from him. Did she also fear that he would come for *her?* Drag her back to England to hang? Did that terrify her enough to post a man in the convent with orders to shoot him if he came for the children?

The skiff's bow nosed through the reeds. Adam hopped out into the ankle-high water and pulled the skiff up onto the muddy shore. He looked out at the *Odette*. The boat was nicely hidden from both land and water, cocooned by the sweeping crescent of shoreline thick with trees. He tramped through the underbrush and soon reached the narrow footpath that ran parallel to the shore. Villagers took the path to reach the stream that fed a larger bay to the north. Adam set out in the opposite direction, toward the village. He passed through woods, then across a meadow, and in half an hour he saw the rooftops of the cottages that made up the village. A hamlet, really, just a scatter of humble dwellings. The squat, stone church was the only other building, except for the ostler's ramshackle stable. When Adam had returned the hired horse he had found the ostler cleaning a mare's rear hoof and asked if any message had come for him. He and Fenella had agreed to send a message here if either got delayed.

"Message?" The ostler looked up, the hoof wedged between his knees. A bald old fellow, he looked slightly puzzled.

"Yes, a note? Or letter?"

"My trade is horses, sir, not letters."

The *sir* surprised Adam. How had the fellow marked him as a gentleman? He wore clothes little better than a farmer's and he'd left the sword from Carlos on the boat. "No matter," he said, tossing the fellow an extra coin for the horse. No message meant that Fenella was on her way.

She'll be here by nightfall, he thought now, the knowledge exciting him as he followed the weedy path that wound into the village. He passed two men sawing a bough fallen from a beech tree. They regarded him with a mix of curiosity and suspicion, it seemed to Adam. Villagers everywhere probably watched any stranger the same way. An ox bellowed from an adjacent field. Adam passed a cottage garden where bees hummed in the hollyhocks and pear trees nudged a stone wall. Maybe he could buy some pears. Fenella would like that.

The stone wall merged with the churchyard wall and he strode on, watching people coming out of the church, a farming family, men and woman old and young in clothes as drab as the soil they worked. A stocky young woman held a baby. A christening? A swallow flitted above the mother and child, and the baby chirped and gurgled at it and the people laughed and grinned. Adam's heart twisted. He remembered Kate's christening, her small fist batting at the vicar's beefy hand. He had smiled at her pluck. Now, twelve years later, there was nothing to stop Frances from delivering her and Robert up to the mighty machine of the Catholic church. Adam thought in fury of the nun who had cuffed his son for his tic. And Kate? She would never leave that convent. His lively daughter, a nun . . . shut away from life, from love. The thought cut him so deeply he wanted to howl like a mad wolf.

He gritted his teeth and picked up his pace. He had to accept what he could not change. For now. He would not leave his children there forever. He would find some way to get them away from Frances. But they were not his only concern. There was Fenella. She could not stay in this country. If she did, Alba would track her down for killing his kinsman. Adam had to get her to England. The thought of her took the edge off his wretchedness about his children. It was a stirring consolation. He knew now that he was in love with Fenella. And she had given every indication that she loved him. In England they would have each other.

There was his duty to Elizabeth, too. Before he'd reached Sark he'd sent her his report outlining everything he thought safe to entrust to paper about his meetings with the Dutch prince in exile and with the French Huguenots based in the port of La Rochelle. But Elizabeth would be waiting to hear from his mouth his opinion of how far she dare pledge England to their cause. The prince wanted Elizabeth's military support to free the Netherlands from Spanish occupation, and the French Protestants, too, wanted her to supply them with arms. Adam intended to advise her to do both. For Elizabeth's sake, and for Fenella's, he had to get home without further delay. Later, somehow, he would come back for Robert and Kate.

The village, Adam found, did have a market of sorts today. Farmers had set up a half-dozen crude stalls beside the church. Strings of onions, baskets of turnips, wheels of cheese. Homemade brooms, a workhorse harness, a used butter churn. A few villagers strolled, inspecting the offerings, haggling, buying. A boy sat on the dusty ground skinning a rabbit. Farmwives stood gossiping beside a donkey that munched discarded cabbage leaves. Men ambled to and from the alehouse across from the church.

The cheese looked good. A stout farmwife stood beside a ripe, golden wheel of it on the back of her cart. Fenella would enjoy that, Adam thought. "How much for a good thick wedge?" he asked.

The woman was all smiles. "Sir, you can have a whole wheel for ten penningen."

He smiled back. "Half will do me." He dug in his pocket for coins. "Shall we say five penningen?"

As she was cutting the cheese, a hand tapped his shoulder. He turned to see the black-whiskered face of his agent, Tyrone! Before Adam could think, his hand shot to the blackguard's throat and grappled it. "You!"

Tyrone raised his hands in surrender, but his look was hard, unrepentant. "Hold on, now. You may want to throttle the life out of me, but then you wouldn't hear about your wife."

Adam released him with a furious jerk. "So you're working with her, you admit it!"

Tyrone rubbed his neck, glaring at Adam. "A man has to make a living, my lord. You were tardy with your silver."

"So the two of you set a trap for me, put my daughter in that church."

"Your wife told me she wanted to talk to you is all. Just talk. How was I to know she'd bring a troop to nab you? Anyway, they *didn't* nab you and you got away, so we're quits."

"How did you know I was here?" Had he followed him from Brussels? Was Tyrone the gunman on the roof?

"Your wife went to the abbey when she got word of the commander's raid and I went with her. She quizzed her children about you—"

"*My* children."

"Aye, aye, yours. No one questions that."

Adam grabbed the man's jerkin in both fists. "Who shot at me? You?"

"Me? What do you take me for? I make no bones about raking in some silver on the side, for I saw no harm in it. But killing? Murder? No, that's not what I do." His look turned sly. "It was *you* the commander was looking for in the abbey, wasn't it? You tried to get your young ones, I warrant. After that, well, I reckoned you'd come to this village. I knew you'd landed nearby."

Questions roiled in Adam's mind, but he and Tyrone were getting glances from the passing villagers. He let go of the man's jerkin and said under his breath, "Why are you here?"

Tyrone's eyes glinted. "Thought I'd make a little more silver. You're hell-bent on getting back the young Lord Robert and his sister, and I can tell how you might yet get hold of them. That's information you'll want to pay for, my lord."

"Don't call me that," he said in a fierce whisper. "Not here."

Tyrone, chastised, looked at the people milling around them. "Christ, you're right," he growled. His gaze went toward the alehouse. "See that portly fellow all in black? His smug face? That's a churchwarden's face if ever I saw one. Bible men, they saunter about watching their village folk, sniffing for lewdness or thievery or anything untoward. You and me, we're two strangers, and that's enough to prick up his ears. I don't want him coming and quizzing me. Do you?"

Adam inwardly cursed his hostile action with Tyrone. He could not afford to draw attention. "No."

"Over there," Tyrone said, nodding at the churchyard. "We can talk there, away from the Bible man's eyes."

"Right. Come on." He didn't trust the man, but if he had even a shred of information about how to get Kate and Robert, Adam wanted it. They made their way past the knots of villagers and reached the churchyard wall. The lych gate was open for the christening party who lingered, chattering, by the church door. Adam followed Tyrone in through the lych gate and they walked together along the path through the graveyard. A crow lifted from a tombstone, wings flapping.

"Here is good," Adam said the moment they'd turned the corner of the church and were out of sight of the villagers. "Now tell me. How can I get my children out?"

"Shhh." Tyrone's eyes flicked to a spot behind Adam.

Adam glanced over his shoulder. An old couple had left the christening party and were moving toward them, eyeing him and Tyrone. The couple were apparently heading for a grave across the grass. They shuffled on. When they were out of sight behind the rows of tombstones, Adam turned back.

He saw Tyrone's knife just in time. The blade glinted in a savage underhand stab. Adam's heart jolted and he kicked the knife from Tyrone's hand. It flew through the air and speared the grass. Tyrone lunged for it, but Adam tripped him and he tumbled.

Adam whipped out his own dagger from his belt. Tyrone jumped up and charged him with such force he almost knocked him down. As Adam stumbled, Tyrone grappled his wrist that held the blade. They wrestled on their feet, arms straining, Tyrone struggling to get the dagger, Adam struggling to turn the blade. Locked in the power struggle, they crashed against a tombstone, knocking Adam backward, off-balance. The tombstone scraped his cheek as he fell with a thud on his back, the breath knocked from him. Tyrone leapt on top of him and snatched the dagger. He pinned Adam's arms to the ground with one hand and one foot. He raised the dagger high to plunge it into Adam's throat.

Willing a surge of strength Adam wrenched his arm free and grabbed Tyrone's wrist. He hacked Tyrone's hand against the tombstone's edge. He heard the wrist bone snap. Tyrone cried out and the dagger tumbled. Adam snatched it and lifted it and rammed the blade into Tyrone's side.

Tyrone's face above him contorted. Adam yanked the blade out. Tyrone groped for his bleeding side. Adam stabbed again. A trickle of blood seeped over Tyrone's lips. His eyes rolled in their sockets. He collapsed onto Adam.

Adam pushed him off. He got to his feet, the bloody dagger in his hand. He twisted around. Had anyone seen?

There was no one. Tombstones. Silence. Blood from Tyrone's body seeping into the grass.

Adam's hand was not quite steady as he swiped the blade on Tyrone's jerkin to clean off the blood. He sheathed it at his belt. There was a fire of pain in his shoulder. Dampness soaking through his shirt, his almost-healed wound bleeding afresh.

He turned and quickly walked away. Across the graveyard, then through the lych gate. He heard faint laughter. The christening party. He kept walking, making for the path that would take him back to the boat. He could not stay in the village. As soon as Tyrone's body was found they'd be looking for him. The woman selling cheese had spoken to him. The men sawing the beech bough had watched him when he'd arrived.

He would slip out of the village and get to the boat and wait aboard for Fenella. She would arrive by nightfall and the moment she did they would weigh anchor and sail out of the cove. They'd be free of this country and soon in England.

He was on the path, wiping a trickle of blood from his scraped cheek, and was walking toward the men sawing the bough, keeping his pace steady so he wouldn't attract their interest, when a voice behind him shouted, "Stop!"

He stiffened. Maybe the command wasn't meant for him.

"Stop, sir, please!"

Sir. He halted. Turned. It was the ostler. He was breathing hard from hurrying, wiping a hand over his bald head. "Glad I am I caught you, sir. My wife says this came for you yesterday evening." He handed him a paper, folded and dirty from its journey. Adam opened it.

> *Master Adams,*
> *I have no further need of your services. I have met*
> *an old friend and will stay where I am.*
> *F.D.*

He tried to make sense of it. F.D. It could only be her. Fenella Doorn. But . . . staying? He felt a needle of pain in his chest, not from his wound but from her words. *My services?*

Voices. He looked up. Beyond the ostler the old couple he'd seen in the graveyard were shuffling past the garden of hollyhocks. They seemed to be arguing, the man pointing at Adam, the woman tugging his raised sleeve as if to rebuke him. The men sawing the beech bough looked to where the old man was pointing. To Adam.

Can't stay here. His fist balled around Fenella's note. He turned and hastened for the boat.

❧ 13 ❧

The Fire Ship

Adam had slept little on the three-day sail alone to Sark, fighting headwinds that buffeted the little fishing boat and fighting his own private turmoil. It was with relief that he raised the island, a welcome landfall. He nudged the tiller to starboard and lowered the mainsail, letting the *Odette* ghost into La Coupée Bay. Razorbills swooped over his head toward the cliffs that rose in a semi-circle, and sheep grazed on the meadowed cliff top. Smoke curled from chimneys among the cottages that hugged its base. Adam saw some of his crew moving around the boatshed and other outbuildings. The morning was still, the breeze warm, carrying earthy smells of pine and sawdust and spring flowers. And a bitter whiff of burning charcoal. Always the bitter with the sweet, he thought. Three days had not been enough to quiet the questions raging in his mind.

Tyrone had come after him to kill him, but who had sent him? Frances? Or was he working for Alba? But surely if Alba had known where he could find Adam he would have sent more than one man. More likely, Tyrone had done it for pay, Frances's pay. She had already tried to kill Adam by posting that gunman on the abbey roof. This time she'd sent Tyrone. Twice now she had caught Adam off-guard. He swore he would not let her do it a third time.

Torturing him, too, were questions about Fenella. *I have no further need of your services.* How could she write such words after all they'd been through together, after what they'd been to each other? And why had she suddenly decided to stay? Her brief message gave no hint that she felt herself in danger, though she'd been well aware that she should get to the safety of England. He could not understand her. It was as though she'd suddenly become a different person. And who was this *old friend?* A man, Adam's blood told him. A man she wanted to be with. *More than she wants to be with me.* A cankerous thought gnawed: *Was I just a dalliance for her?* That was hard to take.

Let her go, he ordered himself. *You have a mission to complete for Elizabeth.* He went to the foredeck and heaved the anchor overboard, which sent pain shooting through his tender shoulder. As he watched the anchor sink he told himself to drown his bitter disappointment about Fenella. Nothing could come of loving a woman who didn't want him.

"Ahoy, my lord!"

He turned to see a boat rowing out from shore. He knew that brawny back hauling at the oars. His longtime mate, James Curry. "Ahoy!" he called.

The thought of seeing his ship again sent fresh energy coursing through him. The *Elizabeth* had been a wounded hulk when she'd limped in here over two weeks ago, but by now his crew working with Fenella's shore crew would have completed the overhaul. New planking on her hull, a new mainmast, new sails. In fact, since he didn't see her alongside the jetty, he assumed Curry must have sent her out for a sea trial of the repairs. It was exhilarating to think he'd soon be aboard his own ship carving the Channel northwestward, the wind in her teeth.

It was time to get home. Time to get back to the business of his queen. On the *Elizabeth* he'd done his share of harassing Spanish shipping alongside the Sea Beggars, damaging Spain's chain of supply to Alba's regime in the Netherlands. England and Spain were in an uneasy standoff, and the menace of Alba's Spanish armies less than a hundred miles off Elizabeth's coast was a constant threat to her. Spain could invade her overnight. Adam's aggressive actions had been to keep England safe, but now he needed to turn his attention to peace. And to his friendship with Elizabeth, because that just might get Kate and Robert home. Elizabeth had powerful diplomatic tools at her disposal. Despite England's tension with Spain, trade between the Netherlands and England was supremely important to both countries, and he might be able to exploit that current to carry his children back to him. Quiet diplomacy. Elizabeth might manage it. At Whitehall Palace he would put his case to her.

The rowboat bumped alongside the *Odette* and Adam caught the line his mate tossed up. "You're well met, Curry," he said, belaying the line around a cleat. He added in jest, "But where's my ship, man? Have you sold her to the Barbary pirates?"

Curry was climbing aboard, and the moment he straightened up on deck his grim face told Adam that something was very wrong.

"I had no way to get word to you, my lord."

"About what? What's happened?"

"They came two days ago. It was pitch night. They sent a fire ship." Curry plowed a blistered hand through his hair. "I'm sorry, my lord. We could not save her."

The charred hull lay at anchor like a floating corpse. Burned to the waterline. Adam stood on the beach staring at it, his stomach heaving. Threads of oily black smoke curled from the stern of what was once his ship. The acrid smell of scorched timbers—that was the charcoal he'd smelled when he'd sailed in.

He struggled to speak through his shock. "You posted no guard?"

"I did," Curry said beside him. "Two good men, Cole and Withrow. The Spanish devils slit their throats."

Fury shuddered through Adam. He saw it. Cole and Withrow lying in their own blood. The fire ship crashing into the *Elizabeth*'s stern. Flames leaping up on deck, scurrying up the masts, bursting into a frenzy at the canvas, whipping the rigging. He saw spars snapping. Rigging tumbling. Masts ablaze. Everything crashing down to the deck into the maw of the roaring fire.

"By the time we got to the beach it was too late. We jumped

into boats with pumps, but we couldn't get near. She was an inferno. Then the fire reached the gunpowder and the blast blew off the sterncastle. Timbers flying like knives. One sheared the side off Heywood's face. He was in my boat. We took him to the Seigneurie, but he's not going to make it."

Adam's hands balled into fists at his sides in rage. Rage at the Spaniards who had done this. Rage at his powerlessness. "How many dead?"

"Just those three. Then the dagos scurried away like the rats they are. After the gunpowder blew we got aboard, a few of us, did what we could." Curry's voice was a bitter growl as he looked at his blistered hands. "Which was nothing."

"Who were they? What ship?"

"We didn't see. They hit us and then they were gone."

Adam tried to speak again, but his throat felt parched, scorched. *My ship.* Fifteen years ago he had overseen every inch of her creation. Planned her with his shipwright, instructed the carpenters, caulkers, riggers, sailmakers. He'd brought the *Elizabeth* to life, a taut, fast, lovely ship, and when he'd stood on her deck she was a proud, living thing beneath him. She had taken him thousands of miles with Hawkins's trading expedition, their small fleet voyaging to the New World. A hurricane had blown them off-course into Spanish territory, to Mexico, and there, in San Juan de Ulúa, the Spaniards had butchered them, a vicious, treacherous attack. Four ships lost, hundreds of men. Adam had seen cannonballs rip off his men's arms, shatter their legs, splatter their brains. Yet the *Elizabeth*, a wounded veteran, had brought him safely home with his handful of survivors. Now the Spaniards had struck again, leaving more corpses. *And one is my ship.* Amputated of masts, she was a flattened rubble of charcoal and ash, of twisted metal and crippled cannon. She was dead.

He forced out a word. "Salvage?"

Curry shook his head. "The guns are warped. Useless."

"Where's the seigneur?" Sark was the fiefdom of Seigneur Helier de Carteret. He was the authority here. Why had his security been so lax?

"Away on Jersey, sir, at his manor of Saint-Ouen. Been there since you left." Curry turned and growled at someone, "Not now."

Adam realized his men had gathered around. He turned. They stood watching him, waiting. He'd left England with forty-two seamen and gunners. After his skirmish with the Spanish galleon *Esperanza* he'd reached Sark with twenty-nine. Now, they were twenty-six. He saw bandaged hands. Blistered faces. Eyes hard with anger. These men had signed on for spoils. Not for humiliation and defeat.

"You men tried to save her," he said. "I won't forget that."

A few nodded, though sullenly. There was grumbling. One man ventured, "Beggin' your pardon, my lord, but how—"

"Shut your hole, Peacham," Curry said. "You'll get your orders when His Lordship's ready."

Adam knew what Peacham wanted to ask: *How do we get home?* They would all want that answer from him. He looked again at the charred wreck. Grief at her loss welled up in him. *My dead ship.* Then a monster wave of rage. *She was murdered.* Like his two men, their throats cut. He lengthened his gaze beyond the dead *Elizabeth* to the only other ship in the bay. Fenella's caravel lying at anchor. Swedish, by her rigging. Named *Gotland.*

"Master Curry, pass the word. I want that caravel ready to weigh anchor by nightfall. With all hands aboard."

Curry's eyes widened. "To sail for home, my lord?"

"No. We're going to get some guns."

By late afternoon the next day pewter-gray clouds had rolled in and the seas had kicked up, and Adam widened his stance for balance on the *Gotland*'s quarterdeck. His eyes were locked on the ships he was chasing.

Six vessels. They were a motley fleet. Two beamy, workaday coastal ships bucking in the chop. Three swift pinnaces. And in the lead an imposing carrack, her masts festooned with colorful, streaming banners. All were powered by billowing canvas so shabby it was as gray as the sky. They sailed in a ragged formation, but all were steadily following the carrack, the flagship of William de La

Marck, who called himself Admiral of the Sea Beggars. This pack was only part of his fleet. His command reached over thirty vessels in the Channel.

Adam's seasoned crew had quickly familiarized themselves with the Swedish caravel on their overnight sail from Sark, and when he now gave the order to overtake the vessels following La Marck his men swiftly manned the lines and braces, and soon the *Gotland* was skimming alongside the flagship. Curry hailed them. The caravel might be unfamiliar to La Marck, but he knew Adam, and within moments his crew hoisted flags to message the other ships to heave to. Adam gave the same order to his men. He and Curry lowered the skiff, and with Curry at the oars they rowed through the chop for the flagship. A spattering rain began to fly, cold on Adam's face. The crew on the ship lowered a rope ladder over the side and Adam grappled it and climbed.

"Thornleigh!" La Marck boomed from the quarterdeck. "I thought by now Alba would have your head on a pike!"

Adam could not help smiling. He called up, "It's good to see you, too, my friend!"

La Marck came down the steps and strutted across the deck to greet him. The fellow had been born strutting, Adam thought, glad to see the wily rogue looking hale. La Marck was neither tall nor powerfully built. A paunch swelled beneath his narrow chest, and his skinny legs reminded Adam of a grasshopper. His cheeks were chubby and his curly hair, feather thin, danced like a baby's in the wind. He had once been a man of property in Flanders and he still dressed like a lord, though one who'd lost his tailor. Gun grease smeared the crimson silk scarf wound around his waist, and cinder marks pocked his yellow brocade breeches above the faded peacock-blue silk garters at his knees.

But Adam knew that the sword at the Dutchman's hip was of the finest Toledo steel and knew the blade had often been slick with blood. Only a fool crossed swords with La Marck. He was a ferocious fighter and had attracted scores of his countrymen to follow him, men who'd been outlawed under Alba's reign of terror, their homes and property and businesses confiscated. They had come to him with ships and guns and bloody-minded resolve, and had proudly dubbed themselves the Sea Beggars. Others had joined them. French Huguenots. Rogue corsairs from Portugal. The prince to whom they swore their allegiance, William of Orange, living in exile in the German lands, had been quick to see their usefulness to his cause of one day pushing Spain out of the Netherlands, so he'd issued them letters of marque, which as a sovereign prince he was entitled to do. Letters of marque, issued by any country, authorized the bearer who had suffered a hostile action by a foreigner in time of peace to recoup his losses by boarding and ransacking foreign vessels. With over thirty ships under his command La Marck had built a fleet that was the scourge of Spanish shipping.

"Bloody hell, Thornleigh," the Dutchman said, embracing him with vigor, "we heard you sank the *Esperanza*. I thought Alba would hound you down and fry your balls with butter. I swear, you've got a cat's nine lives."

"You've got a few yourself," Adam said. The Admiral's crew had sauntered near to watch. They were a dirty, hard-looking lot, none of them shy at leaving their stations to come and gawp. The lax discipline did not impress Adam. He had some hard men in his own crew, but he and Curry kept order.

"Come, let's have a drink," La Marck said, slapping Adam's back, "and tell me where you've been."

They settled in the Admiral's stern cabin. The walls were scuffed, the bulkhead splintered from action the ship had seen, but the berth was plump with a feather mattress and tangerine satin pillows. The ship rocked in the swell. Up on deck wind whistled in the rigging. Adam and La Marck sat across from each other, a sea chest between them, as a boy served them Madeira. Two of La Marck's captains stood flanking him. Adam had seen both captains fight bravely, fair-haired, youthful-looking William Bloys and brooding, dark-bearded Lenaert Jansz. Curry stood beside Adam, enjoying the wine but alert. From up on deck came the sound of men laughing.

"Look at this." La Marck threw open the chest and pulled out a crucifix as long as his arm. "Solid gold," he said proudly.

Adam saw that the chest was crammed with costly objects, including some used in the Catholic mass. Silver goblets, gold plates engraved with religious symbols, a gold sacring bell, lace vestments, a priest's embroidered silk stole. Plunder. "From a galleon?" he asked. Wealthy Spanish churchmen often traveled with such things.

"No," his host said with a wink. "This pigsty was on land. Lauwersmeer. The canting little priest and his bum boys won't be doing their Sunday shows for a while."

Adam knew of the place. A small coastal town.

"And this," La Marck said, pulling out a rolled canvas, "is from Hellevoetsluis. From the house of the mayor himself." He unfurled it. A fine painting of a Madonna. "It'll fetch a fair price in a Portuguese port."

Adam swallowed wine to keep from showing his unease. La Marck had been raiding Dutch towns. What was the point of that? And no doubt blood had been spilled, the blood of innocent townsfolk. But he held his tongue. He hadn't come to argue.

The men's laughter up on deck had subsided and the muffled voices sounded angry and heated now, some kind of argument. Adam had been around seamen most of his life. When they weren't arguing over dice they were fighting about women. "Where are you bound?" he asked La Marck. Adam was hungry for action. Hungry to take on the Spaniards. "Have you some fat galleon in your sights? Maybe one carrying troops to Alba?"

The Dutchman didn't answer. He regarded Adam quizzically. "What's that caravel you're sailing? Has your queen declared war on Johan of Sweden? Did you take the caravel as a prize?"

"Not at all. Her Majesty enjoys cordial relations with His Majesty King Johan."

"Spoken like a prating courtier. Face it, Thornleigh, you're a rover, an adventurer, same as me. Come on, where's the *Elizabeth*?"

Adam gritted his teeth. It was hard to talk about his ship. "Burned," he managed. The very word seared his throat. "To the waterline."

La Marck looked shocked. "Hellfire. Where?"

"In harbor. Sark."

"By Alba?"

"By his order, I'm sure."

"So he *did* come for you." La Marck looked at his captains and crowed, "What did I tell you? This man has nine lives. Ha! Only four or five left now, Thornleigh!"

Jansz said, "I knew that caravel looked familiar. I saw her on Sark." He added to La Marck, "Her owner bartered her for repairs to his galleon."

"Aha," said La Marck, "so the Swede made a deal with the fair Mistress Doorn."

Adam didn't like his tone. Or the leer in his eye. "The *Gotland*, yes. I've borrowed her."

"*Borrowed* her, have you?" La Marck looked intrigued, amused. "And yet Mistress Doorn is known to drive a hard bargain. She's a comely wench, Thornleigh. Did you slip her something *hard* to satisfy her demands?"

Adam was on his feet before he knew it, glaring down at the Dutchman's face. "When you speak of that lady you'll keep a civil tongue."

Curry said, "Come, my lord," a quiet warning. "We're all friends here."

"That we are," the Admiral said. "All friends." But his amused look had vanished.

Adam sat down. He knocked back the last of his wine. There were muffled shouts up on deck, then the sound of men scuffling. A brawl? *Not my business*, he thought. "I asked you, La Marck, where are you bound?"

"What do you care? Are you not bound for England?"

"I'll send some Spaniards to the bottom first."

"Is that why you've come to me?" He looked surprised. "You always fought alone."

"When I had the *Elizabeth*. With gun power."

La Marck brightened. "Ah, so it's *guns* you want."

"The *Gotland* is a merchantman. I need eight cannon. Six at the least."

La Marck held Adam's gaze like a bargainer weighing his prospects. "We might make a deal. Come along with us. We're bound for

Oostduinkerke. Good weather for it, townsfolk indoors in the rain. Then we're off to Dover to sell the swag."

Adam didn't want any of that. Not the raid on innocent Dutchmen or Dover, either. He had advised and approved Elizabeth giving the Sea Beggars safe harbor in her Channel ports—she found them useful for the havoc they caused to Spain—but what he itched for now was action. "How can you be satisfied with mere booty, man?" he said, unable to hide his scorn. "It's Spaniards you need to fight, not Dutchmen."

The Admiral spat on the floor. "Dutchmen who let themselves be slaves to Spaniards." He eyed Adam with a hard look tinged with contempt. "We need victualing, Thornleigh. We've been at sea for three months. You're a rich man. You don't know what it is to go hungry."

"I'll pay you for the guns. We can put in at Calais, transfer the guns there. It's not two hours away."

"I don't want your money."

"What *do* you want?"

"You. My fleet's a damned pack of wolves." He glanced up, indicating the rowdy din on deck. "I could use a tough leader. What do you say? Equals, you and me."

Adam's hope shot up. "That's fine. That's what I came for. Let's give the Spanish devils some pain." A new thought stirred him. "If we can come together as a fighting force there are rebel bands ashore we could unite with, become a force for Prince William to break Spain's grip."

"Hmm. Later, maybe. First we'll lighten the dago-loving burghers of some of their goods."

"Raiding towns? No."

"Why not? A few ports of call and in a month we'll be rich enough to stay in Dover for a year."

"You've gone soft, La Marck."

"And you have no guns." He got to his feet. "Go back to your borrowed merchantman, Thornleigh. And think about my offer."

❧14❧

A Reckoning

On horseback, Fenella kept well behind the man she was following on his fine, gray military mount. She could not let Carlos Valverde see her.

She found it hard to maintain his pace, for he kept his well-trained horse at a fast trot even in the crowded main street leading away from the Grote Markt. At ease in the saddle, he didn't slow as he edged around people and carts, while Fenella clumsily dodged those obstacles and then kicked her mare to keep up with him. People gave Fenella odd looks. No wonder—a woman alone, riding with purpose like a soldier, dressed like a shabby courtesan. The gaudy clothes she wore were a necessary part of her plan for Valverde. But she hated attracting attention in public. She could not afford to have anyone in authority stop her to ask her business, ask where she was from. That was risky enough, yet she was courting even more danger with her plan.

Plan? she thought anxiously. More like a desperate hope. Nothing was certain. She was so nervous, the clammy sweat of her palms made it hard to keep a grip on her reins.

Valverde turned down one street after another, passing shops, a church, crossing a bridge, passing a long wall that enclosed a monastery, then turning again, and again, until Fenella, with her eyes locked on him, was no longer sure in which direction they were going. A glance at the sun hanging low between a rooftop and a church belfry told her they were heading north. The bell clanged and birds burst from the belfry. Evening service was about to begin. It turned her stomach to think of the priests and sheep-like people praying for the health of Alba, their governor, while he tortured and murdered at will. Fenella prayed only that she could finish what she'd set out to do before it was too late . . . before they executed Claes. On Sark she had killed a Spaniard. Now she would kill another.

She had waited for Valverde outside the barracks behind the King's House across from City Hall, the center of Spain's authority here. She had stood by the barracks wall all afternoon, scanning the soldiers who came and went through the gates. She wasn't the only woman—whores idled, chatting and sharing drink from a wineskin, eyeing Fenella, who kept her distance—but she was the only one with a horse. The mare munched grass in the ditch as Fenella waited. A shiver of excitement rippled through her when, not long after suppertime, Valverde trotted out, hard to miss in his steel breastplate and helmet with its white plume that identified him as one of Alba's commanders. She ran to her mare and followed him, growing more nervous and uncertain as he made his way through the city. She'd got a good look at his face when he'd left the barracks, a weathered, unsmiling face that had seen butchery on and off battlefields. Valverde had done hard things to men. He was no fool. Her task would not be easy.

Now he slowed, approaching a walled house fronted by a line of spring-green bay trees. She stopped, watching him pass through the open gate into the courtyard. She glimpsed a fat maidservant waddling by with a brace of bloodied pheasants and halting to let him pass on his horse. A stable groom hurried to meet him. Fenella thought, *This has to be his home.* Just as she'd hoped.

She slid off her horse. She stood still in the street, unable to move, her heart thudding painfully, her hand still gripping the saddle pommel. If she failed, Valverde would have her arrested. She would hang. Claes would die.

Claes.

"At Terneuzen," Jacques had said. "That's where Alba's men captured them. In a rye field north of the abbey."

"And took all the guns?" another of the Brethren asked, a big man with a bristling sandy moustache, named DeWitt. This late-night meeting was in the Beaumonts' printing press room behind their shop. Jacques and Marguerite, red eyed from lack of sleep, were sweating at their work, hastily printing pamphlets that denounced Alba's tyranny. Fenella was helping, doing whatever they asked of her. Anything to keep from curling into a ball in the corner and weeping.

"All," said Jacques, hoarse from the tension they were all living with. "They didn't get a single gun across to Vlissingen."

"Guns," Marguerite said, wiping her brow with her sleeve as she set fresh type on the press. "How can we talk of guns when fifteen of our Brethren are scarcely cold in their graves? And Brother Domenic will be next."

At the mention of him they all looked at Fenella. Her fingers were cold as she adjusted the type the way Marguerite had instructed her. Claes—Brother Domenic—was a leader in their movement, and her statement that she was his wife had likely spread to the Brethren throughout the city. Under the eyes of eight of them now, she said nothing. Johan's agony on the gibbet never left her thoughts, nor the more terrible agony that Claes was condemned to suffer soon. But as for words, she had none.

"Cold they are, our Brethren," DeWitt said gruffly, "and so, beyond our care. It's not the dead we need to think of but the living. And that means guns. Nothing will change until we get enough men and munitions to Prince William to *force* a change."

"Not in time to save Brother Domenic," Jacques muttered grimly.

"Is there not some way to rescue him?" a young man asked, stacking pamphlets as they came off the press.

"How?" an old man scoffed from his chair. "That prison could withstand a hundred cannon. Which is a hundred more than we have."

"The prison's just a building and Brother Domenic is just one man," DeWitt insisted, pacing. Fenella gathered that he was the leader of the Brussels group. "Neither its fall, if that were even possible, nor his rescue would change anything. Not while Alba continues to rule."

"Brother Clarence is right," another man said. "The way to destroy a monster is to cut off its head. Our countrymen are cowed by their terror of Alba, but his corpse might rouse the people to action. Send them to rally round the prince."

"Corpse?" the young man said, incredulous. "Impossible. No one could get close enough."

"Brother Jerome did last year. With poison."

The young man said grimly, "And look what they did to him."

Fenella looked to Marguerite beside her, a question in her eyes: *What did they do?*

"Alba had him strung up by his thumbs," Marguerite answered quietly, "and his wife and children brought before him. They told his wife to drink the poison or see her children killed. She drank it, and as she was dying in front of Brother Jerome's eyes they slit the children's throats. Then disemboweled him and left him to die."

An icy shudder shot through Fenella.

Jacques lowered a lever and the press thumped down. He raised it again and the young man whisked out the newly inked sheet. The Brethren talked on, not of guns now but of moving the press to a new location. That was their priority. They were a brave group, but Fenella heard the fear in their voices. The capture of Claes and fourteen of his rebels might have put these people in grave danger if the captives under torture had revealed information about them. It was not safe to keep the press here, behind the shop. They had come tonight to dismantle it after this final printing and move it to a house outside the city. Fenella's gold had bought the house. Jacques was in charge of the operation. It had been decided that he and Marguerite would split up. She would tell their neighbors that he had gone to Lille to buy the fancy French materials needed for the shop. Lace, silver thread, ribbons.

Fenella watched Marguerite's ink-stained fingers set the type. She didn't want to look into the Frenchwoman's eyes, for she

knew what Marguerite was suffering at the thought of being separated from Jacques, a separation that would begin this very night.
Ink, metal type, paper—these were the concrete objects they dealt
in, creating pamphlets that had inspired their fellow rebels and
that they now hoped would rouse the people to stand up to Alba.
Their life as a couple had to come second to this consuming, es-
sential endeavor.

Fenella was afraid to see Marguerite's pain because the same
pain clawed her own heart. *Adam*. He would have got her message.
By now, he would be gone. Had he sailed with his children, as he'd
hoped and planned? She knew how much his son and daughter
meant to him and it gave her a small quiver of joy to imagine the
three of them reaching Sark to get his ship, repaired and ready for
him, and then sailing to England. They might even be back in
their English home by now. A family. Her misery flooded back.
She would never see Adam again. Sending him that awful message
had been the hardest decision she had ever made. Tears had
clouded her eyes when she'd written it. What must he think of
her? How he must hate her!

Well, let that pass, she told herself as steadily as she could. She
had to deal with reality. The dream she had concocted of a life in
England with Adam—Lord Thornleigh—was sheer fantasy, as in-
substantial as the frothy gauze in Marguerite's shop. Fenella had
built a golden castle in the air, had floated within its glow when
Adam had held her in his arms, but now she had returned to earth.
Adam was gone. She had sent him out of her life forever. Sent him
home.

Home. Her home was here. Because of Claes. She had taken him
as her husband eight years ago, gladly joining her life to his to
build a business together, build a future. That life had shattered
when the Spanish soldiers thundered into Polder, butchering and
burning, and she'd watched them heave Claes into the river,
watched him sink, and she had wept for him and grieved for him
and hated Alba for his savagery, hated all of Alba's henchmen.
Since then she'd lived as a widow. But ten days ago, in shock and confusion, she had found Claes alive, her husband, now a leader of men.

He was her husband still. Her brief, bright time with Adam Thornleigh had not changed that reality. For a few days she had been blind to it, like a child at the fairground bedazzled into a dream of running off with the magic man. But her eyes had been opened by Johan's death, by the mass hangings, and by the terrible death sentence passed on Claes. But by something else, too—the example of Marguerite and Jacques. The simple, unshakable bond of their marriage, no matter what hardships life hurled at them. Fenella recognized the bond, felt it in her bones. By every law of Christendom and every probing of her conscience, Claes was her husband. They were man and wife. Bound together. Whatever the hardships. When she had awoken in bed at the Beaumonts' shop after the hangings and heard Jacques report the fate that awaited Claes, she had known. As long as there was breath in her body, she had to try to save her husband.

The gate to Valverde's home remained open. Fenella tethered her horse to one of the bay trees and walked through the gate. No one stopped her as she crossed the small courtyard. At the open kitchen door a scullery maid tossed out a panful of bread crumbs, her eyes on the hens that came pecking for the morsels. A rich smell of roasted meat wafted from the kitchen, boar perhaps. Music sounded from an upper window, the flute-like notes of a recorder, the tune thin and wavering as if played by a child.

Fenella made for the low brick building where the wide wooden door stood open—the stable, unmistakable from the glimpse she caught of a groom inside leading a black horse. She heard voices as she approached. She slipped inside, keeping to the shadows. Beyond her, the pale gold light was thick with motes of straw. Smells of hay and horses and dung. The lazy shuffling sound of hooves in stalls.

Valverde stood talking to a couple of grooms while lifting off his helmet. His breastplate was already off, held by the younger groom who then took the helmet, too, and walked away with the master's gear. Valverde led the other groom to the black horse, a muscular stallion with a bandage wrapped around his foreleg. A warhorse, Fenella thought, bred for speed and agility on a battlefield. And for chasing rebels? She imagined it, Valverde and his troop galloping after Claes and his men as they ran through the rye field. Ran for their lives, terrified, exhausted, stumbling, falling. No match for horsemen.

The groom unwrapped the linen bandage, revealing a red cut. Valverde gave instructions about a poultice. Fenella could not hear the exact words. Her mind was in turmoil, her skin clammy with sweat. *Step out now,* she told herself. *Confront him.* She balled her fists, closed her eyes, summoning the resolve to carry out her plan.

"Call me in if there's any change," he said, his voice faint.

Fenella's eyes sprang open. Valverde was already out the door. *Fool! Get him back!*

The house smelled of roast boar. Striding through the hall, Carlos was disappointed he hadn't got home in time to have supper with his family. But the business that had detained him had been worth it, a talk with Alba's secretary, who'd come with a commendation from Alba and an invitation. Carlos had made haste to get home, eager to tell Isabel that a pension from the king of Spain would soon be his. He had earned it, bringing in fifteen rebels, including their leader, Claes Doorn. He hadn't felt so hopeful in months. The pension would save him from bankruptcy. Finally, he could take Isabel and the children back to England.

The laughter of his little girl, Nell, guided him to the parlor. There he found her and Isabel kneeling over a basket where five puppies born two weeks ago squirmed to suckle their mother, Isabel's spaniel bitch. Nell squealed when she saw Carlos and grabbed a puppy and ran to him.

"Papa, look! Their eyes are open!" She hugged the animal against her face. "He's my favorite."

"You picked the runt." Carlos tousled his daughter's hair. "Like you."

"Mama says I can keep this one. I named him Jasper. Because his face is wrinkly like Jasper at home." Carlos had to smile. Jasper Winch, the old footman Isabel kept employed though the fellow was lame.

"She wanted to keep them all," Isabel said, getting to her feet, not easy since she was so heavily pregnant. Carlos went to help her up. She took his arm with a grateful smile.

Nell murmured to her puppy, "Do you like your name, Jasper?"

"He can't hear you, my sweet," Isabel said. "His ear canals aren't open yet."

"When will they open?"

Carlos said, "Another week."

"Oh, before I forget," Isabel said, "Piers asked to speak to you about Fausto's leg."

"I just saw Piers. He showed me."

"And? I know how much that stallion means to you."

"The wound's not healing as fast as I'd like. We're trying a different poultice." It wasn't horses he wanted to speak about. "Isabel, there's news."

"From Adam?" she asked eagerly. She threw a glance at Nell to ensure that the child could not hear. "Did he get away safely with Katherine and Robert?"

"No, it's not about him. I haven't heard from him." He saw her disappointment. "But that doesn't mean anything; he's not likely to contact me." Because of Alba. "You, maybe."

"Either way, I thought he'd let us know."

"Be patient. He's traveling with two children. He hasn't had time."

She nodded. "I'm sure you're right. He'll send word once they're home." She kissed him. Love shone in her eyes. "Thank you for helping him. I know what a risk it was for you."

The risk had been worth it, just to see that look in her eyes. They hadn't quarreled about Alba since the night Carlos had ridden into the convent with her brother. He kissed her. Now, his news. "Isabel, I'm getting the pension."

Her eyes went wide. "Oh, that's wonderful!" Questions poured out of her. How had he heard? When would the pension start? How had it all come about? When could they go home?

He laughed, holding up his hands to forestall her. "It's not definite yet. But Alba was very pleased about the recent pack of rebels I brought in. He's sent a special commendation about me to the

King. His secretary just brought me a copy. So it's just a matter of time until the pension comes through."

The smile faded from her eyes. "Rebels? The ones who call themselves the Brethren?"

He nodded. "They've been a big problem. This will slow them down."

"You mean, that mass hanging in the market square? Lady Quintanilla spoke of it yesterday. Fourteen men hanged. She said the crowd was the biggest ever. And the Brethren's leader will be next, she said. A show execution." She shuddered. "And *you* captured them?"

He suddenly wished he hadn't told her.

A knock on the door. "Come in," Carlos called, glad of the interruption.

It was Piers, the groom. "Sir, could you please come to the stable?"

Fenella watched him come into the stable with the groom, Valverde asking, "She didn't give her name?" In her nervousness she hugged herself, pulling her shabby yellow taffeta shawl tighter over her chest.

The groom pointed her out to Valverde.

"Sir," she said, "I just want a word with you."

He looked at her intensely, then said, still in obvious puzzlement, "I know you, don't I?"

He recognizes me. Good. She was about to speak when he said abruptly to the groom, "That's all. Leave us." The man nodded, a rudimentary bow, threw a last intrigued glance at Fenella, and walked out.

Valverde came to her, his rough face alive with curiosity. "Edinburgh," he said. "The garrison at Leith. Right?"

"So you remember."

He said with some warmth, "Hard to forget." A frown tugged his brow. "What the devil are you doing in Brussels?"

Her nerve plunged. Was she brainsick to think he would help her? It had been eleven years. And their brief coupling had meant little enough to both of them. He'd been married and resisted her advances, but Fenella had been desperate for his help to escape, so she'd practically thrown herself at him. Now, his wife was likely in the house just a shout away and his quick pace to get home spoke of a happy marriage.

But she had come this far. Claes's life was at stake. She looked Valverde in the eye and forced a cheeky smile. "You don't remember my name, do you." She scoffed, "How like a man."

He looked flustered. She was right. He didn't remember.

"It's Fenella," she said.

He nodded. "Right." His discomfort almost made her smile in earnest.

"Fenella Craig, when you met me. I got married later."

"Ah, good. I wondered how you'd made out. I'm glad to see you're all right." He indicated the scar on her cheek. "That healed well."

She flinched at the reminder. "Plenty of men have thought otherwise."

"Then they're fools."

The way he looked at her with open admiration sent her emotions into a bewildering tumble. She wanted this man's goodwill, *needed* it, but she reminded herself that days ago he had chased down Claes and taken him captive. Steeling herself, she focused on that.

"You've done well for yourself," she said, making her tone friendly. "A commander of the Duke of Alba. Quite high-and-mighty now, aren't you?"

He gave a terse nod as though it was the last thing he wanted to talk about, then asked again, "But what the devil brings *you* here?"

She took a deep breath. The Brethren could not rescue Claes, so it was up to her. The words of one of the Brethren still echoed: *To destroy a monster . . . cut off its head . . . rouse the people to action.* Her plan for saving her husband was to create chaos. By killing Alba.

"I need a favor," she said.

Valverde looked startled but answered forthrightly, "All right. If I can."

"Like I said, I got married. To a Dutchman, a shipwright. He died. He left debts. It's put me in a bad way. I'm alone, no family, no money. It's hard to make ends meet. There's nights I go to bed hungry. So I've decided to . . . do what I must." She added wryly, "I've found that men soon get over this scar when there's something else they want."

She unwrapped the coarse shawl to uncover her bosom, showing him the bodice cut just below her nipples, with only see-through gauze covering her breasts. She had rouged her nipples the way French courtesans did, a visible red lure beneath the gauze. Valverde's eyes dipped to take it in. Everything she had told him was a lie, but she saw that he believed the tale. Why wouldn't he? When he'd met her she'd been a kept woman. And his for the taking.

He raised his eyes to hers. "I can help you with a little money."

Was this a proposition? She quickly rewrapped the shawl, covering herself again. "In exchange for what?"

He shook his head and said gently, "You misunderstand. Just to help. I'm not rich, but I can give you something."

She was moved despite herself. She hadn't expected kindness.

A door slammed inside the house. He looked sharply in that direction. It snapped the tender moment and cleared Fenella's mind. She thought again of him galloping after Claes. She lifted her head with a show of pride. "Keep your charity," she said. "I mean to make my own way. I have a plan. Do you know the house on the canal under the sign of the Golden Angel?"

She saw his surprise. He knew it, of course, the elegant underground brothel frequented by the city's rich men. Its courtesans were especially popular with Spanish dons. Including, so Fenella had learned, the Duke of Alba. The Brethren knew a great deal about their adversary, and when Jacques had told her that Alba often visited the Golden Angel she knew that's where she could see him face-to-face. Close enough to shoot him.

"I want to work there," she said. "But it's so exclusive, they only take women who've been recommended. That's why I've come to you."

He held up his hands, a clear refusal. "I'm sorry. I can't do that."

His curtness unnerved her. "Maybe you don't understand. All I want is an introduction. Nothing more."

"No. I'm sorry."

Anger flared in her. She had debased herself to convince him, and this flat *No* was all her answer? She was asking so little! *Well,* she thought, *I can* make *you.* "I don't suppose you ever told your wife about us."

Their eyes locked. The steeliness in his made her shiver. This was a man who had hacked off enemies' heads with his sword. "You'd be wise to take what I'm offering," he said steadily. "I've told you, I'll help you with some money. That's all."

"Just an introduction! It's so little to you, and so much to me!"

"I have a position. It's not whoremaster."

Position? It was all she could do to hold her tongue. *I owned a business, damn you! Employed twenty-two men! I made enough gold to keep me in comfort as long as I live.* But she could not bewail the life she had lost. She had to think of Claes. He would be dragged to the market square bound to a hurdle, a steel pin shot through his mouth to silence him. They would haul him up to the scaffold before the crowd. Hang him, cut him down still breathing, castrate him, slice his abdomen and draw out his entrails in his dying agony, cut out his heart. The thought rocked her so horribly she reached out for Valverde's arm. "Please—"

"Carlos?" a voice called from the door. "Is Fausto all right?"

They both turned. A woman walked in. Fenella drew back her hand from Valverde's arm. The woman, though heavily pregnant, moved with grace and purpose. Shaken, Fenella thought, *Is this his wife?*

"Oh," she said in surprise, seeing Fenella. She reached them and looked at her husband. "I thought it was about the horse."

Fenella saw that Valverde was rattled, but he quickly recovered. He turned to Fenella, the look in his eyes a warning to her as he indicated the lady. "My wife." Then to his wife, "Isabel, this is Mistress Craig. From Edinburgh."

Fenella was unnerved as she looked into a face that felt startlingly familiar. This was Adam's sister. The same lively, curious eyes. Fenella gathered her wits and bobbed a curtsy. "It's a pleasure to meet you, madam."

"Edinburgh?" the lady asked, intrigued.

"Long ago," Valverde said.

"Oh, not so very long," Fenella said smoothly, surprising even herself. The thought had sprung itself on her that there might be a way to turn Valverde's tension to her advantage. "It was in the garrison at Leith."

"Leith?" The lady looked at her husband. "When you went to advise the Queen Regent?"

He gave a stiff nod.

Fenella went on boldly, "Your husband did me a great service, madam."

Valverde's eyes flicked to her, anxious.

"Oh?" his wife asked.

"I was living with the garrison commander. His doxy. I hope that doesn't shock you, madam." It did not, she saw from the lady's obvious, earnest interest. *Good,* she thought. "He was a brutal bastard, pardon my language. I wanted out, but I was young and poor. You see this scar?" she said, touching her cheek. "He cut me with a bottle. Your husband came to my defense. Beat the bastard senseless."

His wife blinked at him. "Goodness."

"It was the night we got Adam free," he said quickly, clearly wanting to move on. "Mistress Craig's help was crucial."

The lady's eyes went wide as she looked back at Fenella. "Really? What did you do? My brother told me little about his escape from the garrison jail, and my husband even less. I suppose to them it was all part of soldiering, but I've always wanted to know more. What happened?"

Valverde said, looking Fenella in the eye, "She got hold of the commander's jail keys."

"That I did," she agreed, "and your husband set fire to a storeroom to distract the guards, and together, madam, your brother and I scrambled down to the beach and jumped on the boat your husband had wangled for us and the two of us sailed here to the Low

Countries." Emotion welled up in her, remembering their harrowing escape, Adam so weak from his captivity yet so kind to her. She had fallen in love with him then and there. She swallowed hard. This was not about Adam. It was about Claes. She added pointedly, "I've been here ever since. Married a Dutchman."

The lady seemed moved. "I see that my brother owes you his life." She reached out and squeezed Fenella's hand. "We *all* owe you."

"Thank you, madam." The bond was real. Fenella felt it, too. It gave her courage to forge on. "I'm sorry if I've disturbed your evening, but the truth is I'm in need of a favor from your husband."

"Yes, of course. How can we help you?"

"I was just telling him my husband died and left no money, only debts. So I'm in difficulty. But that's not the whole story. He got mixed up with the rebels. Brainless of him—the Spaniards own the world, don't they?—but there it is. He was caught in a raid." She looked at Valverde. "A raid that you led, sir. He was hanged."

Valverde stared at her. "What was his name?"

"I'd rather not say, sir. You might feel it's your duty to investigate further and that could get some folks into trouble whose only crime is stupidity, like my husband. He paid for his folly with his life. Let that be an end of it." She turned to Valverde's wife. "Trouble is, his passing is just the start of *my* difficulty. I need money, that's the hard truth. Your husband has kindly offered me some, but I don't want that. I'm ready to do what I must to support myself in the age-old way. I can see you're a wise woman, madam, so you know my meaning. I've supported myself in the past, and I'm ready to do it again. But, like I said, I need one small favor."

"Carlos, you *must* help," the lady said. "Won't you?"

He looked caught, lost for words.

"Of course he will. Depend on it, Mistress Craig. Now, tell us, what do you need?"

"An introduction." Fenella looked Valverde in the eye, triumphant. "That's all."

❧15❧

Banished

The moon was full but the night fog so thick Adam could scarcely see the men ahead running with him for the beach. He could make out seven. The others were hurrying to catch up. He'd led the landing party of twelve into the coastal village of Koksijde, the raid had been swift, and now they were making their escape. But a church bell pealed the alarm, and Adam knew the townsmen coming for them could not be far behind. A huge sand dune loomed out of the fog. He was glad to see it. It meant they were almost at the boat.

They scrambled around the dune, the sand slowing them, sucking at their boots. Adam heard his men grunting from the weight of the sacks of plunder they carried. He carried only his sword. Had he got everyone out? So hard to see. The last he'd seen of Morrison, the skinny boatswain had been dragging a strongbox past a draper's smashed door. Then the church bell had begun to clang and Adam had rounded up the others, calling out names in the fog and cursing La Marck for insisting on making the strike in such conditions.

"Fog worked for us when we raided Lauwersmeer," the Dutchman had said, handing out axes from the *Eenhoorn*'s arms chest to his men. "It'll work again tonight."

It'll have us running around like blind mice, Adam had thought.

The business disgusted him. He wanted to be attacking Spanish troopships and pay ships, not plundering Dutchmen's shops. And churches—La Marck never passed up a chance to lighten a church of its Catholic treasures. Adam swore that he'd hold him to his bargain, that after this raid La Marck would give him cannon to arm the *Gotland*.

Dogs barked. Townsmen shouted, their voices muffled by the dune. Adam and his men splashed into the shallows, hurrying for their boat that bobbed in the surf, tugging at its anchor like a nervous colt. Out in deep water stood the *Gotland*, the faintest shape in the fog, a specter alone on the sea. La Marck on the *Eenhoorn* was raiding a town a few miles south.

Adam counted five men climbing into the boat, each one heaving his sack in first, and five more coming fast. Heywood's nose looked broken, dripping blood from a skirmish with a watchman. Adam had forbidden the use of arms on the townsmen except in defense and was relieved there were no casualties. Curry stood in the bow, preparing to haul up the anchor. Adam, in the knee-high water, sheathed his sword and gripped the gunwale, about to hop aboard. "Where's Morrison?" he called above the noise of the surf and clatter of the men.

"Right behind us!" Toth called back, scrambling into the stern.

Adam saw no one coming. Was Morrison on his way, out there in the fog? Or had he collapsed on the beach, wounded? Or been captured?

A townsman's shout crested the dune.

"They're coming!" Toth said, flopping aboard.

"Get in, my lord," Curry told Adam. "I'll weigh anchor."

"No. Hold on. I'm going for Morrison."

He splashed back through the shallows and loped along the beach, peering into the misty gloom, half-expecting to trip over the wounded man. "Morrison!" he called. Every step took him closer to the strident jabber of the townsmen surging this way and the barking of their dogs. The sand dune loomed out of the fog. At the top of it, a man's shape, looking huge, his arms thrown wide. A weapon in his hand? "Stop!" he shouted to Adam, and came barreling down the dune.

Adam drew his sword, but the assailant came at him so fast Adam stumbled backward, almost losing his balance in the sand. The huge man lunged and Adam felt the impact on his chest like a tree trunk hurled by a hurricane. He hit the ground on his back, the breath knocked out of him, the man sprawling on top of him. The man staggered to get up, grunting, clumsy with his bulk. Adam got to his feet, struggling to catch his breath. He had not let go of his sword, and though still half-stunned he raised it.

"Adams, no!" the man cried. "It's me!"

He halted. *Adams?* "Who are you?"

"Verhulst! I'm Berck Verhulst. Brussels, remember? My barge!"

Adam blinked at the black-bearded face in the gloom. *Good God, Fenella's friend!* "What the devil are you doing here?"

"Looking for you." Verhulst bent to grab what he'd dropped. Not a weapon, a sack. He looked over his shoulder in alarm. The townsmen's voices were loud, shrill. "They're coming." He turned back to Adam. "I hope you've got a boat, Englishman!"

Adam could make no sense of the bargeman being on this beach. But there was no time for questions. He heard labored breaths behind him and twisted around, sword raised, to see a shape emerge from the fog. Morrison! He was staggering from the weight of the strongbox he held with both hands, puffing like a bellows. He staggered up to Adam. "Present and accounted for, my lord!"

Adam almost laughed, shaken but relieved. "Come, both of you. Verhulst, take that strongbox; you're bigger. Morrison, take his sack. Both of you, fast as you can!"

They made it to the boat and clambered aboard. Curry weighed anchor. Toth and five others hauled on the three pairs of oars. The boat, crowded with men and treasure, bucked out through the surf. Everyone looked back at the beach where a straggle of towns-men converged, shouting curses and shaking their fists. A pistol shot cracked the air. The bullet splashed behind the boat. Past the surf now, the boat skimmed toward the ship and Adam's men let out nervous laughs at the thrill of their escape.

"Ha! Look at those poor bastards," Heywood said with satisfac-tion, dabbing his bleeding nose with his sleeve.

"Poor, my ass," Morrison growled. "Poxy collaborators in bed with the dagos." Morrison had been Adam's boatswain on the *Elizabeth* with Hawkins's expedition to the New World, and Adam shared his bitterness. They both bore scars of the Spaniards' vicious attack on them in the Mexican harbor of San Juan de Ulúa.

"Who's this, my lord?" Curry asked, eyeing Verhulst. They all looked at the big stranger who was still breathing hard from his exertion.

"A refugee," Adam said, though far from sure. His chest still hurt from the bargeman tackling him. His thoughts lurched to Fenella. Did Verhulst know where she'd gone?

"Lord . . . ?" Verhulst asked, bewildered by Curry's address.

"Your story first," Adam said. "Why've you washed up on this beach?"

"I've been looking to join the Sea Beggars."

"Huzzah," Curry said sardonically. "You found 'em."

"Truly?" Verhulst looked as though he couldn't believe his luck. "I've been asking up and down the coast. An alehouse brewer said Admiral La Marck's ship was sighted off this town, so here I tramped. Didn't make it until after dark, though, and found you lot looting." He looked at Adam. "Saw *you*. The bastards deserved it, so I slipped into an alley to watch." He added with a nod at Morrison, "He's right; that town's a rat's nest of collaborators. The whole country's rotten with 'em."

"You've changed your tune," Adam said, skeptical. "You draw Spanish pay. You warp boats on the Brussels canal, don't you?"

"Not anymore," Verhulst said defiantly. "I've had my eyes opened." Even in the murky light Adam saw the fervent look on the man's face. The zeal of the convert.

"Ahoy!" came a shout as the *Gotland* loomed. A lantern hanging from the yardarm blazed a nimbus in the mist.

"Ahoy!" Curry called back. The oarsmen sculled, bringing the boat alongside the ship, and the men readied their sacks of plunder, talking and chuckling. Crew on the *Gotland* threw the rope ladder over the side and the men in the boat stood, ready to board. Adam stayed seated. They knew he always boarded last.

As they began climbing up in turns Verhulst said to Adam, "Fenella, she's the one who made me see. Told me to stop brooding and do something with my life." His eyes shone, and there was a new tone in his voice, one of tenderness and pride. "Fenella cares about old Berck after all."

Hearing her name shot a spark through Adam. "Where is she, do you know? Is she all right?"

"Haven't seen her since you left my barge. But don't worry, Fenella always lands on her feet." Verhulst looked up eagerly at the ship, slinging his sack over his shoulder, readying to climb the ladder after Curry, who was next. "That's a fine caravel, Adams. And you're her captain?"

"The name's Thornleigh."

"Not Master Adams?"

"Not Master anything," Curry sternly told him, his foot on the ladder. "He's Lord Thornleigh."

Verhulst looked amazed. "Not . . . the English baron? I've heard the stories about you! I surely hope you won't hold it against me, knocking you down . . . your lordship."

Adam almost smiled. "No harm done."

"Would you consider taking me on as crew, my lord? You'll be doing a shipwrecked man a favor."

Adam didn't need to consider. An experienced hand was always welcome. "Curry, find him a berth."

"Aye, my lord."

The bargeman grinned. "Much obliged . . . your lordship." He gamely followed Curry up the ladder, the rope creaking under his bulk.

Adam stood, the last man in the boat. Time for the *Gotland* to weigh anchor and rendezvous with La Marck. But he did not move to climb the ladder. He had no will to. Regret surged through him, a tidal wave of frustration and grief at all he had lost. Fenella, gone from his life as suddenly as he'd fallen in love with her. His children, left in the controlling hands of Frances. His ship, destroyed, dead. Up on deck his crew welcomed Verhulst with friendly curses and the bargeman guffawed at their rough banter. Adam envied him. *Do something with your life,* Fenella had told her friend, and he was. Brimming with zeal at joining the Sea Beggars, Verhulst was bent on action.

Action. Adam craved it. Against the Spanish. They had butchered his men in San Juan de Ulúa and now they ground their boot on the neck of the innocent Dutch. And they were a menace to England, holding over Elizabeth the constant threat of invasion. What England needed was a mighty navy, powerful enough not just to form a protective wall but also to attack and smash rapacious Spain.

A vision gripped him. A vision of action. Elizabeth could give him ships. Merchant ships. She felt that she could not openly antagonize Spain, that she did not dare, but Adam could, privately. With her clandestine help he could overhaul a fleet of merchantmen as men-of-war armed to the teeth and lead them forth, unleashing them as England's covert weapon. He could hit Spain so hard up and down the Channel it would cripple their trade and their military supply lines. He could be the terror of the Narrow Sea.

The boat wallowed under his feet, challenging his balance. The fog suddenly felt clammy on his neck. His fantasy sank. He could take none of the actions he wanted. Elizabeth would never invest in such a radical plan; it would unleash diplomatic chaos, maybe outright war. And even if he could afford the massive investment personally, which he could not, she would forbid him using a private fleet aggressively. His dream was impossible, an illusion. This caravel he was roaming in could do little damage, even with the few cannon that La Marck promised him. Adam didn't even own her. She belonged to Fenella.

And the Sea Beggars? He despaired of La Marck ever unleashing their untapped power. The Dutchman was happy to raid collaborating Dutch villages and then run to safe English ports, thanks to Elizabeth's goodwill, and live there off his plunder. He'd been doing it for three years, he and his men making Dover and the creeks and bays along the south coast their home. Why would he change?

Everything that had happened in the last few weeks suddenly

felt as disorienting, as sick making, as an anchor dragging him to the depths by the neck in a nightmare. His hope of happiness with Fenella, dashed. His plan to rescue his children, stillborn. The knowledge that Frances, his own wife, was intent on seeing him dead.

The only action open to him was retreat. He told himself grimly that he had to accept it, though everything in him chafed. He must return to England, make his report to Elizabeth, and sink into the tame life of a courtier. Attend her council meetings about patronage appointments and trade treaties and the ongoing machinery of government. Advise her. Keep a watchful eye for her on the jockeying factions at court. Manage his own estates. Be content. He would try to persuade her to pull diplomatic strings to get Robert and Kate sent home and with luck he might succeed. That was the best he could hope for, he told himself.

He climbed the ladder, his feet as heavy as his heart.

"Two ships starboard ahead! Hull down!" the lookout called from the *Eenhorn*'s crow's nest.

The morning sun had burned off the last of the fog, and Adam, bleary-eyed from lack of sleep, crossed the *Eenhoorn*'s quarterdeck. He had come aboard La Marck's ship to confer about transferring the guns once they reached Dover. *For what it's worth*, he thought gloomily. The *Gotland*, under Curry, kept pace with them, almost abeam.

Adam went to the starboard rail to look at the two sails the lookout had announced. At this distance they were mere moth wings on the horizon. La Marck followed him. The fresh breeze snapped the sails above them with a sound like a muster master's clap, but on deck La Marck's men slouched and shuffled, groggy from late-night carousing in celebration over their spoils. A few less fortunate lay below, suffering wounds. Unlike Adam, La Marck had not forbidden his men violent action in the town they had raided. He'd handed out axes.

The *Eenhoorn* carved steadily through the low waves that rode out from the English coast not yet visible. Adam could smell the land. He thought of all the times he'd felt cheered at sighting the chalk cliffs of Dover. Home. Not this morning. England seemed almost like a prison waiting to hold him.

Five, he thought, as three more sails popped up on the horizon close behind the first two. The lookout shouted, "Five sails now, starboard ahead!"

Adam and La Marck watched in silence until the two lead ships were hull up. La Marck said, "That's the *Vrijheid* and the *Bruynvisch*." Sea Beggar vessels.

As for the three other ships, even before they were hull up Adam saw that they flew England's colors, the cross of St. George. "That's the *Tiger* nipping at their heels," he said. "Captain Wynter's flagship." He and La Marck looked at each other. Adam spoke the question that was clearly on both their minds. "What's afoot?"

"I don't know," La Marck said, "but I don't like the look of it. Your man's chasing the *Bruynvisch* like a thief in the night."

"Looks like we're going to find out. Wynter's spotted us." The *Tiger* was veering away, leaving the two other English ships in pursuit of the two Sea Beggar vessels. Heading straight for the *Eenhoorn* and the *Gotland*, the *Tiger* signaled a request to parley.

"Look alive!" La Marck kicked a slouching seaman's foot and cursed at the others. He yelled orders to heave to. The crew loped to their posts. Adam saw with satisfaction that Curry was also trimming the *Gotland*'s sails to heave to. The *Tiger* reached them and sent a boat, the oarsmen ferrying an officer to parley.

Adam stood beside La Marck as the man came aboard. A spry fellow no more than twenty, he made a sour face at the dirty condition of La Marck's ship and made no effort to hide his distaste as he introduced himself to La Marck as Captain Wynter's lieutenant. He handed La Marck a paper folded and sealed. "Compliments of Captain Wynter."

The Dutchman read it and Adam saw a storm cloud darken his face. La Marck looked up, clearly disturbed. "It can't be true." He handed the paper to Adam. "What's the meaning of this?"

Adam read it and was stunned. An expulsion order, handed down from the commissioners of the Cinque Ports: Hastings, New

Romney, Hythe, Dover, and Sandwich. It expelled all Dutch privateers. The reason the officials had given was for "*plundering ships belonging to friends of England and impeached the trade of merchandise to the slander of the realm.*" Adam looked at La Marck. "It means the Sea Beggars are ordered to quit Dover and quit England."

"Impossible!" La Marck lashed out with curses at the lieutenant, who bore the abuse with a silent sneer.

"Hold on, La Marck. I'll clear this up," Adam said. "Lieutenant, I'll come and speak to Captain Wynter."

"And you are . . . ?"

"He's Baron bloody Thornleigh, you poxy sea slug!" La Marck blustered.

The man's sneer vanished. He blanched and said in a groveling voice, "My lord . . . of course . . . forgive me. . . ."

The boat was readied. La Marck insisted on coming, too. The three of them were rowed to the *Tiger*. On board the trim English galleon they crossed the gleaming, holystoned deck past the orderly crew and Adam quietly told La Marck, "I'll do the talking." They were taken below and ushered into the captain's teak-lined cabin.

Wynter rose from his desk. Stocky but fit, he had a face weathered by sun and wind and the burdens of leadership, and small blue eyes bright with intelligence. He was Master of Ordnance for the Navy and had recently taken a fleet to subdue the latest rebellion by the Irish. Adam had known him for years. Over a decade ago, when the Scots under Knox were fighting their French overlords, Adam had taken the *Elizabeth* into the North Sea with a small fleet commanded by Wynter to prevent French ships from landing in Edinburgh. Adam had been captured at Leith. Then set free by Carlos and Fenella. "Thornleigh," Wynter said now in greeting, "it's been a while."

"It has, William. You look none the worse for what they threw at you in the Irish Sea."

Wynter allowed himself a small smile. "We pounded some sense into the blockheads." He looked pointedly at La Marck. The two had never met.

Adam introduced the Dutchman. "Admiral La Marck." He

used the honorific in the hope it conferred weight, for he feared La Marck was on shaky ground. "William, this order from the commissioners, there's surely some misunderstanding. Her Majesty gives safe harbor to the Admiral and his fellow captains. You know that. They've been welcome in Dover ever since Spain rolled into the Low Counties."

"Aye, welcome," La Marck burst out, "and with good reason. Your queen hates the dagos and we Dutch have been doing her dirty work for her!"

Wynter said with diplomatic control, "Be that as it may, sir, on the commissioners' orders we escorted eleven of your fellow vessels out of Dover and Hastings yesterday. Five more this morning. And any approaching from now on will be intercepted and turned."

"Turned?" La Marck blustered. "What will you do, fire on us?"

Wynter's blue eyes were cold. "I will obey my orders. Dutch privateers will no longer be admitted into any English port." He added to Adam, "Englishmen, of course, are welcome to come home."

"William, this makes no sense," Adam said. "It goes against Her Majesty's interests. The Sea Beggars are her allies. You understand that—you've done your own share of privateering in the service of the Queen."

"You've been absent from court too long, Thornleigh. Her Majesty's view has changed. She will no longer countenance illegal hostilities against subjects of the king of Spain."

"You mean she's giving in to his howls. Appeasing him."

"I'd be careful what you call it," Wynter advised, a quiet warning. "It is her proclamation."

"And what's to become of us?" La Marck demanded. "We need victualing, damn it. Water and food. And I've got wounded men. We can't go back and put in at home; the Spaniards would slaughter us. So where are we to go? Or does your queen mean for us to roam the sea until we starve?"

"That, sir, is not Her Majesty's concern."

* * *

Back aboard the *Gotland,* Adam strode across the deck and up the steps to the quarterdeck, his thoughts awhirl. Curry stood at the binnacle awaiting his orders. Word of the expulsion order had swept through the lower decks like gale spray, bringing all the crew up to catch what news they could. Some stood by the main-mast, some on the forecastle; some had climbed up into the rig-ging—twenty-six faces with their questioning eyes on Adam, their captain. As English subjects they knew they would be welcome home, but they had come to know La Marck and his men.

Adam's heart was beating fast, as though he were about to order his men to battle stations. "Loose sail, Master Curry. Mizzen-, main-, and foremast. Courses, topsails, t'gallants, and royals."

"Aye, sir." Curry shouted the orders. Crewmen loped to their posts.

"That's canvas aplenty for beating into Dover, my lord," Curry observed. "You'll soon be home abed."

A natural remark, Adam thought, since Dover lay dead ahead and he hadn't given a change of course. He was still wrestling with himself. From Dover it was a day's ride to Whitehall Palace and then, once he reported to Elizabeth, a short wherry ride into Lon-don and a walk to his house on Bishopsgate Street. He looked be-hind him. Beyond the *Gotland*'s stern the *Eenhoorn* was sailing away, her grimy sails bellying, for she was running before the wind. But running where? Outlawed in the Low Countries, forbidden to enter English ports, the Sea Beggars would be mistrusted and un-welcome everywhere else, because any nation showing kindness to Spain's enemies could suffer reprisals from Spain. That very fear had obviously pushed Elizabeth to close her harbors to them. In parting from La Marck, Adam had seen the Dutchman's silent rage but also his deep alarm. Standing on the quarterdeck of the *Eenhoorn* now, La Marck must be as unsure as Adam about where to steer his ship. Where *would* the Sea Beggars go?

Maybe it was wind snapping the *Gotland*'s sails above Adam, and the thrumming vibration of the deck under his feet as the ves-sel gathered speed, and the mix of excitement and peace that he always felt in captaining a ship as it carved the waves. Or maybe it was the thought of dreary days among backbiting courtiers at Whitehall, and nights in his quiet house empty of love, of children. Or maybe it was simple pity for the Dutchman and his homeless followers. Whatever the spark, Adam was suddenly sure. He could not abandon La Marck. And there was something more. An idea was gathering speed in his mind.

"Change of course, Master Curry. Hard about. We'll run before the wind. Our course is with the *Eenhoorn*."

Curry blinked, but there was a twinkle in his eye as he called out Adam's new orders. A cheer went up from the crew. These men might be English, but they had signed on for spoils.

By evening the wind had dropped and the sun was sinking toward the placid water in a wash of red and gold that made one vast mirror of water and sky. The two ships were abreast and all but becalmed. Two other Sea Beggar ships limped along to starboard, captained by William Bloys and Lenaert Jansz, who had fallen in behind their admiral when La Marck left English waters. Adam stood at the taffrail with La Marck, who was gazing out in grim silence. Adam had just explained his plan and the Dutchman was absorbing the surprise, the blaze of the sunset reddening his face as he considered his options. This had been a bleak day for him, and his anxious men were sullen and grumbling. Still, Adam wondered: Was their situation bleak enough to make La Marck see he had no option but one?

"Attack, eh?" the Dutchman said as though struggling to accept Adam's plan.

"Extremis malis extrema remedia," Adam said.

La Marck looked at him. For all his coarse swagger, he was an educated man and knew Erasmus's Latin proverb. *Drastic measures for drastic times.* "Maybe," he allowed.

"We'll call all the Sea Beggars together," Adam said. "How many men does that give us?"

"Thirty-two ships. Over four hundred men. Many of them louts."

"A lout can be trained. Manpower is manpower. And if we succeed, if we can just gain a toehold, the prince of Orange may send troops to help us. It's the breakthrough he's been waiting for."

"But attack where? They have fortified garrisons in every port of any size."

"I don't know, not yet. But with so much territory to defend they must have a weakness somewhere. We need information. That's why we have to make contact first with the Brethren." They had talked before about the rebel landsmen. La Marck was well aware of the Brethren's work. "Then," Adam went on, "we'll be able to combine and coordinate our forces."

They talked until the water swallowed the sun. The sky was a luminous gloom and the night breeze rose, cool on Adam's neck. The first gleam of interest shone in La Marck's eyes. "All right, Thornleigh. I'll send boats to take the message to our other ships up and down the Channel. The sooner we do this thing, the better. My men need food."

"Good. I know an ideal spot to make landfall. It's a sheltered cove, not a day's ride from Antwerp. A safe hiding hole for two or three ships. From there we can sortie to make contact with the Brethren."

It was a risk. The village wasn't far from the cove and the people there knew he'd killed the other stranger who'd come among them, Tyrone. Adam would have to be very careful. But the possibility of raising a countrywide revolt was well worth the risk.

❧16❧

"Señor Grande"

It was a busy night in the subterranean rooms of the Golden Angel. In the candlelit reception area two naked, nubile courtesans swung their wooden bats in a sprightly game of shuttlecock, giggling at the half-naked customer who played the role of their net, his arms outstretched. Male spectators laughed and wagered bets. A yapping lapdog scampered back and forth between the girls, frantically jumping for the flying feathered shuttlecock. The dog stopped behind one girl and hopped up with paws on her rump and sniffed. Laughter erupted.

Fenella, her nerves frayed, stood apart from the group with the brothel's manager, Mevrouw Dekker, bearing the brunt of the woman's displeasure. The other day when Valverde had introduced them Mevrouw Dekker had been all smiles, full of compliments for Fenella's beauty, but of course the smiles were for Valverde since the connection with him, as one of Alba's commanders, could bring lucrative trade. She was smiling no longer. "Sick *again?*" she asked.

"It's this cursed flux," Fenella said, a hand on her belly. "I can't keep anything down."

A lie. This was her third night at the brothel, keeping an eye out for Alba. She came only in the evenings and for the first two, pleading sickness to Mevrouw Dekker, had managed to evade servicing any customers. She had served them food and chatted with the other women and kept out of Mevrouw Dekker's way. But tonight a customer who'd seen her last night had asked for her specifically. He was known here as the Inchworm. Despite the amusing name, Fenella sensed fear in the other women when they spoke of him.

That wasn't her only worry. She'd heard a rumor from a girl named Sophie, Alba's favorite, that he was hosting guests from Spain at his palace and so might forgo visiting the Golden Angel for a while. Fenella felt almost desperate. This was the only place she could get close enough to Alba to kill him. In the chaos his assassination would create, the Brethren might have a chance to rescue Claes. The plan was wildly uncertain enough . . . and now, what if Alba didn't come to the brothel for days, weeks? Claes could be dead by then. The not knowing . . . it left Fenella in agony. She could only wait and watch and pray that Sophie was wrong. But how much longer could she evade doing what she'd been hired for?

Mevrouw Dekker regarded her with a scowl. "Well, you'd *better* keep it down," she ordered, "at least until the Inchworm gets it *in*. This can't continue. I'm losing money on you. Clothes alone." Making her point, she flicked at the lacy décolletage of the gown she'd loaned Fenella, a garment of scarlet silk so gossamer thin it clung to her every curve. She poked a finger at Fenella's cheek where the white makeup Fenella had applied barely masked her scar. "Don't forget," she warned. "With that cut face you are not for all markets." She tugged the gown lower off Fenella's shoulders to emphasize her bosom and pointed down the corridor. "He's waiting. Give him what he wants, or leave the gown and don't bother coming back."

Fenella could have slapped the woman. But that would not help Claes. She swallowed her disgust, feeling sick in truth. "Yes, madam."

Down the corridor she went, her eyes raking the guests in the frantic hope that she might spot Alba. His appearance, described by his favorite girl, Sophie, was etched in her mind: sixty-four, thin as a cadaver, lean face, cropped gray hair, beard like an iron spade.

A couple strolled past her, the man nuzzling the woman's neck. A little boy dressed like Cupid hurried by, delivering a platter of fruits to one of the private rooms where the door was open and lute music lilted. Two drunken men lumbered past, one grazing Fenella's elbow. No sign of Alba. Her fingers were cold with worry as she fussed with her wig, a fanciful concoction of blond curls. Marguerite Beaumont had given it to her, thrilled by the possibility of removing Alba after hearing Fenella's plan. Together, in the shop, they had created this disguise so that if she could manage to get out after doing the deed and remove the wig and makeup there was a chance she could escape. The Brethren would hide her.

The deed, she told herself, *focus on that. Get through tonight, and hope for tomorrow.*

She reached the closed door of the room Mevrouw Dekker had assigned her two days ago. The Blue Room. It was where Fenella had hidden her flintlock pistol. She opened the door. The candlelit space was cozy. Blue-tapestried walls. A four-poster bed with a blue brocade coverlet. A bedside table with pewter goblets and a decanter of wine.

A stout man, florid faced, sat on the foot of the bed. He wore a gray robe that hung half-open in a V where his paunch bulged. Thin gray hair hung in limp fingers below his ears. He stood up, scowling. "You're late."

"Am I? Well, I'm here now."

"Don't talk back, woman. Close the door."

Fury and disgust roiled in her. But she told herself, *I've come this far.* She closed the door.

He threw off his robe. He was naked. White hairs curled across his sagging breasts and the thatch around his flaccid cock. "Take that off," he said with a flick of his hand at her gown.

Fenella's nerve almost deserted her. "There's plenty of time, lover," she said, moving to the bedside table. "Let's have some wine first. Here, I'll pour you—"

"No." He snatched her wrist. "I'm a busy man. And never again call me by that odious word."

She winced at the pain of his grip. The thick ring he wore dug into her flesh. Furious, she glared at it, an amethyst as big as an acorn set in gold crafted with crucifixes, and suddenly she realized its significance. This was a ring that people kissed. The man was a bishop!

"Come." He pulled her to the bedpost. She saw that he had tied a leather cord to the post. He lifted the cord, still holding her wrist. "Hands together."

She now saw what lay on the bed. A whip, the brown leather coiled languidly like a snake.

"You're mad," she said, pulling free.

"And you, doxy, are paid for." He added with a dark smile, "Don't pretend you've never seen the like." He pointed to her scar. "Someone's already had sport with you." He grabbed a fistful of her gown between her breasts, about to wrench it off.

She lurched back. "Keep your hands off me." She glanced at the whip. "And that thing, too." She was breathing hard. Everything in her wanted to get out, get away, but this wretched place offered her only chance with Alba.

His hand was at her throat faster than she could gasp. "*These* hands?" he said, savagely squeezing. The ring dug into her windpipe. She could not breathe.

She groped for the table behind her, knocking the decanter. It fell with a crash. She groped and snatched a goblet. Raising it high, she brought it down hard on the top of his head. He staggered back from the blow. His hand flew to his head, to the bleeding cut. He looked at his hand, at the bright blood. Fenella dropped the goblet, cursing herself. Impossible to stay here now!

Voices sounded in the corridor. Mevrouw Dekker's, warmly welcoming. A man's, deep, calm, accented. A Spanish accent?

The bishop grunted in shock and rage. "What have you done?" He stumbled a step toward her, then stopped, swaying, weak with shock. He sank to his knees. Fenella hardly saw him. She was straining to hear the voices past the door.

Mevrouw Dekker's: "My dear sir . . ."

The Spanish man: "Where's Sophie?"

Another man: "I'll be in the card room." Fenella stiffened. That third voice she knew. Valverde.

"Here's my Spanish knight!" a woman called gaily. It was Sophie.

Fenella's heart thudded. *Alba!* She went down on all fours and fished under the bed for her pistol. Behind her the bishop, still on his knees, snatched the back of her dress and yanked. "Cunt!" She tumbled backward and fell. Kneeling, he loomed over her, still half-stunned from the blow to his head, blood trickling down his neck. She struggled to get up and made it to her feet, but the silk skirt was tangled between her legs. He swiped at her like a maddened bear and his fingers raked the silk with a loud rip. She got her leg free and kicked him in the chest. He sprawled onto his back with a cry.

The voices past the door faded. She heard a door close. She looked at the bishop who was sprawled on the floor, groaning in pain from her kick. She couldn't risk him stopping her. She grabbed one of his arms and raised it to the bedpost where the leather cord hung. He gaped at her, still dazed. She wound the cord around his wrist and tied a knot. Snatching the whip off the bed, she grabbed his other hand and bound the whip around his wrist and tied it to the other bedpost, snugging it tight. Arms outstretched, on his knees, naked and bleeding, he looked like a fanatic mimicking Christ.

It took her only a minute to load the pistol with the finger-sized powder charge, then the ball. Long enough for the bishop to come to his maddened wits. As she opened the door he bellowed obscenities at her.

She shut the door and looked up and down the corridor, holding the pistol at her knee in the fold of her gown. A couple of women sauntered past and she greeted them loudly, smiling, to cover the bishop's voice. The little spaniel trotted by. No sign of Sophie. Or Alba. The two doors opposite were closed. She opened one. Empty. Then the other. A couple writhed on the bed, the man young and blond. She shut the door. The bishop kept bellowing from the Blue Room. Fenella hurried to the reception area, then around the corner to the card room. Valverde sat dealing cards to a fat man and a pretty girl with a monkey on her shoulder.

Fenella forced herself to look calm as she approached them.

Forced her hand with the pistol to stop trembling. "Señor Valverde, how nice to see you."

He offered her a slight smile, a hint of pity in his eyes. "How is it working out for you?"

"Fine. Have you seen Sophie? My gentleman likes a three-some. He's asked for Sophie."

"Not likely," the girl with the monkey scoffed. "Not when she's got Señor Grande."

The girl's glance over her shoulder at a room to the right was all the information Fenella needed. The Gold Room. She rejoiced. The Gold Room had a private staircase that curved up to the busy street. With luck, she could escape up those stairs, toss the wig, and hurry away among the foot traffic.

She threw open the door. Beside a table laden with food stood Sophie, in green gauze, serving sweets to a well-dressed man in an armchair. He was thin as a cadaver, with cropped gray hair, beard like an iron spade. Alba.

Startled, they both looked up.

"Your Grace," Fenella said, closing the door.

"Yes?"

It was so easy! He sat not fifteen feet away. The staircase was right behind him.

Voices sounded in the hall. Pounding feet. Shouting. A cry from Mevrouw Dekker. Fenella told herself, *Do it now!* She raised the pistol. Aimed at Alba's forehead. He jumped to his feet.

"No!" Sophie cried. She lurched in front of Alba, arms spread wide to shield him.

Fenella's heart leapt to her throat. She could not shoot the girl.

Two men pounded down the stairs, swords drawn. Fenella stiffened. *His guards. Of course. Idiot!*

Alba pushed Sophie aside, a ferocious look on his face as though he would tear Fenella apart with his bare hands. He came at her. It gave her a clear shot. She steadied her hand. Aimed.

The door burst open and a man lunged for her, chopping her arm with his hand. The blow was like an axe. Pain seared and the pistol flew from her hand, clattering to the floor. She turned to go for it. The man tripped her. She tumbled and sprawled on her back, her wig falling off. He stomped on her arm, pinning her to the floor.

With a gasp of pain she looked up into the furious face of Valverde.

Church bells chimed across Brussels. Frances Thornleigh thrilled to the sound as she made her way through the governor's palace with her two children. It was as though the city were celebrating the Duke of Alba's narrow escape from the assassin last night.

No one was more relieved than Frances, for she felt her whole future lay in Alba's hands. She needed him alive. If he could persuade King Philip to back an invasion of England they would topple Elizabeth and install Mary Stuart, the realm's rightful, Catholic queen, and then, finally, Frances could go home. And now, if the would-be assassin last night was who she suspected it was, she might forge an even stronger bond with Alba. She was edgy with anticipation as she nudged her son and daughter to follow the footman who ushered them into the duke's private suite.

Kate obstinately resisted, gripping Robert's hand. "How long do we have to stay?"

Frances pinched the girl's ear. "Hush! You'll stay until you're told." Her fury at her daughter had simmered for days, ever since the girl had dared to plead Adam's cause. Frances had slapped her and forbidden her to speak his name again.

Robert looked nervously from his mother to his sister. Frances shoved them both. "Move! The duke is waiting!"

They found Alba bidding good-bye to a trio of city magistrates. He leaned on a cane, a sufferer of gout, and looked very tired. The visitors appeared anxious. No wonder, Frances thought. All of Brussels was abuzz about the attempt on the governor's life. She held back her children as the magistrates walked out. Alba then noticed her and beckoned her.

"Your Grace," she said, bustling forward with the children. "I rejoice to see you in health. We all praise God for sparing your life."

"God's plan, madam. He knows I must finish my work in this

heretic land before He calls me to His rest." He regarded the children with vague interest. "Your son and daughter?"

"Yes. Robert and Katherine." She prodded Kate, who curtsied, though with an icy look. Robert made a bow stiff with awe and fear. "My lord," Frances said, "I trust my dear Duchess of Feria made clear to you my dreadful plight?"

"She did, yes, in her note. I sympathize, madam. A mother naturally wants to ensure her children's safety."

"Oh thank you, my lord! I am quite beside myself with worry. *Twice* their father has tried to abduct them. He is dogged and devious. The abbey simply is not secure enough."

"The duchess suggested they take sanctuary here. Is that, in fact, your wish?"

"I would be eternally grateful."

"Your Grace," Kate said, a quaver in her voice, "may I speak?" He smiled thinly. "Of course."

"My father is a good man. He only wants—"

"Quiet!" Frances ordered, aghast. She caught the look of distaste in Alba's hawk-like eyes. "His Grace wants none of your foolish prattle! Not one more word! Do forgive her, my lord. The upheaval has left her confused."

He let it go. Frances got him back to the matter at hand and the details were quickly settled. The children would stay, a young priest would tutor them. Alba called for his secretary, and as they waited for him Alba said, "I hope you will excuse me if I sit, madam. I am a martyr to gout." He hobbled toward an easy chair.

Kate whispered fiercely to Frances, "I will not stay here."

"You will," she replied through clenched teeth, "and you'll behave yourself."

"No. I will find some way out. To Father."

"Bah, then do it and be gone." Having the girl out of her hair would be a blessing. It was Robert she needed. Robert she was careful to keep close. Through him she could regain everything she'd lost—rank, position, wealth—if the blessed day ever came when they returned to England. With Adam dead, her son would inherit his title. *Robert, Baron Thornleigh. Frances, the Baron's esteemed mother.*

The boy was silently crying. "Don't leave me, Kate."

His sister squeezed his hand. "Of course not, Robin. I never would; you know that."

Frances tugged them apart. "His Grace does you an honor," she firmly assured the boy. "You will prove yourself a fine, brave little man, won't you? For Mother's sake?"

The secretary came padding in. "Albornoz," the duke said to him, "take Lady Thornleigh's children to the chamberlain. They are my guests. Indefinitely."

Watching her son and daughter go, Frances breathed a tight sigh of relief. She turned to Alba. "Your Grace, how can I ever thank you enough?"

He regarded her from his chair. "The duchess's note said you've had news about your husband."

This was what Alba wanted, she knew. Adam, dead or alive. Frances only wanted him dead. "I have," she confirmed. "When he failed to abduct the children I sent my man Tyrone after him. I've now heard that Tyrone was found murdered in a village near Antwerp. Kloster, it is called, near the sea. From witnesses' descriptions, I believe the killer was my husband. It means he may still be in the country."

"No, but he is not far offshore."

She didn't understand. "Pardon, Your Grace?"

"I've had reports that he is with the criminals who call themselves the Sea Beggars."

She hadn't thought of that but wasn't surprised. "He has rejoined them?"

"In a vessel he stole. We found his English ship on Sark and burned it."

The *Elizabeth*! Frances felt a strange mix of exultation and pity. How Adam had loved that ship.

"They've been marauding coastal towns," Alba went on. "Koksijde and Lauwersmeer last week. Several villagers claimed the English pirate baron was among them." He pointed his cane to a tall window that looked west. "Thornleigh's lurking somewhere along the coast; I can feel it. Perhaps in that maze of islands northwest of Antwerp. There are bays there that could hide a ship or two."

The chilling thought crept over Frances that Adam meant to try again to take the children. Thank God she had brought them here.

Alba's cane thumped on the floor. He looked at Frances with weary forbearance as though disappointed. "I had hoped you knew your husband's whereabouts. But it seems we are still in the dark." He pushed himself to his feet. "Now, you must excuse me. Business calls."

"But I *do*," she blurted.

He looked annoyed, impatient. "Do what?"

"Know where he is. At least, I think we may be able to find out."

His hawk's eyes fixed her with keen interest. "How?"

"The person arrested last night, the one who tried to shoot you, I've heard it was a woman. A foreigner. Is that correct?"

He looked puzzled. "Yes. They tell me she is Scottish. Why?"

"Did you get a close look at her?"

"Close enough."

"A redhead?"

He shrugged. "Under a wig, yes."

"With a scar? Here?" She ran her fingernail over her cheek.

"I could not say; her face was painted." He frowned. "What do these questions signify?"

"When I hired Tyrone he reported that my husband first arrived in this country with a woman. A red-haired woman with a scarred cheek." Jealousy pinched her heart despite her will. She swallowed her humiliation and pushed on. "He thought she might be my husband's lover."

Alba's keen look sharpened. "And you think . . . that woman is the one who tried to kill me?"

"I don't know. But if she is, and if she will talk, she may know where Adam is hiding."

Alba smiled, a cold smile that even Frances found unsettling. "Oh, I assure you, madam, she will talk."

❧ 17 ❧

Death in the Great Hall

Fenella struggled against the ropes that bound her to the plank. For the second time the water chute thudded open above her face. She tensed in terror. *Not again . . . no . . . no!*

Water roared down. It beat her face. Pounded her clamped-shut mouth. Blocked her nose. *Suffocating!* Sputtering, she strained against the hands that pinned her head. *Stop! . . . Sweet Jesus, make it stop!*

Alba's lean face swam above her. His voice rumbled through her water-plugged ears. "Tell me where Thornleigh is. Then this ends."

Make it stop! . . . Let me breathe!

The chute grated shut. The torrent slowed to a trickle. Fenella gasped air. The hands let go of her head.

She coughed out water, gasped more breath. Fire seared her chest. Water still blocked her hearing . . . blurred her vision . . . stung her nostrils. Panting, she struggled against the ropes. Too weak. The hemp bit into her arms, her thighs. The black dungeon wall glistened with splashed water. The henchman who'd pinned down her head was red bearded, his beard glistening with water drops. He shifted his feet . . . a spongy sound of boots on the watery floor.

Alba said, "Tell me. Then you won't have to suffer through that again. Where is Thornleigh? We know he's somewhere along the coast north of Antwerp. You know *him*. You were his accomplice. You know his haunts."

Accomplice? she thought wildly. How could Alba think that?

"Where is he hiding?"

The cove. She was sure of it. That snug indent of the sea, scythe shaped, hidden by the crescent of trees crowding the shore . . . water-weeds nodding in the shallows. *If he's hiding, he's there.*

"Tell me," Alba demanded. "Or the next deluge may drown you."

She shivered, frigid with fear. The chute dripped water on her forehead. She willed herself to submerge the terror . . . forced her courage to resurface. But it was so hard to be strong! She summoned the memory of Adam to give her strength. *Adam, smiling at her . . . moonlight in his eyes.* Twice under the torrent of water she had clung to that memory and had not told Alba what he wanted.

"Speak, woman."

She blotted out the image of the cove. Plunged it back down into the dark depths. It took every shred of strength she had. She concentrated on an image of Adam . . . free, beyond Alba's reach . . . *Adam, standing tall on his ship, sailing into the sun. . . .*

"Don't know him," she said, her voice a trickle. "Don't know anything about him."

Alba nodded to his henchman, Redbeard. He clamped Fenella's head again. Her heart kicked in terror. The water chute thudded open. The torrent crashed on her face, roared in her ears. She sputtered, choking. Her starved lungs screamed. Her heart crashed at her ribs. *Dying . . . I'm dying!*

"Speak now. Your last chance."

The chute grated shut. The torrent stopped. She gasped air. Coughed. Sputtered. Sucked breaths that felt like knives in her throat.

Alba's voice sounded underwater through the gurgle in her ears. "Whom does he meet among the Brethren?"

Brethren? She lay shaking, uncomprehending, gulping breaths. She could not focus on Alba for the water stinging her eyes. *Next time he'll drown me. . . .*

"We have the Frenchman and his wife. The wig you wore led us to their shop."

Marguerite! Jacques!

"Friends of yours, are they?"

She thought her heart would crack. Those good people . . . *are they in a dungeon, broken, moaning for God?* The water that stung her eyes mingled with her own tears.

"I see that you care about them," Alba said. "So I propose a bargain. Tell me where to find Thornleigh, and I won't hang your friends. In fact, tell me what I want and I won't hang *you*."

She blinked up at him, trembling. "Liar."

"You're wrong. The bargain is worth much to me, your worthless life for Thornleigh's. It's him I want. So, tell me. Then you'll live."

The cove rose up in her mind. The rustling trees . . . the lapping waves. "I will tell you the place—" She coughed up water and phlegm.

"Yes? The place . . . ?"

"Where you can go." She spat at him. "To hell."

He grunted in anger. Nodded at Redbeard. The hands clamped Fenella's head. Terror seized her. *Don't betray Adam! Please God, before I do that let me die!*

The chute thudded open.

Was it night? Morning? Fenella had struggled to keep a mental grasp on what day it was, but her mind wandered, lost in misery and pain. The cell was icy cold. She lay in a tight ball on the frigid stone floor, shivering. She wore nothing but the thin gown of scarlet silk she had been arrested in at the brothel, the top of it clammy-wet from the water chute, the skirt ripped at the knee, the hem foul with her vomit. Her hair was coldly damp, tendrils plastered to her neck like snakes. Her teeth chattered.

Sewage gurgled in the shallow trench that ran under the wall from other cells and snaked out under the far wall. The stench made her stomach heave, and watery vomit shot to her mouth. She spat it out as far away as she could without moving, desperate to stay coiled, trapping what little body heat she had. The acid taste of bile made her choke. Tears of shame stung her eyes . . . shame and fury and fear. To be left here like an animal . . .

Her tears spilled, stinging her cracked lips. *So thirsty!* She craved water, but the memory of the torrent clogging her nose and mouth brought back a wave of horror. Thirst and horror clashed in her mind . . . craving water and terror of water. . . . *I'll soon go mad.*

The door clanged open. She froze, eyes straining in the gloom to make out the man who walked in. Redbeard? Would he drag her back to the room with the water chute? She couldn't bear it again . . . the agony of near drowning . . . she felt she would tell Alba about the cove even before the chute opened!

The man came to her and stood over her. Not Redbeard. It was Carlos Valverde.

"Can you stand?" he asked. He offered his hand.

Hope stabbed her. Was he taking pity? He had before, at his stable. Would he give her water? A blanket? Even . . . dear God . . . free her? She took his rough hand. It felt so warm she knew how icy hers was. She struggled to get up. Once she was on her feet Valverde let go of her hand. His face was unreadable, a stony mask, but did she see sympathy flicker in his eyes?

"You didn't tell me you were working with Adam Thornleigh and the rebels."

"I'm not."

He frowned at her, not believing. "So you decided all by yourself to kill Alba? To use me to get near him and shoot him?"

"Yes, by myself. He deserves to die."

"He believes you're Thornleigh's accomplice."

Again, it stunned her. "Who told him that?"

"I don't know. *Are* you?"

She closed her eyes, hugged herself at the cold realization that she was utterly on her own. "You wouldn't understand."

"I'm not sure I want to." His eyes went hard. "Are you ready to cooperate?"

Why had she thought there could be any hope? Valverde was Alba's creature. "I suppose you're a hero for saving his life," she said bitterly. "Ha. You're just another of his murdering henchmen."

He ignored her malice. "*Do* you know where Thornleigh is?"

"I didn't tell Alba, so why would I tell you?"

"Don't fight me. I'm trying to help you."

"By betraying your brother-in-law?"

"He's used to looking out for himself. Alba's got patrols checking every beach and every bay for miles up and down the coast and they haven't found him yet. You need to think of saving *yourself*. Tell Alba what he wants and he'll spare your life."

She suddenly understood, and it startled her. "Spare me . . . for *your* sake?"

He nodded. It amazed her, and she felt a warm wave of gratitude. Then reality came roaring back. "What's the point? He'd never let me go. I'd live out my days in a dungeon as a bag of bones."

He said nothing for a moment. He knew it was true. "Where there's life, there's hope. Take this offer. It's your only chance."

Hope. Perhaps one day a pardon? Or escape? It was possible . . . *freedom.* Her legs felt weak at the glorious thought. Suddenly, she hated Valverde for offering it, torturing her with it. The price of hope was delivering Adam to his enemy. She forced what strength she could into her voice. "Never."

He let out a ragged breath of regret. Then he motioned to a man behind him. "Bring her." The man stepped forward. Redbeard. "No manacles," Valverde said.

Redbeard took her elbow, pulling her toward the door. Fenella balked, fear swamping her. "What's happening?" Neither man answered. Redbeard pushed her out the door.

They walked down the dim stone corridor, Fenella shakily following Valverde, with Redbeard behind her. Valverde stopped at a scarred wooden door, closed but with its iron bar lifted. The door was new to Fenella. *Not the water chute room, thank God.* Then the thought struck her: *Something worse? The rack?* Would Alba tear her arms and legs from their sockets to get what he wanted? Fear made her tremble. Valverde opened the door. Redbeard prodded Fenella, and when she resisted he shoved her inside.

The room was not much bigger than the cell she'd come from but not as dark. A torch blazed from a wall sconce. Fenella shuddered, seeing Alba, his granite-gray eyes. The torchlight sheened his black satin doublet like the wet black walls of the water room. She caught the look that passed between him and Valverde, saw the question in Alba's eyes, and the answer in Valverde's as he shook his head. Their collusion horrified her. *How do they know so much about me?* She looked around the room. No rack. No instruments of torture at all, just a barren space. But in the far shadows stood another man, a guard beside him. The man stepped forward into the light.

Fenella's heart leapt to her throat. Claes!

How thin he was! How filthy, his fair hair matted, his beard crusted with dry blood, his lips scabbed. His dingy shirt hung like a rag from his bony shoulders, and bruises darkened his eyebrow ridge and neck. He stared at her as though in disbelief, and she read in his face the same wild mix of emotions that coursed through her. Confusion. Joy. Dread.

The joy won out. *He's alive!* She rushed to him and threw her arms around his neck.

His body trembled. Slowly, his arms enfolded her. He tightened his embrace, and she felt he was straining to hold back a sob. He said in her ear, his voice a rasp, "I'm sorry . . . so sorry. My fault. They only brought you because of me."

She realized: *He doesn't know.* "No," she whispered back, her heart breaking. "You're not to blame. It's me. . . . I tried to shoot him."

He released her, gaping at her in wonder. "What? How—"

"Very touching," Alba interrupted. "The happy couple."

Fenella stiffened. How had he found out that she and Claes were married? A thought clawed at her. *Marguerite . . . Jacques. Had one of them shrieked the truth under torture?*

"Now," Alba said, "let's proceed to business."

Claes tore his eyes off Fenella and turned to him. "Let her go. You've got me."

Alba snorted in derision. Dread crept over Fenella. Why had he brought her and Claes together?

"Let her go," Claes repeated, "and I promise I'll recant on the scaffold before I die. I'll tell the world I've been wrong to oppose you."

Alba ignored him, his whole attention on Fenella. "As I said, to business. Where is Thornleigh?"

Claes looked amazed at the name. "The English baron?" His eyes flicked to Fenella, a question burning in them: *Why is he asking you?*

She felt them both staring at her. She could not think.

"The pirate," Alba said. "Tell me where he's hiding and I'll let your husband keep his ears."

She froze. *His ears?*

Claes grabbed her hand. His fingers were bones of ice. "Tell him nothing, Fenella."

Redbeard pulled her away from Claes. "Take your hands off me!" she cried, and shook off his grip.

Alba beckoned the guard behind Claes. The man stepped forward and took hold of him. Alba pointed to the floor, and the guard forced Claes down to his knees and bound his hands behind his back. Alba turned to Valverde. "He's your prize; you brought him in. Take his ears, if you want."

Valverde growled, "I'm no butcher." He shot a last look at Fenella, one of furious frustration. He turned and stalked out.

Alba beckoned Redbeard, who stepped between Claes and Fenella and unsheathed a long knife. He held the knife an inch above Claes's ear and looked to Alba, waiting for the order.

Alba said to Fenella, "What's it to be?"

Her breath stopped. She stared at Claes. His body was rigid, his mouth clamped tight, readying for the pain. He looked up at her with haggard eyes. "Tell him nothing."

She could not move, in awe of Claes's courage.

"Nothing," he urged. "Or what did Johan die for?"

Redbeard kicked him in the stomach. He doubled over with a groan. Redbeard snatched his hair and yanked his head up, the knife poised again over his ear.

Fenella looked in agony at Alba. He was unyielding, his face as cold as stone. No plea would move him. She swallowed. She looked straight into his eyes and said steadily, "I don't know the man you mean."

Don't look away. She turned to Claes. Her only hope—*his* only hope—was to show Alba that this wouldn't work.

Alba motioned to Redbeard. The knife sliced. Claes screamed. The ear tumbled. Blood spurted.

"Claes!" Fenella cried.

Redbeard let go of his hair and Claes swayed, moaning, eyes glazed in pain.

Fenella lurched to him and dropped to her knees and took him in her arms. "Claes . . . Claes," she murmured in anguish. His head lolled on her shoulder. His warm blood soaked the silk, wetting her skin.

"Where is Thornleigh?" Alba demanded.

With a snarl she twisted around on her knees and lunged for him. Her fingers raked his knee. Redbeard behind her snatched her shoulders and yanked her so hard she sprawled on her back with a cry of pain.

"Every time you refuse to answer," Alba said, "my man will hack another part off your husband. His other ear. A hand. His nose."

She struggled to get up. She was too shaky to get further than her hands and knees.

"Answer now," Alba said, "or watch him bleed to death."

"Don't believe him," Claes breathed. His voice was feeble, but he stood tall on his knees now, blood streaming down his neck. "He wants me alive . . . until the execution. My death . . . a show." He struggled to keep upright, to focus his eyes on her. "You won't change that."

She gaped at him. He knew he was doomed. She sank back on her knees, stunned. Her heart bled for him.

"Say nothing," he breathed.

Tears stung her throat. *If he can be strong, so can I.* She looked up at Alba, wishing she could claw out his eyes. She said again, "I know nothing."

Was it morning or night? Fenella no longer cared. Sleep was fits of exhausted stupor shattered by wakefulness. Her nerve was shredded, her passionate fury drained. In her dank cell she lay curled up on the floor, clinging to her knees for the thin warmth it gave. They had brought her crusts of bread, but barely enough to fill her mouth, and her empty stomach roiled. They had given her water, but never enough, and thirst burned her throat. The constant headache hammered. Images of Claes tormented her . . . the bleeding, ravaged side of his head . . . his heartbreaking bravery. Alba had not mutilated him further. Claes had been right about that. Alba could not let him bleed to death. He wanted him alive for the grand public spectacle of his execution.

The door clanged open. She scarcely flinched. Hope for herself did not even cross her mind. She knew she was going to die one way or another. The certainty of that gave her a strange sense of peace. It took the place of fear, even of strength. She would die, and so would Claes. Nothing could change that. The only hope she still held on to was that she would not tell Alba about Adam and the cove no matter what agonies he had in store for her. She had to stay silent. For Adam . . . for Claes, too, to honor the suffering he'd so bravely endured.

There were four guards this time and their faces were new to her. Their clothes were far better than Redbeard's. Peacock-blue doublets, all cut the same. She had seen these blue uniforms outside on duty in the market square. Soldiers of the palace guard. This prison lay beneath Alba's palace.

"Get up," the captain told her. He tossed a bundle beside her. "Get dressed."

She felt the bundle. Clean clothes! It so enticed her, a spurt of strength pushed her to her feet and with trembling fingers she untied the shawl that wrapped the folded garments. There was a shift of clean, sweet-smelling linen. A wool dress of sage green, simple, warm! Worsted wool stockings. A forest-green shawl. It was like a gift from heaven . . . but why? She looked at the captain's disinterested face and knew it was pointless to ask. She hardly cared, so eager was she to get out of her thin, filthy gown and into the clean, warm things. Her hand was on the lacing of her sleeve, ready to untie it and undress—she was waiting only for the guards to step outside. They did not move. *No privacy*, she realized bitterly. Did they think she could fly out of the cell like some witch? "Will you turn away, at least?" she asked.

Silence. *To hell with the bastards. Let them look.* She stared straight back at the captain as she stripped naked. Slipping into the fresh clothes felt delicious, as soothing as balm.

As soon as she was dressed and wrapping the shawl around her for its welcome warmth, they marched her out of the cell, the captain ahead of her, the other three behind. Marched her along the windowless stone corridor the opposite direction of the way she'd been taken to Claes. The corridor went on so long she realized it must be a tunnel. She stumbled several times, her muscles weak. They went up a stone staircase that wound around and around, going up two stories. Then along another corridor, this one with a wooden floor and plaster walls and daylight let in by some unseen window. She tugged the shawl tighter around her. "Where are you taking me?"

Silence. The captain opened a door, and when Fenella and the soldiers followed him through it she took in a startled breath. The corridor was gorgeously paneled in gleaming hardwood, lined with colorful religious paintings, bright with sunshine from tall windows. She squinted in the light like a mole flushed from the dark earth. She was inside Alba's palace.

Maidservants in starched livery walked this way and that, going about their tasks, eyes down in subservience. A young clerk cast a curious look at Fenella as he bustled past, a thick ream of paper tucked under his arm. Two black-robed priests ambled ahead of them, deep in private talk. Fenella was unnerved by the casual, workaday atmosphere, everything so jarringly normal when she was likely on her way to die. She heard a lady's faint laugh down a connecting corridor and caught a scent of rose-water perfume. It sent a shiver of longing through her, a longing to live! She squelched it. She had signed her own death warrant when she'd aimed her pistol at Alba. She accepted that. She'd known the risks of capture, and the consequences. As for Alba's offer of sparing her life, allowing her to live out her days in madness in a dungeon in exchange for Adam's whereabouts, that was easy. She would rather slit her own throat.

The captain opened a door. He jerked his head, an order for Fenella to enter. She stepped through the door alone. It closed behind her. She was in a long gallery that overlooked a soaring great hall; the gallery ran all the way around it. The length of the gallery that she stood in was spacious, colonnaded and chandeliered, but quiet, empty of people. Between two nearby columns nestled a luxurious private oasis: two opposing settees cushioned in gold velvet. Fenella saw, past the near column, the edge of a small dining table whose white damask tablecloth was spread with silver platters of food. She took a curious step forward, and stopped abruptly when Alba came into view around the column. He sat at the table, his gouty foot resting on a gold velvet footstool. Before him was a platter of dark-sauced meat. On a small, silver plate he was cutting an orange into sections.

"Come," he said, beckoning her. "Join me, won't you?"

Fenella did not move, bewildered, confused. Why had he brought her here? Everything in her recoiled at the thought of coming near him. Then a thought gripped her: *Grab a knife and stab his throat.* But a glance at the gallery behind the colonnade revealed a half-dozen soldiers spread out against the wall. They stood on guard, as still as the paintings ranged above them. One word to them from Alba, one look, and soldiers would surround her.

"Do join me," he insisted. "This roast venison with tarragon sauce is very good."

The rich aromas made her mouth water. Roasted meat. Oniony, herbed gravy. A macabre thought came to her: *the last supper.* The dark humor of it almost made her smile. Since death was coming anyway, why not enjoy the bastard's fine food? *And show him a brave face.* She came to the table, glad she could hold her head high, though hating that her legs were still shaky.

"Excellent." He indicated the orange he was cutting. "Here, let me offer you some of this. Do sit."

She stayed on her feet. "What have you done with my husband?"

"Nothing. For the moment." He finished cutting. The orange lay in a star of six sections. "From Seville. Delicious. Tangy sweet."

"The only good thing you Spaniards brought with you."

"Do have some." He impaled a wedge and offered it up to her.

She took it. Bit into it. Orange sunshine burst in her mouth.

"Do sit," he said.

She stayed on her feet, letting the juice run cool and sweet down her throat. She swallowed it. Her stomach gurgled at the shock.

"We bring far more, you know," he said soberly. "Centuries of civilization to enlighten these crude people. The glories of the one true Church. Salvation for their heretic souls."

"You've brought terror." She tossed the orange rind on the floor. "You are hated."

He smiled thinly. "Terror is an effective start to establishing order. Frightened people do as they are told." He heaved a sigh. "The fact is, I have sacrificed four years of my life to this wretched place and would like nothing more than to return to my quiet villa in Spain and play with my grandchildren and eat oranges. But my king still needs me here, to bring harmony and stability to these fractious people, and I am but a servant of my king. So here I remain." He cocked his head at her. "Enough about me. Let's talk about you." He moved the platter of venison closer to him, thin slices bathed in glistening red-brown sauce, and picked up a serving spoon. "I've learned quite a bit about you, Mistress Doorn. You're an intelligent woman, and enterprising. I admire how you built your ship salvage business on Sark."

A *business I'll never see again*, she thought with a pang.

"We know that's where Thornleigh went after he sank the *Esperanza*. To Sark." He lifted a slice of the venison with the serving spoon and slid it onto a plate. "And we know that you then sailed with him to His Majesty's lands here. Is that where you two became close, you and Thornleigh, on the voyage? Is that when you fell in love with him?"

She gaped at him. *How could he know that?*

He smiled. "Your face tells me I'm right. I thought it must be so. Why else would you keep so loyally silent in the face of my . . . persuasions?"

"Is that why you've brought me here? For more persuasion?"

"If you call kindness persuasion, then yes." He spooned sauce over the meat. "Tell me where I can find Thornleigh and you will never see a dungeon again. You will enjoy dishes like these, the most succulent fare my kitchens offer, and tonight you will sleep in a soft feather bed." He held up the plate, offering it to her.

Did he really think a full belly would make her betray Adam? "You're a fool."

"I fear you underestimate me." He set down the plate, nudging it closer to her. "A feather bed not just for tonight, but every night for the rest of your life, back in your native country. Edinburgh is a fine city for starting again. How does that sound?"

"Like the words of a liar."

He settled back in his chair, studying her. "He's married, you know. Thornleigh."

She sneered. Of course she knew.

"And has children," he added. "A boy of nine and a girl of twelve. Did you know that his wife, Lady Thornleigh, lives here in Brussels with them? Thornleigh tried to abduct the children. He failed."

She stifled a gasp. *Failed!* It wrenched her heart. *Poor Adam . . . getting his children meant so much to him.* She felt a sting of tears. *He loves them so.*

Alba was watching her closely. "After that, his wife feared for their lives, so she brought them to me. The boy and girl are now my guests. Right here in the palace."

What does this have to do with me? she thought, forcing back her tears. The smell of the rich food suddenly made her queasy, her stomach rocky. Alba's talk was sickening and pointless. She would rather be back in her frigid cell than listen to his gabble. She took the plate of venison and gravy and dumped it on the tablecloth. It slewed across the damask in a lumpy, glistening pool. "I am not hungry for meat bought with the blood of Dutchmen. Nor for a feather bed bought with their heads. I'll keep to my solitary cell, if you please." She glared at him. "The company is better."

His face was as still as stone. Except for a twitch of his mouth. "Perhaps you do not understand how important capturing Thornleigh is to His Majesty. The man is a scourge to Spain. When he pirated His Majesty's pay ship carrying gold for my troops, he almost sparked a war, and he continues to attack our peaceful merchant mariners, robbing them and killing them. I have sworn to rid the seas of his evil, for my king." He added with quiet menace, "And for the honor of my house. When Thornleigh sank the *Esperanza* he captured Don Alfonso Santillo de Albarado de Cavazos, my nephew. Don Alfonso has not been seen since. Thornleigh murdered him."

"Ha! You're wrong." She itched to tell him. "It was me. I shot your nephew's damned head off." The words were out and she did not regret them. At Alba's look of amazement, satisfaction swept through her, a rush of warmth like brandy. He was going to hang her no matter what, and Claes would die, too. Nothing would change that. But for this moment, she savored her small victory. "I'd do it again," she said.

He did not take his eyes off her as he raised his arm to beckon a soldier. A lean, helmeted captain with a pockmarked face came immediately to his side, his sword clanking in its scabbard. Alba nodded to him, a silent command. The captain turned and left them.

Fenella held her breath. What was happening?

Alba ignored her. He served himself a slice of venison from the platter and cut a bite. He chewed it thoughtfully, then drank some wine, a small mouthful, a slow swallow, then set down the goblet. He lifted the damask napkin from his lap and dabbed his mouth, then used the napkin to wipe a trace of gravy from his fingertips. Then he stood. "Come with me," he said. "I want to show you something."

He did not wait for Fenella. But he did not go far, only to the gallery railing that overlooked the great hall. Though it was just steps away, she did not follow him. She would not give him the satisfaction.

"Handsome children, are they not?" he said, looking down at the hall. "Thornleigh's young ones."

Her ears pricked up at the sound of a child's voice. Curiosity leapt in her. She went to the railing and looked down. The hall was vacant except for the pock-faced captain strolling in with two children, a boy in a russet velvet doublet and a tall, slim girl in a violet-colored satin gown, her chestnut hair hanging loose. Both were looking around as though surprised to be there but curious and eager, as though playing a game of hide-and-seek. Fenella watched them, transfixed. Were they Adam's son and daughter? The captain was speaking to the boy, who said something in return. Their voices echoed up from the marble floor, the man's deep, the boy's light, their words indistinct.

"I daresay you have never met them," Alba said, glancing at Fenella. "Just as I have not met the father. Are they like him, would you say? I've heard that Thornleigh has dark hair and eyes, like his boy there."

She could not take her eyes off the children. They were so like Adam! Their names came to her. Katherine—so pretty!—and Robert. The sight of his tousled dark hair and inquisitive eyes squeezed Fenella's heart. Two more soldiers walked in and flanked the girl, who looked up from one to the other, a question in her eyes and a faint smile on her lips, like someone who'd been promised a treat.

"So young and innocent," Alba said.

Fenella looked at him and dread seeped into her like ice water. *Why has he brought Adam's children before me?*

"Too young to die, I'm sure you agree."

She froze. "You would not."

"And *will* not, if you tell me where their father is hiding."

Her gaze flicked to the children in horror.

"The girl first, I think. It will require a story for their mother, but so be it." He shrugged. "Lady Thornleigh thinks she is important to me. She is not. I entertain many English exiles, and most have titles far grander than hers." His eyes bored into Fenella's. "Speak now. Or see the girl die."

A hoarse sound came from Fenella's throat, a dry laugh of total disbelief. No, he could not mean it. It was impossible, even for him!

"Obstinate woman," he growled. He jerked a nod to the pocked captain. The captain grabbed the girl from behind, his arm like a bolt across her narrow chest, and unsheathed his sword with a screech of metal. He drew the blade across the girl's throat, slow and smooth. Blood spurted. The girl twitched. Then slumped to the floor.

Fenella's heart stopped. *No . . . No! . . .*

The boy was screaming. The soldiers held him between them.

"Tell me now," Alba said, "or the boy is next."

She could not breathe. The sight gutted her . . . the rag doll girl . . . the pool of blood. . . .

Suddenly Fenella was climbing. She planted a foot on the top of the railing. Grappled it to swing herself up. *Up and over. Jump. Die. End this. He'll let the boy go. . . .*

"What?" Alba cried. "What are you doing?"

She made it to the top, stood with both feet on the railing, her stance wide, swaying for balance. *Jump. Die. End this!* She spread her arms, closed her eyes, ready to pitch forward.

He snatched the back of her dress and yanked. She tumbled backward, flailing at air. The side of her head and her hip struck the floor. Her vision swam bloodied. Sprawled at Alba's feet, she clutched his ankle. He clamped the back of her neck and twisted her head, forcing her to look down between the posts. "Look."

She blinked at the horror. The dead girl . . . the captain, sword raised as he held the squirming, screaming boy, waiting for Alba's command.

Vomit shot up Fenella's throat. "Stop! . . . I'll tell you. . . . Don't!" She gagged on her vomit. Forced it down. Swallowed it. Sucked in air that cut her throat like a knife. "Cove . . ." she moaned, "village of Kloster . . . hiding . . . cove . . ."

❧18❧

The Duchess's Coach

Into the lion's den, Isabel Valverde thought with a shiver as she entered the hall in the Duke of Alba's palace. Alba's torturers mauled people as viciously as any lion. Gentlemen strolled past her, greeting one another, exchanging pleasantries. She felt almost ill at being here.

The footman she was following guided her up to the second floor and down a corridor to a small suite of rooms. Isabel steeled herself. She had come to see her brother's wife and must show Frances a brave face. The baby inside Isabel kicked, and her hand went to her belly. In five or six weeks she would have this new babe to protect as well as Andrew and Nell. Thinking of her children gave her strength for what she was about to do. Today was her last day in Brussels. Never again would she have to stomach Alba's hideous regime. She was going home to England. Without Carlos.

Frances came out of the adjoining room, fastening her cloak. Leaving already? Yet Isabel had been prompt in arriving for the appointment. The note she'd sent Frances early this morning at the Duchess of Feria's home asking to visit had brought her sister-in-law's terse reply, an instruction to wait on her at the palace at ten o'clock. It was not yet ten.

Seeing her, Frances stopped and regarded her coolly. "Isabel. Your message took me very much by surprise."

"I daresay, Frances. But after all, family is family."

Kate and Robert came out of the adjoining room, and relief rushed through Isabel at seeing her niece and nephew safe. Last night, when Carlos had told her of Alba's horrifying action of having a child killed in front of the Scottish woman, it had almost made Isabel sick to her stomach. Alba had had two child beggars brought from the street, Carlos had learned, and dressed them in fine clothes to convince the woman they were Adam's son and daughter, a hideous ploy to induce her to reveal Adam's whereabouts. The girl's throat had been slit. Reeling at this atrocity, Isabel had then been amazed to learn from Carlos that the woman was believed to be an accomplice in Adam's work with the Sea Beggars. It was dizzying. . . . Isabel knew no details, only what Carlos had brusquely outlined. But she'd been galvanized by the horror of the girl's death to take action to get herself and her own children out of this cursed country. Alba had ordered another mass hanging for this afternoon in the Grote Markt. So much death . . . it rocked her. She *had* to get out before the killings began.

Kate's eyes went wide with surprise when she saw her aunt. "Madam!" She rushed to Isabel and bobbed a curtsy. "Oh, it has been so long!"

What a young beauty Adam's daughter had become! Isabel had to smile despite her anxiety. "Too long, my dear." She embraced the girl as closely as her pregnant state would allow.

Kate's hand flew to her mouth in concern. "Have you brought word of my father? Is he in England? Is he ill?"

"Enough!" Frances snapped. "You know I will not hear him spoken of."

Kate held her tongue, but with a look of furious resentment. Her mother glared back at her. The girl's spirit moved Isabel, and her heart ached for Adam's sake. She wished it were in her power to take his children home with her. What would become of them here, fatherless? Robert was staring at her, and she saw confusion in his eyes. He had been only five when he'd last seen her four years ago, and she guessed that he was struggling to remember who she was. He made a childish bow to her, then continued to stare, his head jerking oddly. A tic, she realized, feeling pity. The boy was without a father and had a traitor for a mother.

A traitor that I must now charm.

A young priest appeared at the door. "Lady Frances, we are behind our time."

"Quite right, Father." Frances clapped her hands at the children. "To your lessons now with Father André. Katherine, at my next visit you will recite the Order's rules on the patience and perseverance of prayer, or your meals will be bread and water until you can. The Sisters will not take a dunce for a novice." She turned to Robert with a motherly smile and patted his cheek. "Go."

The children bowed to her and to Isabel, then trudged out the door after the priest.

"I am glad to see my niece and nephew so hale," Isabel said. "I can only imagine the depth of your own relief."

"Pardon?" Frances gave her a quizzical, impatient look that made Isabel wonder: *Has she not heard of Alba's abominable act?* It seemed impossible; gossip was rife. More likely she did know and was unmoved—a chilling thought. Frances's consideration for the young did not extend to beggars.

"They are hale indeed, and I was just leaving," she said, adjusting her cloak. "Why did you ask to see me? What do you want?"

Isabel forced a smile. "Peace, Frances. I hope we can mend the rift that has kept us apart. There was a time when we were friends."

"Long past."

"Yet I remember those days fondly. Don't you?" She had helped Frances through her difficult first labor, had delivered Kate, placing the babe into Frances's exhausted and grateful arms. "I'll never forget your face at that first sight of your daughter."

"Ah . . . yes." There was a softening in her voice, a note of regret. "You were kind."

"You were brave." Isabel smiled.

Frances, however, looked newly wary. "Come, Isabel, what has brought you? You must want something."

"I have heard that your friend the Duchess of Feria is ill. I hope it is not serious?"

"An ague. It will pass."

"She keeps to her bed, though, I'm told."

Frances's eyes narrowed in suspicion. "What concern is that of yours?"

"I have not met the duchess, but I'm sure she is aware that my husband is a trusted commander in the governor's service."

"Yes, Alba holds Valverde in high regard, I believe. What on earth are you getting at?"

"I need your help, Frances. I am leaving Brussels. With my children."

"What?" She was all astonishment.

"I will not pretend to you. Carlos and I feel very differently about the Spanish occupation, and have for some time. He sees honor and duty in keeping his commitment to Alba. I see suffering and unrest, an uprising in the making. Danger. I do not want my child to be born here. So I am going home, and taking Andrew and Nell. We'll sail from Antwerp." Her hand went to her belly. "But I am almost eight months gone, Frances, and you know how punishing thirty hard miles on horseback would be in this condition. It's not my comfort that concerns me; it's the safety of the babe. So I have come to ask a favor. Your friend the duchess has a coach. Given her illness, she has no need for it at the moment. Would you intercede on my behalf, and ask her for a day's use of the coach to take us to Antwerp? I warrant the coachmen will have it back overnight."

Frances regarded her sister-in-law thoughtfully, as though considering her dilemma with some sympathy but weighing what benefit the favor would bring to herself.

Isabel said with feeling, "We may have different beliefs, Frances, but we share one thing in common. We have both fallen out with our husbands for their actions on opposite sides of the Spanish cause. Broken marriage . . . it's a cross we both bear." She reached out for her hand. "Please, be my sister in this? Be a friend to my unborn child, as I once was to yours."

Frances blinked at her. Whether she was moved or dismayed Isabel could not tell. "When would you want the coach?"

"Today. Right now."

"But your children—"

"They're packed, ready. I shall collect them on the way. If you'll just help us with the duchess . . ."

A wistful look came over Frances. "I knew her when she was simple Jane Dormer, you know, long before she caught the eye of the late duke. We are old friends."

"Then you'll ask her?"

"No need. I take the coach whenever I wish. Come back with me to her house. You shall have the coach. If you will do me a favor in return."

Isabel hesitated. "If I can."

"Oh, it is not difficult. I would merely have you deliver a letter. To a friend in London."

Caution pricked Isabel. She had heard enough to suspect that Frances was scheming against Queen Elizabeth with her fellow Catholic exiles here. It was no secret that they wanted to see their favorite, Mary Stuart, Queen of the Scots, on England's throne, and rumor said that they hoped to entice Philip of Spain into backing them with troops. Frances had likely forged her friendship with Alba to further this plan. And no doubt the exiles kept their English friends abreast of developments. If Isabel delivered her sister-in-law's letter, would she herself be an accomplice to treason?

That's unknowable, she decided. *While my present mission is clear.* She could waste no more time. "Certainly, Frances. It will be my pleasure."

They took the litter Isabel had come in and reached the duchess's mansion with its granite columns facing Balienplein Place. The business of ordering the coach was quickly done. It clattered up to the front entrance, an impressive sight: two white horses drawing a vehicle gorgeously painted in primrose and forest green, two coachmen in livery of the same color scheme, the coach doors emblazoned with the gold crest of the Duchess of Feria. Frances gave Isabel the sealed letter, then told the coachmen they would be picking up the lady's passengers. "Follow her instructions."

The two women shared an awkward, tense moment, both of

them aware that this might be the last time they would see each other, both silent about the man in their thoughts, Isabel's brother, Frances's husband. A brisk "Good-bye" from Frances, a gentle "God be with you" from Isabel, who then climbed into the primrose velvet cushions of the coach.

She had never been inside such a conveyance—popular with the Continent's rich, coaches were still not common in England—and she was thrilled by how swiftly it flew down the street, for she had told the coachmen to make all haste. People on foot and on horseback quickly moved aside to let the noblewoman's coach pass. Isabel took a grateful, nervous breath. She would be in Antwerp by evening.

Church bells all over the city were ringing the mid-afternoon hour as the coach jounced toward the Laeken Gate, the most northern exit in the city wall. Isabel knew the tolling bells summoned citizens to attend the executions at the Grote Markt, and her heart was beating fast as she watched people leaving their houses and shops. She was not clear of the city yet, but on one score she took comfort. She had lied to Frances when she'd said she would collect Andrew and Nell. They were already gone. Early this morning Isabel had sent them to the canal wharf in the care of Hughes, a loyal manservant, to take the Antwerp-bound barge. At the port they would embark for England, and there Hughes would deliver them to Isabel's mother in London. No matter what happened now, Isabel could trust that her children were safe.

But was Carlos? Was she in time? The questions drummed inside her head as the church bells clanged. Were the executions in progress? Carlos had faced past dangers on battlefields and Isabel had often feared for his life, but never as acutely as she did at this moment. If he failed, Alba's wrath would be terrible. She feared . . . and she hoped. And never had she loved her husband more.

The crowd's too thin, Carlos thought, feeling on edge. *I need a bigger turnout.* On horseback he was leading his small execution party toward the Grote Markt, dead ahead at the end of the house-lined street. Behind him his four mounted soldiers escorted the horse-drawn wagon that held the two prize prisoners, the rebel leader Claes Doorn and his wife.

A boy darted across Carlos's path and he reined in Fausto. The stallion snorted, as edgy as Carlos himself. He touched his spurs to Fausto's flanks and trotted on. The street widened into the broad square of the Grote Markt and Carlos saw with relief that he'd been wrong about the crowd—it was as large as usual. *Good.* The air hummed with the people's excitement. Two corpses already hung from the gibbets. Over a dozen more prisoners were corralled in a pen, awaiting their turn. On one side of the scaffold an executioner stood beside a butcher's block where Doorn's special agony would take place: castration, then his abdomen would be slit and his entrails drawn out before his dying eyes.

Guards cut down the two dead rebels. A roar went up from the crowd. Church bells rang.

Carlos looked to the side of the square. Stands had been erected for the Spanish dons and the city's magistrates and leading burghers. On the top tier, under a canopy, sat Alba with his cane. As usual he was flanked by his Spanish advisers. He looked relaxed, chatting with one of them.

Carlos glanced behind him. The wagon was open, its wooden sides cut down to waist height so that people had a good view of the prisoners. The condemned couple stood on either side, their hands bound behind them and tied to the wagon side. Doorn, the earless side of his head crusted with dry blood, looked delirious from his ordeal, barely able to stay on his feet on the jostling platform. Fenella was white-faced, her haggard eyes on her husband. Men and women jeered them as they passed. The soldier driving the wagon grinned vacantly. He was a slow-witted veteran who'd suffered a head wound that left him good only for menial tasks. Carlos had picked him specially for this job.

They had reached the rear edge of the mob. Most of the crowd were looking forward, eyes on the scaffold where the next two prisoners were being led from the pen to the gibbets. Few had noticed Carlos's party yet. Carlos's instructions were to escort the condemned in a wide circle around the crowd toward the scaffold, moving slowly so that everyone could view the prize couple in the wagon. He would bring them past the dignitaries' stand for Alba's viewing. When they reached the scaffold, trumpeters would announce their arrival.

Carlos turned in the saddle and held up his hand to his men. "Halt."

The dull-eyed veteran on the seat tugged the reins, stopping the draft horse. The wagon creaked to a halt. The four mounted men stopped, too, and looked at Carlos, awaiting his order.

"We turn west." He pointed down the street that led to the canal.

His horsemen exchanged puzzled looks.

"Now," Carlos ordered.

The driver, mindlessly obeying, flicked the reins and the wagon began moving. The horsemen, too, turned their mounts to the street Carlos indicated.

He led them, uneasy, a prickle of sweat on his back. Was the crowd big enough after all to mask his detour? He heard the wagon creak behind him, heard the slow-clomping hooves of the nag and of his men's horses. He longed to order them to speed up, but that might raise suspicion—not from his men, who would do what he commanded, but from people in the street who were heading in the opposite direction, toward the execution square. If even one of them mentioned the odd occurrence to a guard there and the guard sent word up to Alba's lieutenants, Alba would send men galloping after Carlos.

He dared a glance back. Fenella gaped at him in stunned wonder. Doorn seemed unaware, feverish, barely conscious. Behind them, Alba's form in the stands was small as it receded, and Carlos could not tell where the man was looking. Was he watching in astonishment as his prize prisoners were taken away? *If so, I'll soon be kicking from one of those gibbets.*

Willing that thought away, he turned and straightened in the saddle. Last night, telling Isabel about the murdered beggar girl, he'd known she was right about Alba. No pension was worth working for such a man. Back in England Carlos would have to deal with his rocky finances, but that lay in the future—that is, if he lived to see England again. Right now, the decision to try to save

Fenella and her husband made him strangely exhilarated. Death might be his reward. But he had faced death before. *As long as Isabel got away, it's worth it.*

The canal was not far—it ran through the city center—and in five minutes they reached the wharf. It was busy, bustling with merchants and barge hands, travelers with baggage, customers at chandlery sheds. A few looked with curiosity at the prisoners in the wagon led by the breast-plated commander and his men, but the Spanish martial presence throughout the city was too familiar a sight to raise concern.

Carlos halted the party. He turned Fausto. "The prisoners are going to Antwerp," he told his men. "From there they'll sail to Spain to be executed for His Majesty's view. The Antwerp Guard on the barge will take over from here. You're dismissed." He ordered them back to barracks.

They looked mildly surprised at being freed from duty so early in the day but far from unwilling. They nodded to him and turned their mounts. Carlos watched them trot away.

He dismounted. "You too, Freyer," he told the veteran on the wagon seat. "Back to barracks. Down you get."

Freyer made no objection to the unusual command that would leave the wagon driverless. He climbed down.

"Walk straight back. No stopping."

The man blinked at Carlos for a moment. Then, obeying orders as he had done all his life, he turned and trudged down the bustling wharf.

Carlos led Fausto to the back of the wagon and tied the reins to it.

"Spain?" Fenella said, her voice weak, hoarse with horror. "To burn?"

He swung up onto the wagon and went to her.

"Have mercy," she said. "Kill us now." Her haggard eyes begged him. "Quick and clean. Please."

He unsheathed his sword. Doorn blinked at him with fever-fogged eyes. Fenella straightened with a spurt of strength, ready for death. "Thank you," she whispered.

Carlos sliced the blade behind her arms, severing the leather tie, cutting her free.

She rocked on her feet, gaping up at him. "What . . . ?"

He crossed to Doorn and cut him loose. Doorn slumped at the sudden freedom. Fenella rushed to him and caught him in her arms.

"Lay him down," Carlos said as he hopped off the wagon. "You too." He pulled a tarpaulin from his saddlebag and tossed it up to her. "Cover yourselves. And be prepared for a rough ride."

She blinked in shock. In hope. "Where?"

No time to talk. Guards might already be galloping this way. He left her and climbed up onto the wagon seat and flicked the reins. The horse lurched and the wagon creaked into motion. Carlos glanced back. Fenella was spreading the tarpaulin over herself and Doorn.

Carlos drove the wagon north, making for the road to Antwerp. He whipped the nag and it broke into a startled canter. The rickety wagon rattled and groaned, lurching at every turn, jouncing the couple on the hard floorboards. People lurched out of their path and Carlos glared at anyone who was slow to make way. He heard Fausto cantering in train with his smooth, powerful gait.

The Laeken Gate rose dead ahead. Two soldiers of the city guard stood viewing all who came and went. Carlos gritted his teeth and slowed the horse.

The guards were deferential to Carlos; his steel breastplate and plumed helmet were his permit. But their duty was to question all who passed on execution days. One walked to the back of the wagon, asking Carlos as a courtesy, "Where are you bound, sir?"

He mentioned a town and added loudly, "The cemetery."

The guard idly lifted a corner of the tarpaulin. Carlos threw an anxious glance over his shoulder. Would Fenella take his cue? Yes, thank God, she lay as still as death. Doorn looked unconscious, his grisly wound apparent. "The governor wants them out," Carlos said, and added quietly, as though to forestall panic lest any of the public heard, "in case it's plague."

The guard dropped the tarpaulin in revulsion. The other one had heard, too, and quickly waved Carlos through. "God speed you, sir."

As soon as they were clear of the gate he whipped the horse and the wagon rattled northward. Traffic coming onto the city was thin since it was an execution day, with many shops and markets closed. The land was flat, sparsely treed. Fields stretched out on either side, blue-flowered flax, golden barley. *No place to hide.*

Carlos reached the bisecting road that ran east toward Maastricht and the German lands and west toward Ghent and the coast. Just north of this crossroads the road rose slightly over a bridge, allowing a stream to run beneath.

Once over the bridge Carlos slowed, taking the wagon to the side of the road. The verge leading down to the stream was weedy, the water sluggish and brown. Besides the bridge, the only structure in sight was a windmill lazily moving to the east. In a distant field, men were scything grain. Behind, to the south a half mile across the flatland, the Laeken Gate was still visible. A black-robed priest on a donkey was ambling toward the bridge. In a few minutes he would reach it.

Carlos hopped down from the wagon, leaving the winded nag breathing hard. Fausto, in train, was frisky. The couple in the wagon lay unmoving under the tarpaulin. "Get down," Carlos told Fenella. "Be quick."

She looked out from under the covering, her gaunt eyes hopeful but wary as she scanned the flat countryside. Her husband lay beside her, blinking at the sky.

"Bring him, too. Can he walk?"

She helped Doorn to his feet. He groaned, as much in bewilderment as pain, it seemed to Carlos. *Fevered from his wound, for sure. Would he make it?*

"What's happening?" Fenella asked Carlos as she led Doorn to the edge of the wagon.

"Take him down there, under the bridge," Carlos told her, helping the man down. Doorn felt all bones. But there was a core of strength about him, a fierceness to resist the fever. Carlos glanced toward the oncoming priest. "Quick."

Together they led Doorn down into the tangle of weeds under the bridge. There, on the shadowed slope where the weeds were thinner, Fenella got her husband to sit. He was shivering, disoriented, pale of face.

"What's happening?" she said again to Carlos. "What are we doing here?"

"Waiting."

"For what?"

Carlos was not superstitious, but a voice inside him warned that telling the plan might curse it. He couldn't let himself think of the consequences. "Where there's life, there's hope," he said, and saw from her face that she remembered. He'd said those words to her in her dungeon cell.

"Thank you," she said shakily.

Doorn moaned. They both looked at him. "He needs water," she said.

Carlos had a wineskin of water strapped to Fausto. He was glad to be active. "Stay here," he told Fenella. He went to his horse and fetched the wineskin. The priest on his donkey was nearing, close enough now that Carlos could hear the faint clomp of the hooves. He brought back the water and Fenella helped Doorn drink it. Some dribbled over his parched lips. He raised his eyes to her as though recognizing her for the first time. He motioned for her to drink, too, an impulse more instinctive than conscious. The gesture struck Carlos. Even in extremity the man was concerned for his wife.

Isabel. Worry gripped Carlos's heart. *Did she get away?*

Fenella took a swallow of water. She looked unsteady, exhausted, beaten. Carlos had seen soldiers with that look, too traumatized to go on. She needed some good news. "The girl that Alba ordered killed," he said. "She wasn't Thornleigh's daughter." He explained that Alba had brought two beggar children from the street and dressed them in fine clothes to convince her. She looked horrified. She sat down beside Doorn, stunned, taking it in. When she looked up at Carlos again he saw a flicker of joyful relief in her eyes. She cared about Thornleigh; that was clear. Did Doorn know? No time to think about that now. "Stay here," Carlos said again, and left them to go back up to the wagon.

The priest reached the bridge, a wrinkled old man, slumped from lack of muscles. He nodded to Carlos.

"Good day, Father," Carlos said, tucking the tarpaulin into his saddlebag. The stallion blocked the priest's view of the end of the bridge and the fugitives beneath it.

The priest halted his donkey. "Trouble with your wagon, Commander?"

"Just giving the nag a rest."

"Ah," the priest said with a chuckle, "we old nags do need that from time to time." He pulled a handkerchief from his sleeve and wiped his eyes of dust from the road.

Fausto tossed his head. Carlos held the saddle horn tight to keep the stallion from moving. He could see, in the distance to the south, some movement at the Laeken Gate. A wagon coming this way. Too far to make out any details.

"Are you bound for Antwerp as I am?" the priest asked. "I'll rest with you, and then we can travel together."

"I'd like that, Father, if I weren't going the opposite way. I'm for the capital. So don't let me keep you. You'll want a bed before sundown, and your beast is slow."

The priest nodded with a sigh. "Too true." He tucked away his handkerchief, wished Carlos good day, kicked his donkey, and plodded on.

Carlos did not look at the slope beneath the bridge. The priest might glance back. Instead, Carlos watched the wagon coming from the Laeken Gate. It was coming fast.

His pulse picked up. Not a wagon. A coach. Two horses, hooves pounding the road. He watched it come on, half-hoping, half-dreading. In the silence, the windmill creaked.

Then, sunlight glinted off the door's golden crest. *Yes! The duchess's coach!*

Just before the bridge the coach clattered to a halt. Carlos swung open the door. Isabel was already on her feet, arms outstretched to him. Her smile thrilled him. So did her bravery. This rendezvous had been her idea. He'd been afraid for her safety, but she had insisted. "Are you all right?" he asked as he lifted her down.

"Yes, fine."

"Andrew and Nell?"

"Safely away this morning with Hughes."

He let out a breath of relief. All was going as they'd planned. So far.

"Where are they?" Isabel said, taking in the empty wagon in dismay. "Could you not get them?"

He glanced at the two coachmen side by side on the seat, one holding the reins, both looking at him with interest. He said in a low voice, "What about the coachmen?"

"It's all right," she assured him. "I had Frances instruct them to pick up my passengers."

Carlos had to smile. Isabel had managed things so well. "They're here. Hold on." He went down the slope and under the bridge. Fenella sat huddled in fearful anticipation with Doorn, her arm around him protectively. She must have heard the coach stop. "Don't worry," Carlos told her. "It's a friend. Come."

He got them on their feet, brought them up to the coach. "You remember my wife?"

"Madam!" Fenella exclaimed in amazement.

"Mistress Doorn," Isabel said warmly, "I heard what you've suffered, you and your husband." The sight of Doorn's blood-scabbed gash clearly rocked her.

Carlos had his eyes on movement at the Laeken Gate in the distance. Horsemen, leaving the gate. Ten or twelve of them. Galloping.

"Get in, and help him in," he told Fenella. "If anyone stops the coach my wife will say you're her servants and she's taking Doorn to a doctor. You're going to Antwerp. Then, get yourself and your husband on the first ship for England."

"Yes . . . yes." Tears sprang to her eyes. "Oh, how can we ever thank you?"

"By staying alive. Now get in."

She was so overcome, she kissed his cheek. He looked at Isabel. She saw the kiss and looked surprised, then blinked it away as though aware that in such a crisis who would *not* be overcome?

Fenella helped Doorn into the coach, then got in herself. Isabel said to Carlos with a quick smile, "I'm so big, you get in first and help me up, will you?"

He held her back. "I'm not going."

She looked appalled. "What?"

He glanced at the riders coming this way. Sunlight glinted off their breastplates and helmets. They would reach the bridge within minutes. Isabel followed his gaze. She stiffened. "Alba's men! Carlos, come! Hurry!"

"No. Get in quickly now, and go. You'll be fine."

She balked. "No! You can't stay here. They'll take you!"

"I won't stay." He untied Fausto from the back of the wagon. "I'm going to lead them away from you. When they find the wagon empty they'll come after me to find Doorn."

"But if they capture you, Alba will—"

"They won't. You know how fast the stallion is."

It was a boast inflated only with hope, and Carlos saw that she knew it. But she said nothing more, and he blessed her for that. "I'll lead them west, then turn and head for France. From Calais I'll sail home. Now go. There's no more time."

Holding Fausto's reins, he wrapped his other arm around Isabel and kissed her. A kiss to tell her all that she meant to him. A kiss to last him until he saw her again. If he lived.

"Help her in," he told Fenella.

He made sure Isabel was safely aboard, despite her look of anguish at leaving him; then he told the coachmen to drive on with haste. The coachman flicked the reins and the vehicle clattered forward.

Carlos swung up into the saddle. He watched the coach go, dust spitting from the rear wheels. Then he turned Fausto and faced the oncoming horsemen. He waited just long enough for Alba's men to spot him. His black stallion would be familiar to some of them. Waiting, he considered his chances. Fausto *was* fast. And with Isabel's kiss still on his lips he made a vow. If he lived through this he would tell her what had happened between him and Fenella in Edinburgh. Tell her before she heard it from someone else. Tell her it had meant nothing.

He kicked his spurs into Fausto's flanks and galloped west.

❧ 19 ❧

The Cove

A full moon shone over Antwerp. In the harbor, moored ships slumbered. On the wharf, fishmongers' stalls lay deserted.

Fenella tightened her arm around Claes as she led him down the fishmongers' dock, a spur of the main wharf. He was so weak she was half-dragging him. "Almost there," she promised. She looked over her shoulder in dread of seeing someone come after them. Her arm around him trembled from the strain of holding him up.

She made for the battery of fishing boats, skiffs, and rowboats bobbing in the water alongside the dock. The bright moonlight made her feel horribly exposed, like a furtive harbor rat. Thank God they were in the shadows of the harbormaster's tower. But Claes shambling beside her was so slow, like an anchor being dragged. She hated herself for thinking that about him after all he had suffered, but they had to *move*. She had to get to the cove to warn Adam. Alba's men were surely coming for him. *Because I told.* The horror of the beggar girl's murder, and the horror of how Fenella had betrayed Adam because of it, gnawed her without mercy. How she hated Alba for his unspeakable trick! She prayed that she might be wrong about Adam taking refuge in the cove, prayed that he was sailing somewhere, free, and far from Alba's reach. But if he *was* in the cove, Alba's men would soon swoop down on him.

"Just a few more steps," she assured Claes. She knew he was trying hard to keep pace. On the coach ride from Brussels he had surfaced from the worst of his fever, had regained his mental bearings at least. Valverde's wife had taken linen from her luggage and Fenella had used it to bandage the ghastly wound where Claes's ear had been severed, winding strips around his head. The journey had given him a chance to rest, enough to croak his wishes when the coach reached the wharf at sunset. Valverde's wife was preparing to board a merchant ship about to sail for Portsmouth, expecting them to come with her, but Claes had balked. "No, not England . . . not me," he had said hoarsely. "I'll stay . . . and fight."

Fenella had not anticipated that. Her thought had been to get him away to safety and then she would follow after she'd warned Adam. But Claes's refusal did not completely surprise her. He had made the rebels' cause his life. She sensed that as long as he had breath he would fight the Spaniards. As for her own plan to reach Adam, she had not told Claes, nor told Valverde's wife. Fenella couldn't bear to admit to Adam's kind sister that she had betrayed him. Besides, she was far from sure that she could warn him in time. "Madam," she had said, "I am staying, too."

"What? But you'll be safe in England. Both of you."

"Thank you, but no. There's business to be done here first. God be with you, madam, and our heartfelt thanks."

The lady had to get to England to join her children. She sailed away. Fenella and Claes waited until dark, hiding behind a wharf alehouse amid its crates and trash until the fishmongers' dock was deserted. It had meant losing a precious hour but had given her a chance to explain to Claes where she was taking him, and why.

"The English baron?" His haggard eyes were suddenly bright with anticipation. "And he's with the Sea Beggars?"

It was hard to hide the depth of her feelings for Adam. "That's what Alba told me. And I believe it."

"Good. *Very* good. We'll join them."

After that, Claes's fever seemed to drag him under again. He fought it—Fenella *saw* him fighting to stay lucid, stay strong in spirit—but his body was so weak.

Now, half-dragging him along the dock, she prayed that they weren't too late.

She chose a skiff small enough to sail single-handed. Claes was in no condition to help. The skiff was a grimy, slapped-together thing, its gunwales splintered, more a cracked cockleshell than a boat. She lugged Claes aboard, breathing hard at the weight of him, thin though he was. She settled him on a mat of rope in the stern, and he gave her a faint smile of relief that squeezed her heart. Poor Claes, what hell he had been through.

The cramped craft stank of fish, and its rigging was frayed, and as she raised the sail she saw that the canvas was patched. Her fatigued muscles were trembling as she took the helm. After the torments of the dungeon she hoped she still had the strength to sail. Blessedly, the breeze was on her starboard beam, pushing her away from the dock, and the bright moonlight now became her friend, illuminating the moored ships that she had to navigate around to get to the harbor mouth. Once clear of them she hardened the sheet and the wind caught the sail, and the skiff ghosted swiftly out of the harbor. Fenella took her first deep breath, relishing the fresh sea breeze. Freedom might not last long, but for this moment it tasted sweet.

The passage down the estuary and out to the scattered islands took six grueling hours. Claes spent it in restless half sleep. Fenella was bleary-eyed from *no* sleep and tense with worry. Had Adam already been discovered and dragged to prison? Dawn was a smudge of pearly light on the horizon when she spotted the whitish swirl of water over a rock shoal that told her she was near the cove. She stayed well clear of the shoal and scanned the aspen-thick shoreline, looking for the tall dead birch tree that marked the narrow opening to the scythe-shaped cove. Birds awaking in the trees chorused a liquid warble.

There it was, the dead birch! "Claes, wake up! We're here."

He struggled to sit up and watched as Fenella tacked the skiff and steered into the narrow opening. The wind lightened in the lee of the trees. The sail flogged, and the drop in power made steering difficult. The passage into the cove curled like a nautilus, and as Fenella rounded the last of the curve she saw two ships lying at anchor. *Adam!*

But no . . . her heart plunged. Neither vessel was the *Elizabeth*. Who were these interlopers?

Horror surged through her. Spaniards? Had they taken Adam away?

Fool! I've sailed right into the arms of the enemy! Terrified, she scrambled to tack the skiff, desperate to sail out again before they saw her and Claes. Too late! A crewman on the near ship shouted of her approach. She was still straining to bring the bow around in the light wind when she heard Claes say weakly in surprise, "It's Verhulst!"

Fenella whipped around and followed his gaze to the crewman on the ship's foredeck. She stared in amazement. Berck Verhulst? How was it possible? But there was no mistaking Berck's huge bulk and black beard. A memory flashed of him buying rope in her Polder chandlery, he and Claes discussing rigging. Now Berck stood pointing at her, and crew were coming to the rail to see. Fenella took another look at the ship, a caravel. Her terror of Spaniards had blinded her before. The caravel was startlingly familiar. The *Gotland* . . . from Sark! *She's mine!*

"Fenella!" Berck called. "Ahoy!"

The men at the rail moved aside and suddenly Adam was there. Stunned, Fenella could make no sense of any of it, but the sight of Adam was all she needed. "Ahoy!" she cried. She tacked back and in a moment brought the skiff alongside the *Gotland*. As she tied her bowline to the ship's chain plate the crew tumbled a rope ladder over the side for her. She went to Claes to help him to his feet.

"Friends?" he said, struggling to get up. "Verhulst . . ."

"Yes, friends." She helped Claes get a foothold on the ladder. He climbed, shaky but determined, and she kept a steadying hand on him as long as possible, then climbed up after him. On deck Berck had hold of him by the shoulders and gaped at him in amazement. "Claes, my friend! Back from the dead, as I live and breathe! And Fenella! What the devil are you doing here?"

"I could ask the same of you!" she said.

Claes blinked, looking around him. "Are we with the Sea Beggars?"

"You are, my friend." Berck pointed across the deck to the other ship where crewmen, gathered at the rail, had made way for their captain, a gaudily dressed man with a baby face but fierce eyes. "That's Captain La Marck!" Berck said, and pulled Claes into an embrace.

"Fenella . . ." Adam was gazing at her in wonder.

Shaken, she was hardly able to steady her voice. "I see you went to Sark."

"And found they'd burned the *Elizabeth*."

She gasped. *His ship!* "So you took the *Gotland*."

"If I'd known where you were I—"

"No, it's all right. You joined the Beggars."

"To kill Spaniards." He seemed about to say more but stopped as though questions crammed his throat. He looked at Claes, at his bandaged head, his neck and shirt stained with dried blood. "Who's this?"

Claes struggled to stand tall. "The name is Doorn."

Fenella held her breath. But Adam did not seem to make the connection. Naturally—he believed her husband was dead. And Doorn was a common Dutch name. "I'm Thornleigh," he said.

"I know," Claes managed, and added with clear admiration, "and I know of your work, my lord, in the cause of our country's freedom."

The two men regarded each other with open curiosity.

"There's no time to talk," Fenella blurted to Adam. "You're in danger. The Duke of Alba has sent men to capture you."

A murmur of alarm rose among his men, and she wished she had taken him aside to quietly give him the news. But it was hard to think clearly, standing between him and Claes, their eyes boring into her.

"Thornleigh!" La Marck called from the other ship. "What's going on?"

Adam had not taken his eyes off Fenella, and he said in bewilderment, "Alba knows we're here?"

"Yes."

"How?"

She dreaded explaining. And there was no time! "I'll tell you everything, but right now you must believe me. We've come from Brussels to warn you. His men are on their way. You must go. Now!"

Adam looked at her for a long moment as though judging her words. Then he turned and gave the order to his mate to weigh anchor. The mate called out the order, and Adam crossed the deck to tell Captain La Marck. They had to raise their voices, ship to ship, and Fenella heard La Marck say, incredulous, "Leave? Before we've even got ashore? Are you sure the woman knows what she's talking about?" Adam replied that he trusted her word and would trust her with his life.

"And ours," La Marck growled, glaring at her. But he, too, ordered his men to weigh anchor. "Bah," he grumbled, "what a pointless landfall this was."

Adam came back to Fenella. His face was grave. "Surely it's not safe for you to go ashore."

"No. We're coming with you."

"I'm afraid you have no choice. Though I'm sorry to put you in danger."

"Nothing like the danger we've just escaped."

He looked from her to Claes as though burning with questions, but there were a hundred eyes on them and he had a ship to get under way. "Move!" he told his men.

Crewmen jogged to stations. Two turned the handles of the big windlass, hauling in the anchor cable. Others climbed aloft, readying to loose the sails. Fenella stood with Claes, who held on to the rail for support. She knew he was trying to appear strong, but she saw the strain in his face.

Adam said to Berck, "Take our guests below." He indicated Claes's bandage. "Have Westwood see to this man's injury."

"Aye, my lord." Berck slung his arm around Claes to support him.

Adam started for the quarterdeck. "And give the lady my cabin."

"Then your berth will do for both, my lord. They're together."

Adam stopped. Fenella did not breathe. Berck was leading

Claes away. Adam turned back to Fenella, pinning her with his eyes. The anchor cable, slowly coming up, creaked and groaned as it wound on the windlass. Adam said, "It seems Verhulst knows more about you than I do, you and your friend." He gave a hollow laugh. "And to think I waited for you."

"Please, I can explain—"

"No need. I understand now why you sent that note. Obviously he's the friend you prefer."

"You don't understand—"

"Oh, I think I do." He started for the stairs to the quarterdeck.

"Adam, stop. Claes Doorn is my husband."

Adam turned. He stared at her. "Doorn . . ." He said it like a man awaking.

"And he was my husband when you first came to Sark."

"But, you said . . ." He looked at Claes being led toward the companionway to the lower deck. His eyes flashed back to Fenella. "You told me . . . he was dead."

A loud *crack!* A scream. They both whipped around. A man tumbled from the mainmast and thudded on the deck, blood spurting from his neck. Another *crack!* Gunshots! Fenella looked ashore. Men were swarming onto the beach from the trees. Men with harquebusses. Men on horseback. Spaniards!

Adam ran up the steps to the quarterdeck shouting commands. "Hand gunners to starboard quarter! Master Curry, make sail!" Adam's mate bawled the orders across the deck.

In the storm of action that followed, Fenella lurched out of the way of running crewmen. A shot from shore hit one of the men turning the windlass, throwing him backward, clawing at his shoulder.

"Cut the cable!" Adam ordered. "Hand gunners, fire at will!"

He shouted more commands and his mate bawled them up to the men aloft, who scampered to loosen the sails, monkey quick in the rigging. On La Marck's ship men had been hit, too, and the crew had burst into action. All around Fenella was a din of barked orders and thudding feet and gunshots from shore and from the ships. Men with axes ran to the anchor cable to cut it. One cut loose the skiff Fenella had come in. She looked around for Claes.

Men were pouring out from the companionway, but she could not see Claes or Berck. Had they made it below before the shooting started?

"Fenella, get below!" Adam shouted.

A man hauling a mainsail line beside her jerked like a puppet and dropped to his knees, blood blooming on his shirt at his collarbone. The line ran slack, like a panicked snake twisting in the air. She snatched it. The rope burned her palms, but she tightened her grip and got the line under control. She hauled, coughing from the acrid smell of gunpowder all around her. A man was suddenly beside her, grabbing the rope, taking over. "I've got it!" he said. Fenella stepped away.

Crewmen chopped the anchor cable. The ship was finally free! Above Fenella the sails unfurled, a waterfall of rolling canvas that sounded like thunder. Catching the wind, the ship lurched. Fenella fought to keep her balance. Wind ruffled her hair, a smooth, steady breeze. She exulted in it. They were under way!

The din of shouts and gunfire boomed around her, and as the crew frantically manned lines and sails and helm they left the dead and wounded where they fell. Fenella ran to help a wounded young man snagged in the ratlines at the rail. He thrashed in the web of rope, moaning, his blood-soaked elbow shattered by a bullet. Fenella wrenched him free and sat him down beneath the rail. She unsheathed her dirk and used it to cut her skirt hem and tear off a strip, and she wound the makeshift bandage around his bloody arm.

She glanced up at Adam. He stood on the quarterdeck directing his helmsman at the wheel, and fear twisted her heart to see him so exposed to the marksmen ashore. He was their target. By the time she had tied off the bandage Adam had got the *Gotland* moving steadily. The light wind made the going excruciatingly slow. La Marck's ship was at their heels, trading gunfire with the Spaniards onshore. The *Gotland* followed the nautilus-like curving of the passage out toward the sea. They reached the opening and the wind picked up, billowing the sails, and the *Gotland* broke free of the land. Fenella almost cried out in relief at the glorious, wide sea room ahead. She glanced back at La Marck. He was right behind them.

The wind at their stern grew stronger with every yard they put between themselves and the shore, and when she turned again to look at the beckoning sea the wind at her back blew her hair around her face. That's when she saw the ships. Three of them. Spanish men-of-war. Fanned out, they sailed in a disciplined line coming straight at the *Gotland*. A shudder ran through Fenella. *A blockade.* Now she understood Alba's strategy. He had sent the harquebusiers by land to flush Adam out of the cove so he would be slaughtered by these ships' cannon.

She looked at the crewmen around her. Every anxious eye was on the Spanish ships coming toward them. Then, every eye turned to Adam.

Fenella looked up at him on the quarterdeck. Would he turn to starboard? The land bulged there, leaving an impossibly narrow gap between the shore and the Spanish ships. Turn to larboard? The rock shoal lay there and would snag the *Gotland*. Death by cannonballs fired at the *Gotland* pinned against the shore or death by shipwreck and drowning? Horrible choice! Fenella watched Adam, her heart in her throat. Which way would he turn?

Adam's eyes were fixed on the Spanish ships. He did not move. Did not speak. Had he frozen in fear? Fenella could not believe it. She looked back at La Marck. He had made his decision, boldly turning his bow to starboard. Adam's crew watched in grim suspense. The helmsman glanced at La Marck, then at Adam with a pleading look as though desperate to follow the Dutchman.

"Steady on," Adam commanded.

Suddenly Fenella understood what he was going to attempt. The wind was strong in the teeth of the Spanish ships. They were clawing their way forward, moments away from being close enough to open fire. They would be calibrating their cannon to fire broadsides at the pinned enemy. Adam was putting his trust in those few moments before the enemy could get into position. He was going to try to plow the *Gotland* straight through the blockade. It seemed a mad gamble. The Spanish cannon could rubble a cathedral.

Adam turned and shouted, "La Marck, stay close! Open your gun ports!" then turned back to his helmsman and repeated, "Steady." He told his mate to send men to the rails with all the handguns they had. The mate barked the order and men ran to the rails, loading pistols. *Pitiful*, Fenella thought, trying to hide her desperation. The *Gotland* had no cannon.

The *Gotland* plowed on, running fast before the wind, sails bellying, water roaring past beneath the rails. Fenella watched the enemy ships close on them. The Spaniards were moving slowly, the wind on their nose, but the *Gotland* was flying. Adam aimed his ship between two of theirs. Fenella glanced behind. La Marck had understood the tactic and turned back and was following Adam. His half-dozen gun ports were open on either side.

The two Spanish ships were now so close they rose like massive buildings, dwarfing the *Gotland*, the wind screaming in their rigging. Fenella could see faces aboard, saw their yawning gun ports, twenty and more big black maws in long lines along both ships' sides. Her knuckles were white, gripping the shroud above the prostrate wounded man she had helped. She saw the Spaniards on the starboard ship swivel their deck-mounted culverin, saw them touch a flame to the gun. The culverin blasted. Fenella gasped and dropped to her knees, covering the wounded man to protect him. The ball tore off the head of a crewman, then struck the base of the mainmast, sending splinters flying. Fenella watched in horror as the headless man toppled. The ball embedded in the mainmast smoked. Fire! Someone heaved water on it from a bucket. The ball hissed and steamed.

The *Gotland* shot between the two massive ships. Adam's men fired their pistols as they flew past. Through the gun ports Fenella glimpsed Spanish cannon crews inside the vessel frantically ratcheting down the big guns' muzzles. Adam was right—they'd been preparing to fire on a floundering enemy trapped against the shore, not one flying past them a stone's throw away.

Behind, La Marck's cannon boomed. A red-hot missile hissed through the air toward the larboard Spanish ship, tore through the leach of her mizzen, and plowed into the sea. The Spanish culverin blasted back. The ball whizzed across La Marck's deck, ripping off a chunk of his stern rail.

In a moment, both the *Gotland* and La Marck's ship were through the blockade. Shouts came from the Spaniards behind them, the captains giving orders to come about. The Spanish ships gave chase. But Adam and La Marck, running with the wind, had a long head start.

In the next hours Fenella helped tend the wounded. Adam and his crew, with the Spanish menace now far behind them, sailed north and tended to the damage on the ship.

The fo'castle where the crew had their berths was dark and dank as Fenella did her best to ease the agony of five casualties, assisting Westwood, the boatswain's mate, a grim-faced veteran who did the office of ship's doctor. Bandaging wounds, she held back her nausea at the protruding shards of bone and the glistening gore and the men's groans. She gave them cups of water and encouraging words. When she and Westwood had done all they could, she made her way out to the waist of the ship, her back aching, her skin sticky with sweat. On deck the carpenter's crew hammered at repairs and sailors coiled lines. She took a deep, grateful breath of the sea air.

The evening was chilly. With daylight dying, fog had crept around the ship. The seas had become lumpy, making Fenella's gait clumsy as she crossed the deck. The sails drooped and billowed by turns in the erratic wind, the hemp lines creaking in the lulls, then snapping taut in the gusts. Two corpses shrouded by canvas lay beneath the ratlines, awaiting burial in the deep. Fenella looked up at the quarterdeck. Adam was not there, only the helmsman and the mate. She looked out at the heaving gunmetal sea. La Marck might be near, but in the murk of fog and fading light she saw no sign of his ship.

She went the opposite way, across the deck and down the companionway, then aft to the stern cabin. She had left Claes sleeping there. *Adam's cabin.* That thought brought a kind of ache to her heart. Adam was busy elsewhere, would sleep elsewhere. He had a ship to manage. *I have my life to manage.*

She opened the door slowly to avoid a creak that might wake Claes. He lay unmoving on the berth. She came in and carefully closed the door behind her. The moment she turned, his eyes fluttered open. She came to the side of the berth. The cabin lay in half gloom, lit by a single hanging lantern, and its flickering light probed the hollows of his cheeks and the bony ridge of his brow. His fair hair stuck out in loops out from under the bandage wrapped diagonally around his head.

"I slept," he said apologetically.

"It's what you needed. You look much better for the rest." It was true. There was a new composure about him. He regarded her with clear, calm eyes. "I think your fever's passed," she said.

He offered a slight smile. "Escaping death is a great restorative." His look turned sober. "Sit down, my love. You look like you need rest too."

She sat on the edge of the berth. *Adam's berth.*

"Where is Thornleigh headed?" Claes asked.

"I don't know. North."

"And La Marck?"

She could only shrug in ignorance. Where *were* they going? She'd heard Westwood say something about the Beggars being no longer welcome in England. So where *could* they go? She looked around the cabin. Everything in it spoke of Adam. The gimballed brass compass on the bulkhead. The narrow shelf of navigation books. The desk where his log would be safely stowed in a drawer. The stern window that looked out on the sea behind, though all she saw now was a foggy gloom.

"Fenella." Claes pushed himself to sit up. He was still weak and lay back against the pillow again, half-sitting. "You got us here. I give thanks for you."

"For friends," she said quickly.

"Friends indeed. Thornleigh's sister. Thornleigh's brother-in-law." He was looking at her as though trying to decipher a puzzle. "*Your* friends."

She rubbed the back of her stiff neck, turning away. A tray with two wooden bowls and two wooden cups sat on the desk. Had Adam sent food? She realized she was hungry. All she'd had to eat since morning was some biscuit and water while tending the wounded. "Have you had something to eat?" she asked, getting up and going to the tray.

"Verhulst brought me some broth."

So, Adam had told Berck to take care of them. *He wants nothing to do with me.* She looked down at the bowls and her hunger shrank away at the sight. Gray broth with knobs of gristly meat. In the cups, scummy-looking small beer. One hard biscuit lay beside. Were the ship's stores so depleted? The Sea Beggars . . . beggars indeed.

"Fenella, come, sit down. I'm only hungry to talk to you."

She forced a cheerful look. "Drink a little, at least. You need to build your strength." She brought him a cup of beer and sat beside him and helped him drink. He finished half, then shook his head to say he could drink no more. She swallowed the rest. In the silence between them the ship carried on her lonely conversation with herself, rope creaking on rope, wood groaning on wood, the sigh of the sea against the hull.

"It's a long time since I've been on a ship on the deep," Claes said. "It feels good. Free."

"It's my ship." She set the empty cup on the floor. "From Sark."

His eyes widened. "Really?"

She told him about the bargain she had made over a year ago with the *Gotland*'s Swedish owner. He'd been aboard when his captain had stopped at Sark to repair a snapped bowsprit and replace its lost sails, but the owner was too low on funds to pay, so Fenella had offered a trade: a German carrack she had salvaged and restored to some beauty. He'd agreed and she sent him away happy. "I got the best of the bargain. The *Gotland*'s worth twice that old carrack."

They shared a small smile.

"You built quite a business, didn't you?" Claes said. "You must miss Sark."

Sadness washed over her. "I miss Johan."

"Ah," Claes said quietly. "So do I."

She was bone weary. "You should rest again now, and I'll have some of that pathetic broth." She started to get up. He caught her hand.

"Fenella, wait." She looked at him. "How did you know Thornleigh was in that cove?"

"Know? I didn't. I guessed. He'd said it was an ideal hiding hole."

"When was that?"

"He sailed with me and Johan from Sark. We anchored in that cove."

He looked down at her hand in his. He spoke as if piecing the puzzle together. "So, Alba held you in his dungeon to get that information from you." He shook his head with sorrow. "And made you suffer for it."

"It's *you* who suffered." She remembered him kneeling, grim faced, to bear the mutilation. His ear hacked off.

He looked up at her. "For my countrymen. You suffered to protect Thornleigh."

She looked at his hand holding hers. His felt cold.

"That time you spent together, you and Thornleigh," he said. "You . . . got to know each other well?"

She looked toward the door. Her skin prickled.

"Fenella, I want you to know . . . I understand. You spent five lonely years on Sark. You thought I was dead. And Thornleigh is . . . well, I imagine he's a man most women notice." Claes tightened his grip on her hand. "But now, things are different. Aren't they."

The last was a statement. But she felt him waiting for her to answer. The silence between them widened.

"Fenella, look at me." He pulled her gently to turn back to him. She made her eyes meet his. "Aren't they?" he asked.

The bandage around his head had slipped. The edge lay aslant across his eyebrow. She reached out and lightly tugged the linen up and tucked it back in place. "Different, Claes? No, the same." She squeezed his hand. "The same as five years ago."

She slid her hand free. "Now, rest."

She awoke early the next morning to the sound of men shouting. Feet tramped the deck above her head. Claes lay asleep beside her and she rose quietly so as not to disturb him. She dressed quickly, a matter only of pulling her dress on over the shift she had slept in and scuffing her feet into her shoes. The ship was unusually still. A glance out the big stern window showed a sea of long swells like low hills, the morning sun shining on the vastness of blue.

She came up on deck to find the full crew of perhaps thirty men massed in the waist, and the ship hove to, stopped in the water. Many of the men were grumbling; all looked agitated. Some had climbed the ratlines to watch; some perched farther aloft, on the yards. A long stone's throw away lay La Marck's ship, also hove to. La Marck's whole crew, it seemed, lined the rails, as agitated as the men around Fenella. And another ship lay hove to just beyond La Marck's. What was going on?

She spotted Berck by the starboard main brace and made her way to him.

"Berck, what's happening?"

"That's what we all want to know." He jerked his bearded chin aft. Up on the quarterdeck Adam stood with La Marck and another man. "Captain La Marck and Captain Bloys have come to parley. But it seems they and Lord Thornleigh don't see eye to eye."

"Bloys? The Sea Beggar captain?"

"One with a hungry crew."

Adam came forward to the quarterdeck rail and looked out at the gathered seamen. "This is up to you men. I say the time for running and hiding is over. The time for burying our dead at sea is over. It's time to attack. If we gather the Sea Beggars together we have the strength. If we can break Alba's grip, the prince of Orange is ready to send an army to smash him."

"I'm all for it," La Marck said, "but attack where?"

"Rotterdam!" someone shouted.

"Enkhuizen!" another shouted from La Marck's ship.

"No, we need victualing!" Bloys insisted. "My men are near starved."

"That's God's truth," La Marck said to Adam. "My men have only maggoty biscuit. It's meat we need and freshwater. We can't fight with starving men."

A yell from the ratlines: "Let's raid the ports, like before! Plenty of victuals!"

Adam said, "If we keep roaming and raiding, the Spaniards will just pick us off one by one. We need to stand together, and attack."

That brought a thunder of shouting, men calling out on all three ships. Adam was saying something and Fenella longed to hear him, but the clamor of voices drowned him out. Furious at the disorderly uproar, she glanced at Berck and saw a pale face beyond him moving among the men. It was Claes. He was coming toward her.

"Claes, no," she said, "you should get below."

He reached her, saying something, but his voice was faint in the din. From the expression on his face it was clear he felt his words were urgent.

"Claes, what is it?" She put her ear to his mouth.

"South," he said. "Sail south for Brielle. No time to lose."

Something in his eyes sent a shiver up her backbone. *He knows something.* "Why Brielle?"

"Attack."

That's what Adam wants. She turned and shouted, "Listen to this man!"

The men ignored her or didn't hear, carrying on with their clamor while the three captains went back to arguing among themselves. La Marck drew his sword and shouted something about a raid for gold to buy weapons. He brandished the sword high in a show of resolve, and a cheer went up from half the men. Fenella feared La Marck would soon win them all over. She saw the pistol in Berck's belt. She grabbed it. "A ball," she told him, an order. Startled, he dug out a ball from the pouch at his waist, and Fenella loaded the pistol. She raised it, pointed at the sky, and fired.

At the shot the deck fell silent.

"Listen to this man!" she said, pointing to Claes.

All eyes turned to him. He raised his face to address the three captains. "Brielle," he said, his voice stronger, clearer. "We can take Brielle."

"Bah!" someone shouted. "There's eight hundred dago soldiers at that garrison. It'd be suicide."

"No," Claes said, "they're not—" He stopped to cough. The grumbling voices rose again, ignoring him.

"Listen to him!" Fenella shouted. "He's Claes Doorn, leader of the Brethren!"

They all looked again at Claes, this time with clear curiosity.

Adam came to the quarterdeck's forward rail. He stared down at Claes, looking surprised. He seemed skeptical yet eager all at once, and called across the deck, "Doorn, why Brielle? What do you know about Brielle?"

"In prison the Brethren got word to me. Alba has sent the Brielle garrison to Utrecht to put down an uprising. The town is practically defenseless. Attack, now. The Brethren will join you."

20

The Eve of Battle

Fenella could not sleep. She pulled on a cloak that Berck had earlier scrounged for her, checked that Claes was sleeping soundly, and left the cabin. She wanted air. Wanted something to take her mind off the perils that lay in store when they attacked Brielle. It wasn't fear that made her so jumpy. She'd felt worse fear in Alba's dungeon. This was something else. She hardly knew what, only that her nerves were wound so tightly she needed to get out.

She came up on deck into the waist of the ship. The night was clear, the deck moon-drenched, white. The *Gotland*, bearing southeast, was making good progress in the fresh breeze, sailing on a smooth beam reach. She thought, *If the wind holds we'll make landfall by morning.* Ahead of them La Marck's flagship, the *Eenhoorn*, was a ghostly form beyond the *Gotland*'s foremast and bowsprit, her lanterns winking on the stern. Fenella looked up at the stars caught among the sails. Wind hummed and thrummed and whistled in the rigging. It was as if the *Gotland* were restless, eager to get to Brielle. She felt the same restlessness. *I must be brainsick,* she thought, *because God alone knows what awaits us.* She remembered once telling Johan that rebels going up against Imperial Spain were like minnows attacking a shark. Well, at least these minnows were not going to be swallowed without a fight.

Claes seemed eager for the fight. The last three days of rest had done much to restore him to health. His ravaged ear was healing well, and Fenella saw that every hour more of his vigor returned. It had felt strange to lie beside him these nights. She sensed he was giving her time to get used to him again. He had not touched her.

She scanned the quarterdeck, wanting to go up and look out from the stern. She would not if Adam was there. She had been avoiding him and was sure he was steering clear of her, too. Not difficult for either of them, since he had the ship to captain and she'd been nursing Claes as he got his strength back. She saw two figures standing on the quarterdeck in the silvery moonlight. One was Adam's mate, James Curry, who had the watch. He stood at the windward rail, one hand on the ratline, looking out at the night. Behind him was the helmsman at the wheel. No Adam.

She went up the stairs. Curry turned to her. "Everything all right, Mistress Doorn?"

"Yes, fine, Master Curry. I just wanted some fresh air. I won't disturb you."

"No disturbance at all, ma'am," he said gallantly, and made a sweeping gesture that said, *Be my guest.*

She went aft and looked out over the taffrail. In the ship's dark wake, lights flickered like a ragged spray of fireflies: lanterns on the twenty-one Sea Beggar vessels that followed the *Gotland* and the *Eenhoorn*. It had taken three days to hail them all and gather them together, and what a motley fleet it was. Three big carracks robust enough to voyage to the New World. Lively pinnaces. Beamy, workaday coastal ships. Refitted fishing smacks. The crews aboard them, perhaps four hundred men in all, were equally diverse. Some had enjoyed status and property before the Spaniards invaded, like Captain William Bloys, who'd once had the lordship of Treslong and whose brother had been executed by Alba. Others had been shopkeepers and artisans and common seamen, and some were mere opportunistic rovers only after spoils. All were exiles. For over three years they had roamed the Channel preying on Spanish shipping, granted safe harbor for victualing in English ports until Spain had rattled its swords at the Queen and she, acquiescing, had expelled the Sea Beggars. Homeless now, they were on the brink of starvation.

Fenella watched them in the moonlight, a small forest of masts atilt to larboard, canvas bellying, hulls carving the low waves. This sight was what she had left her berth for, she realized. A sight to fortify her. Four hundred men with one goal. She *needed* to see them, because doubts gnawed her. Did these men stand a chance in the fight ahead? Few had any experience as soldiers. La Marck had proved a crafty admiral of his pack of vagabonds, but could he lead a disciplined assault on a fortified city? And what if Claes's information was wrong and they found the Spanish garrison at full strength with a thousand or more battle-hardened troops? Yet she had to trust his judgment. Claes was no green recruit; he had fought Spaniards, had led the Brethren on dangerous missions. Soon he would be fighting alongside the Beggars. So would Adam. She admired the courage of both men . . . and feared for them both. The restlessness churned within her. She wished there were something *she* could do.

Her restless frustration had begun during the meeting that La Marck and Adam had held with four of the captains and Claes, assembling in Adam's cabin. Fenella had stayed, eager to hear their plans, unsettling though it was to see Adam and Claes together. She knew it unsettled them, too.

"I know Brielle," William Bloys had told them. His father had been governor there before the Spaniards came. "It's a fine, wide port on the River Maas. Their shipping sails to Zeeland, Rotterdam, Dordrecht, and they have a trade agreement with the Hansa towns, even have their own trading post in Sweden." He'd drawn a detailed map, and as the others examined it he explained the layout of the city. "It's on Voorne Island and lies at the southern tip. It's not a large city, but it is well walled. And when I was last there, about eight years ago, it was fortified."

"Who's the mayor?" La Marck asked.

"I don't know."

Claes did. "His name is Koekebakker."

"A Brethren sympathizer?" Adam asked.

The others looked at Claes hopefully. "I'm afraid not," he said. "Koekebakker's a Spanish appointee. But he's not popular. He rigorously enforces the Spaniards' ten percent tax on all goods bought and sold. My information is that there's support for the Brethren among the people."

"Support for the prince of Orange," La Marck sternly clarified. "If we do this, we do it in the Prince's name. We may be beggars, but we're not brigands." There were arch looks from the other captains. They had all been raiding small seaports. La Marck added gruffly, "Well, not anymore."

"I suggest we break into two parties," Adam said, studying the map. "One takes the southern gate, the other the northern gate. We only need one group to break through."

They discussed landing parties, group leaders, munitions, boats. Listening, Fenella felt a squall of emotions. She longed to help but had nothing to contribute. And to see Claes and Adam working together as comrades in arms was disconcerting but also inspiring.

On deck now, footsteps sounded behind her in the moonlight. She turned, expecting to see Curry come to join her at the taffrail. Her breath caught. It was Adam.

"I'd like a word," he said. His cool, aloof tone stung her. He stood a pace away from her as though unwilling to come near. "We'll enter the mouth of the Maas by morning. I'm going to put you ashore before we reach Brielle."

Hope sparked in her that they had some special mission for her. "Why?"

"It's going to be bloody. Even if your husband is right about the garrison, Brielle will defend itself. A walled city under attack heaps corpses at its gates. So I'll put you ashore first."

She felt insulted. "And what would I do ashore?"

"Live."

The intensity he forced into the word startled her. Was he really so unforgiving? Or was it warmth she'd heard? She collected herself. "Thank you, but no, I'll stay." He opened his mouth to argue, but she said firmly, "You may be captain of these men, but the *Gotland* is my ship, remember? I'll stay."

He looked at her for a long moment, and she saw a struggle thrashing in his eyes. Then he made a terse bow of the head. "As you wish." He turned to start back across the quarterdeck.

"Wait." She could not bear to have him leave with such cold reserve. It might be her last chance to talk to him. She touched his arm. "Please, wait. There's so much to say."

He turned slowly. "Is there?"

How to begin? She glanced at Curry. He had moved to the quarterdeck's forward rail, his back to them. He couldn't hear. "Your son and daughter," she said. "When we parted . . . you were going to get them. What went wrong?"

A look of pain flickered in his eyes. "I failed."

"You could not find them?"

He seemed about to answer and she sensed that he wanted to explain, but he stopped. "Curry," he said, raising his voice across the quarterdeck. "I'll take the watch. Stand by." Curry nodded and left them, going down the stairs into the shadows of the waist. The helmsman at the wheel continued to watch the sea, eyes ahead. He was far enough away that he could not hear. Adam turned back to Fenella. "I did find them. And they were eager to come with me. I *had* them, but . . ." His tone was bitter. "My wife was prepared for that. She'd sent a gunman. He fired on us. I had to leave Kate and Robert, for their own safety."

Fenella was amazed. "Your wife sent someone to *kill* you?"

He jerked a nod, and she saw that the memory tore at him.

"I'm so sorry. About your children."

They stood in awkward silence. He looked out over the taffrail at the Sea Beggar fleet. So did she, watching the *Gotland*'s wake as it swirled and whispered. Adam's words whirled in her head. *My wife . . . your husband.*

"I meant to thank you," he said, looking out.

She didn't understand. "For what?"

"Warning me about Alba."

"Ah. Thank the wind. For hobbling his ships."

"No, you. If you hadn't come when you did we'd all be in chains in Alba's prison."

She remembered the hideous water torture and shivered. "We may be yet."

Adam turned to her. "What happened after we parted? How did you know Alba had sent his men for me?"

She watched the ships but felt his eyes on her. To explain meant to confess that she had betrayed him, and she shrank from that. But part of her wanted him to know and understand. So she began, and told it all, starting with the bizarre day she saw Claes in Polder after five years of believing him dead. Told how she'd offered to take some of her gold to his Brethren friends in Brussels. How only days after she reached the capital she saw Johan hanged and Claes sent as a captive to await execution. How she set out to shoot Alba.

He listened, rapt, and at her last words he asked in astonishment, "Shoot him?"

"Your brother-in-law stopped me."

"Carlos?" His surprise was even greater.

"He made up for it later." She wanted to get the awful part over with, and barreled through how she'd been held in the dungeon and Alba had interrogated her. "He wanted to know where you were." She was dry mouthed as she told how Alba had brought in a girl and boy and told her they were Kate and Robert. How he'd again demanded the information about Adam and, when she refused, how he'd had the girl killed before her eyes.

"Good God," Adam whispered.

"They were beggar children he'd dressed up. I thought they were yours. It was so ghastly . . . that poor girl. And he would have killed the boy next. So . . ." Fenella was so shaken she was clenching the taffrail, the skin of her knuckles as taut as a windward sheet. "So I told him where I thought you were."

He let out a kind of moan. She could not look at him. She plowed on. How even after her confession Alba had sent her to hang. How she'd been put in a cart with Claes . . . his ear mutilated . . . taken to the Grote Markt for execution. How, to her amazement, Carlos Valverde had then taken charge of the cart and managed their escape.

"Carlos freed you?" Adam said in wonder.

"Your sister helped." She turned to him and told him about the coach. His eyes went wide with surprise. "Claes was fevered . . . his ear . . ." Her stomach felt rocky, her legs weak, from reliving these horrors. As she looked into Adam's eyes, tears pricked hers. "We took a boat . . . hard sailing. I had to get to you, because . . . because I told Alba. Can you ever forgive me?"

Suddenly his arms were around her. "Fenella . . . Fenella," he moaned. "What hell you've been through. I had no idea."

A thrill ran through her. He didn't hate her! Her hands slid up his back and she held him tight, her cheek against his shoulder, his heartbeat pulsing against hers. She closed her eyes, heady with the hardness of his body, the strength that throbbed in him.

"I'm sorry," he moaned. "So sorry." He pulled back, still gripping her arms, his eyes searching hers. "Can you forgive *me?*"

"For what?"

"How I've acted. I was so angry. That you had let me think your husband was dead."

"On Sark, I thought he was."

"But in Brussels. On Verhulst's barge . . ."

She nodded in misery. "Yes." She had seen Claes by then, knew the work he was doing. "I should have told you, but . . ." She dared to hold his gaze. "I wanted you so much."

He pulled her closer. His eyes searched hers. "As I wanted you. And loved you."

Happiness coursed through her, a wave of joy.

His voice was tense with hope. "And now?"

"Now?" She tried to think straight. Hard to do with his arms around her, his eyes on her, too, so warm. The warmth was love! The wave of joy crested, then ebbed, and in its wake her tears welled. *Now . . . ?* A rope creaked beside them. Water whispered below them. Lanterns flickered in the strung-out fleet. Twenty-one ships. Four hundred men, all knowing that tomorrow they could be facing death. "Now," she managed, "so much has changed."

He released her, slowly, reluctantly. His arms dropped to his sides. Fenella's heart was breaking, because he understood her meaning. "Your husband is a fortunate man," he said. It was too much for her. Her tears spilled.

Gently, he wiped a teardrop from her cheek. "*You've* changed. You used to say the rebels were fools. Now look at you."

At his touch she longed to kiss him. A longing so strong she had to force herself not to move. Tomorrow he would face the defenders of Brielle. Tomorrow night he might be dead! A storm rose in her. *Damn the Sea Beggars!* She hated them all for endangering Adam. "They *are* fools," she said harshly, swiping away her tears. "So are you. English, and a lord, by God. You could be safe at home and yet you've joined them."

He nodded with a faint, sad smile. "Some gambles are worth the risk." As he looked at her, love shone in his eyes. "I've never regretted the times I've been a fool."

A bell rang in the fo'castle, startling her. She looked down at the shadows in the waist of the ship and saw two men come sleepily across the moon-drenched deck. They spoke with Curry. The change of watch, she realized. In a few moments they would come up here to the quarterdeck.

"You should get some rest," Adam said.

She struggled to collect herself. "You too."

"Fenella, if things don't go well tomorrow . . . if something happens and I don't come back—"

"No, none of that. I'll say good night now and—"

"Listen to me. I want you to take the ship—*your* ship—as soon as we go ashore. I'll leave crew enough on board. Just go. Any survivors among us will be welcome aboard the other vessels. Or, if we lose, taken prisoner. So get away before then. Sail to England. Wait for your husband there." He was tugging a ring off his finger. "And take this. It will get you an audience with the Queen. Show it to her. She'll take care of you."

Fenella spent a sleepless night in the berth alongside Claes. He slept soundly. *If something happens and I don't come back*, Adam had said. She could not bear the thought. His touch lingered from the moment he'd placed the ring on her palm and closed her fingers around it. A gold signet ring with the seal of a thorn bush, his family's symbol. *It will get you an audience with the Queen,* he had said.

A new thought stole over Fenella. The restlessness that had plagued her quieted, its turmoil turning into something more calm but also more intense, like a flame, small but steady. She lay listening to the ship whisper to itself: the moan of ropes, the murmur between sea and hull. In Fenella's mind, an idea was forming.

There *was* something she could do.

❧ 21 ❧

The Walls of Brielle

The Sea Beggar fleet lay at anchor in the broad River Maas and the *Gotland* rang with the voices of men preparing the attack. Boats splashed into the water, lowered by the boatswain's crew. Weapons clanked through the lower deck where the crew was being issued pistols and pikes, and boots thumped as men hustled out from the fo'castle. Voices rang across the water from ship to ship as the rest of the Sea Beggars prepared.

Fenella stood amidships with Berck, both of them loosening ropes on blocks that held a rowboat on a boom. Spring sunshine swept the forward deck, but she and Berck stood in the shadows of the mainmast and its furled sails.

"Are you sure about this?" he asked her with a frown of concern.

"Lord Thornleigh's orders," Fenella said. A lie, or near enough. She glanced shoreward at the city of Brielle rising up just beyond the beach. Its walls looked impregnable. Fortified towers rose beside the two main gates. The gates were closed. *Sure about this?* No, she was sure only that the blood of men would spill if the Sea Beggars attacked. Maybe Adam's blood. Maybe Claes's. "His Lordship said he'd put me ashore before the assault," she added. "Ask him, if you want."

Berck glanced toward the stern where Adam, his back to them, was giving commands to a gang of men. "He should have done it before now," Berck muttered.

"Not his fault, I said no at first. I've changed my mind."

"So Claes wants this?" Berck asked, skeptical. "Seems you'd be safer staying aboard."

Claes was belowdecks helping with the preparations. To avoid answering Berck she glanced at the activity around Adam. "Time for you to join them. And for me to push off." She nodded to the line he held. "Lower it." Together they let the rowboat down and it hit the water with a splash. Fenella swung her leg over the bulwark, about to descend the rope ladder.

"Wait," Berck said, stopping her. "Claes couldn't mean for you to go alone."

"I'll be fine. His Lordship needs every man here."

Berck looked torn. "Say the word and I'll come with you, Fenella. I'll get you safely away, to Brussels or to the coast."

His offer touched her, because she knew how eager he was to take part in today's action. The change in her old friend still amazed her: Berck, once so stolid and morose, leaving his barge and his beer to join this band of desperate men. *He's not the only one,* she thought with a shiver of surprise, recalling Adam's words last night: *You've changed.*

"Berck, I've been taking care of myself for a long time," she assured him. She forced a smile. "Next time we meet, you and I, we'll share a pot of ale and you'll tell me what a hero you were today."

She took a last look at Adam. He was busy organizing a load of pikes for a boat and hadn't seen her. She went quickly over the bulwark and down the ladder.

Rowing toward shore, she felt the sunshine like a hand on her back to halt her, warning her to stay away from the city. She glanced over her shoulder at the walls and towers coming closer, then back at the Sea Beggar fleet getting smaller. The sounds from the fleet thinned, and the city seemed silent, too, its stone walls blocking the sounds within. Rowing, she could hear only the squeal of her oars in the oarlocks and the creak of a windmill on the beach.

The rowboat slid up onto the sandy beach. She shipped the oars and hopped out and dragged the boat farther up onto the sand. To her left a stone pier jutted into the water, the fishing boats tied to it bobbing alongside beneath a crane for loading cargo. To her right stretched the beach, where a damaged two-masted bilander lay careened beside a couple of skiffs hauled up on chocks for refitting, one with the top of its mast snapped off. There was a scatter of gear common in any harbor: ropes and nets, barrels and barrows. She saw no one on the beach. Farther down it, the big windmill's arms lifted and fell, groaning.

She looked up at the city's stone wall. The crenellated top was like a castle wall, spiked with square stone teeth. In one of the rectangular gaps a man stood watching her. The sun behind him made him a silhouette, but sunlight glinted off something metal that he held. A harquebus? A pistol? Her heart knocked. There could be no doubt that the townspeople were aware of the fleet that had invaded their river.

She walked toward the southern gate that rose before her. It was almost as wide as the *Gotland*'s beam, a massive wooden barrier, arched and studded with iron. A tower dominated the corner that overlooked the gate, its walls hatched with arrow slits like black crosses. Was the tower filled with soldiers? Were archers standing ready on platforms behind those slits? As she reached the gate she heard a sound from the sally port, a narrow door in the wall beside the gate. A plate behind a metal grill at face level scraped open. Eyes glared at her through the grill. "Who goes there?"

"My name is Doorn. I've come from the Sea Beggar fleet. Admiral La Marck has sent a message for your mayor. Please, let me in."

The plate scraped shut. There was muffled scuffling behind the door. Fenella waited, unsure, nervous. The big windmill groaned. Overhead, a seagull screeched.

A bolt or bar behind the sally port clanked and the door opened. A thin man eyed her. He wore a burgundy velvet robe like an alderman. "Enter."

The moment Fenella stepped through the doorway noise engulfed her. A crowd of townspeople, who must have been standing silent as she'd spoken outside, moved in on her, clamoring with questions. A sergeant in a helmet shouted at them to move back. Dogs barked. A shutter slammed open on the upper story of a house, and along the street people leaned out from windows to watch. The thin alderman was urgently conferring with three men who had come forward to join him, fellow officials by their fine dress. They glared at Fenella.

She tried to ignore the clamor and spoke directly to the officials. "Is one of you Mayor Koekebakker?"

"I am Magistrate Duervorst," said the thin man. "You say you've brought a message for the mayor?" He held out his hand. "I'll take it to him."

"I'll speak it to his face, sir."

The officials exchanged tense looks. Then the magistrate nodded to Fenella. "Come."

She followed him and the other officials up the street, the whole party led by the sergeant. Townspeople hustled after them in their wake. Men and women gawked from house windows and shop doorways. Fenella looked around for soldiers, trying to gauge the city's military strength. All she saw was citizens and shopkeepers, men and women who looked frightened. *No more frightened than me*, she thought. The officials led her past a church where monks stood clustered at its door, gabbling to one another as they watched her go. A yeasty smell reached her, the aroma of baking bread wafting from a bakehouse. Her stomach gurgled with hunger. Like all the Sea Beggars she had eaten nothing in two days except gristles of salt pork as tough as shoes. Another tower rose at the far end of the street behind houses at a bend in the route, the tower's crenellated top just visible behind the house roofs. That had to be the northern gate.

Townspeople crowded the steps of the City Hall and more were milling inside it. Guards held the people back as the officials hurried Fenella into a council chamber and shut the door on the crowd. Several finely dressed men stood waiting—councillors, Fenella reckoned. They flanked a man as though he was their leader. Surely this was Mayor Koekebakker. He was a beefy, florid man with a mane of gray hair and piercing gray eyes, and Fenella felt at once that he was no fool. Magistrate Duervorst reported to

him and the councillors what she had said at the gate, and Koekebakker greeted her warily. Like the others, he was clearly nervous.
They were no doubt aware of the Sea Beggars' reputation for plundering coastal towns, and never before had the Beggars come in
such strength. Koekebakker's questions were quick and to the
point: What were Admiral La Marck's intentions? Why had he sent
her? The implication of the second question, sharp with surprise
and disdain, was clear: why a woman?

"I played loose with the truth," she said. "The Admiral did not
send me. He does not even know I've come. He is busy preparing
his men to take your city."

They gaped at her. The mayor repeated her word, incredulous,
"*Take* it?"

"And hold it. And when they do, they will be joined by the
fighting men of the Brethren." That was a lie, too. Back in the
cove, Adam and La Marck had not even made it ashore to try to
contact the Brethren when the Spaniards arrived. But she saw the
alarm that her mention of them had on several of the councillors
and she plowed on. "I see you know the Brethren, sir, at least by
reputation. Good. Their leader is Claes Doorn, and he is out there
right now, on the Admiral's flagship."

"That cannot be," a councillor protested. "Doorn is locked up
in the Duke of Alba's prison."

"He is not, sir. He escaped. How do I know all this, you wonder? Because I escaped with him. Claes Doorn is my husband."
That brought a swift change in them, looks of a new, grim respect
for her. It gave her the courage to press on. "He and I have traveled with the Admiral's fleet, which, as you can see, is formidable.
And I'll tell you something more. They know your garrison is woe-
fully understrength."

She paused, her heart in her mouth. Koekebakker, stone-faced,
did not contradict her. Did that mean Claes was right about the
garrison? Or was the mayor craftily keeping silent about the Spanish troops standing ready in the city's towers?

Magistrate Duervorst, however, could not hold back. "How
many ships? How many men?"

"Sixty-eight ships," she said. "Three thousand men." The lie was so brazen, so incredible, she feared they would scoff or even laugh. Instead, they looked afraid. They believed her! Her ploy was working! She masked the thrill she felt. "And that's not all." She pulled Adam's ring off her finger, the signet ring of the House of Thornleigh. "The English baron Lord Thornleigh sails alongside Admiral La Marck. This is his ring."

Koekebakker took the ring and examined it gravely. The councillor nearest him said in awe, "The pirate baron."

"The same," Fenella said. "He has come with three warships sent by the queen of England."

Duervorst looked frightened but bewildered. "But . . . the English queen has abandoned La Marck's Beggars. She expelled them from her ports."

"Only to unleash them. The whole world knows Queen Elizabeth is no lover of Spain. She supports the Dutch people's rightful leader, the prince of Orange. Baron Thornleigh has come as her fighting arm, and his warships are now almost at your harbor. When they reach it their cannon fire will obliterate your walls."

The men gazed at her in agonized silence. She could not afford to give them time to think. "I have come here to reason with you. The Admiral and his men have no quarrel with you or the citizens of Brielle. They are Dutchmen, too, and would rather not harm you. Their only goal is the overthrow of the tyrant Duke of Alba. So open your gates to them. Welcome them as the liberators they are. Yield to them now, and there will be no bloodshed."

Silence. Stony faces. Then all the men seemed to speak at once.

"Their strength is vast."

"What shall we do?"

"Resist!"

"No, no, surrender."

"Flee! Gather our families and flee!"

"And abandon our property? To go where?"

"There is no time! We *must* surrender!"

Fenella said quickly, "Permitting entry to your fellow countrymen is not surrender." She had frightened them just as she'd hoped and she hid her exultation. All she needed to do now was calm them. "Simply open your gates and let them in. I assure you, they will neither harm you nor despoil your city. They are your friends!" She smiled. "In fact, your shops and alehouses will profit by their stay. Think of them as paying guests."

They fell silent, staring at her as though wanting to believe her. She kept smiling, *willing* them to believe. Gradually, all eyes turned to Mayor Koekebakker. He was the only one who had not spoken. Fenella watched him turn Adam's ring in his fingers, deep in thought.

He looked up at her. "We could flee, as Councillor Jurdens would have us do, but as Councillor Poelman says, by doing so we would forfeit our property. Or we could throw open our gates to the visitors, as Councillor Roehorst and this lady would have us do, and indeed she paints a rosy picture of them enjoying the city and our citizens happily pocketing their gold. But despite her honeyed words for it, that *is* surrender. Surrender to rebels. Treason. Make no mistake, gentlemen, that is exactly what the Duke of Alba will call it. And I assure you that if we willingly let in this rebel horde, the only rosy hue will be the blood spurting from our necks when Alba's executioner strikes our heads from our shoulders."

They gaped at him. "Dear God," Duervorst murmured in horror, "he's right." The other men, white-faced, seemed to shrink into themselves.

Fenella felt her victory sink like a man washed overboard. "Wait, please—"

"No, enough," Koekebakker ordered. He tossed the ring back at her. She fumbled it. It fell and clattered on the floor. As she snatched it up Koekebakker said sternly to his councillors, "We will resist the rebels. Agreed?" No one objected. He strode to the door and opened it and the voices of the crowd in the corridor became a roar. He gestured for the sergeant, and when the man pushed his way in through the people Koekebakker said, "Inform your lieutenants: They are to stand firm and repel the attack."

"Yes, my lord."

"And have guards escort this woman to my house. She is not a guest; she is a rebel. Lock her in."

* * *

Adam was rowing as hard as his men, pulling toward shore. With the ox-strong Berck Verhulst at the oars they were three boat lengths ahead of the others, twenty-seven boats in all. Each had four to six pairs of oars splashing in unison and held fifteen to twenty men crammed together, their pikes upright, looking like a flotilla of porcupines. Adam hauled at his oars, his back to the beach, his eyes on Claes Doorn in the following boat. Only the strongest men rowed, so Doorn sat motionless in the bow, gripping his pike. On board the *Gotland* he had been hurrying past Adam to get into the boat when Adam angrily grabbed his arm to stop him.

"How could you let her leave the ship?"

"What?"

"Your wife, man! When you *know* it's not safe."

"What are you talking about?"

"You don't know? She's gone ashore. Verhulst just told me."

Doorn looked shocked. "Why?"

Adam didn't know. "She told Verhulst it was my order, which is nonsense." His eyes locked with Doorn's, both of them struggling to understand. What could Fenella be thinking? What could she be *doing?* But there was no time to talk. The boats were loading.

Now, Doorn sat gripping his pike, his face skull-thin but shining with zeal for the mission. Adam grudgingly admired the zeal. Doorn had experience with this kind of fight. Adam didn't. He had hacked and slashed his way across Spanish decks slippery with blood but had never taken part in a land battle. He feared it more than he'd expected now that they were nearing the beach. He had always vaguely assumed that when death came it would be at sea, since he'd spent most of his life there, and he had found the thought of oblivion on the water oddly comforting. Now, as the Beggars' ships receded and the walls of Brielle loomed, he felt a gut-sharp pang. *This isn't where I want to die. Never to see Fenella again.*

No time to dwell on it. To the right La Marck and Bloys and two other captains were leading half the flotilla around the pier. They would attack the northern gate. Taking the southern gate was up to Adam and two other captains with a hundred and seventy men.

It suddenly seemed far too few. *If Doorn's information is wrong, a thousand Spanish soldiers could be waiting for us behind that wall.*

His boat crunched up onto the beach. He and his men jumped out. Then the other eleven craft hit the beach, Doorn's first, and men poured out of them onto the sand. La Marck and his boats disappeared around the pier. Adam looked at the city wall that rose dead ahead, its gate closed. The tower overlooking it rose into the pale blue sky. No movement on the tower. The beach, too, was deserted. Nothing stood in their way.

He turned to his mate, Curry, and pointed to a bilander on the beach. From the *Gotland* Adam had spied it, a small two-masted ship that lay careened on the sand, its hull stove in. He drew his sword. "Foraging parties, go!" Thirty men set off along the beach to carry out the plan, Curry's group with axes, a group of young Captain Lueb's men spreading out. "The rest of you, to the gate!"

A hundred and forty men swarmed across the beach toward the wall. Adam's crew was the vanguard and he led them at the run. The two other captains followed at their heels, leading their men. The sun was hot on Adam's face, bright in his eyes. Then it darkened, eclipsed by the wall.

The gate was a massive arched portal of wood studded with iron, and when the throng reached it they halted with a clatter of pikes. They stood catching their breath, looking up, looking around. Still no soldiers atop the wall. The tower was silent as an obelisk. Adam raised his sword and thumped its handle against the studded wood. *Thud! Thud!* A hundred and forty men waited as the hollow thumps reverberated. Adam was about to call out to demand entry when suddenly Doorn was beside him, brandishing his pike, shouting, "In the name of Prince William of Orange, open the gate!"

His voice was so vigorous, the men caught his fervor and several yelled, brandishing their weapons, "In the name of the Prince, open the gate!" Some banged their fists on the wood. "Open! Open! Open!"

Muffled shouting behind the gate. "Quiet!" Adam called to his men. Their voices died, everyone straining to listen. The shouting inside the city died, too. Nothing stirred.

Captain Lueb came to Adam. "Burn the gate, my lord?"

Adam nodded. This was the plan, and the foragers among Lueb's men were coming forward on the run with combustibles they'd collected from the beach: crates, ropes, barrows, spars. All joined in now, heaving this material at the base of the gate, piling it high. Adam saw Doorn dragging a barrow, so he picked up the other end and together they hurled it up onto the pyre. Lueb set the pyre alight. Orange flames licked the gate and black smoke boiled, giving off a reek of fish oil.

Adam wiped sweat from his brow as he watched the bonfire burn. It would take a long time to eat through the solid gate, time for Spanish archers to man the walls and rain arrows down on them. He glanced up, expecting to see steel helmets appear atop the wall. So far, no one. He turned to see how Curry and his men were progressing at the bilander, chopping its mainmast down for a battering ram. Adam beckoned Verhulst. "Come. We'll help haul it!"

They took off at the run and reached the bilander, where Curry and his men were hacking with axes at the two-foot-thick mast, wood chips flying. Doorn had followed Adam and Verhulst, and Doorn now scrambled up onto the vessel to help two more of Curry's party who were knifing through rigging that hung in fouled loops. They tugged it down, stripping the mast clean.

The mast creaked, about to fall. "Stand back," Adam ordered. It toppled, crashing like a felled oak. Curry and the others grappled it and lifted it. Adam took the position by the masthead and slung his arm around it.

"We should get the other mast, too," Doorn said. "Use it to scale the wall."

Adam nodded and told Verhulst, "Cut down the mizzen."

"Aye, my lord." Verhulst wiped his brow as he moved to the mizzenmast with his axe.

Adam raised his voice to the five men behind him holding the battering ram. "Up with her now!" They hoisted it up onto their shoulders and started across the sand toward the gate, laboring under the burden. Doorn kept beside Adam and yelled ahead to the massed men, "Make way for the ram!"

A cheer went up from the throng at the gate when they saw the battering ram coming. They backed away, leaving a corridor between them to the gate.

"You three men, fall in!" Lueb said, and they trotted to the mast and ranged themselves along its length with the other five. They brought the mast to within a few feet of the gate.

"Ready!" Adam yelled. "On three! One . . . two . . . *heave!*"

The masthead thundered against the wood. Adam felt the shock shoot through his shoulder bone. Muffled shouts rose from inside the city. The men with the ram danced back, reversing the momentum, then forward again as Adam yelled, "One . . . two . . . *heave!*"

The ram thudded. Again they danced back.

A *crack!* The man behind Adam fell with a grunt. Adam froze. He knew that *crack!*—a pistol shot. "Halt!"

The man writhed on the ground, moaning. Adam looked up at the tower. Nothing stirred.

"Move that man!" Lueb yelled. "You, take his place!"

Behind Adam, the fallen man was pulled out of the way of the other ram bearers. Adam forced his eyes ahead on to the gate. He yelled, "One . . . two . . . *heave!*"

Crack! Lueb cried out and fell, blood spurting from his neck.

Shouting erupted in the street. *What's happening?* Locked alone inside the mayor's study, Fenella stood on her toes under the window, trying to see out, but the window was so high, the sill level with her forehead, it was impossible. Through the stained glass covered with heraldry she could see nothing but an opaque shimmer of sky.

Again, she heard that muffled *thud!* like a rumble of thunder. She'd heard it several times. It had to be a ram. The Beggars were battering at the gate! With every *thud!* her heart thumped and the shouting in the street got louder. Many townspeople had left their houses and the commotion sounded like they were coming closer. The mayor's house was around the corner from the southern gate. *Is Adam behind that gate? Is Claes?*

A faint sound, a *crack!* A woman screeched. *A pistol shot? What's happening?* Fenella could have screamed in frustration.

Behind her the mayor's house lay silent. A half hour ago when they'd locked her in, the house had been in an uproar, frightened maidservants running this way and that, Koekebakker sending his family out with a few retainers. Fenella had heard enough to know that Koekebakker had personally gone to stand with the city guard, but that was *all* she knew. How many fighters were in the city guard? How many archers? How many guns? Even if the Spanish soldiers had left to quell unrest in Utrecht as Claes had said, the bullets and arrows and pikes of several hundred guards and citizens fighting for their lives could just as surely kill the Sea Beggars.

Thud! went the battering ram. She could hear townspeople outside, on the move. Were they heading for the southern gate? A mob massing to fight the attackers? She had to know!

She looked around for something heavy. On the desk were papers, scrolls, a globe, two pewter goblets. She snatched a goblet and hurled it at a window. The glass cracked, but the goblet bounced off and tumbled to the floor. She grabbed the globe, big as a pumpkin, its lead stand heavy as a rock. Lifting it above her head in both hands, she hurled it. It smashed the glass and sailed through. She jumped back from the rain of glass shards. Now she could hear the voices outside, men and women, loud, strident, and the tramping of feet. The *thud!* of the battering ram thundered. She smelled a faint whiff of smoke, something burning. The gate? Had the Beggars set fire to it? She had to get out!

She went to the desk and started to pull it toward the window. It was too massive, like trying to pull a stalled mule. She came around the desk and pushed it, grunting at the effort, and slowly maneuvered it across the room and beneath the window. She clambered up onto it. The windowsill was now at her waist and she looked out through the hole in the jagged glass. The crowd was tramping toward the southern gate. To fight the Beggars? But none of them had weapons. And there were as many women as men. Could she climb out? The room was at street level, so if she could get through the window it wasn't far to jump down. Using her elbow, eyes closed, she smashed the glass to make the hole big enough to climb through. She swept the residue of glass shards off the sill with her sleeve, then planted a knee on the sill and was struggling to pull herself up into the opening when the door behind her clicked. She dropped back onto the desk and whipped around. The door opened. A young woman came in. She stared at Fenella up on the desk.

"Are you Mevrouw Doorn?"

How did she know? Fenella was wary. Was this woman from the mob? *Do they want me as a hostage, maybe?* But the open door offered her the fastest way out. She jumped down off the desk. "Yes," she said.

The woman beckoned someone and a burly man appeared and the woman said, "See?" She turned to Fenella. "Is it true your husband is out there, at the gate? Claes Doorn?"

Fenella hesitated, eyeing the man in the doorway.

"Don't worry about him. He's my uncle. The devil duke hanged my father."

"Been wanting to join the Brethren," the man said shyly.

Hope surged in Fenella. *Friends!* "The other people out there, do they feel as you do?"

"Yes, they're for the Beggars," the woman assured her.

"And for the Brethren," the man said.

Fenella could have kissed them both. "Then you *shall* join them! Come!"

When they stepped out into the street Fenella found that the crowd was even bigger than she'd thought. They were moving toward the southern gate, and with every *thud!* of the battering ram their pace picked up more boldly. Fenella and her companions fell in with the people. "To the gate!" someone shouted. Other voices rose, picking up the cry, "To the gate!" It became a chant as they marched: "The gate! The gate!" Fenella glimpsed a half-dozen helmeted guards holding pikes at the edge of the street under the eaves of houses, but they looked on in silent dismay as the crowd marched past them. The city walls rose above the heads of the people. Fenella could see the arched top of the gate. Smoke billowed above it and the smell bit her nostrils. *Thud!* went the battering ram.

A shout. Someone pointed. Fenella looked to the top of the wall beside the gate. Three Sea Beggars were crawling up onto the wall from the other side. One got to his feet, crouching, pulling a dagger from his belt. Grim-faced, he eyed the people as if they were lions about to spring at him.

"The Beggars!" someone shouted. A cheer went up.

"Down with Alba!" a woman yelled. The crowd took up the chant. "Down with Alba! Down with Alba!"

The three men on the wall stood frozen, amazed. Fenella wanted to shout to them in glee, *Brielle is yours!* Two more men crawled over the edge. One was Berck Verhulst.

"Berck!" Fenella shouted. She pushed her way through the people, eager to welcome him. "Berck! Over here!" He heard her and scanned the faces, looking for her.

There was a crash of splintering wood as the ram smashed through the gate. People cheered, even as they lurched out of the way. Axes outside the hole hacked it to enlarge it, and in a moment men were scrambling through, pouring into the street.

Crack! One of the men on the wall beside Berck tumbled forward and pitched down to the street. A woman screamed.

Fenella looked to the tower. Saw a man behind an arrow slit. He had a pistol! The four men on the wall had crouched, looking swiftly around for the gunman. Berck alone stood upright. He hadn't seen his comrade get shot and he was grinning, waving with his own pistol to the Sea Beggars below, exuberantly beckoning them in.

Berck, get down! Fenella shoved people out of her way, trying to get to the wall.

"Down with Alba! Down with Alba!"

Crack! Berck slapped his neck as though stung. Blood spurted from under his ear. *Crack!* He reeled on the wall. "Berck!" Fenella cried. He collapsed, tumbling down to the street.

She pushed past shoulders, arms, backs, and finally broke free and ran. Sea Beggars streamed past her, pouring into the city. The tramp and clatter of their boots and weapons was drowned in the roar of the people swarming them, welcoming them. Fenella reached the spot where Berck lay on a dusty strip between houses in the shadow of the roofs. He lay still, blood pooling in the dust from the wound in his neck and soaking his breeches from the wound in his hip. She fell to her knees beside him. He blinked at her. "Berck, I'm here . . . you'll be all right."

Crack! One of the Beggars in the oncoming stream lurched. Blood fountained from the side of his head as he fell. His comrades around him stopped and bent to him, but the oncoming tide of them kept coming amid the welcoming roar of the people. Fenella looked up at the arrow slit in the tower. A star of sunlight glinted off the gunman's weapon. She looked back at the Beggars streaming in. There was Adam, striding ahead with sword raised. Men kept scrambling in through the opening. She saw Claes.

Crack! Another Beggar fell feet away from Adam. Adam stopped and bent to help the man.

"Down with Alba! Down with Alba!"

Fenella looked up at the tower. The star of sunlight glinted. *Adam could be next!* She saw Berck's pistol lying in the dust. She grabbed it. Scrambled to Berck and dug a ball out of the pouch at his belt. She stood. Steadied her trembling legs. The man's face behind the arrow slit turned to her. She aimed at him. Fired.

Something bit her side, a wasp at her rib. She swatted it . . . but her hand had lost its bones, a floppy thing with no power. Something wet oozed between her fingers over the rib. She raised her hand weakly and looked at her fingers. Bright red . . . a metallic, salty smell like the sea. Her legs buckled. Blackness engulfed her.

22

Departures

Swimming upward . . . slowly upward, her limbs weightless but weak. Up Fenella drifted, up . . . up.

She broke the surface of consciousness with a jolt. Pain gouged her side. Her eyes flicked open. Sunlight stabbed them. She lifted her head. Pain gouged her rib again and she fell back. A battering ram beat inside her head.

Where am I? She lay on a bed. Soft, warm. Lavender-scented pillow. Blanket a blue hue like violets. Gauzy bed-curtains, gathered at the four posts of shiny, carved oak. A chambermaid stood at the foot of the bed, engrossed in folding lace-edged linens into a trunk.

A barrage of raw laughter. Wincing, Fenella turned her head. An open window, the brash laughter outside. Men's coarse, ribald voices, one of them singing drunkenly. She smelled something oily, thick. Gun grease? Shards of memories cut her mind. Acrid smoke billowing above the gate . . . the battering ram's *thud!* The gate smashing . . . men scrambling through . . . Adam, his sword raised. Sunlight flashing off the gunman's weapon. *His target, Adam!*

With a shudder she turned her head the other way on the pillow. Her breath caught. Adam sat in a chair, absently cleaning a pistol with a rag streaked with gun grease. In sheer relief, tears pricked her eyes. Not even a scratch on his handsome face!

"Oh!" the chambermaid said with a start. "She's awake."

Adam jumped up, the pistol and rag in his hands forgotten. "Thank God!"

"You're—" Fenella had to stop, her throat as rough as canvas. "You're alive."

He smiled. "How are *you?*"

Every muscle hurt. Pain throbbed through her left side as though an arrowhead were embedded, grinding. "Thirsty."

"Water," he told the maid. "Quickly." She bobbed a curtsy and hurried out. Adam turned back to Fenella and shook his head in wonder. "The doctor said you wouldn't make it. Said fever would claim you. You've proved him wrong." He smiled, gazing at her. "Poor fool, he doesn't know the woman you are."

She wanted to swim into the warmth of his eyes. But the pain in her side anchored her. The battering ram pounded in her head. "Where am I?"

"The mayor's house."

She struggled to remember . . . the mayor's study . . . smashing the window . . . the couple freeing her. It was a blur, like peering through a wet windowpane. Adam still held the pistol and she suddenly recognized it, that pocked handle of horn. Berck's pistol. "Is Berck all right? He was shot. Can I see him?"

Adam's smile vanished. He set the pistol and the rag on the bedside table. "Fenella . . ." His voice was low with sympathy. Something in her shrank back from knowing. *Please, not Berck.* "I'm sorry," Adam said. "We lost seven men to that gunman in the tower, including your friend."

She closed her eyes, cutting out the sunlight. She wanted no sun. No soft bed. She could see Berck standing beside her on the deck of the *Gotland*, offering to come with her to Brussels or the coast, to keep her safe. If she had let him she might have kept *him* safe.

The mattress jostled. She opened her eyes. Adam had sat down beside her. "I'll tell you this. He lived long enough to know that your shot killed the gunman." He laid his hand gently on hers. "Fenella, you saved a lot of lives. The men are calling you their heroine." He picked up something from the bedside table and showed her an iron ball the size of a large pea. "The doctor took this from your side. Wedged between ribs."

She stared at it, the memory still a fog. "We attacked . . . today?"

"No, yesterday. You've been unconscious."

Something he'd said clutched her. *We lost seven men.* She swallowed and asked, "Claes?"

Adam drew back his hand. "He's fine. And something of a hero, too. He was the first to storm the City Hall and he ripped down Alba's flags. Made a bonfire on the steps and burned them. The men loved it." He stood up. "You must be in awful pain. What can I do for you? What can I get you? Another pillow? Something to eat?"

She was still trying to grasp what had happened. "So . . . we won." Elation washed over her. *Down with Alba!* And yet the victory felt thin, shallow, like water, Berck drifting away, a corpse.

"Amazing, but true." Adam indicated the open window. Through it they could hear the men's singing and laughter carrying on. "Hear that? They're celebrating. La Marck and his Sea Beggars occupy the city. They're swaggering around as if they'd taken Brussels."

"No one fought them?"

"A few stalwarts of the city guard, but after the leading citizens fled, the guard surrendered. The councillors lit out to the Antwerp Road with all the property they could lash to their horses. Only the mayor stayed. He's in the garrison lockup. La Marck and his captains have taken over the best houses. I told them not the mayor's house. Told them it was for you."

Adam said it as though he would have fought them for it, for her. She couldn't help smiling. Though he'd got to his feet he was so near she could have reached for him. She longed for him to sit by her again.

"Fenella!" Claes came through the door, the chambermaid behind him. He came straight to the bedside. "Great heaven, it's true, you're awake." He took her hand and held it in both of his and said with feeling, "I feared we'd lost you."

"No . . . though it seems I lost a day." She glanced at Adam. He tore his eyes from her. He beckoned the chambermaid, who'd brought a jug, and told her, "Give the lady some water."

Claes said to him, "Thank you for sending me word."

Adam looked about to reply. He hadn't sent for him. But he just nodded, turned, and walked out.

Claes pulled the chair close to the bed and sat. "You look well. Better than I dared hope."

She felt far from well. The grinding pain in her side, the pounding headache, the fogginess in her mind. The maid offered her a cup of water and she struggled to half sit up. She drank a mouthful. It felt blessedly cool going down her parched throat. A couple more mouthfuls, then she lay down again, her strength sapped by the simple effort. It gave her a stab of panic. Would she be an invalid forever? No, that's nonsense, she told herself. People recovered from such wounds all the time. So would she. *He doesn't know the woman you are*, Adam had said. That warmed her but tormented her, too. Watching him walk out, that was the torment. She looked up at Claes. Bathed and rested and dressed in fresh clothes, he looked healthier than she had ever seen him. "The victory, Claes. I've heard. It's wonderful."

He nodded, his face shining. "And this is just the beginning. Brielle gives us a base. We—" He stopped and turned to the maid who was setting the jug and cup on the table, and he told her to leave. Didn't want her to overhear. When she was gone he turned back. "It's exactly what we needed. A base that we can get supplied by sea. A base we can attack inland from. La Marck and I have sent a joint message to Prince William in Dillenberg, telling him of our victory. It's just the beginning—and what a beginning! I've contacted the Brethren in Rotterdam, and with our combined strength, Sea Beggars and Brethren, we'll take more ports throughout Holland and Zeeland, all in the name of the Prince. We plan to start with Vlissingen. Just think of it, Fenella—it controls the channel that the entire trade of Antwerp sails through. With Vlissingen we can take the whole western region!"

"Yes . . . that would be wonderful," she managed, but in fact it made her heavyhearted, the thought of tramping from town to town, following him and his troops of rebels. She didn't want to think of it. She was weary, so very weary.

"You're tired; forgive me." He glanced at the window and grinned. "Listen to them. Once they sleep off their celebrating, those men will be ready to fight."

"I think . . . I need to sleep, too."

"Yes, yes, of course. And I must get back to La Marck. We're planning the attack on Vlissingen. Get back your strength, Fenella." He patted her hand, smiling. "The men think you're very brave, you know." He smiled awkwardly. "Why, I believe they would follow you before me or La Marck."

She tried to smile at his jest. Her eyes closed as he left the room, closing the door behind him.

She slept right into the night. A dream of Berck falling into a chasm, falling forever into a gale-tossed sea, jolted her awake, sweating. She fell back into a dull, dreamless sleep.

The next day she sipped some broth and ate a little rye bread. The fog in her mind cleared and the headache faded, though the pain in her side was still intense. The doctor, a wheezing white-haired fellow, changed her bandage, and the maid helped her into a fresh nightdress. Claes visited, spreading out a map on the bed to explain the tactics the Sea Beggars were planning. Adam came to ask if she was feeling better. She said she was. He stayed only a moment.

The following day she felt quite a bit better. Stronger. Hungrier. Interested. She ate a dish of rabbit stew and an apple and drank some ale. The maid told her Lord Thornleigh had gone to a neighboring town and had left word that he would not be back before nightfall.

Claes did not come to see her all day. Too busy with the plans, Fenella thought. She tried to ignore the voice inside her that wondered why he would not take a few minutes to look in on her. Lying in bed had become boring, irritating. *Tomorrow I'll get up*, she told herself, *even if just for a short walk*. She had a hankering to see her ship, the *Gotland*. A hankering to be useful again.

* * *

"Your husband left this," the maid told her when she awoke the next morning. Fenella opened the letter.

> *My dear wife,*
> *By the time you read this I will be halfway to our destination by sea, with our Rotterdam friends on their way to join us by land. The doctor advised me that you should not travel, nor do I wish to subject you to such rigors. Wish us well. When I have good news I will send for you. Until then, may God keep you well.*
> *Your loving husband,*
> *C. Doorn*

Claes had sailed! She asked the maid if the whole fleet had gone. The girl confirmed it. "Yes, they left before dawn with the tide."

It stunned Fenella. Why had Claes not woken her to tell her? Was a quick good-bye so impossible? She chided herself for the thought. He was on an important mission, a dangerous one, and had a thousand details of organization on his mind. Naturally that consumed him. Her heart beat fast with excitement and alarm. The rebels were on the move! And now that she'd had a moment to absorb the news a guilty shiver went through her, a shiver of relief that she had not had to go with Claes.

Had Adam gone, too? "Did the *Gotland* sail with them?"

The girl shrugged. "All ships look the same."

Fenella needed to see the harbor. She struggled out of bed, her bandaged ribs feeling like they were grating together, and went to the window. It overlooked the mayor's garden, and she found that the neighboring houses masked the harbor. She could not get even a glimpse of the water. Infuriating! She turned back to the girl. "The *Gotland* is Lord Thornleigh's ship. You've heard nothing of him?"

"Oh yes. Pieter said at breakfast that the English lord has gone to talk with the mayor."

Fenella sank down on the edge of the bed, a little shaky from the exertion, the relief. Adam was still here. She knew she had no business being happy, but happy was how she felt.

There was a scent of pear blossoms in the air. Four days had passed since La Marck's fleet had left, and Fenella was very glad to be outside after so long in bed. She reveled in the freedom of the open air as she and Adam climbed the stairs from the street up to the city wall. She didn't mind the weakness she still felt, for it gave her an excuse to take his arm.

"Sure you want to go to the top?" he asked.

She nodded with a smile. She wanted to see the harbor and could wish for no better guide. Adam had stayed to assist the people of Brielle in resuming their daily lives.

He and Fenella reached the top. They were alone on the wide walkway. Throughout the city spring greenery frothed the gardens of citizens' homes and the monastery precincts. Fenella drank in the pear blossom scent. In the harbor, boats skimmed to and from the pier, sails atilt in the fresh breeze. Bright sunshine beamed, then darkened as a flotilla of clouds sailed by, then beamed again. In the quick-shifting play of light and shadow Fenella fancied the sky was displaying the emotions that wheeled through her. She could not have more of Adam and that was something of a torment, but just to be near him satisfied her heart.

"You look well," he said. "You look . . ."

She pushed back her hair tickling her cheek in the breeze. "Look what?"

"Happy," he finished.

She could not tell him that he was the reason. She covered her feelings with a cheerful change of subject. "As happy as the Admiral's men?"

He smiled. "Aye, there won't be a drop of wine left in Vlissingen tonight, I warrant."

She laughed. "True, they're a thirsty lot." The news had reached them this morning. The Sea Beggars had taken Vlissingen! The city was a strategic port that guarded the entrance to Antwerp, the trading capital of Europe, and it had opened to them, just as Brielle had. Astonishing! And wonderful. Immediately after, word came of a proclamation by Prince William from his exile in Dillenburg. Praising the victory, he called on all the Dutch people to rise up against their cruel and bloodthirsty foreign oppressors.

"Do you think the Beggars can do it?" Fenella said, looking out at the wide river that led to the sea. "Take back their country?"

"It could happen, if they can hold these naval bases, Brielle and Vlissingen. They'll have access inland, and access to the sea for arms and supplies and food. And men. Victory is a great recruiter."

She nodded, delighted by the possibilities. Already rumors were galloping in from other towns that they, too, were eager to open to the Beggars.

"But Alba will strike back like Zeus from Olympus," Adam said. "He's got battle-hardened armies, and his rage will be fierce."

As if hearing Adam, the clouds suddenly blotted the sun. Fenella shivered. She had personal knowledge of Alba's ferocity. Memories of his dungeon chilled her.

"You're cold," Adam said. "Shall we go back?"

She turned to him. "Why didn't you go with La Marck?"

He looked at her soberly. "It's time for me to go home, Fenella. Past time. I must report to the Queen. I shouldn't even have stayed this long, but I wanted to make sure you were all right."

Part of her was thrilled at his last words, but another part felt like she was falling, tumbling off the wall as Berck had tumbled. She had known that Adam would eventually go, of course, but she had pushed that reality to the back of her mind. It lurched out now, and the blow spun her like chaff in the wind.

"Will you stay here?" he asked. "Until . . ." He didn't finish. *Until your husband comes back.*

"No. My gold is still with the Antwerp banker." She forced a smile. "I'm quite rich, you know." She looked out at the water. Her smile faded. "I'll go to Antwerp."

"Good, I'll leave some men to escort you. After that you'll go to England, I hope. As long as you're in this country you won't be safe from Alba. Doorn must understand that."

She needed no persuading. She had already given this a lot of thought. From England she would send word to Claes that she had gone there to wait for him. Her stay would be temporary. As soon as he sent for her to rejoin him, she would do so.

"You know I'll do anything I can to help you in England," Adam said.

"I know. Thank you." *Anything,* she thought sadly, *except be my love.*

That night, she could not sleep. A shutter somewhere in the house kept banging. The wind had built all day. It moaned past Fenella's window. She tried to ignore it, but sleep still evaded her. Her body had almost healed, but she doubted her heart ever would.

A knock on her door startled her. Who would come knocking so late? It was closer to dawn than midnight. Perhaps . . . news from Claes? She got up and whirled on her robe. She opened the door.

"Fenella." Adam's voice was an urgent whisper. "I must talk to you. Can I come in?"

"Of course, what is it?" He strode past her. She had never seen him so agitated. She shut the door.

"This letter came," he said, holding up the paper. He plowed a troubled hand through his hair. "I had to tell you. Before I go."

"Go . . . to England?"

"To Brussels. I'm riding out tonight. Now." He thrust the letter at her. It was grimy and crushed from its travels. "Read."

She quickly scanned the few lines.

> *Dearest Father,*
> *Brussels is in an uproar. They say the Sea Beggars have taken Brielle. They say you led them to victory. I pray it is true and that you are safe. And I pray that this letter finds its way to you there. Yesterday Robert and I escaped the duke's palace. We want to go home to England and be with you! My hope was to get us to a ship bound for London, but we had to run from the palace before I could get any money, so we came to Uncle Carlos and Aunt Isabel's house. But we found they had gone and the house was closed. We got inside*

and are hiding here. But we cannot stay. Mother will
surely come to look for us. Can you come for us?
Please? We will wait here until the Feast of Saint
Hedda. If you cannot come by then we will set out for
Brielle to find you. I do not know what else to do.
Please, Father, come for us.

Fenella looked up in wonder. "Clever children! Adam, you can get them back at last!"

"Or get killed. It may be a trap."

"What? How?"

"My wife used the children to bait me before."

Fenella gasped. "But why would your daughter agree to such a thing? She and Robert were both ready to flee with you."

"I don't think she did agree. Frances likely made her write this. Or Frances may have written it herself." He shook his head, bewildered. "Or maybe it's all true and they really *have* escaped. That would be wonderful. But I just don't know." He slipped the letter into his pocket. "Either way, I'm going to find out. I only came to tell you. If they are on their own I have just two days before they start tramping here on foot, with no money, prey to every evil on the road. I have to get to them before they leave the house."

"But if you're right about your wife she'll be lying in wait for you. Adam, you must not go alone. You need help."

"No. I've told Curry I'm going, but my men didn't sign on to risk their lives for this. Besides, I may have a better chance alone."

"No, you won't. Your wife will be looking for you, expecting you." She tugged off her robe. "Just give me time to get dressed. Saddle a horse for me."

"What? No, Fenella, don't even think of—"

"I'm coming with you, and that's that. You need someone your wife doesn't know."

✒23✒

The Commander's House

Rainclouds threatened Brussels, darkening the evening sky. The air was sultry, humid, sticking Fenella's thin muslin skirt to her legs as she reached the walled property of Carlos Valverde's house. She stopped where the line of bay trees stood like sentries along the wall. She saw no armed men standing guard. Saw no one at all except an old woman on a donkey plodding farther up the street. The gate to Valverde's house lay open.

A trap? That's what Adam believed, and maybe he was right. Maybe his wife had left the gate open to lure him inside. On the other hand, if Kate and Robert were hiding alone in the house they might have left the gate open in the hope that Adam was coming for them.

If they're even here, Fenella thought. That was what she had to find out. The only thing she knew for certain about the house was that Valverde and his family were long gone.

She tramped through the gate and into the courtyard, her gait a little unsteady, not from the few swigs of brandy she'd taken, which hadn't been enough to make her drunk, but from the clumsy wooden clogs on her feet. And she was terribly nervous. Despite the evening's humid warmth she felt chilled in her thin, drab dress. The muslin, once poppy colored, was faded to a dingy pink, and grease stains mottled the bodice, cut low almost to her nipples. Passing through the twilit courtyard she pushed her mob-cap farther askew on hair made blowsy to complete the effect. She saw no one, heard no sign of life, not even a dog. She reached the front door. The windows visible from here were dark, including the ones upstairs. She felt a sliver of hope. If Kate and Robert were camped inside they would be careful not to proclaim their presence with light. She took a deep breath. *Do it.*

"Let me in!" she yelled. She made her eyes lazy like a drunk's, raised her fist, and banged on the door.

It opened. A grizzled man glowered at her above his breastplate, one hand on the handle of his sheathed sword. Fenella's heart jumped to her throat. Adam was right: soldiers! Beyond this one three more stood watching in the dim hallway, a small lantern casting the only light. Boots thudded behind her and she glanced over her shoulder to see five more soldiers fall in between her and the street. Where had they come from? *If they arrest me it's the gallows this time.* Her mouth was so dry her lips stuck together until she forced out her voice. Fear made it easy to slur the words. "Where's the poxy commander? I've got a bone to pick with him."

The grizzled soldier glared at her. "What do you want, woman?"

"Commander bloody Valverde! He got *his* bone in but never paid for it." She barged past him. "Let me at him!"

"Hold on." He grabbed her arm, making her stagger.

"Whoa there, lover." She groped for his shoulder as if she were so drunk she needed his support.

He relaxed with a smirk now that he understood. "Back out you go, doxy. You can't come in here."

She shrugged out of his grip with such force it tugged her left breast free above her bodice. The men's eyes went to it and she made no move to cover herself. "I *am* in, and I'm not leaving till I get what Valverde owes me. Where is he?"

"Not here."

"Ha!" She let her brandy breath hit his face and he winced at the vapor. "This is his house, right? And you're his men, right? Maybe one or two of you know me, came round for some fun behind the barracks." She pointed to a bearded fellow down the hall. "You there. Jurgen, isn't it? I'd know that big salami of yours anywhere. Oo, look at it grow!"

A couple of them chuckled. The grizzled one didn't. He held the door wide open. "On your way, now."

Fenella tucked her bodice up to cover her breast, eyeing a staircase that led to the upper floor. "Valverde!" she bellowed. "Where is the rat?"

"I said you can't—"

She stormed for the staircase and dashed up the steps. "Valverde, you pisser, come out! You know you owe me!"

The grizzled fellow shouted in irritation, "Stop that stupid doxy!" and two soldiers hurried up after her.

"Valverde!" She threw open a door. A bedchamber lay in gloom. Empty.

The soldiers reached the top of the stairs with the grizzled fellow right behind them. "Hey there, halt!"

She dashed on and threw open another door. A half-dozen soldiers looked up from a table where they sat playing cards, a single lantern burning, the window shutters closed tight. She shut the door just as the three who'd come upstairs reached her. Two grabbed her arms. She bellowed again, "Valver—"

A door opened. A woman frowned at the commotion. Rich clothing, a sharp-featured face, arrogant bearing. "What's going on?" She glared at Fenella. "Who is this?"

"No one, Lady Thornleigh," the grizzled man said. "Sorry, my lady."

Fenella froze in the men's grip. *Adam's wife!* She pulled her frazzled wits together and blustered on. "Is Valverde in there with you?" Her eyes raked the room behind Frances Thornleigh. A bedchamber. Perched on the edge of the bed a girl and a boy, holding hands. Her heart told her this could only be Kate and Robert. Their pale, worried faces moved her. They were frightened—by their own mother. Fenella channeled all her loathing for the woman into a dark jest. "Make sure he pays you, dolly bird."

Frances Thornleigh made a face of disgust. "Throw this trollop out."

Fenella shouted curses as the soldiers dragged her down the stairs and pushed her out the front door. "To the street with her," the grizzled fellow told the soldiers in the courtyard, and two of them manhandled her out through the gate. The last thing she saw as they turned back was a third soldier, a lanky man with a pock-marked face who ambled over, curious about the whore they were tossing out. Fenella ducked her head and hurried down the street.

That pockmarked face. Never would she forget it. The captain in Alba's palace. At Alba's command, he had slit the beggar girl's throat.

A thin rain, warm as blood, spattered the Zenne River, which wound through the center of Brussels. Fenella hurried across the bridge to the island of Sint-Gorikseiland in the twilight, then down the jetty to Berck's barge. She took a last look to make sure no one had followed her, then stepped aboard, opened the hatch, and slipped down the companionway to the cabin.

Adam and three of his men, weapons ready, stood watching her descend. Curry was closest to the steps.

"Don't skewer me for a Spaniard, Master Curry," she said wryly.

They relaxed. "Never fear, mistress. I may be jumpy, but I can tell a pretty woman from a poxy dago."

She smiled, grateful that these men had come with her and Adam from Brielle. He had not asked them to, but they'd said they would not let him go alone, proof of the loyalty he inspired. Fenella knew how they felt, for she felt the same. He came to her and gently took her face in his hands. "I should never have let you go there. If anything had happened to you—"

"I'm fine," she assured him. The love in his voice made all the danger worthwhile. "I saw them. Robert and Kate. In the house."

"Alone?"

"No. You were right; your wife is there. And she has hired soldiers."

"Soldiers? Not the duchess's men?"

"No. From what I saw—" She stopped, not sure of the real meaning of what she'd seen. If it was what she thought, the danger was worse than Adam had expected.

"Sit down, rest," he said, indicating the bench at the cabin table. "You've been through hell."

She sat, grateful after her long walk. The scuffed table was grimy, sticky with ale, exactly as Berck Verhulst had left it the day he'd set out to join the Sea Beggars. It weighted her heart to think of her dead friend who'd given his life in the attack on Brielle. But she knew Berck would have welcomed her and Adam using his barge. An ideal place to hide.

Adam sat down across from her, waiting for her to go on. Curry took a stool beside the cold galley. The others, Morrison and Toth, sat on the narrow berth, and Morrison took up a mug of ale he'd apparently been interrupted in enjoying. Toth went back to whittling a stick with his dagger. Rain pattered on the deck above. All of them listened as Fenella continued.

"Your son and daughter are kept under guard. I counted fourteen men. They wore plain clothing, but I believe they're soldiers of the palace guard."

"Sweet Jesus," Toth murmured in dismay, his whittling hand still. "Alba's men?"

"What makes you say that?" Adam asked her.

"I recognized one of them, a captain from the palace." She explained, getting through it quickly. The slaughter of that girl at Alba's order made her sick. "I could be wrong, though, about him being from Alba. Your wife might have hired him privately, and the others, too. Mercenaries. But—"

"But if Alba did send them, he's part of Frances's scheme."

"Do you think he masterminded it? Suggested it to her?"

"Or she went to him. To offer me."

Fenella was appalled. That the woman's hatred could go so deep!

"Either way, my lord," Curry said grimly, "this makes black odds for us."

He and Morrison and Toth waited in tense silence. Adam ignored their eyes on him and asked Fenella, "Where are they holding Robert and Kate?"

"I saw them in a bedchamber, at the rear of the second floor. They looked well enough, though frightened." She explained about the soldiers she'd seen playing cards, and the ones in the courtyard, and gave the layout of the house, as much as she'd been able to see. "They kept it dim, I warrant to make you think there's no one there but the children." When she'd finished she said, "The Feast of Saint Hedda is tomorrow. They'll be waiting for you."

"And Alba's no fool," Adam said. "He'll be expecting me to come with men of my own. Which means the fourteen you counted are just the guard. He'll likely send more." He looked at Curry and Toth and Morrison. "I want you to know what we're up against."

The three looked at one another, sober faced. "Pardon, my lord," Morrison said, "but the four of us can't fight a troop of battle-hardened Spanish *tercios*."

Fenella saw the pain in Adam's eyes. To have come so close to getting his son and daughter, to hear of them being held captive, but then to be forced to slink away, leaving them behind, this time forever—it was killing him. But Morrison was right. Alone, they had no chance against the might of Alba.

Adam told the men he'd give them his answer in the morning. They moved off to the forward berths, leaving him and Fenella alone. She said to him in sad wonder, "Your wife is the very devil. How can she hate you so much?"

"It's more than that. I think it's her way of keeping hope alive."

"Hope?"

"That she might one day get home to England. If I'm dead, Robert inherits my title, my lands. She knows she can control the boy."

Fenella shuddered. "But she must know she can *never* go back. She's a traitor. She'd hang."

"Not if the Queen was dead, too."

What a dark, twisting labyrinth! It was beyond Fenella. She shook her head. "She's mad."

"Madness doesn't stop people from trying to get what they want." He plowed a hand through his hair. "I can't leave without trying to get the children, Fenella. But you can. As for Curry and the others—"

"They're still with you. So am I." She reached across the table and took his hand. "And I've asked someone to visit us."

❧ 24 ❧

The Cellar

The fire-tipped arrow blazed like a comet against the blue morning sky. Loosed from the neighbor's roof, it sailed over the wall that surrounded the house of the departed Valverde family. Plunging, it pierced the stable's thatched roof. Flames from the arrowhead scurried along the thatch.

On the street outside the house, Adam watched the fire arrow's arc, then watched it disappear behind the wall. Standing among the leafy bay trees with Curry and Morrison and Toth, he waited, jumpy with frustration, for all he could see was a patch of the courtyard through the open gate. *Open for me to walk into Alba's trap.* The leaves above him rustled in the breeze like voices whispering a warning. He scanned the top of the wall where the arrow had disappeared. What was happening? *Curse it, has the thing hit the ground and died?*

"There!" Curry said quietly, pointing.

Adam saw it now. A thread of black smoke. Morrison, tense as a bearbaiting dog, started to unsheathe his knife and lunged a step toward the open gate, but Adam caught him and held him back. "Not yet."

The four of them watched the smoke thicken and billow, the column listing leeward in the wind. Adam could smell the smoke now, and he heard the first shout from the house behind the wall, the words unclear but the meaning unmistakable: an alarm. Not panicky; a disciplined military call to action.

"That's cut into their breakfast," Toth muttered with a dark grin. They heard a bang like a door kicked open, and soldiers' voices rose, several now. Adam caught the clipped words of a call for water buckets. Toth, tense but eager, said to him, "Now?"

"Not yet." Adam turned toward the street and shouted, "Fire!"

Curry turned and took up the call. "Fire!"

Down the street a bald head craned from an upstairs window. A few houses away a door opened and a woman stepped out, wiping her hands on her apron. "Fire!" Adam yelled. "Help!" Up and down the street window shutters were thrown open and people appeared at doorways. Two men came running, and three more jogged from the opposite direction, two of them with buckets. "Commander Valverde's house?" one called as he ran.

"Yes!" Adam said. "Please, help us!"

The small throng of neighbors reached them, with more heading toward them every moment: men in homespun work clothes, a blacksmith in his thick leather apron, three young apprentices, a baker dusted with flour, a couple of sturdy housewives. Several immediately hurried through the open gate. Adam turned to his men. "Now."

They ran in with the anxious neighbors. The courtyard rang with the voices of over a dozen soldiers trying to contain the fire that now blazed all along the stable roof. Some must have been sleeping in the stable, for they were dragging out their belongings, stamping at teeth of flames on sacks and satchels. A half-dozen more soldiers poured out of the house to join those at the well in an elbow of the wall, passing buckets down a line of men and up to two on a ladder against the stable wall who tossed the water onto the blazing roof. Adam and his men blended with the excited people from the street who kept streaming into the courtyard, twenty or more neighbors now. The soldiers' disciplined actions gave way to disorder as the neighbors, milling pell-mell, pitched in to fight the flames. Adam counted over two dozen soldiers, a frightening number, because he knew there would be others in the house obeying their orders to guard his children. He'd been right: Alba had sent a troop. Adam caught the alarm in the eyes of Curry and Morrison and Toth, who were surely thinking the same thing. How many soldiers altogether? Thirty? More? *Don't think about that. Just get into the house. Get Robert and Kate.*

The front door of the house was open, two more soldiers hurrying out to join their fellows. Adam skirted the bucket line, scanning the neighbors until he spotted the blacksmith, a big fellow with a bristling sandy moustache. Their eyes met. Adam nodded to him. The blacksmith gave a terse nod back. Adam turned and beckoned Curry and Morrison and Toth, who followed him as he strode toward the open front door, passing laboring soldiers and neighbors. His heart beat furiously as he glanced behind him at the blacksmith who suddenly bellowed, "In the name of Prince William!"

Instantly the blacksmith and most of the male neighbors drew weapons—daggers, dirks, axes, knives. There were twenty at least and they fell on the unsuspecting soldiers with battle cries. Adam drew his sword and his three men drew theirs and they ran for the door, Adam inwardly blessing Fenella for inviting the visitor last night to the barge, the blacksmith DeWitt, leader of the Brussels Brethren. These "neighbors" were his fellows. One had loosed the fire arrow.

Adam reached the door with his three men as weapons clanged behind them and men shouted and the stable blazed. With a last glance over his shoulder he saw a star of fire, windborne, sailing from the burning stable toward the roof of the house.

He burst into the house. Soldiers came at him, seven of them, but having been taken by surprise they were ill organized and he and his men hacked and slashed in a ferocious attack. Curry and Toth felled three. Morrison battled another. Adam parried with an expert swordsman whose blade sliced his forearm, drawing blood. Adam rammed his sword into the attacker's belly. The man crumpled and fell. So did Morrison's opponent.

As Toth and Morrison fought on against the last two, Adam bolted for the stairs with Curry right behind him. He raced up the steps and down the hall toward the door of the bedchamber where Fenella had seen the children. He was almost there when the door flew open. He glimpsed Kate, her face white with alarm. She was still in nightdress and robe. She saw him and her face lit up with joy just as two guards lunged out at him, swords drawn. Adam slashed and parried with manic vigor now that he'd seen Kate. Curry was beside him and together they cut down the two guards.

"Father!" Kate cried.

Adam went to her, catching his breath. "Where's your brother?"

"Here," Robert said faintly.

Adam whipped around. Across the room Frances had hold of the boy. How pale and pinched Frances looked! Three years since he'd seen her this close, and she met his gaze like an enemy, her eyes flashing with hate. Or was it fear? Adam didn't know and didn't care. She was gripping Robert's shoulders, his back to her, holding him against her. Adam's eyes didn't leave her as he said to Curry, "Take my daughter. Kate, go with this man."

She ran to Curry. Adam stalked across the room to Frances. "Let the boy go."

Frances looked wildly toward the door for help. But there was only Curry standing with Kate beside the bodies of the fallen guards, one dead in a pool of blood, the other moaning as he died. Shouts and the clang of weapons in the courtyard rang downstairs. Robert stared up at his father's blood-smeared sword. His head jerked, again and again. The tic.

"Robert," Adam said gently, holding out his hand. "Come with me."

Trust shone in the boy's eyes. He broke from his mother's grasp and took a step toward Adam and Adam caught his arm. But Frances snatched the boy's collar, making him lurch to a stop. Robert, quaking, stood between his parents, who each had hold of him with one hand.

Adam raised his sword above Frances's fingers curled on the collar at their son's neck. The blade hovered over her wrist.

"Release him, madam, or lose your hand."

She held his gaze. "You would not," she challenged. "And now they'll put you in chains! Alba will have your head!"

He hesitated, though hating himself for yielding. He was about to wrench the boy to him to break Frances's grip, when a drop of blood slid from the blade and hit her wrist. She flinched in revulsion. It was enough, and Adam jerked the boy to him. Robert threw his arms around his father's waist and clung to him. Adam quickly led him to Curry and Kate at the door. "Come!" Down the stairs they ran, Adam first, sword ready, the children hurrying after him, Curry at the rear.

"Stop them!" Frances screamed down from the top of the stairs. "Captain Ramos, *stop them!*"

Soldiers from the courtyard were running in, led by a lean, pock-faced officer. *Ramos,* Adam thought. *The captain Fenella described. The child killer.* Eight or ten soldiers were with him, but Morrison and Toth were ready for them, and on the soldiers' heels some Brethren were attacking from the rear. Ramos's men turned to fight the Brethren. DeWitt bolted in, holding a jagged timber as long and thick as his arm, the end of it ablaze. After Adam and the children reached the bottom of the stairs and ran on, DeWitt hurled the burning stick onto the steps. Flames licked the newel posts.

"To the cellar!" DeWitt shouted to Adam, beckoning.

Adam led his charges past soldiers and Brethren battling all along the hall. The soldiers were strong now that they had rallied, but the Brethren were fierce in their zeal. Adam glimpsed Toth battling Ramos. Toth ducked and Ramos's sword slashed air. Toth lunged at him with his long knife, but Ramos parried savagely with his sword, disarming Toth, his knife clattering to the floor. Ramos's sword slashed Toth's throat. Blood spurted. Toth fell.

Rage exploded in Adam and he lunged with his sword for Ramos as Ramos turned to face one of the Brethren. But Curry grabbed his elbow, spinning him around. "Too late, my lord, Toth's dead. Come!"

"To the cellar!" DeWitt shouted again across the hall.

It brought Adam to his senses. He grabbed the terrified children and headed for DeWitt. Ramos turned and saw them and yelled, "After them!"

Adam and the children and Curry followed DeWitt through to the kitchen. DeWitt held open a door. "Down to the cellar!" he shouted. "Quick!"

A soldier charged Curry from behind and Curry whipped around to fight him. Adam gritted his teeth at leaving Curry, but he barreled on through the door, making sure Kate and Robert were behind him. It led on to a staircase and as he ran down the steps, the children scurrying after him, he heard Ramos shout again, "After them!"

The cellar's gloom enveloped the three fugitives. Dim light, dank air. Adam stopped at the bottom of the stairs just long enough to usher Kate and Robert into the shadows where barrels and casks and crates were ranged like irregular tombstones in the murky light. Above, the scuffling sound of men fighting told him the Brethren and Curry and Morrison were keeping the soldiers at bay. *Keep them back for just a few more minutes!*

"Father," Kate cried, breathless with fear, "there's no way out!"

"Come!" He plunged ahead, pushing over crates and casks that smashed and rolled as he cleared a path all the way to the far wall. A high stack of crates rose beside a shadowy door. Adam rapped on the door and said the password: "Brielle." The door opened and Kate and Robert gasped as two men with pistols stepped out. Then Fenella.

Adam had never loved her more—nor been more afraid for her safety. She was risking her life for his children. But now she and Kate and Robert could flee. That was the plan Fenella and Adam had agreed on. He gripped her hand and felt how cold hers was, yet her face shone at him even in the gloom. How brave she was, and how clever! The Brethren knew their enemy. All residences where Alba's commanders were billeted had escape passages in case of insurrection. Fenella had explained it to Adam last night. The tunnel that she and these two Brethren had come down led to a church. That's where she would take Robert and Kate, then to the canal and away. "Thank you," he said quickly to her and her friends.

A thunder of boots sounded above in the kitchen. Ramos and his soldiers were coming. Adam pulled the children toward Fenella. "Go with this lady," he told them. "Down the tunnel."

Robert froze in fear. "What?" he cried. Kate looked just as apprehensive. Fenella was a stranger to them, and the tunnel was a frightening black maw. Robert's tic claimed him, his head jerking frantically.

"Go!" Adam told them. "There's no time to waste!"

Ramos burst onto the top step, a monstrous ghostly form in the gloom. Robert lurched backward in mindless terror. He ducked behind the stacked crates. Adam tried to snatch him—they were steps away from freedom!—but the boy was frantic to hide and skulked back farther. He squatted down, huddling, his arms wrapped around his knees, eyes closed, head jerking.

Panic swarmed over Adam. *No more time!*

"We have to close the other door," one of the Brethren grimly told Fenella. "Now. This is our only chance."

She cast Adam an agonized look. "Adam?"

He almost choked. But the man was right. Unless they dealt with Ramos and his soldiers no one was getting out. "Do it," he told Fenella. He grabbed Kate and pushed her to her knees beside Robert. "Stay down!" he whispered fiercely to the children. "Don't make a sound."

"Close it!" Fenella commanded down the tunnel, her voice a croak of dread. The boy's terror had exploded the plan! "Bolt it!" she said. The door midway along the tunnel banged shut. *No way out now*, she thought.

She dashed back and ducked behind the stacked crates where Adam and the children and the two Brethren were hiding. She hunkered down with them, her heartbeat pounding in her ears.

Ramos and his pack thundered down the stairs. Fenella's muscles trembled as she peered through a crack between crates. Ramos didn't even pause as he charged into the gloom, his bloodied sword raised, and set out across the path of overturned crates and barrels toward the open door to the tunnel. "Don't let them escape!" he yelled to his men.

They raced past the stack of crates so fast they sent a draft of dank air that hit Fenella like a net. Sixteen men . . . seventeen. They poured headlong into the tunnel . . . twenty-three in all. Then, no more. Fenella held herself back, felt Adam and the Brethren holding themselves back, too, until she heard a shout of surprise down the tunnel. The first soldiers had reached the door midway. The Brethren on the other side had already closed it and bolted it.

Adam sprang to his feet. So did the two Brethren. Adam slammed the cellar door shut, then dropped the iron bar to bolt it. Ramos and his soldiers were now trapped between the two doors. Fenella felt a dizzying flood of relief. This part of the plan had worked. Adam had lured the soldiers to the cellar and straight into the tunnel.

The two Brethren cocked their pistols. One slid his barrel into the spy hole in the door, a hand-sized square at eye level. He fired. A scream sounded beyond the door. He stepped back and the other man took his place, aimed his pistol through the hole, and fired. He stepped back. They took turns, each one with his pistol reloaded as soon as the other had fired. Faint pistol shots sounded from the far end, too. Fenella knew the Brethren there were firing through the far door's spy hole. The muffled cries and thuds and scuffling told her that Ramos and his men were dying, one by one. She and Kate and Robert were on their feet, still behind the crates, the children white-faced at the sounds of the slaughter. Fenella took hold of the girl's icy hand and wrapped her other arm around the boy's shoulders. He was trembling. So was Fenella.

It was over in minutes. Adam lifted the bar and opened the door. The two Brethren stepped into the corpse-filled tunnel, and Fenella heard one of the Brethren shout the password, then heard the far door scrape open.

Adam came to her and the children. "Hurry, take them out now," he told her. They shared a look of apprehension that the children would have to go past the soldiers' bodies, but that horror could not be helped. "Kate, Robert," Adam said, "you must go with this lady. She's our friend. You'll be safe with her. Do exactly what she tells you. Understand?"

Fenella thought she had prepared herself for this good-bye with Adam, yet she felt her heart crack. She managed a sham smile. "We'll see you at the harbor."

He nodded and said quietly, "God keep you."

"What?" Kate cried. "But, Father, you—"

"I can't leave my men," he said. Backing up toward the stairs, he pointed to the tunnel. "Go with the lady! *Now!*" He bolted up the steps.

Fenella took the hands of the two children and they watched him disappear through the open door at the top. She heard the scuffling of men fighting above. And she smelled something. Smoke—an unmistakable acrid whiff snaking down the stairs. *Fire. Dear God, what is Adam heading into?* She squeezed the children's hands as much to steady herself as them. "My name is Fenella. I'll get you safely out, I promise." Letting go Kate's hand, Fenella pulled her dirk from its sheath at her waist, ready to take them into the tunnel. "Come along now."

Kate balked. "Listen to that! They're attacking Father! We can't just leave him!"

"Your father is a strong fighter. He'll get through this and meet us at the canal. Come!"

"No!"

"Kate, it's what he *wants*." She turned to Robert, who was trembling so much she bent to reassure him. He looked as dazed as a sleepwalker in a nightmare.

"No!" Kate snatched the dirk from Fenella's hand.

Fenella said as steadily as she could, "Kate, give me that. You're not thinking clearly. You cannot fight soldiers."

"I can't leave him!" She turned and darted up the stairs.

"Kate!" Fenella tried to think. She had to go after the girl but could not send Robert into the corpse-filled tunnel alone. He would never go. Nor could she leave him here in lonely terror. "Robert, we have to get your sister." She grabbed his hand and together they ran after Kate up the stairs.

At the top the sounds of voices and scuffling feet got louder, the smell of smoke stronger. Holding Robert behind her, Fenella looked out into the kitchen. She saw no one. But danger blazed on the far side. The hall was in flames.

The smoke was so thick Adam was coughing painfully as he swung his sword at a young soldier. The soldier parried weakly, as exhausted from the smoke and heat as Adam was. Flames leapt around them, the heat so intense Adam felt as though his face were cracking. A chunk of blazing ceiling crashed between them. The soldier flinched, cast a frightened look at the wall of flames getting closer, then turned and ran.

Adam stumbled, gasping for breath, looking around for more of the foe. Looking for Curry and Morrison. Were they dead? The fire roared like ocean rollers. He saw no one, only smoke and fire. No one but corpses. Four soldiers. Two Brethren.

Then, through the acrid haze, a shape he knew. "Curry!" Adam bolted toward him. Curry was staggering, a vicious gash in his thigh, blood soaking his leg. Adam slung his mate's arm around his shoulder and hauled him toward the front door. It was hard to see through the blanket of smoke . . . hard to breathe. Adam stumbled on a body and almost slipped on blood by the man's head. It was the blacksmith DeWitt. Glistening blood smeared his neck. His throat had been slit.

Coughing, his chest on fire, Adam guided his limping mate on toward the air they both craved. Soldiers might fall on them the moment they stepped outside the burning house, but they had no choice. Adam only prayed that Fenella and Robert and Kate had made it down the tunnel. From the church the Brethren would get them to the canal. Staggering on with Curry, Adam saw a rectangle of misty light looming through the smoke. The front door. Open.

"My lord!"

Adam whipped around. "Morrison!" He rejoiced to see his skinny boatswain stumbling toward him through the smoke. Morrison was bleeding from a wound on the side of his head and Curry was hobbling from his gashed thigh and Adam's forearm bled, but they all were still standing. "We've licked 'em, my lord," Morrison said with grim glee, panting.

"All?" Adam asked, hardly daring to believe it.

"All this lot. When the troop went down after you, the Dutchmen and me and Curry made quick work of the ones up here."

"But where *are* the Dutchmen?" The Brethren.

"Gone, vanished, soon as the outcome was clear. And now we'd better get our hides out, too."

Curry coughed. "He's right, my lord. We already lost Toth."

Adam was barely listening, his eyes on three faint figures near the staircase that led to the second floor, mere shadows in the haze. Fenella? And Robert! "Morrison, take Curry. Go!" Transferring his mate to the boatswain, Adam plunged back into the smothering smoke.

"Kate!" Fenella found the girl on all fours, coughing, overcome by the smoke. "Robert, help me. We have to get her on her feet." Fenella took one of Kate's arms and the boy took the other, though the heat of the fire around them was so painful even Fenella's clothes were baking and Robert's face was a horrible red. He helped her lift Kate and she silently blessed him. The boy had found his courage in the need to save his sister. They dragged Kate to her feet.

Dizzy from the choking smoke, Fenella felt a hand on her shoulder and jerked around, ready to claw at the soldier. She gasped. "Adam!"

"I've got her," he said, lifting Kate in his arms.

"Father . . ." Robert fell against Adam's side, coughing, almost too weak to stand.

Fenella was stunned with joy at finding Adam alive, then saw Morrison dragging Curry through the smoke, joining them. She'd never been happier to see two salty seamen!

"Come with us, Robert," Adam said. "Fenella, the door's this way. Follow me."

Fenella took the boy's hand, about to follow Adam with Kate in his arms, when a shriek stopped them all. A figure hurtled down the stairs, screaming—a woman, the back of her dress on fire. Adam's wife. Fenella stood transfixed by Frances Thornleigh's eyes, a lurid orange, reflecting the flames. Robert pulled his hand free. He seemed caught by an impulse to run to help his mother, who threw off the blanket around her as she ran. It was the blanket on fire, not her dress. She reached the bottom of the stairs and Fenella saw a beefy soldier following her, coughing, his face streaked with soot.

"My son!" Frances cried, pointing. The soldier lumbered forward and snatched Robert. He threw the boy over his shoulder and turned and disappeared with him into the smoke. Frances Thornleigh staggered after them, disappearing, too.

"No!" Adam cried. He set Kate down. The dazed girl rocked on her feet. "Fenella, take her!" Horrified, Fenella saw that Adam was about to plunge into the smoke and flames to go for his son. A blazing post toppled across his path. Flames on it leapt higher than his head. Morrison grabbed him, stopping him. Fenella held him back, too. She was breathless from the heat, the horror of seeing Robert taken. Adam strained in their grip. "Adam," she said, "I know you would die for your son, but these men will follow you. They will die for *you*."

Kate whimpered, fainting. Fenella caught her to support her. Adam turned, and Fenella saw the anguish in his red-rimmed eyes. He picked up his daughter again in his arms.

"Back the way we came," Morrison said, hauling Curry.

They made it to the front door. As they staggered out, no soldiers fell on them. Fenella gasped breaths. Never had pure air felt and tasted so sweet.

The courtyard was a chaos of people running and shouting, neighbors streaming in—real neighbors this time, eager to stop the fire spreading to their houses. They ran with buckets of water, some already sloshing water up onto the walls.

Fenella and Adam and the others merged into the mêlée. Adam had carried Kate out, but he was as weak as the rest of them from the near-smothering smoke and he set her down. The girl looked as white as sea foam, but the fresh air revived her enough to stand on her own. She clung to her father, though, and he kept his arm around her shoulders.

"We can slip out to the street," Morrison said, tense but eager as they watched the noisy activity of the people around them.

"And right quick, my lord," Curry said grimly. "More soldiers will come soon."

Fenella saw that Adam had frozen. She followed his gaze past the running people, all the way across the courtyard. Frances Thornleigh, bedraggled as a witch, stood beside a horse, frantically pushing Robert up to the rider, the soot-streaked soldier, who dragged the boy up by his collar. Robert looked dazed, tears of confusion glinting on his cheeks, as the soldier flung him on his stomach between the saddle and the horse's neck. The soldier kicked his mount and the horse bolted through the crowd. Out the open gate he flew and cantered up the street.

Fenella looked up at Adam's white face. People ran this way and that with their buckets, shouting about the fire. When she looked back, Frances Thornleigh was gone.

❧ 25 ❧

Home

The French ship had sailed through the night and reached Gravesend as dawn streaked England's pewter-colored sky. Carlos had been up before dawn and was the first to disembark. He was eager to finish his journey. His fast ride out of the Low Countries into France to shake off Alba's men had been wearying, and in Calais, Carlos had laid low in a rat-hole alehouse for a week in case they were watching the port. But that was all behind him now. He'd sent Isabel a message to her mother's house, telling her he was coming home.

For the final leg upriver to London he took the long ferry, as Londoners called the big barge, crowding in with fellow passengers and a cargo of bawling calves. He could have hired a private barge with four rowers for five shillings, but he saw no reason to waste even that much money. In Calais he'd had to sell his stallion, Fausto, to raise enough to buy passage. Having burned his bridges with Alba, he would have to watch every penny from now on.

Despite the early hour, the Thames was busy with watercraft on the approach to London. Small boats under sail skimmed past oared wherries and tilt boats, the watermen calling out to one another. London snugged close to the river, and as the turrets of the Tower came into view the city's familiar smells wafted across the water: sawdust and fish, wood smoke and dung, the pungent tang of the tanneries, and a whiff of brewhouse hops. The passengers' chatter around Carlos got more excited as London's three great landmarks loomed ahead: the Tower, the Bridge, and St. Paul's. The Bridge was a prime location for commerce as the city's only viaduct, and the three-story buildings that spanned it were so tightly packed together that not a sliver of daylight squeezed between. Sheep bleated on the Southwark end, their drover waiting for the Bridge gate to open. On the other side swans rocked by the water stairs of Billingsgate, and from a wharf came the creak of a crane lifting barrels from a wherry. Smoke curled from the chimneys of bakers and brewers and housewives. London was starting its working day.

Carlos watched a squadron of swallows flit across the roof of St. Paul's, the massive church that lorded over the sprawl of houses and shops, alehouses and livery companies. When he'd first arrived in England as a landless mercenary eighteen years ago he'd been impressed by the church's magnificent spire, one of the tallest in Europe. It was gone now, struck by lightning a decade ago, the roof rebuilt without the spire. Still, that roof was an imposing sight, long as a battlefield, its lead expanse glinting in the strengthening summer sun.

The long ferry was headed for the legal quays just before the Bridge, where its cargo would be landed and assessed for customs. They passed the crowd of oceangoing ships forced to anchor in the Pool before the Bridge, and the rigging on the forest of masts jingled tunes in the breeze, a cheerful discord. To Carlos it sounded like a welcome. It was good to see boisterous, easygoing London after a year in occupied Brussels. Though God knew he had little enough reason to be in such a happy mood. He was hobbled with debt, his lands mortgaged, and the only way out was to start selling some of his encumbered property at a low price. That or ask Isabel's mother for money. Isabel had assured him the lady would happily oblige, but Carlos loathed the idea. He pushed the money worry to the back of his mind as the barge came alongside the quay. This was the kind of morning that made a man feel glad to be alive. Soon, he'd be with his family.

The gangway was lowered and he and his fellow passengers started disembarking.

"Carlos!"

He almost lost his footing on the gangway when he saw Isabel. She was hurrying toward him through the stream of passengers getting off. Too impatient to wait his turn, Carlos shouldered sideways past people on the gangway and hopped off the edge and hurried to meet her. When he reached her his heart skipped. She held a baby in her arms. "My God," he said.

Isabel grinned. "Meet your daughter, two weeks old. A bumpy passage across the Channel hurried things along. She came the day after I landed." The baby was asleep and Isabel beamed at her, then at Carlos.

In awe, he ran his thumb tip across the baby's tiny rosebud mouth, soft as a petal. The little lips began sucking, even in sleep. It gave Carlos a glow of joy. This child was their fourth, but the marvel never staled.

"I've named her Anne," Isabel said. "Do you like it?"

"I love it. I love her. I love you." He took his wife in his arms, baby and all, and kissed her. As their lips parted he asked, suddenly sober, "She came early. You're all right?"

"Right as rain," she assured him.

The baby stirred and her eyes blinked open. She frowned at Carlos as if to say, *Who are* you? He laughed. Then kissed the babe's forehead.

"Let me look at you," Isabel said. "Oh, we were so worried. Three weeks, and not knowing. But here you are!" She kissed him again.

"Where's Nico? And Andrew and Nell?" He couldn't wait to see them. "With your mother?"

"No, we stayed with her at first, but now she's gone to Rosethorn House. She's getting it ready for a visit from Her Majesty." He knew the Queen and the Dowager Lady Thornleigh were old friends. "So we're staying at Adam's house."

"Adam! He's back?"

"Oh, you'll hardly believe the news." She rattled off a tale that amazed him. Adam attacking Alba's soldiers to get his children from his wife. The Brethren supporting the attack. "In our house! He got Kate safely out and brought her home, but he had to flee before he could get Robert. Frances has him still. Oh, Carlos, Adam grieves for the boy."

Sad news. To leave a child behind. Carlos felt even more eager to see his own. "Come, tell me all about it on the way." With a grin at the baby he wrapped his arm around Isabel and led her past the people on the quay. Adam's house on Bishopsgate Street was not far.

"We're invited to Rosethorn, too," she said as they walked. "Her Majesty arrives the day after tomorrow. She'll be in good spirits— she always is with Mother—so it might be a good time to ask her again for a post."

"After helping Alba?" He shook his head. "She'll think me more of a Spanish sympathizer than ever."

"But you turned *against* Alba. That might move her."

He doubted it.

"And you saved Claes Doorn, who's fighting the Spaniards. Oh, Carlos! I didn't tell you about that. Doorn stayed in Antwerp, but Adam brought Mistress Doorn home with him and Kate. Brought her to stay with Mother."

"What? Why?"

"She helped him organize the attack on our house. And that's not all. I'm sure Adam's in love with her. Anyone with eyes can see it, and see that she feels the same about him."

Good God. "You mean she's left her husband?"

"No, I don't think so. He's with the Brethren fighting Alba." She smiled at him, excitement in her eyes. "And there's more. It turns out that Mistress Doorn has quite a lot of money, and she told me she intends to give you much of it for saving her life and her husband's. Five thousand pounds, she's promised us! Isn't that wonderful?"

He was astounded. But it took only a moment for relief to flood in. It *was* wonderful. Five thousand would halve his debts.

"God bless Mistress Doorn," said Isabel heartily. "I like her very much. She's a courageous soul. And yet . . ." She shook her head, bewildered. "This thing between her and Adam is rather sad. They're both married. I don't quite know what to make of their . . . relationship."

Neither did Carlos. Adam with Fenella—it was a surprise. They were both fine people who'd suffered, and Carlos hoped they might find some happiness together, if only in private behind closed doors. He suddenly remembered the decision he'd made while sending Isabel off in the duchess's coach with the Doorns, a decision to one day tell her about his moment with Fenella years ago, tell her just so that everything between them was aboveboard. It had been a meaningless tryst in Edinburgh, born in the crisis of war and long forgotten. Now, though, hearing about Adam, he came to the opposite and firm decision. For everyone's sake, that bit of the past must stay hidden forever.

"Nico still limps a bit from his broken leg, but the bone has healed well," Isabel chattered on as they crossed Thames Street, busy with wagons and foot traffic. "And Nell has made a silk sash for you. And Andrew can't wait to show you the pony Mother has given him, and . . ."

Carlos squeezed her shoulder, eager to hear it all. It was good to be home.

Fenella took the letter from the Rosethorn chambermaid, thanked her, and closed the door. The sun was barely up and Fenella was still in her nightdress. She'd been awake when the maid knocked and about to dress, but the delivery of the letter jolted her as though from sleep with a clanging alarm. It was sealed, but she recognized the outside handwriting. From Claes. She had sent him word of where she was staying. Now, he would want her to come home.

She needed air. She went to the window and opened it. The bedchamber overlooked the Dowager Lady Thornleigh's rose garden, and the blossoms' fragrance drifted in around her on the soft summer air. She took a deep breath of it to steady herself. She watched bees drowsing among the roses and iris and gillyflowers.

She sank down on the soft window seat of moss-green velvet and turned the letter over in her hands. She dreaded reading it. The moment she did, this sweet dream she'd been living at

Rosethorn House would burst like a bubble of sea foam. She would find herself cast on the rocky shore of reality. Claes was her husband. Her place was with him.

Her gaze drifted across the beautiful room. The cherrywood linenfold paneling. The four-poster bed with its curtains of moss-green brocade. The man-sized chest of carved, gleaming oak. The dressing table with its looking glass crowned with a spray of fresh roses, damask red and white. The silver bowl heaped with lavender and sage. Though she'd been here for only two weeks, she had come to love this house. A safe harbor from the madness she'd been through. A haven of tranquility and peace. How kind old Lady Thornleigh had been. She was Adam's stepmother, a widow, and Fenella sensed the lady's deep personal acquaintance with grief. Yet her house was a cheerful place where servants were at ease and where the toy boats and poppet dolls of her grandchildren were as cherished as her costly works of art. Today, the household folk were up early to prepare for the Queen's visit tonight and Fenella suspected that Lady Thornleigh was, too, supervising it all.

Fenella was nervous about meeting Queen Elizabeth. Lady Thornleigh's seamstresses had created a gown for Fenella for the grand occasion, a lovely thing of silver satin, the bodice embroidered all over with pink rosebuds, and she felt she looked well in it, but she had no experience with courtly ways and feared that despite the finery she might seem like a fishwife among the lords and ladies. Dozens of guests would be coming. So would Carlos and Isabel Valverde. The Queen had offered to be their newborn baby's godmother, an extraordinary honor and one that Fenella suspected they owed to Adam. Her Majesty valued Adam's friendship, and this was his way of thanking Valverde for saving Fenella's life. She had offered her own thanks to Isabel Valverde in the form of five thousand pounds and Isabel's delight had touched her. Such a wonderful family. She felt blessed for everything they had done for her.

Adam would be here tonight, too.

She looked down at the letter in her lap. She could no longer put off opening it. She slid her finger under the seal, pried it loose, and unfolded the paper.

My dear wife,

I rejoiced to read your letter. Praise God for keeping you safe. Our noble English friend and his kin are gracious people and glad I am that you are in their care.

I trust you will have heard the news from here. After Brielle and Vlissingen three more towns in Zeeland have opened to us. Everywhere, our countrymen are panting to throw off the yoke of the oppressor. Many have joined us. We have word that Prince William will soon send an army. We are resolute. But this is only a start. Our enemy is strong, a many-headed monster that will devour hosts of men before it dies. This work will take time. It may take years. Many years.

The work consumes me, Fenella. I must roam the land to prepare our people, and go wherever I am needed to fight, to build a country free from tyranny, to die if that is God's plan. And because I must do this, I cannot have you with me. I cannot be a husband. I pray that you will understand. I think perhaps you do already, and will forgive me. Mine will be a lonely life.

For my sake, do not be lonely, too. Stay in England. Be happy. You have my blessing and my love.

Your faithful husband,

C. Doorn

She got to her feet. The letter slid to the window seat. Emotions tumbled inside her, a whirl of joy and relief, gratitude and confusion. A hummingbird darted in front of her outside the window, whirring its jeweled wings, hovering. It seemed to look right at her as if to say, *Rejoice! He has set you free!*

She *felt* free. Clearly, Claes did, too. For years he had been living as if he had no wife. He had known she was on Sark but had left her there. And after she'd been wounded at Brielle he had left her to go and fight. He *had* to go, she knew that, but she also knew that she did not matter to him the way the rebels' cause mattered. *Rejoice. He has set you free.*

The hummingbird darted away as suddenly as it had appeared.

Fenella felt adrift. *Was* she free? Marriage was a legal bond ac-knowledged by all of Christendom, and nothing that Claes had said, nor all the love she felt for Adam, could change that fact. *Until death do us part.*

The open air was a welcome respite after the ladies' cloying perfume in the great hall of Rosethorn House. Perfume made Adam's eyes itch.

He crossed the terrace in the twilight and headed for the rose garden. Behind him, strains from the Queen's musicians in the house quivered on the warm air. He was still savoring the effect Fenella had had on his stepmother's guests. He doubted that any of them had ever seen anything like Fenella, a woman of humble birth so vibrantly independent, so stunning in her confidence, so *herself.* They were whispering about her and him, of course, no way to stop that, and he hated to think the gossip might hurt her. But she'd been magnificent this evening. Before being presented to the Queen, Fenella had quietly told him she was nervous, but he hadn't noticed it. Hard to notice anything except how beautiful she looked in that silver gown.

He noted Elizabeth's guards standing sentry at the base of the terrace, and he set his mind to business. Why had the Queen sum-moned him to this private meeting when supper was about to be served? Urgent news from the Low Countries? She'd already told him she wanted him to be an intermediary in her clandestine deal-ings with the prince of Orange. Or could it be word about Robert? *No,* he told himself soberly. That was his private cross to bear, not Elizabeth's.

He reached the rose garden and passed under its brick entrance arch. Inside, the trellised walls reached as high as his shoulders, the dusky red blooms climbing the trellises. The voices and music in the house sounded ever fainter as his boots crunched the gravel path. Two ladies-in-waiting bobbed curtsies to him, Blanche Parry and a new one he didn't know. Blanche gestured down a rose-sided alley. Elizabeth stood with her head bent to sniff a blossom. She wore her favorite colors, black and white, all silk, bejeweled all over with rubies and sapphires. She turned when she saw him coming.

"Lady Thornleigh will be glad her roses cheer you, Your Grace," he said, bowing.

"They do. The variety she cultivates has a lovely perfume. I warrant it's a kind that even *you* do not turn up your nose at."

He smiled. She knew him well.

"You take after her," she said.

"I, Your Grace? I'm afraid I am no gardener."

"Yet you have brought a new kind of bloom into our court."

Ah, Fenella. "I take it you refer to Mistress Doorn. A brave and valiant lady."

"Indeed. I like her spirit well. But take heed, my friend. With roses come thorns." She flicked her fingers toward her ladies. Obeying, they turned and moved away, out of hearing. "I am hungry for supper, Adam, so I will get to the point. I have considered your request and have an answer for you. You will find it bittersweet. Which part will you hear first, the bitter or the sweet?"

"I'll take the sweet, Your Grace. To gird myself for the bitter."

"Very well. At your request I am granting you an annulment of your marriage."

The relief was so powerful it jolted him. Frances had been an anchor grounding his ship on a lethal reef. Elizabeth had cut the cable. He was free!

"Annulment is a grave matter," Elizabeth said, "for marriage is a sacrament. But this is an extreme case. Your wife is a vicious traitor who tried to murder me, and would have succeeded but for you."

He bowed deeply. "I am your very grateful servant."

"Good. Let service be your guide as I tell you the bitter part. You will now do something for me, something very difficult."

"Anything, Your Grace."

"You will disown your son."

The words startled him. Had he misheard? "Disown . . . ?"

"Robert is the boy's name, I believe?"

"Yes, but—"

"Renounce him. Disown him. Wash your hands of him."

He gaped at her. She could not be serious. What possible cause could she have?

"I demand this, Adam, for your own safety. Your wife tried to have you killed. You told me so yourself. And we know why. Your son would inherit your title, your lands. Your wife controls the boy and she holds that dream ever in her mind, of being the mother of the new Baron Thornleigh. But if you cut him off, you kill her dream. She will have no reason to hazard another attempt on your life."

He could find no words. He saw Elizabeth's reasoning . . . but reason faltered in the face of a demand that cracked his heart.

"The boy is lost to you, Adam. You know that. She will never, ever let you near him. She has Alba on her side."

"I might yet try . . ." His words trailed. He felt their hollowness. *Try what?*

"No. You shall not. And I will tolerate no debate on this. You are too valuable to me. Though you would risk your life, I will not. Disown the boy. It is my command."

Their eyes locked. Inside the house, the music ceased.

Elizabeth laid a gentle hand on his shoulder. Pity softened her voice. "However, I have a sweet to give you yet, my friend. Honey to salve your wound." She beckoned Blanche Parry and told her, "Bring me Mistress Doorn."

Fenella could not tame her tumbling thoughts as she followed the Queen's lady-in-waiting across the terrace and down to the rose garden. Mistress Parry had said only, *Her Majesty wishes a word*, and Fenella could scarcely imagine what that word would be. Perhaps, *Who do you think you are, you foolish woman?* Or, *How dare you impose on this noble family's goodwill?* Or, *Quit my kingdom this very night!*

But nothing prepared her for the sight of Adam standing with Her Majesty. They watched her coming. The Queen looked grave, Adam bewildered. Fenella reached them and sank into a deep curtsy before the Queen.

"Rise, mistress. I have a question or two to put to you. Kindly make your answers brief, for I am hungry and eager to sit down to Lady Thornleigh's roast pheasant."

"Yes, Your Majesty." Her voice was so thin she barely heard herself.

"How do you like England?"

Fenella blinked at her. "Your Majesty?"

"Do you find the country pleasing? Salubrious to your health? Overflowing with wise and gentle people?"

"England is . . . all that, Your Majesty," she stammered.

"Ha, she is a born courtier, Lord Thornleigh."

Adam gave Fenella a look that said he was as mystified as she was.

"I have just rid this gentleman of his troublemaking wife," said the Queen. "He is in love with you. Do you love him?"

Fenella was astounded. Adam clearly was, too.

"It is not a difficult question, mistress. Do you love him, yea or nay?"

Stunned though she was, Fenella could not help admiring the bluntness. "With all my heart, Your Majesty."

Her Majesty seemed slightly startled. "My, you do speak your mind. Good. Then, it's settled. You like England, and England has given you a protector in Lord Thornleigh. I therefore proclaim you forthwith a denizen of my realm, with all the rights, privileges, and duties of an English subject. My people, my nobles, and all the world will henceforth consider you an Englishwoman."

Fenella blinked again. What did all this mean? "I . . . thank you, Your Majesty."

"No need for thanks. You've provided me a fine opportunity to somewhat pacify the bellicose king of Spain. I *must* pacify him, you know, for with one lash of his fury he could send an army to our shores. So I intend to have it known far and wide, here and abroad, that I make you my subject for one reason only." She turned to Adam, a twinkle in her eye. "Can you guess it, sir?"

He seemed lost for words. "I cannot, Your Grace."

She looked triumphant, turning back to Fenella. "It is because your husband has taken up arms against the lawful authority of

Spain, something no subject anywhere must ever do. Your husband is therefore a rebel and a traitor, and any connection to such evil rabble I will not abide. Which is why, mistress, since you are now my subject, I hereby annul your marriage."

Fenella gasped. Adam gasped.

"The rest, sir, I leave to you. And now," said the Queen with impatience, "let us sup." She beckoned her ladies, a signal that she was leaving.

Fenella could scarcely bend her knees to curtsy, too buffeted by joy, too caught up in grinning back at Adam's grinning face.

The Queen bade her rise. Their eyes met. The Queen stepped close and whispered four words in her ear.

What did she say to you? Adam had asked Fenella that evening when the Queen had left them alone among the roses and they'd embraced, laughing in joy. Fenella did not tell him then. She did not tell him in the sixteen days that followed, just enough time to publish the banns in church on three successive Sundays. She did not tell him during the whirlwind of wedding preparations with his sister and his daughter and the Dowager Lady Thornleigh. The gowns, the gifts, the jewels, the banquet, the throng of guests, the toasts. The love in Adam's eyes when he and Fenella exchanged vows as man and wife, making her heart sing. The shy, sweet smile from Kate that made Fenella want to cry.

Now, as she came to him in bed for the first time at his house, she wanted to tell him, to give him this gift. "Do you want to know what Her Majesty said to me?"

He was kissing her neck, scarcely listening. "What?"

"That night in the rose garden, my love. She said four words."

He looked at her, curious now.

She kissed him, more happy than she'd thought it was possible to be. Then she put her lips to his ear and whispered the words. "She said this: *Give him a son.*"

AUTHOR'S NOTE

Readers of historical fiction are often keen to know how much of a book is fact and how much is fiction. Regarding *The Queen's Exiles*, let me fill you in. First, the facts.

Spain's ruthless occupation of the Netherlands, sixteenth-century Europe's rich mercantile hub, is well documented, as is the brutal governorship over the Dutch by the Spanish Duke of Alba, the "Iron Duke." In 1567, Alba set up a special court called the Council of Troubles to crush Dutch resistance, and under its authority he executed thousands. The people called it the Council of Blood. Here are Alba's own words: "It is better that a kingdom be laid waste and ruined through war for God and for the king, than maintained intact for the devil and his heretical horde."

The scene of cruelty in Chapter 3 of *The Queen's Exiles* after a Dutch boy throws dung at the Duke of Alba's statue is an invention, but Alba did in fact commission a life-sized statue of himself showing him trampling rebellion. It was made by sculptor Jacques Jonghelinck and in 1571 was erected in the market square of Antwerp. (For the dramatic purposes of my story I set the statue in Brussels, twenty-seven miles from Antwerp.) The people loathed the statue, and it did not long outlive Alba's regime; his successor pulled it down. However, Jonghelinck also sculpted a bronze bust of the duke and it survives today in the Frick Collection in New York.

The story of the Sea Beggars, the Dutch rebel privateers, is fascinatingly true. Led by William de La Marck, they were a motley fleet of about thirty vessels who harassed Spanish shipping and raided coastal towns. The origin of their name is intriguing. Before the Duke of Alba's arrival in 1567, the governor was the king of Spain's sister, Margaret. In 1566, a delegation of more than two hundred Dutch nobles appeared before her with a petition stating their grievances. She was at first alarmed at the appearance of so large a body, but one of her councillors exclaimed, "What, madam, is Your Highness afraid of these beggars?" The Dutch heard the insult, and after Margaret ignored their petition, they declared that they were ready to become beggars in their country's cause and adopted the name Beggars with defiant pride. When the Spanish persecution worsened, scores of these rebels took to the sea to harry Spanish shipping and proudly called themselves the Sea Beggars.

For several years England's Queen Elizabeth gave safe conduct to the Sea Beggars, allowing La Marck and his rebel mariners to make Dover and the creeks and bays along England's south coast their home as they continued their raids on Spanish shipping. England was far weaker than mighty Spain, so Elizabeth was playing "a game of cat and mouse" with King Philip, says historian Susan Ronald in her fascinating book *The Pirate Queen:* Helping the Sea Beggars was "the only course open to her to show her defiance of Spain." But Philip's fury grew dangerous, and in March 1572, Elizabeth ordered the expulsion of the Sea Beggars from her realm, an act that people assumed was to placate Philip. It turned out, however, that Elizabeth had struck a lethal blow at Spain: By expelling the Sea Beggars she had unleashed these fierce privateers' latent power. For a month they wandered the sea, homeless and hungry, until, on the first of April, they made a desperate attack on the Dutch port city of Brielle, which had been left unattended by the Spanish garrison, and they astounded everyone, even themselves, by capturing the city, just as depicted in the novel. Their victory provided the Dutch opposition's first foothold on land and launched a revolution: the Dutch War of Independence. The capture of Brielle gave heart to other Dutch cities suffering under Spain's harsh rule, and when the Sea Beggars pushed on inland they rejoiced to see town after town open their gates to them. The exiled prince of Orange now sent troops to support them. But Spain ferociously struck back. Taking the rebel-held cities of Mechelen and Zutphen, the Duke of Alba's troops massacred the inhabitants; in Mechelen the atrocities went on for four days. The town of Haarlem bravely resisted during a long siege, but finally surrendered. Alba's troops methodically cut the throats of the entire garrison, some two thousand men, in cold blood.

By 1585, Elizabeth could no longer tolerate Spain's tyranny in the Netherlands and she openly supported the Dutch revolution, sending an army under the Earl of Leicester to fight alongside the Dutch resistance. Nevertheless, it took almost six more decades until the people of the Netherlands won their freedom, in 1648. To this day, on the first of April every year the Dutch people still exuberantly celebrate the Sea Beggars' capture of Brielle. (In writing about these ragtag but committed rebels I often thought of the French Resistance fighters in World War II who stood up to the Nazi occupation of France.)

Here are a few notes on the fate of four real people who appear in *The Queen's Exiles:*

The Duke of Alba was a military legend in his own time, a stupendously successful general in Spain's many European wars, but after six years as governor of the Netherlands even his master, King Philip, felt Alba had been too hard on the Dutch and he was recalled to Spain in 1573 at the age of sixty-six. His glory days, however, were not over. In 1580 the seventy-two-year-old duke led a force of forty thousand across the Spanish-Portuguese border and defeated the Portuguese army. He triumphantly entered Lisbon, making his king, Philip II of Spain, also Philip I of Portugal. Alba died in Lisbon in 1582 at the age of seventy-four. For information about him I am indebted to Henry Kamen's fine biography *The Duke of Alba.*

William, Prince of Orange, the popular Protestant leader of the Dutch resistance, does not make an appearance in *The Queen's Exiles,* but the Sea Beggars fought in his name, and after their victory at Brielle he openly supported them. He led the resistance movement until 1584, when he was assassinated, shot in his house by a Catholic Frenchman, Balthasar Gérard.

Elizabeth I was in the fourteenth year of her reign in *The Queen's Exiles: 1572.* She went on to rule England for the next thirty-one years, an extraordinary age of peace and prosperity for her people, and of bold exploration and an unprecedented flowering of the arts. Elizabeth's intervention in the Netherlands was a feature of her foreign policy of supporting Protestant rebellions to destabilize the Catholic regimes that were her adversaries: Spain and France. Working with her ever-loyal first minister, William Cecil, whom she elevated to the peerage in 1571 as Baron Burghley, Elizabeth forged this successful policy, eloquently described by historian Conyers Read, of "keeping England safe by making fires in her neighbors' houses." In 1603 Elizabeth died peacefully in her bed at the age of seventy.

Jane, the English-born Duchess of Feria, was a real person (though her friendship with the fictional Frances Thornleigh is my invention). Born Jane Dormer, the daughter of a prosperous Catholic Buckinghamshire landowner, she was at the age of sixteen a maid of honor to England's Queen Mary, and when the Spanish Count of Feria came to Mary's court as Spain's envoy he fell in love with Jane and married her. They settled in Estremadura, Spain. In 1567 he was created Duke of Feria, which made Jane a duchess. After her husband died in 1571 she moved to the Netherlands, where she was a champion of the English Catholic exiles, many of whom, including the Countess of Northumberland, enjoyed pensions from the pope.

Novelists do wide research to mine the "telling details" of everyday life that ground our fiction in reality, and one such detail I unearthed is rather fun. In *The Queen's Exiles* Fenella visits a Brussels shop owned by a French Huguenot couple who sell headdresses and perukes (wigs). I based this scene on information in historian Charles Nicholl's delightful book *The Lodger Shakespeare: His Life on Silver Street*. Nicholl describes the "head tyre" shop on Silver Street in London owned by a French family from whom Shakespeare rented a room in 1612. That was forty years after the events of *The Queen's Exiles*, but according to Nicholl the kind of fanciful headgear I describe in the novel was popular decades earlier as well. Clearly, the whimsy of women's fashion is ageless.

A note regarding geography: In Elizabeth's time, people used the terms "the Low Countries" and "Flanders" to refer to an area that included modern-day Belgium and the Netherlands. I have called this area the Netherlands throughout *The Queen's Exiles* to avoid confusion for the reader.

Now, the fiction.

Fenella Doorn, the Scottish-born heroine of the novel, is my invention. She made her first appearance in a small but crucial role in *The Queen's Gamble*, a previous book in my Thornleigh Saga, and her spirited character stayed with me when I began planning *The Queen's Exiles*, set eleven years after *The Queen's Gamble*. I was delighted to give Fenella the starring role as an entrepreneur, owner of a ship-refitting business on the island of Sark. The Channel Islands, including Sark, were in fact notorious havens for pirates and privateers throughout the Tudor/Elizabethan period. Sark was a possession of England, and in 1565 Elizabeth granted Helier de Carteret the fief, naming him the Seigneur of Sark.

The seafaring Adam Thornleigh and his embittered wife, Frances, are fictional, as are former mercenary soldier Carlos Valverde and his intrepid wife, Isabel. They all feature in my five previous Thornleigh Saga books. Each book is a stand-alone story. Many readers have written me to ask the order in which the novels were written, so I give it here:

The Thornleigh Saga begins with *The Queen's Lady*, featuring Honor Larke, a fictional lady-in-waiting to Catherine of Aragon, Henry VIII's first wife, and follows Honor's stormy love affair with Richard Thornleigh as she works to rescue heretics from the Church's fires. *The King's Daughter* introduces their daughter, Isabel, who joins the Wyatt Rebellion against Queen Mary, a true event, and hires mercenary Carlos Valverde to help her rescue her father from prison. *The Queen's Captive* brings Honor and Richard back from exile with their seafaring son, Adam, to help the young Princess Elizabeth, who has been imprisoned by her half sister, Queen Mary, another true event. *The Queen's Gamble* is set during the fledgling reign of Elizabeth, who, fearing that the massive buildup of French troops on her Scottish border will lead to an invasion, entrusts Isabel to take money to aid the Scottish rebellion, led by firebrand preacher John Knox, to oust the French. *Blood Between Queens* begins with the arrival of Mary, Queen of Scots, in

England in 1568, fleeing her enemies who have usurped her, and follows the Thornleighs' ward, Justine, in her dangerous mission to spy on Mary for Elizabeth. I hope you'll enjoy the adventures of all these characters, who live in that best of all possible worlds, the reader's imagination.

Readers have sent me wonderfully astute comments and questions about the characters, real and invented, in my books and I always enjoy replying. This partnership with you, the reader, makes my work a joy. If you'd like to write to me, I'd love to hear from you. Contact me at bkyle@barbarakyle.com and follow me on Twitter @BKyleAuthor. And, if you'd like to receive my occasional newsletters, do sign up via my Web site at www.barbarakyle.com.

ACKNOWLEDGMENTS

The team I work with at Kensington Publishing is truly a dream team. Foremost among these dedicated experts is my editor, Esi Sogah. *The Queen's Exiles* is my sixth book with Kensington and my first with Esi. Her keen talent and solid professionalism are deeply appreciated. I could not ask for a more enthusiastic advocate or a happier working relationship.

Production Editor Paula Reedy guides my books through the production process with skill and grace. Copy Editor Sandra Ogle brought her eagle eye to the manuscript. Kensington's fine Sales and Marketing teams are a collective powerhouse, and Alexandra Nicolajsen brings her special flair to digital marketing. The savvy and indefatigable Vida Engstrand expertly manages my books' publicity. I sincerely appreciate the work of all these dedicated professionals. In addition, I'll be forever grateful to Audrey LaFehr, who first championed my books, and I wish her joy in her new home in a new state. To Martin Biro, kudos and thanks.

A huge thank-you to John Rosenberg, whose tremendous book-business expertise has made my books such a success in Canada, and to the lovely, ever helpful Jeannine Rosenberg.

In Al Zuckerman of Writers House I'm blessed with a literary agent whose achievements are celebrated. To me, Al is a valued friend and long-time mentor. I'm also indebted to Al's assistant, the hardworking and unflappable Mickey Novak, and to Writers House's able foreign rights specialists Maja Nikolic and Caitlin Ellis.

A happy nod to my fellow authors in the Historical Novel Society, who are a fount of support and knowledge and fun.

My husband, Stephen Best, is my creative partner in art and in life. My gratitude to him knows no bounds.

THE QUEEN'S EXILES

Barbara Kyle

ABOUT THIS GUIDE

The suggested questions are included to
enhance your group's reading of Barbara Kyle's
The Queen's Exiles.

DISCUSSION QUESTIONS

1. Fenella's troubles all spring from her moment of fury when she rashly shoots the Spanish don who years ago massacred the people of her village. Did you think she was justified in killing him? Can murder ever be right?

2. Adam sails to Spanish-occupied Antwerp to hunt down his wife, Frances, and take back his young son and daughter. But there's a price on his head in Antwerp. Did you feel Adam was right to risk everything, even his life, to get his children away from Frances? What other options might he have explored?

3. Carlos and Isabel argue heatedly about staying in Antwerp. He says he must remain loyal to the governor to secure a needed reward for his family. She says they must get out before Alba's regime leads to bloodshed that endangers them and their children. How did you respond to their fiercely opposing views?

4. Frances is so frightened of Adam coming for her she hires a gunman to kill him. Were you disgusted by her act, or do you think she had to do it to save herself and the children?

5. Fenella makes a hard decision to give up future happiness with Adam in order to stay with her husband and help his work with the rebels. How did you feel about Fenella's personal sacrifice?

6. Fenella, held captive by the Duke of Alba, won't betray Adam by telling Alba where Adam is, though she knows her silence may cost her her life. Do you think you could muster that kind of courage to protect someone you love?

7. Carlos risks everything by rescuing Fenella and Claes from hanging by the Duke of Alba. Do you think this makes up for Carlos's previous allegiance to the brutal duke?

8. Adam casts his lot with the rebel Sea Beggars despite the edict of his own queen, Elizabeth, expelling them from England. Was Adam foolish or justified in joining the rebels' desperate fight?

9. *The Queen's Exiles* explores three marriages in crisis: of Adam and Frances, Fenella and Claes, and Carlos and Isabel. All three couples face life-and-death challenges. Which person in each marriage do you sympathize with most? Do you agree with the choices they make?